Praise for
THE DEATH OF VISHNU

"A wonder of a book. From the first page I could tell that this is an astonishing debut."

—Amy Tan, author of *The Joy Luck Club*

"Manil Suri's *The Death of Vishnu* finds the Universe in a block of Bombay flats; it is tender, caustic, witty, and inspired."

—Jim Crace, author of *Being Dead*

"Sympathetic, penetrating, comic and moving, this fine and unusual first novel . . . draws on the best storytelling traditions of both East and West."

—Andrea Barrett, author of *Voyage of the Narwhal*

"Enchanting. . . . Suri's penetration of his characters' lives is as precise and cunning as that of a master surgeon like J. M. Coetzee."

—*Boston Globe*

"Manil Suri has created an intimate and intricate portrait of life in this metropolis [Mumbai]."

—Vikram Chandra, author of *Love and Longing in Bombay*

"A considerable achievement . . . shows what a writer working with memory, moral vision, an instinct for comedy, and technical skills can do."

—Pankaj Mishra, *The New York Review of Books*

"[A] literary accomplishment. . . . Reading Manil Suri's ambrosial first novel, *The Death of Vishnu*, affords an aesthetic pleasure akin to the gustatory one of eating an Indian mango . . . eloquent, refined, and tasteful."

—*Washington Post Book World*

"Suri, at his best, reveals not only a collision of modern and mythic India but a commingling of them. . . . Suri contributes to our understanding of what it means to believe."

—*San Francisco Chronicle*

"Marvelously life-embracing. . . . *The Death of Vishnu* is a seamlessly constructed, quietly eloquent work of art."

—*Newsday*

"The reader is swept away by Suri's fresh, witty observations and tender, comic moments."

—*Seattle Times*

"A delightful and rich first novel . . . lyrical."

—*Wall Street Journal*

"Suri . . . unlayers the jealousies, vanities, longings, and embarrassments of ordinary people with a combination of ruthlessness, insight, humor, and wickedly perfect pitch, as well as an almost tactile sense of language that can neither be faked nor learned."

—*Entertainment Weekly*

"More than anything, there is an exquisite beauty in Suri's prose."

—*USA Today*

"Manil Suri's debut novel is a wonder."

—*Time Out* (New York)

"Enchanting."

—*Time*

THE DEATH OF VISHNU

Manil Suri

HARPER PERENNIAL

NEW YORK • LONDON • TORONTO • SYDNEY

THE DEATH OF VISHNU

HARPER ● PERENNIAL

First Perennial edition published 2002.

First Harper Perennial edition published 2008.

Designed by Antonina Krass

The Library of Congress has catalogued the previous edition as follows:

Suri, Manil.
The death of Vishnu : Mani Suri.—1st Perennial ed.
p.   cm.
ISBN 0-06-000438-X
1. Apartment houses—Fiction. 2. Bombay (India)—Fiction. 3. Servants—
Fiction. 4. Death—Fiction. I. Title.
PS3569.U725 D43 2002
813'.6—dc21   2001036961

ISBN: 978-0-06-146706-6 (pbk.)

08 09 10 11 12 ID/RRD 10 9 8 7 6 5 4 3 2

For my mother and father

AUTHOR'S NOTE

Although the persons and events depicted in this novel are fictional, the central character was inspired by a man named Vishnu who lived on the steps of the apartment building in which I grew up. He died in August 1994 on the same landing he had occupied for many years.

"I am Vishnu striding among sun gods,
the radiant sun among lights. . . .
I stand sustaining the entire world
with a fragment of my being."

From Krishna's discourse to Arjun, Chapter Ten
The Bhagavad-Gita
Translated by Barbara Stoler Miller

THE DEATH OF VISHNU

Chapter One

Not wanting to arouse Vishnu in case he hadn't died yet, Mrs. Asrani tiptoed down to the third step above the landing on which he lived, teakettle in hand. Vishnu lay sprawled on the stone, his figure aligned with the curve of the stairs. The laces of a pair of sneakers twined around the fingers of one hand; the other lay outstretched, as if trying to pull his body up the next step. During the night, Mrs. Asrani noted with distress, Vishnu had not only thrown up, but also soiled himself. She had warned her neighbor, Mrs. Pathak, not to feed Vishnu when he was so sick, but did that woman ever listen? She tried not to look at the large stain spreading through the worn material of Vishnu's khaki pants, the ones that her husband had given him last Divali. What a mess—the jamadarni would have to be brought in to clean up such a mess, and it would not be free, either, someone would have to pay. Her large frame heaving against the sari in which it was swaddled, Mrs. Asrani peered at Vishnu from the safety of the third step and vowed it would not be her.

A more immediate problem had to be dealt with first—what to do about the cup of tea she brought Vishnu every morning? On the one hand, it was obvious that Vishnu did not have much need for tea right now. Even yesterday, he had barely stirred when she had filled his plastic cup, and she had felt a flutter of resentment at not having received her usual salaam in return. On the other hand, giving tea to a dying man was surely a very propitious thing to do. Since she had taken this daily task upon herself, it would be foolish to stop now, when at most a few more cups could possibly be required. Besides, who knew what sort of repercussions would rain down upon her if she failed to fulfill this daily ritual?

Pressing the edge of her sari against her nose to keep out the smell, Mrs. Asrani descended gingerly to the landing. Using the scrap of brown paper she had brought along for the purpose, she fished out the cup from the small pile of belongings near Vishnu's head, taking care to always keep the paper between her fingers and the cup, so as not to infect herself with whatever he had. She placed the cup on the step above the landing and poured tea from the kettle. Hating the idea of good tea being wasted, she hesitated when the cup was half full, but only for a second, filling it to its usual level to fulfill her pledge. Then she ascended the steps and surveyed her handiwork. The cup lay steaming where she had left it—but now Vishnu looked like he was stretching out across the landing to try and reach it, like a man dead in the desert, grasping for the drink that could have saved him. She thought about moving the cup to correct this, but the scrap of paper she had used now lay on the landing, and she couldn't be sure which surface had touched the cup. There was nothing she could do anymore, so she turned and climbed up the remaining steps. At the door of her flat, it occurred to her that she still didn't know if Vishnu was alive or dead. But it didn't really matter, she had done her duty in either case. Satisfied, Mrs. Asrani entered her flat and closed the door behind her.

THE STEAM RISES lazily from the surface of the tea. It is thick with the aroma of boiled milk, streaked with the perfume of cardamom and clove. It wisps and curls and rises and falls, tracing letters from some fleeting alphabet.

A sudden gust leads it spiraling down to the motionless man. It reaches his face, almost invisible now, and wafts playfully under his nose. Surely the smells it carries awaken memories in the man. Memories of his mother in the tin-and-cardboard hut, brewing tea in the old iron kettle. She would squeeze and press at the leaves, and use them several times over, throwing them away only when no more flavor could be coaxed out. Memories of Padmini, the vapor still devoid of cardamom or clove, but smelling now of chameli flowers fastened like strings of pearls around her wrists. After they had made love, and if she did not have another person waiting, the tea would be carried in by one of the children at the brothel, and they would sit on the bed in silence and sip it from metal tumblers. Memories of Kavita, the steam finally milk-rich and perfumed, her long black tresses framing her smiling face as she bends to fill his cup. For almost a month last year while Mrs. Asrani was sick, it was her daughter Kavita who performed the daily ritual. Vishnu would scrape a broken comb through his knotted hair every morning and wait to deliver a toothy "Salaam, memsahib!" when she came, winking at her with his good eye.

All these memories and more the steam tries to evoke in the man. His mother discarding all her used leaves on festivals, even scooping out a few spoonfuls of sugar to sweeten the tea. Padmini pressing her lips against the metal rim, laughing as she offers him the tumbler stained with unnatural red. Kavita trying to keep her dupatta from falling off as she bends down, passing the kettle from hand to hand so as to not burn her fingers.

A breath of exhaled air emerges from the man's nostrils, fraying the steam into strands. The strands shimmer for a second, then fade away.

IT HAD BEEN almost eleven years now that Mrs. Asrani had been bringing Vishnu his morning tea. Before that, it had been Tall Ganga for whom she had brought the tea, the old woman who had slept on the landing between the ground and first floors since as far back as anyone could remember. One day, Tall Ganga had announced to Mrs. Pathak and Mrs. Asrani that she would no longer be bringing them their milk bottles in the morning or cleaning their dishes in the afternoon. She had finally saved up enough money to have the last of her daughters married and would be going back to her village to live out the rest of her days with her eldest son. It would be Vishnu who would be taking over these duties in a week, and sleeping on the landing as well, so they should pay Vishnu and bring the tea and left-over chapatis for him after she had left.

The news had been received with dismay by both Mrs. Pathak and Mrs. Asrani. The problem was that Vishnu was a drunk, lolling around every afternoon on the small ground-floor landing that was a few steps above the street. They had entreated Tall Ganga to find a more reliable replacement, to leave their milk bottles and dishes in better hands. "You've been staying here with us all these years," Mrs. Pathak had reminded her reproachfully. "Surely you owe us this much."

The last statement had outraged Tall Ganga. "What do you think, I've been staying here due to your generosity? I came here long before you did, Pathak memsahib. Every family that's ever lived in this building has eaten off dishes washed by my hands. I may not be rich like you, but I have more right to be here than anyone in this building!" The hot tears in Tall Ganga's eyes had silenced both Mrs. Pathak and Mrs. Asrani. Tall Ganga had straightened out from her old woman's stoop and stretched to her full height, until her head was actually pinning the sari covering her hair against the ceiling. "I've already given my word to Vishnu," she had declared, staring down at them, "that he is to be my replacement. And I hope, as the person who brought the milk that your children grew up on, that you will preserve my dignity." Mrs. Pathak and Mrs. Asrani had been unable to do anything but nod their heads. It was only later, when Vishnu was entrenched on the new landing, that they learned from the cigarettewalla downstairs that Tall Ganga had exacted the sum of two thousand rupees from Vishnu to designate him as the official replacement.

Within a week, it had become clear that Vishnu was not cut out to perform the duties of a ganga. The milk bottles, if delivered, would arrive late in the afternoon, their blue foil caps bulging from the pressure of the curdled milk inside. The dishwashing was a disaster, with pots dented, cups chipped, and plates covered with grease stacked up in the kitchen cupboards. Once, Mrs. Asrani had screamed upon finding a giant green cockroach with white innards squished between two dishes in the cupboard—they'd had okra the night before, and Vishnu had left an entire pod stuck to a plate. And almost every day, Vishnu would "borrow" a tumbler for his evening drink and Mr. Pathak or Mr. Asrani would have to go down to the landing to retrieve it. ("Glass affects the alcohol, sahib, gives it more of a kick.")

They'd tried, without much hope, to dislodge Vishnu from the landing. But all the shopkeepers on the ground floor, from the electrician to the tailor, from the paanwalla to the cigarettewalla, knew about Vishnu's contract with the ganga. Since nobody actually *owned* the landing, it was clear that all inhabitation rights to it now belonged to Vishnu; it would have been ridiculous to usurp this order. Vishnu was perfectly entitled to store his meager belongings there, to eat, drink, and sleep there, even to spit paan juice on its crumbling walls if he wanted. (He did.) And at night, the occupants of the building were expected to carefully feel their way past the thin edge of his blanket in the dark, just as they did for the inhabitants of landings higher up along the stairway, even though Mrs. Asrani could not help prodding his reposing form accidentally a few times, such was her frustration with the situation.

They did, of course, cut Vishnu off, both from his duties and the tea and chapatis. In his place, they hired Short Ganga, who while not particularly short was called that to differentiate her from her predecessor. Short Ganga wanted neither a place to sleep nor stale chapatis to eat; in lieu of these perks, she insisted on a higher salary, and this caused both Mrs. Pathak and Mrs. Asrani some agony.

It was Mrs. Pathak who finally integrated Vishnu back into the scheme of things. Noting that her stale chapatis (which she had started giving to the woman who begged next to the paanwalla shop) were not really getting her anything (except, she supposed, peace of mind), she brought the topic up with Mr. Pathak one day. "It's impossible to starve him out, you know—all he does is drink, anyway—he doesn't care about food. Why don't you tell him we will start feeding him again—even pay him once in a while—he can help in return—stand in the ration line, take the wheat to the mill, that kind of thing. We might as well make some use of him, if he's here to stay." Mr. Pathak, who had not been aware that they had been trying to starve Vishnu out, or even that they had cut off his chapatis, dutifully talked to him later that afternoon. Vishnu started performing chores for the Pathaks, then the Asranis, then the Muslim Jalal family on the second floor, and then for Vinod Taneja, the widower who lived alone in the large third-floor flat at the top of the building. Within a month, Vishnu had been able to pay back the first installment of the two thousand rupees he had borrowed from the cigarettewalla.

Thus was Vishnu rescued from starvation, and, more importantly, from the rigors of sobriety.

THE LIGHT SHINES through the landing window. It plays on Vishnu's face. It passes through his closed eyelids and whispers to him in red.

The red is everywhere, blanketing the ground, coloring the breeze. It must be the red of Holi. He is nine, hiding behind a tree, fistfuls of red powder in each hand. He has been waiting for the festival for so many weeks. All morning he has played Holi—his hair is purple, his clothes blue, bright red and yellow streaks run across his face. He can taste the color on his lips—it is gritty, like mud, but more metallic.

His father sits with friends on the other side of the tree. They have been drinking bhang since morning, the milky liquid in the earthenware pots is almost gone. They are all quite intoxicated by now; some of them are weeping, some are laughing. His father lifts a pot to his mouth, drinks deeply, then lets it smash at his feet.

Vishnu has been saving the powder for his father. He emerges from behind the tree and runs to the squatting men. He opens one fist and hurls the powder at them, then goes over to his father and rubs the powder from the other fist on his face. He tries to run away, but someone catches his foot. He trips, his lip splits open on the ground. He feels himself being dragged back by his leg. The men are all over him, laughing and weeping, holding him down to the ground. He sees his father's face, all round and bloated, there is a pot in his hand. "Open his mouth!" his father says, and someone pulls his jaws apart. Fingers press into his torn lip, the blood trickles out into his mouth. His father tilts the pot and a stream of bhang splashes against the inside of his throat. He gags and tries to swallow; the liquid burns down to his stomach. The hands are pulling his mouth open wider, he feels the bones in his jaws will break. The liquid is spilling from his mouth, gushing through his nose, washing the color from his face. Finally the stream stops, he sees his father look down at him. Laughing, his father lets the pot go—it descends, and bursts on his forehead.

WHEN MRS. PATHAK opened her front door, the first thing she noticed was the smell. "I think their toilet is backed up again," she announced to Mr. Pathak, sitting in the living room. "I'll bet she tries to take some water from the kitchen, you just wait and see!"

The Pathaks were involved in a long-running battle with the Asranis over the first-floor kitchen, which the two families shared. It was the wives who did most of the fighting, except when things got so heated that spousal reserves had to be deployed. The main problem seemed to be the rusty green tank in the kitchen, water from which was supposed to be used for cooking purposes only, but which each side was tempted to raid on days that the terrace cistern allotted to each flat ran out. Coupled with this were the perennial skirmishes over counter and cupboard space—although several formulas had been suggested over the years, at least one (sometimes both) of the wives was always simmering under the suspicion she had been cheated of her rightful share. Frequently this simmer, stoked as it was by the fumes and the heat of the four kerosene stoves in the cramped kitchen, would come to a boil, and then the fight would erupt—charges of stoves being tampered with and dinners burnt, countercharges of utensils being pilfered and spices misappropriated, and accusations of meals being given the "evil eye," or even, on some occasions, poisoned.

"She's going to take the water, you wait and see!" Mrs. Pathak said again, sliding the gold bangles up her arms and licking her lips. Her thin frame twitched. The kitchen had been very hot lately, and almost three weeks had elapsed since the last fight.

"If she wants it, let her have it," Mr. Pathak suggested, without hope. He knew what was coming, this was going to be a big one. Possibly, he and Mr. Asrani would be required to serve as well.

Mrs. Pathak stood at the door and wrinkled her nose. "It seems to be coming from downstairs, though. . . ." There was disappointment in her voice. "I wonder. . . ."

Mr. Pathak heard her shuffle into her slippers and descend the steps. There was no sound for a few seconds, then Mrs. Pathak gasped, and he heard her running back up the steps. He looked up from his paper, just in time to see his wife burst through the door, her face red. "Are you listening?" she shouted. "It's Vishnu. He's gone to the toilet, all over our stairway!" Mrs. Pathak's eyes flashed ferociously. "I told you not to let him come back here."

When Vishnu had fallen ill some months ago, he had come to Mr. Pathak and asked him for money to go back to Nagpur. "My brother said he will look after me, sahib—all I need is train fare—my brother said he can get me into the hospital there. Free." After he had given him the money, and Vishnu had gone, Mr. Asrani had informed Mr. Pathak that he, too, had given Vishnu "train fare." There had been no sign of Vishnu for some weeks, and both the cigarettewalla and the paanwalla had been eyeing the vacant landing. Then one day, Vishnu reappeared at Mr. Pathak's door. "Salaam, sahib!" he had said, saluting Mr. Pathak and giving him his toothy grin. "They said I didn't need to be in the hospital after all."

Both Mrs. Pathak and Mrs. Asrani had been most unhappy at this return. They had just completed negotiations with Short Ganga, promising her the first-floor landing if she agreed to lower wages. (Short Ganga had, in turn, paid off the paanwalla and the cigarettewalla to quell potential claims, and rented the landing to Man Who Slept on the Lowest Step, at a profitable rate.) However, neither Mrs. Pathak nor Mrs. Asrani had been willing to tell Vishnu he could not return; they had nagged their husbands to do it. The plan hadn't worked: Vishnu had been reinstated, much to their chagrin.

He had fallen extremely ill almost immediately. "He was coughing quite badly this morning," Mr. Asrani said to Mrs. Asrani one day.

"TB," Mrs. Asrani whispered to Mrs. Pathak that afternoon. "He was coughing blood when I took him his tea."

"We're all going to be infected!" Mrs. Pathak screamed at her husband that evening. "Blood all over my sari when I went to feed him!"

But the doctor Mr. Pathak had called in, at Mrs. Pathak's hysterical urging, had said there was no sign of tuberculosis, and further tests would be needed to diagnose what it was—tests that cost money, and which Mrs. Pathak quickly declared out of the question, it being bad enough that the doctor had charged his full fee and didn't these doctors have any heart, even for people who slept on the landings?

And now that Vishnu had soiled himself on their steps, on the very day that she was hosting her kitty party, what was Mr. Pathak going to do, and hadn't she warned him?

Mr. Pathak thought about continuing reading his paper, but he knew this would only infuriate his wife further. He put on his glasses to better appraise her anger. "I could call an ambulance . . ." he ventured.

At this, Mrs. Pathak got very excited. "An ambulance! An *ambulance*! We don't have money to send Rajan to a boarding school, and you're going to order an ambulance! For *Vishnu!*" For a second, Mr. Pathak wondered if he had provoked his wife into her occasional ritual of removing the gold bangles from her arms and telling him he might as well sell off her dowry. Fortunately, his infraction had not been serious enough, for Mrs. Pathak's anger seemed to quickly veer away. "We've already paid for a doctor—if anyone pays for an ambulance, it should be them!" She spat out the last word at the wall separating their flat from the Asranis.

"Go talk to them," Mrs. Pathak ordered. "Tell them it's their responsibility now."

Wearily, Mr. Pathak folded his newspaper. Summer weekends were the worst. The monsoons were still two months away.

It is a different red. He knows this color well. It is the red of her room: the ceiling, the walls, drip red. The girls are dancing downstairs, a film song rises through the floor. She dances with back toward a freestanding mirror, her arms swaying above her head. Her fingers caress the chameli on her wrist, they undo the string that holds them. She looks up at the flowers as they cascade over her face. Her hand slides down her arm with the music, her fingers move to her breast. She pulls open a clasp, her dress parts down the front. Rounded flesh peeks out from the cloth, the skin between is powdered white. Vishnu hears the ghungroos on the dancers' feet below chiming to the music.

She turns around quickly and the dress falls to the floor. She grabs a side of the mirror with each hand and presses her body against it. Her back is swaying in front of Vishnu, he has still not seen her breasts.

Slowly, she peels her body off the mirror. Her breasts rise from the surface, like moons emerging from a pool. Her hair swings free, her body arches back, and her nipples turn into view—they ascend into the air, crowning the twin mounds of her body. Vishnu stares at them in fascination: drops of blood against white flesh, they are painted a bright iridescent red.

"Squeeze them," Padmini says, and Vishnu's fingers close over each nipple. He rubs them and the red comes off on his fingertips.

"Taste them," she says, still bent backwards. Vishnu leans over. His tongue traces a path up her white breast and he tastes the chalkiness of the talcum. It reaches the nipple. The red feels sticky on his tongue, it is sweet colored syrup. She laughs as he bites her gently.

"On the bed," she says, and he lifts her up and carries her to it.

"Down below," she whispers, loosening the string of her skirt.

Vishnu pulls down the cloth. Her thighs are powdered white, between them Vishnu sees a triangle of garish red. "Slut!" he whispers.

"Do it!" she says.

"Slut!" he says again, and begins to rise, but she pulls him back into the red.

SQUATTING ON THE floor in front of the dressing-table mirror, Mrs. Asrani was in the midst of applying Tru-Tone to her hair when the doorbell rang. "Can you get that?" she shouted to Mr. Asrani. "If it's the meatwalla, buy a kilo—and don't let him give you all bones like he did the last time."

Around and under Mrs. Asrani, the floor was covered with pages of the *Times of India*. Six years ago, when she had started dyeing her hair, Mr. Asrani and the children had quickly learned that to venture into the territory delineated by the newspaper was to risk terrible consequences. As Mrs. Asrani's ire at her aging had grown, so also had the area she staked out. These days, she was up to the entire Saturday edition.

The dye was not behaving today, it didn't look viscous enough—perhaps she had not mixed the two components in the right proportion. She dipped the old toothbrush wrapped in gauze into the saucer of black liquid by her foot and ran it over her hair. Black drops rolled down onto the faded towel around her shoulders. Her hair was getting grayer, she could tell: time was that a bottle of Tru-Tone lasted her a year, but now Mr. Asrani had to be sent down to the chemist for a new bottle every two months.

Mrs. Asrani sighed. How many more bottles of Tru-Tone would she go through before she finally decided to quit? She hated the whole process—the chemical smell of the dye, the way it stained her fingers, the long wait for it to set while it seeped out into her skin. No matter how hard she scrubbed afterwards, the marks remained for days on her forehead, crude enhancements of her hairline that someone might have painted on to form a more decorative frame for her face. She wasn't even sure why she did it anymore—whom was she trying to fool, whom was she trying to impress? Certainly not Manohar—all he seemed to care about was his gods and his drinks. He had not commented on her looks for—how long had it been? In fact, when was the last time he had even brought her a string of jasmine—the blossoms she had come to expect every evening in those early years, tied around her hair by his own hand? The buds would glow creamily in her tresses, black as kohl back then, and he would squeeze the petals between his fingers to release their fragrance and perfume her hair.

But that had been before her hair had turned, before her looks had thickened, before her body had begun to spill around her every time she sat down. Why had it happened to her? Manohar was no more plump than the day he first came to look at her—hair mostly gone, it was true, but the baldness only accentuating his babyish looks. And Mrs. Pathak, right next door, giving birth to her two children in the same two years she had—how had she retained the slimness of her figure, the immaculate blackness of her hair? It was all so unfair.

She could feel the anger descending again, a curtain falling around, enveloping her insides in its folds. She wondered if it could be a chemical in the dye that caused this reaction month after month. She really had to give the whole thing up. She had tried to do so once last year, going an entire two months without using the Tru-Tone. Squiggles of white had sprouted all over her head, like some crawling infestation, but she had not reached for the bottle. The squiggles had turned into gaping patches, and she had tied her hair tightly into a bun to hide them. But Mrs. Pathak had taken to shaking her hair loose tauntingly every time she came into the kitchen, and she had finally succumbed. She had even tried using henna once, since it did not have a chemical base, but it had turned her hair a bright orange and she had ended up looking like one of the old Muslim ladies who came to visit Mrs. Jalal on Saturdays.

Voices from the door brought her out of her reverie. ". . . and since he's in such a bad state, we thought. . . ." It was Mr. Pathak, not the meatwalla—what was he talking about? Mrs. Asrani put down the toothbrush and held her breath, to make sure she heard every word.

". . . really should do something before Vishnu gets. . . ." Of course. Vishnu. The steps outside. She should have told Mr. Asrani—it was Mrs. Pathak's fault—who'd ever heard of giving such dry chapatis to someone in that condition—her chapatis would make even a well man sick! *Tell them they should pay for cleaning up*, she felt like yelling to Mr. Asrani—what a mess—her head half covered with dye.

". . . and since we paid for the doctor, we think it's only fair that you pay for the ambulance." What a preposterous suggestion. Of course, Mr. Asrani would politely but firmly correct this silliness. The woman must be mad, to send her husband to say this. Poor Mr. Pathak—Mrs. Asrani felt a twinge of sympathy for him.

"Of course." The two words, in her husband's voice, sent Mrs. Asrani into shock. But the situation was too egregious, and she was forced to quickly recover. She tried to speak, but the indignation made the word stick in her throat. "No!" it finally emerged, swinging through the corridor and speeding toward Mr. Asrani.

"No!" Mr. Asrani agreed, as soon as the missive reached him. "Tell them that the only reason Vishnu threw up is because of those chapatis they fed him."

"The chapatis," Mr. Asrani explained. "You see, he ate them and that's what caused the problem. Perhaps you shouldn't have fed them to him."

"If someone is that sick, one can only expect—" Mr. Pathak began. "If someone is that sick, one doesn't feed them food fit for the dogs," Mrs. Asrani interrupted, still speaking only to her husband. "And if one does insist on feeding such things, then one must pay for the consequences." Mrs. Asrani was trying to keep her voice low, but frustration at her temporary incapacitation made it difficult.

"Aruna, let me speak to Mr. Pathak," Mr. Asrani said, trying, without much hope, to sound assertive.

"So really, *they* are the ones who should pay for the jamadarni even."

"Surely you aren't suggesting we should be paying for *everything*. We already paid for the doctor, you know."

"And for what, ask them, for what? What did the doctor say, that he's sick? I could have told Mr. Pathak that."

"Aruna."

"No, tell Pathak sahib that *they* are responsible. *She* is responsible. Tell him he should go to his wife and tell *her*—" Before she could finish her sentence, the door slammed.

By the time her husband entered the room, Mrs. Asrani was calmly applying the Tru-Tone again. "Did you have to be so rude?" Mr. Asrani demanded, the anger giving his face a cherubic flush. "You really should at least—"

"*I* should at least? Don't tell *me* I should at least. *You* should at least. You know how much ghee she's been stealing? Every day the level goes lower and lower, and I can't say anything. I can never catch her. And you're taking her side." Mrs. Asrani's voice faltered, as if she were about to cry.

"Aruna, Aruna, I'm not taking her side. Don't be silly."

"You said *I* should at least—" Again, Mrs. Asrani's voice wavered, threatening to dissolve into a sob.

"All I said was Vishnu—the man's dying—on our steps—we have to do *something*."

"So let *them* do it," said Mrs. Asrani, her voice hardening suddenly, like syrup cracking in water. "What good will it do now anyway? He's too far gone, the poor bechara—any fool can see that. And what makes you such a saint? Coming home drunk at one o'clock last night. Face so red it could have been a traffic light." Mrs. Asrani stabbed malevolently at the dye with her toothbrush. "Now can I please finish this?"

Mr. Asrani fumed out of the room, drawing back the door as if to slam it, but closing it gently at the last instant.

AS MRS. PATHAK dabbed at the sweat on her forehead, she wondered again why she had embarked upon the recipe for Russian-salad samosas. It was all Mrs. Jaiswal's fault, of course—serving those strange Mexican things at the last kitty party—"tocos" she had called them. They had been nothing more than fried chapatis wrapped around salad leaves and cauliflower curry, but the woman had been shrewd enough to mix in lots of mango pickle and chili, and the ladies (including Mrs. Pathak, despite herself) had just gone wild over them. "Rohit tells me that tocos are very popular in Omaha right now," Mrs. Jaiswal had crowed, lest anyone forget that her son was currently enrolled at the University of Nebraska, in the States. This had been particularly galling, given that Mrs. Pathak's elder son, Veeru, had just failed his first-year exams at Bombay University.

Mrs. Pathak melted a quantity of ghee in a kadai, then quickly scooped out and added an extra two tablespoons from the plastic container on Mrs. Asrani's side of the kitchen. She regarded this as compensation for all the water she was sure Mrs. Asrani pilfered from the tankie every day—the endless string of pots that boiled away for hours on the stove—the family seemed to do nothing but take baths all morning. Mrs. Asrani would mark the level of ghee on the container with lines and codes using an eyebrow pencil, but this only served to stimulate Mrs. Pathak, who had become addicted to this daily larceny.

As she waited for the ghee to heat, it occurred to her that her husband still hadn't reported back from the Asranis. Perhaps he had gone downstairs, to have a cup of tea at the Irani hotel. She had never understood why he couldn't just have the tea at home, instead of paying to have it in that tired old place. But at least he didn't get drunk at the drinkwalla like Mr. Asrani did twice a week, so she did not object. She hoped the question of the ambulance had been settled—Vishnu had to be out of there before her kitty party guests arrived this afternoon. She could just imagine the remarks behind her back if Mrs. Jaiswal saw something like that.

Poor Vishnu. She felt bad he was going to die. She was going to miss his "Salaam, memsahib" every time she went down the stairs. Although his return from Nagpur had been a disaster, the years before had worked out well for the families in the building—even better than she had expected. Mr. Pathak had certainly been thankful he no longer had to stand in the ration lines or take the wheat to be ground. And both she and Mrs. Asrani had felt better having someone to look in regularly on Mr. Taneja cooped up alone in his flat upstairs. Even the steps and landings had acquired a cleaner look, once Vishnu had been weaned away from his habit of spitting paan juice on the building walls. She resolved to make an offering for Vishnu at the temple the next day, if he had passed away by then. They would have to decide about the landing, of course—perhaps Short Ganga would still be interested in the deal they had arranged some months back.

The ghee was hot, so Mrs. Pathak rolled back the bangles from her wrist and added the first batch of neatly folded triangular pastries to the kadai. The batter made a sizzling sound which pleased Mrs. Pathak, and her bangles clinked together as she petted some of the samosas encouragingly with her ladle. She was glad she hadn't skimped on the ingredients as she usually did—a whole bottle of Dr. Writer's mayonnaise the recipe had called for, and she had tried to ignore the price tag as she had mixed it in. It would all be worth it, though—just the expression on Mrs. Jaiswal's face, as she brought in the platter piled high with her delicate, perfect, *foreign* samosas. Perhaps she'd even get another bottle of mayonnaise, to serve on the side. She had better hurry though, if she was going to go downstairs for the mayonnaise—she still hadn't selected the jewelry she was going to wear, or even the sari.

Mrs. Pathak looked back into the kadai and gasped. The top of one of the samosas had unfurled. Peas, carrots, potatoes and the precious mayonnaise were being released into the swirling fat. Before she could do anything, the remaining samosas began unraveling as well, almost in choreographed succession, until the kadai was a bubbling mass of vegetables, batter, and rapidly vaporizing mayonnaise.

Mrs. Pathak stood by the stove, her bangles bunching silently at her wrists. She stared impassively at the contents of the kadai. The Russian-salad samosas had disintegrated, they would not be debuting at her kitty party today. There was nothing left to do now but let everything crisp up. Then with lemon and pickle, it might yet taste good—she'd serve it as a side dish for lunch. And if nobody ate it, perhaps Vishnu was still well enough that she could give it to him.

THE RED IS darker, more viscous now. It oozes into the shadows of the hut. It lingers at the cut on his forehead, and darkens the edge of his eye bruised shut. Somewhere through the red he hears a snore, it is his father sleeping in a corner of the hut.

His sister enters through the doorway. She has brought a piece of ice from the market. She gives it to his mother, who wraps her dupatta around it.

"It hurts, I know," his mother says, applying the ice to his swollen eye. "But you must be brave. Remember, you are Vishnu." The ice feels cold against his eyelid, but does not quell the fire underneath.

"Vishnu of the ten avatars," his mother says, pressing the ice against his forehead. "Rama and Krishna are part of you."

Rama and Krishna, he thinks, and tries to remember the other eight incarnations his mother has taught him. *Matsya the fish, Kurma the tortoise, Varaha the boar* . . . His father suddenly snores loudly, and he stiffens.

"Vishnu the fearless, Vishnu the merciful," his mother continues, "the Ganges flows from the feet of my little Vishnu. One day his Lakshmi will descend into his life, and Garuda the eagle will appear to fly them to Vaikuntha."

Vishnu pictures himself with his mother riding the giant eagle above the clouds. In the distance lies their private paradise of Vaikuntha, gold spires glitter in the sun.

"You are Vishnu," his mother tells him, "keeper of the universe, keeper of the sun. What would be the world without you?"

"I am Vishnu," he says, "keeper of the universe, keeper of the sun. There is only darkness without me."

Chapter Two

Mr. Pathak paid the hotelwalla for his package of Gluco biscuits and returned to his table, where his cup of tea was waiting for him. There was a newspaper lying on the table as well, but it was in Gujarati, and he could not read it. He had thought of bringing the *Times* along, but he had not been ready to go back and tell his wife about his failure with the Asranis just yet.

He tore open the wax paper and took out a biscuit, then dipped it halfway into the tea, and bit the wet part off. The warm biscuit melted over his tongue, releasing its intensely sweet Gluco and tea flavors. This was what he liked most about Irani hotels—sitting at a white marble-top table on one of the black cane chairs, staring at the quotes from holy books painted in Urdu on the mirrored walls, hearing the orders being called out by the busboys, letting the tea-soaked Gluco biscuits dissolve one by one in his mouth. It was a shame so many of them were closing down. Just last month, the one down the street had been converted into a clothes boutique (the fifth boutique on their street), while there was talk of this one being sold to make way for a video store. Mr. Pathak stared at the yellowed ceiling through the slowly revolving overhead fans, and wondered how many more times he had left, to escape to this private haven.

A red double-decker bus roared by the open doors of the hotel, and Mr. Pathak smelled the hot dust churned up in its wake. There was so much noise everywhere and things these days seemed to move so fast. All Mr. Pathak ever wanted was peace, and it seemed as if he spent all his free time trying to find it. Even when he thought he had found it, like this morning, there was always something that caused it to be short-lived.

It was not his fault that Mrs. Asrani was so unreasonable. It was not his fault that Vishnu was sick. It was certainly not his fault that Usha had arranged the kitty party for today. Nothing was his fault, yet he knew he would be blamed for everything. A wave of self-pity swept over Mr. Pathak, and the Gluco turned chalky in his mouth.

Already, he could see his wife's face narrowing with anger, lips flaring around a stream of cruel words, eyes darkening with derision— *He had failed her again.* He would slink back to his chair after his chastisement and stare at his newspaper. The words would dissolve meaninglessly on the page as he planned his revenge—little acts of rebellion, tiny nips of retaliation, administered in carefully camouflaged ways, that helped balance things out in his mind. There would be ample opportunity today, what with Usha's impending kitty party. He would sit at the dining table instead of in his chair to read his newspaper, serene in the knowledge that his presence in the middle of all his wife's preparations would drive her crazy. She would bustle around him in increasingly frenetic circles, trying to dislodge him with dirty looks and inaudible mutterings, but he would feign obliviousness while secretly savoring her every move. She would have to finally break down, of course, and tell him to move, at which point he would do so with much reluctance, pulling out that expression of long-suffering, injured misery that he knew she hated so much. And when the friends arrived and were all assembled at the table, he would shuffle into the room, unshaven and in a torn kurta perhaps,

33

to ask after the women's husbands, or to generally hover around, until he was certain his wife's embarrassment was complete, and no more could be squeezed out.

The thought of getting even brightened Mr. Pathak's mood somewhat, but also enervated him. Revenge took too much out of him, it was exhausting to plan and draining to execute. He would much rather have the ambulance pick Vishnu up, so that he didn't have to deal with this issue. Perhaps he should call one and pay the money himself—Usha need never know.

Or perhaps he could call for it, but give Mr. *Asrani's* name instead. Mr. Pathak adjusted his glasses, as if he had just spotted a new and particularly interesting inscription on the wall. Wouldn't that be a surprise! The corners of his mouth curled up devilishly as he inserted a whole Gluco biscuit between his lips. Or better still, *Mrs.* Asrani's name. That would be a riot! Excited, Mr. Pathak crammed the last two biscuits into his mouth as well, and began to chew on them vigorously. He imagined the look on Mrs. Asrani's face when the ambulance driver presented her with the bill, and his lips twisted into a smile. Her eyes bulging like someone being throttled, her mouth opening and closing silently like that of a fish, no sound emerging from it for once, what a sight it would be! Mr. Pathak began to laugh. Bits of Gluco biscuit flew from his mouth, and the imam at the facing table stroked his white beard worriedly and looked away. Then a few of the crumbs flew down Mr. Pathak's windpipe, Mr. Pathak's eyes bulged somewhat themselves behind his glasses, and he was beset by a violent coughing fit.

The coughing subsided, and with it went Mr. Pathak's planned deception. It was too dangerous. He wished Mr. Asrani and he had been better friends, so they could have somehow, secretly, resolved this matter without their wives knowing. When they had first moved into the flat, Usha had invited Mrs. Asrani to a few of her kitty parties. Mr. Asrani and he had talked politics every time they met, and the four of them had even gone to a movie together once—*Main*

Chup Rahoongi, Mr. Pathak suddenly remembered. And when Kavita, just a baby then, started crying in the darkened theater, his wife accompanied Mrs. Asrani to the lobby and waited with her until the crying stopped.

Of course, all that was gone forever now, the kitchen had taken care of that. Any friendliness shown to Mr. Asrani (or worse, Mrs. Asrani) was interpreted as treason by Usha, who was constantly vigilant to prevent things from going too far. Both Mr. Asrani and he had been trained not to linger in the kitchen together, and to exchange only the most cursory of pleasantries when they met. Perhaps it was time to break this silence, Mr. Pathak thought, time to become allies. If nothing else, they could at least settle the problem of Vishnu.

Mr. Pathak drank the last of his tea and used his finger to scoop up the dissolved biscuit pieces from the bottom of the cup. Mr. Asrani, he knew, took the 81 bus every Saturday morning—he had often wondered where his neighbor went. He should be passing by soon on his way to the bus stop. Licking the last of the biscuit mush from his fingers, Mr. Pathak sat back in his chair to wait.

SATURDAYS WERE A day of atonement for Mr. Asrani. He would "make the rounds" as he put it, to ask forgiveness for all his sins over the week. Primarily, he supposed, for all the time he spent at the drinkwalla. He would first take the 81 to Mahim, and pay his respects at the big Ram Mandir temple there. Next, he would stop at the Prabhadevi temple, and the Mahalakshmi temple, and sometimes at the small shrine to Hanuman along the way as well. After finishing with the Hindu temples, he would take the bus all the way to the masjid near Metro, and offer his prayers there, covering his scalp with his handkerchief like the Muslim mosque-goers. On the way back, if nobody he knew was watching, he would make one final dash into the Catholic church across the street. Mr. Asrani believed in not taking any chances where appeasement of the heavenly powers was concerned.

Today he felt a special urgency to get to the safety of the temple. It was bad enough that this was amavas, the dreaded monthly event of no moon. Now, to complicate things further, Vishnu lay dying on their steps. Mr. Asrani shook his head at this awe-inspiring compounding of inauspiciousness.

The stench on the way down the steps was terrible. Mr. Asrani stopped to look at Vishnu and wondered whether to touch him.

"Vishnu?" he called. "Are you alive?" Then he realized how absurd his question sounded, and looked around, but nobody else was there. A bubble of saliva grew at Vishnu's mouth, and Mr. Asrani thought he saw it expand and contract. He decided, finally, not to touch him, partly because of the smell, but more because of an irrational fear that Vishnu would spring to life on contact. Holding his handkerchief to his nose, Mr. Asrani skirted around Vishnu and continued down the steps.

At the door leading to the street, he paused. He hated venturing out on amavas. He wished someone would invent an umbrella that would ward off the rays of misfortune he could feel raining down upon him on such days. His baldness made him feel extra-vulnerable—he could not even count on a layer of hair to protect him. Had it not been a Saturday, Mr. Asrani would have tried to remain ensconced in the protection of the house. But staying in today and missing his weekly round might be even more dangerous. Pulling up his collar around his neck, as if he were preparing to ward off some great chill, Mr. Asrani stepped through the doorway and exposed his body to the insalubrity of the day outside.

"Asrani sahib!" He had been walking toward the bus stop, keeping a wary eye on the cars passing by, to make sure they did not mount the pavement and kill him, when he heard the voice. It was a thin bespectacled man beckoning to him from the Irani hotel. "Why don't you come in, join me for a cup of tea?"

"Pathak sahib, it's you." The surprise showed in his voice. "I'd love to, but I have to catch the bus." What could Mr. Pathak want? On amavas, no less!

"Yes, yes, I know, the 81. Well, you might as well rest a little, two of them just went by, completely empty, it's going to be a while." Mr. Pathak beckoned to the hotelwalla. "Two more teas please. And a packet of your special cream-filled biscuits."

Warning signals were flashing in Mr. Asrani's head as he entered the hotel and sat down, and a cup of tea was placed steaming before him. They grew stronger as Mr. Pathak pushed the cream biscuits toward him, but subsided somewhat as the crunch of the biscuit was followed by the oozing sensation of raspberry filling against his tongue. Although Mrs. Asrani often sent him downstairs to purchase cream biscuits, they were always for the children, and he rarely risked his wife's disapproval by reaching for them himself. It had been so long since he had tasted the raspberry ones—though his favorite had always been orange. What happy memories it brought back of all the different flavors with which his mother would ply him every evening after school.

"About this morning . . ." Mr. Pathak began, and Mr. Asrani looked up in alarm from the biscuit he had split open to lick the cream out. How could he have forgotten the scene with Mr. Pathak and Aruna so completely? He quickly tried to mend the two halves together, but it was too late. The taste of cream was already on his tongue, the incriminating smudges conspicuous on his lips. Mr. Asrani's neck flushed raspberry with guilt.

"Pathak sahib, I don't know what to say," Mr. Asrani started, but Mr. Pathak cut him off.

"No, no, these things happen. The important thing, I think, is not to let them upset us. Or even more important, not to let them upset

37

our wives." Mr. Pathak's pupils seemed to radiate understanding from behind their lenses. "Really, why bother them with such matters, which, really, we should be handling anyway? It's not as if we need *permission* from them or anything." Mr. Asrani winced at the emphasis Mr. Pathak put on the word, and did not meet his eyes.

"Allies, that's what we should be," Mr. Pathak said, and Mr. Asrani wondered why, against his best instincts, he had stepped out on this noxious day. "Friends, really," Mr. Pathak continued, peering through his glasses, and the cream and biscuit began to form a knot in Mr. Asrani's stomach, ready to reemerge as a raspberry bolus. "Friends who can settle things amicably, between themselves," Mr. Pathak purred, and Mr. Asrani looked hopelessly at the packet of biscuits lying on the table. And as he found himself nodding to all the things Mr. Pathak was suggesting, found himself agreeing they should share equally in the cost of the ambulance, even found himself standing next to Mr. Pathak as he spelled out both their names on the phone to the ambulance clerk, Mr. Asrani thought to himself that this was the dearest biscuit he had ever eaten, and wasn't he glad he had only taken one.

THE RED HAS receded into darkness. Light is beginning to appear again, flecks that emerge through the shimmer of gauze.

"Eight," he hears himself saying. "Nine." Through the veil he sees her come.

"Ten," he says. "Eleven." The dupatta she has wrapped around his head is slipping off. "Twelve. Thirteen." She is trying to tiptoe down the stairs past him. "Fourteen," he says. "You know you can't hide down there, you're not allowed down the stairs."

"You looked!" Kavita cries.

"I didn't! Not through my good eye!"

"You looked! Even after I tied the dupatta! What's the use? I'm going to take it off!"

The gauze begins to slide against his eyelids, it quickens and he feels the burn against his skin. His eyes open as it alights from his face and shoots into the air, a long, crinkled swathe, reaching up high toward the open window. The light streaming in sets it ablaze; suspended in the air, it sparks and crackles, like a canal for lightning, like a conduit for the sun, capturing light and energy from the universe and funneling them into her hand. Slowly, she turns, there is gold cascading around her, she turns round and round, and the dupatta floats in spirals above her.

"Kavita." The word plays against his lips, as her form descends past the window again. It is Divali, she has a sparkler in each hand. "Look at my phuljadis," she says, as she waves the sparklers around in the air. Drops of fire fall from them, bouncing and splashing against the stone floor.

Vishnu smells the sulfur burn. The shadows are dancing on the wall, kissed to life by the light of the phuljadis. Up and down, back and forth, they rise and thrust and fall and turn. This is their chance, they know, this is the night of Divali, they whisper, the night when Lakshmi descends through their midst to the earth. They see her come, flanked by flame on either side, they leap into the air with every step she takes. "Will she find her Vishnu," they sing, "will she unite with her destined one?" The firecrackers outside roll to their song like distant drums.

"Do you have one for me?" Vishnu asks.

"This one's almost done," Kavita says. "You can have it." The phuljadi goes out just as the wire stem passes from her hand to his.

"Take this one, then," she says, "quick, before it goes out too." Vishnu takes the sparkler but it too burns out. The wires glow orange in his hands, he holds them up to peer into the darkness. The movement on the walls has stopped, the shadows have fallen back to rest.

"It's dark," Kavita says.

There is a flash from the window. Rockets begin to bloom in the night, they color her face green and blue. She turns around to stare at the sky. The shadows stir a little to life again.

Vishnu gazes with her at the garden unfurling above them. "It's never dark on the night Lakshmi is around," he says.

The years pass, and every Divali, she graces the landing. She gives Vishnu phuljadis, whole ones sometimes. He uses them to light strings of red and green patakas, the ones she likes so much to watch, but is herself afraid to light. They burst in long volleys on the landing, and Vishnu looks at the flashes in her eyes. Always, he sees both fear and fascination. Sometimes he holds on to the top end of the string, and the explosions climb the red and green rungs, creeping closer and closer to his fingers, until she screams for him to let go. Then he tosses the string into the air, the crackers turn fiery cartwheels over their heads; Kavita covers her eyes with her hands, and the shadows are forced down to the floor.

"Kavita." The Divali comes when Kavita descends without phuljadis. Vishnu notices she is wearing different clothes now. He notices her body is different too, it is fuller, with an allure he has not suspected before. He notices many things about her that year. "Kavita," he thinks, as she negotiates the stairs in high heels, trailing a group of laughing friends, their perfume sweet in the landing air. "Kavita," he wants to say aloud, as she passes by, her eyes in a dream, her lips in a faraway smile. "Kavita," he wants to say, and reach out his hand and touch, as she glides by on an invisible plane, the edge of her sari undulating like a wave behind her.

He says it one day, "Kavita," and doesn't realize he has uttered it aloud. She stops, as surely as if he has physically intercepted her. She stares at him uncertainly. A smile plays at her lips, and Vishnu sees the mischief seep into her eyes.

"Kavita *memsahib*!" she says, and looks at him daringly, to see if he will contradict her. Her hands are on her hips, and Vishnu can see the skin of her midriff exposed between her blouse and petticoat.

Vishnu looks into her face, past the defiance, and is struck by her vulnerability. His need to touch her has never been stronger. "Kavita memsahib," he whispers, and folds his straying hands together.

Delight springs to her eyes. She turns from him to hide her smile. "Salaam, memsahib!" Vishnu salutes, as Kavita raises her head, tosses her hair, and begins to ascend the stairs triumphantly.

THE FIREWORKS FADE from the night. In their place are hundreds of bulbs, wrapped in squares of colored cellophane. They light up the sky in bursts of red and blue and purple.

He stands with Padmini at the entrance to the fair. It is two months since the first time he has been to see her. He cannot believe she has come with him. How has he persuaded her to leave her room?

"I love melas!" she says, as they enter the city of stalls made of cloth and rope and bamboo. The lights blink on and off all around, the loudspeakers are blaring an old Shamshaad Begum song. Ahead rises the giant wheel, lifting laughing fairgoers into the sky.

"Look! Carrots!" Padmini says, pulling Vishnu toward a gunnysack stall. A man sits behind a mound of vegetable scraps. He is inserting carrots into one end of a shiny tube and they are emerging in an unbroken spiral at the other end. "And potatoes! Look! Look!" The potatoes have been forced through a slicing machine, a stack of ridged ovals lies spread out before the man.

"Come right up, memsahib, see what the wonders of science can do for you. Every husband should buy one of these for his wife, yes, you too, sir." He points at Vishnu with the implement. "Make your shrimati happy!"

Padmini has put her elbows on the wooden platform on which the man with the vegetables is performing his magic. "Does it do mooli too?" she asks, leaning forward and resting her chin on her palms.

"But of course!" In goes a long white radish; it, too, emerges as a spiral.

Padmini claps her hands. "Here, you try it, memsahib," the man says. People stop to watch. Padmini takes a carrot and puts it into the metal tube. She turns the handle, but nothing happens. A hush passes over the spectators. "You have to push it through," the man quickly says, and shows her how. The carrot emerges in a spiral, Padmini laughs, and a sigh of relief is heard from the crowd.

"It's so easy!" Padmini turns around and exclaims. Dazzled by her endorsement, people surge forward to buy the carrot cutter. The man sells so many that he gives her a new one, still wrapped in plastic, and tells her she can keep it.

"I've always loved kitchen things," she says, as they walk through the gunny-lined corridors.

Vishnu looks at her silver-sandaled feet treading delicately around the puddles of mud. He looks at her dress, studded with sequins, sees the layers of red, red lipstick on her lips, the kohl applied so skillfully, stroke by stroke, that her eyes seem to float white and free. He is still amazed, amazed to be walking with this exquisite creature next to him, this woman with the stainless-steel gadget held so tightly against her sequined bosom. He still cannot believe that she has agreed to be with him today.

"Guddi ke baal!" Padmini points. The cotton candy does look like pink doll's hair, it appears from nowhere, spinning itself into a giant pink puff around the stick waved around inside the bowl of the machine.

"Would you like some?" Vishnu asks, and Padmini nods shyly. Vishnu buys it for her, and they continue.

"Look at that! What a motor!" They are passing a photographer's stall, lined with all sorts of painted backdrops. There is a horse, standing up on two legs, perilously close to the edge of a cliff; an aeroplane with painted-on wings, obviously airborne, as evidenced by the clouds behind; even a crescent moon surrounded by stars, a rocket spaceship about to land on the surface. But Padmini is pointing at the bright red car painted on a wooden cutout, with yellow headlights, and a plate lettered in English, which the man reads out: "Good luck. Made in USA." She runs to the seat hidden behind and leans out of the window. "How do I look?" she says, as she presses on the painted-on horn.

"Only three rupees for a picture," the man says, so Vishnu pays him. He begins to sit in the seat next to her, but she stiffens. "No, just me," she says, "just me, or just you, but not both."

She begins to rise, but Vishnu stops her and gets up instead. There is a flash as the photo is taken.

They have an hour before the picture will be developed. They come to a canvas tent outside which a man stands. "Come see the film!" he shouts. "Cabaret dance by Reshma! Very hot! Up next, five minutes!"

"Let's go!" Vishnu says. "I love seeing the films here."

Padmini is unsure, but allows herself to be led through the tent flap. Inside, wooden benches face a sloping white sheet that has been sewn to the tent. A naked bulb swelters at the end of a wire. The heat has built up with every show, the air is now thick with the smell of perspiration and warm canvas. Vishnu and Padmini join the audience, which waits listlessly in the heat, scattered around the benches like victims of a carnage.

"I'm not used to this," Padmini says. "Usually I get taken out to proper cinemas. Taj, sometimes even Novelty." She shifts around, displaying obvious discomfort on her wooden seat. "And mai, it's so hot!" She tries fanning herself with the carrot cutter.

"It's going to start in a second," Vishnu says. Outside, the ticket seller is making a last all-out attempt to attract customers. "See Reshma's body sizzle like a pataka in the most passionate and revealing dance of her career! See her bare all, her youth, her beauty, her all!"

The light finally goes off, and Reshma appears on the screen, her head unnaturally elongated. She pouts and prances, and boasts that her body is so intoxicating she could even make the priest in the temple worship at her feet if she wanted. Although the promised revealing of her youth does not materialize, the audience is quite satisfied, and there are whistles and catcalls at the screen.

"That fat cow!" Padmini snorts after they have exited. "All she ever does is wriggle that big stomach of hers! Why did you take me to see her?"

"Because you dance so much better than her," Vishnu says quickly. "You should be the one up there."

"You really think so?" Padmini wants to hear more. "But she has bigger breasts than I do."

"Yes, but your face. There's no comparison." Padmini is pleased at this.

It is late by the time they get back to the street where she lives. There is music and light everywhere, young girls and women beckon from windows, from doors, from balconies.

"Can I come?" he asks.

"Depends," she answers, rubbing her thumb and fingers together. "You know what you need if you want to come in."

IT IS LATE afternoon when he awakens. The tide has come in and receded while he slept. The sand stretches to the water's edge, gleaming in the sun's rays as if painted with silver.

He tries to remember the night before. Standing on Padmini's doorstep after the mela. Telling her how much she means to him, telling her how much he loves her. Trying to find the words into her room, into her heart.

Padmini smiles her half-smile. "Wait here till I am done," she says, and runs her fingers lightly across his lips. He tries to catch them, to kiss them, but only her attar remains.

He cannot remember how long he sits outside her building. Listening to the music float by, watching the people file in and out. He gets up when the sound of the ghungroos chiming inside becomes too much to bear.

Is the sky still dark when he makes his way to the beach? Are the stars still out when he lays back his head on the sand? He lies by the water and thinks he has not felt this way with any of the other girls. This desire to be consumed with Padmini in one fiery instant, this feeling that he wants them to spend a lifetime together.

But now the sun is up, and the day demands more practical pursuits. He watches a seagull making its way across the beach in search of food. It hops through the sand, stops to peck at a piece of plastic, then hops on. It stops each time it sees something yellow or orange, and tests it with its beak. A wad of paper, a cigarette butt, a dried mango pit—everything inedible is spit back out.

The bird gets closer and Vishnu sees how ugly it is. The head is dark and shiny, as if dipped in oil. The feathers are streaked with black and look oily too. Gobs of brown cling to the legs.

The gull walks up to where he is sitting and lunges at a crust of bread in the sand. Vishnu watches the bread disappear into the beak, and imagines it traveling in one large piece down the bird's gullet. His own stomach rumbles its emptiness.

The bird stares at his toe, and Vishnu wonders if it will peck at it. He sits completely stationary, tempting the bird with his stillness, hands poised at his sides, ready to twist the white-and-black neck. The bird lifts its head, looks beadily at his face, then turns and hops away.

The sun hovers above the water. The hunger in his stomach rises, a roiling tide inside. He tries to remember when he has last eaten. Did Padmini tear off a bite for him from her cotton candy?

A small boy walks up to him. "Would you like some crabs?" he asks, holding out a bright yellow plastic pail with a toy spade in it. Vishnu notices the boy is wearing bathing shorts made of striped red nylon. They look expensive.

"I caught too many of them," the boy explains, "and Mummy said we can only take one of them home. Would you like the rest?" The boy stirs the spade in the pail and Vishnu hears the contents scrape against the plastic.

"How big are they?" Vishnu asks, looking skeptically at the pail.

"Oh, all sizes," the boy says, and lowers the pail, so that Vishnu can peer inside. "See this one?" He points with his spade at the largest crab, only a few inches wide. "That's the only large one. I'm going to add it to my aquarium."

Vishnu shakes his head and mumbles no. The boy stands there, surprised. "You really should take them—they'd make great pets. Besides, I spent all afternoon looking for them." His voice has an injured tone.

"Go away," Vishnu hisses at the boy. "I don't want your crabs, they're too small!"

The boy goes running toward a man and a woman. They are also wearing swimming clothes. "Mummy," he cries, "the man says my crabs are too small!" Vishnu turns away.

When he looks back, the boy is emptying the pail into a hole dug out in the sand. Vishnu watches as he straightens up and goes running after the couple, the pail swinging by his side.

A fresh knot of hunger tightens in Vishnu's stomach. His vision swims. He suddenly sees Padmini emerge from the water and walk toward him across the wet sand. Drops of water fall from her hair, a platter piled with fish gleams in her hands. The sun blurs and lists peculiarly to one side. He wonders if he should go over to the hole and see if the boy has dumped in the large crab as well.

There is a screech from above. Wings flap above his head, and he looks up to see a blur of oily brown feathers. The seagull circles once, then lands. It hops to the hole and perches at the edge, gripping the wet rim with its claws.

Leaning forward, the gull probes deep into the hole, then straightens out. Vishnu can make out legs and claws flailing through the sides of its beak.

The gull hops back from the hole, then turns toward Vishnu. It stares at him for a second, then spreads its wings wide. Vishnu watches the feet leave the ground, watches the body ascend into the air, watches the head turn lazily toward the sea. He tracks the bird as it completes half a circle, tracks it through the sky, tracks it until it flies toward the sun and is swallowed in its brilliance.

CHAPTER THREE

MRS. JAISWAL WAS cheating again, and as usual there was nothing Mrs. Pathak could do about it. Not unless she was prepared to be banished from the kitty party circle, like poor Mrs. Bawa had been. The scene was still fresh in her memory—the last time anyone had ever seen the hapless Mrs. Bawa, who had not even directly accused Mrs. Jaiswal, just said, "You seem to be getting too too too many good cards today."

It had been the three "toos" that had done her in—Mrs. Bawa could not have made a bolder statement had she pulled three aces from Mrs. Jaiswal's breast and flung them in her face.

"Are you suggesting I am getting these too too too good cards not by my own good luck?"

The chill had been so palpable that the women in the room had hugged their saris tight around their shoulders. Even Mrs. Mirchandani had felt it in the kitchen and rushed back to catch every word.

Perhaps if Mrs. Bawa had been keen enough to perceive the danger she was in, and skillful enough to pretend she'd just been joking, she might have escaped. But she interpreted the silence as encouragement to blunder on. "So much luck you have—last week too your three-three queens to my ninetenjack—it must be something you eat, to get this rosy rosy luck every time." She laughed nervously and looked around the room for support, but no one would meet her eye.

"Never so-so much luck for one person only, never have I seen that." Mrs. Bawa laughed again, more nervously this time.

"You haven't been playing very long then," Mrs. Jaiswal said, and everyone in the room, except Mrs. Bawa, knew what the words foreboded for Mrs. Bawa's cardplaying future. For Mrs. Jaiswal controlled all the top kitty parties in town, and no one who wanted to keep playing dared challenge her.

Poor Mrs. Bawa, Mrs. Pathak thought, she had been so distraught on the phone. "The exact amount that I put into the kitty!" Mrs. Bawa had wailed. "It came in a letter, today only! And now Mrs. Dosh won't let me play in her group either, says her sister has moved into town, and she has to give my place to her."

Mrs. Pathak had clucked sympathetically. She bit her tongue now, as Mrs. Jaiswal plucked the two-rupee notes, several of which had been lying in front of Mrs. Pathak a few minutes ago, from the sheet spread out on the floor. "I was so sure I was going to lose, too—Mrs. Pathak gets such big-big cards, and I only had a small little sequence."

The last of the notes disappeared into Mrs. Jaiswal's big black purse, the one that always lay by her side, the one that Mrs. Pathak was convinced held the secret to her unnaturally good luck. She watched as Mrs. Jaiswal tucked the purse under the folds of her sari, and fantasized again about pulling it out and emptying its incriminating contents over the sheet.

The kitty party had been a disaster from the start. The ambulance that Mr. Pathak said Mr. Asrani had called had not shown up. At one-thirty, only an hour before the guests were to arrive, Mrs. Pathak had sent frantically for the jamadarni, to have the mess around

Vishnu cleaned up. The jamadarni had demanded—Mrs. Pathak still couldn't believe it—thirty rupees! Thirty! The cheek of that woman, taking advantage of her when she was helpless! It had taken all Mrs. Pathak's bargaining power to bring it down to twenty, with the Russian-salad samosas thrown in. (Mrs. Pathak had tried impressing upon the jamadarni that the mayonnaise alone had cost five rupees, but unfortunately, the jamadarni had not known what mayonnaise was.)

After the cleaning had been done, there had been barely enough time to dress up for Mrs. Jaiswal. She had been unable to locate the pearl earrings that went with her necklace, and had been forced to put on a green pair that didn't match. ("What delightful earrings Mrs. Pathak is wearing," Mrs. Jaiswal had remarked loudly between hands. "They must be her lucky pair, that must be why she has them on with that white necklace.") Minutes before the first guests arrived, Mrs. Pathak had remembered Vishnu again, and pulled out an old sheet which she'd been saving to give the jamadarni at Divali (but certainly not *now*). She'd sent Mr. Pathak down to the landing with it to cover Vishnu up as best as he could. "Make it look natural!" she'd shouted after Mr. Pathak. "I want people to think he's asleep, not something else."

But it hadn't worked. The first thing Mrs. Jaiswal had said upon walking in was, "If I'd known I'd see a dead man on your stairs, I would never have come! On a Saturday, no less! How inauspicious!"

"Oh, that's Vishnu. He's just drunk. As usual—we really can't do anything with him."

"Drunk? You have drunk people on your steps? What kind of building have you brought us to here, that there are drunk people on the steps?"

"He's perfectly harmless," Mrs. Pathak had tried saying, but Mrs. Mirchandani had started complaining that Vishnu had lurched towards her as she'd walked past, and Mrs. Ganesh had declared that he had grabbed her foot, and it had only been the sight of the kitty pouch, hurriedly brought out and dangled in front of the women by Mrs. Pathak, that had quieted them down.

It had surely been a sign of terrible displeasure that Mrs. Jaiswal had not asked the hostess, as was the custom, to draw the week's winner, but had assigned the task to Mrs. Mirchandani instead. And now, here was Mrs. Mirchandani, fawning over Mrs. Jaiswal as usual, begging her to repeat the story about how she had come to Bombay on her honeymoon, and been discovered by a film producer, and acted in three films. "Tell us again, Sheila, wasn't one a silver jubilee?"

"*Two* of them, actually. And *Haseena* would've been a golden jubilee, ask anyone, if only the freedom movement hadn't gained force."

Mrs. Jaiswal played with the streaks of henna painted in her beauty-salon-coiffed hair and adjusted the diamond pin in her nose. "They said that if I'd continued, I'd have been the next Meena Kumari." Mrs. Pathak resisted the temptation to remark that at least Meena Kumari had been dead and gone for some years now.

A sudden tickle started up in Mrs. Pathak's right palm. She tried to ignore it, since it was a bad sign, portending more loss of money. While she was growing up, her mother had always called her "the lucky one," the one destined to be married into riches, a bungalow and car. Instead, here she was at forty-three, with two children (one of them first-year fail at Somani College), living in a two-room flat with not even her own kitchen, trying to impress this woman with orange streaks in her hair, who still believed herself to be a film star. The earrings dangled greenly at Mrs. Pathak's earlobes, the itch in her palm seemed to get worse, but still she refrained from scratching it.

Since they had come to Bombay, she had strived to claim her place in the circles her mother had promised her. It had taken work to get this far—she had learned to cultivate and flatter, to aggrandize her family's status and her husband's position, and to gamble away a few hundred rupees she could ill afford to lose. Now that she was recognized in the kitty party circle as one of the women eligible to be a hostess, what was the next step? Start her own kitty party? Try to wrest control of this one? Mrs. Pathak looked at Mrs. Jaiswal displaying the gold-and-blue silk border of her sari to the women around and scratched her palm distractedly. She would never be as rich and powerful (or even as coordinated) as Mrs. Jaiswal, she could never *become* her, so what was the use?

But this was no time for self-pity. There *was* one thing she could do, one thing she *would* do—and that was to make mincemeat of Mrs. Jaiswal's "tocos" from last week. She went into the adjacent room to assemble her tray. After the disintegration of the samosas, she had gone straight to the steel bedroom cupboard, the one where she kept all the valuables she owned. Rummaging under the pile of her Benarasi saris, her fingers had closed around the metal cylinder. She had pulled it out and looked at it—"Kraft" it said, in letters so proudly red and yellow against the bright blue curve of the tin that they practically screamed "Imported," practically screamed "American." (In fact, weren't red and blue the colors of the American flag?) She had been saving it ever since her cousin had brought it for her from his trip abroad—if ever there was a time to use it, it was now.

She had opened the can and peered at the cheese inside—it was definitely more orange, more *rich-looking,* than the pale yellow Amul cheese she was used to. She had decided to cut it into cubes and serve it from the can—better not to take any chances with these old goats, who probably couldn't tell the difference between Kraft and paneer. The taste had been surprisingly disappointing—bland and a little plastic, like something wrapped in cellophane, but without the wrapper taken off. But it was nothing a little hot chutney couldn't fix. Maybe some spicy roasted peas too, she had thought, and some lentils fried with chili powder—that should zip things up. As she had ground together the green chilies and coriander for the chutney, Mrs.

Pathak had wondered how the Americans liked to eat *their* Kraft cheese.

The bell rang just as Mrs. Pathak was putting the final touches on her tray. She looked at the cheese all neatly cut into cubes, at the peas and lentils glistening with spices, at the bowl filled with dark green chutney. There were voices from the other room, but Mrs. Pathak would not be hurried—she carefully turned the tin around until the lettering was facing the front of the tray. She was still adjusting the cubes of cheese when Mrs. Mirchandani burst into the room. "Usha, come to the door quickly. The ambulancewalla is here, and your neighbor is demanding you pay him!"

"VISHNU, WAKE UP!" The words come from far away. He opens his eyes. Kavita is standing over him in the dark. "Wake up! Has Salim come down yet?" Slowly, he remembers. It is the night he fell asleep, waiting for her to come.

"Not yet, memsahib."

"Not yet?" Her brow furrows. "Tell him then I'll be waiting upstairs. Right near the terrace door this time, even above Mr. Taneja's landing—last time we almost got caught. And, Vishnu, warn us again, will you, if anyone comes?" Kavita reaches out her hand as if to touch his cheek. But her fingertips stop just before they make contact with his face, and she waves instead.

Salim descends some minutes later. He is the Jalals' only child. Vishnu wonders why Kavita has chosen this Muslim boy, why she risks her parents' wrath to see him. The moon dusts silver on Salim's hair, and for an instant, Vishnu can imagine himself standing there instead. But then the light catches the boy's face, uncovering the full brilliance of his youth. Eyes so deep and earnest that Kavita must fling herself a thousand times into them, lips so full, so innocent, she must ache to press their sweetness out into her mouth, skin so fair and radiant, it must feel like life itself under her touch. Vishnu is overcome with humility at the boy's beauty.

"She's up there, at the entrance to the terrace, waiting for you."

Salim smiles, and the walls of the landing light up. Vishnu imagines Kavita thinking of that smile all day, waiting for darkness to fall so she can be close to its luminance. He waits until Salim's footsteps have faded, then throws off his blanket and follows.

Vishnu ascends the steps leading up from Mr. Taneja's landing. There is no one at the terrace entrance. A rectangle of light on the floor ushers him through the open door, to the night beyond. He stands just inside the door, his heart racing.

The terrace is white and empty. A shirt hangs torn from a clothesline, twirling in the night breeze. Antennas guard the perimeter, rising like sentinels from the parapet. Beyond them lies the sea, the whites of waves gliding silently over its surface. The moon looms unnaturally close, like a face pressed flat against a giant window.

Twice, Vishnu misses the red of Kavita's blouse. But the third time, he sees a corner, visible between stacks of empty soft drink crates. He crouches and moves noiselessly across the whitewashed surface, into the darkness of the shadows at the far end. From here, he can see the two of them—they are lying between the crates, their bodies tight against each other.

"See that star," Salim says, pointing at the sky, "the big one, blinking there? When I carry you away, I'll follow that star and see where it takes us."

Kavita giggles. "That's not a star, it's an aeroplane. Don't think I'll run away with someone who can't tell a star from a plane."

"All the better to fly you away in," Salim whispers, putting his head on her shoulder.

Kavita presses his face into her blouse. Vishnu sees his lips touch her flesh, sees the red of his tongue dart against her breasts. Wet streaks gleam in the moonlight against white skin. Kavita pulls her blouse lower to uncover more of her bosom. Salim's tongue goes down one breast and up the other, straddling the valley in between, reaching under the cloth to caress the flesh underneath. The streams of wetness merge, in a line of silver that winds its way across her chest and to her throat. Kavita moans and flails, her foot hits a stack of crates and sends it tumbling noisily. Vishnu looks on, unable to break away; he looks on, and feels the moon behind him, looking on too.

A wave of jealousy seizes him. He imagines pulling Salim off, and hurling him over the parapet. The boy grabs for an antenna to save himself, but it breaks, and plunges over the edge with him. Kavita runs screaming to the wall, and tries to jump over as well. Vishnu catches her skirt, and pulls her down to the ground with it. She is shrieking with grief as he lowers his body over hers. He feels the roundness of her breasts press against him with every scream, feels the firmness of her thighs as he pulls down her dress. He buries his face deep into her neck, and lets the smell of her body overwhelm his senses; he traces his fingers greedily over her skin, and covers her mouth with his long-waiting lips.

He looks at the couple again. They are lying in each other's arms, eyes closed, faces dappled by the moon. They seem so peaceful, so at rest, he might walk up to them, and they would not notice. He straightens up from the shadows. The wind seems to have picked up, the waves are sweeping the bay more purposefully now. He thinks he can feel the chill of the approaching winter in the night.

Vishnu turns around and goes back through the door. He climbs down slowly, one step at a time. A cloud covers the moon, funneling the night down the spiral of stairs. His feet feel the familiar stone of his landing. He sinks to the floor. He sits there surrounded by the darkness, allowing it to fill his universe and push all thought from it.

WHILE MRS. PATHAK fought Mrs. Asrani, and Mr. Pathak avoided Mr. Asrani's doom-laden look, the ambulancewalla stood and watched, and silently stiffened with anger.

"How dare you interrupt my kitty party!" Mrs. Pathak shouted, waving the end of her sari accusingly at Mrs. Asrani. "It was *your* husband who called the ambulance!" The earrings flashed and swung through the air with the angry bob of her head.

"Liar!" Mrs. Asrani shouted, launching the word with the full heft and conviction of her bosom. "It was your husband! And don't think I don't know what you do with my ghee!"

"*You* liar! *You* thief! All that water you steal—you can take all the baths you want, but you'll never get rid of the dirt on your face!"

"Thief, thief! I'll teach you, you thief!" Mrs. Asrani turned to the kitty party ladies, who had filled up plates and come out to watch the fight. "Hai, all you women, with the dal sticking to your fingers and to your face. It's fried in stolen ghee, all of it—now how do you like the taste?"

"No!" Mrs. Jaiswal gasped, quick to draw upon her thespian grounding. She allowed her shocked fingers to release the toxic plate, and watched wide-eyed as it shattered with a satisfying crash, sending lentils bouncing everywhere. Mrs. Mirchandani tried doing the same, but inexpertly toppled her plate inwards instead, depositing cubes of cheese in her sari, some of which she only found (and ate) at home, later.

Mrs. Pathak lunged at Mrs. Asrani, but was stopped by the ambulancewalla, who positioned himself between the two women. "No more!" he screamed. "How many hours the driver is waiting on the road for you. You don't have the only sick person in Bombay, you know. Two hundred and thirty-five rupees, right now! Or I'm calling the police. On all of you." He slapped his palms on his knees for emphasis.

"On *all* of us?" Mrs. Jaiswal exclaimed, from behind him. "What rot! We don't even live here! I've had enough of this tamasha—come, ladies, let's go."

But the ambulancewalla spread his hands out and blocked the head of the stairs. "First I want my money. Nobody can go until I get my money."

Instinctively, Mrs. Jaiswal advanced to challenge him, but Mrs. Mirchandani held her back. "He's holding us hostage, Sheila!" she gasped. She turned around, her face flushed, and explained the situation sadly to the others: "Mrs. Pathak hasn't paid him, so he's holding us all hostage."

"Pay him at once, Usha!" Mrs. Jaiswal commanded.

"*I* pay him? *You* pay him, you cheat! Stealing everyone's money, week after week, stuffing your black purse—you think no one can see? Let's have a look—all of us, what's in that purse of yours— what special good-luck charm, for you only, Lakshmi has bestowed—even the ambulancewalla wants to see—" Mrs. Pathak grabbed a strap and tried to snatch the purse out from under Mrs. Jaiswal's arm, but the strap broke and came loose in her hand. Mrs. Pathak stared at it, bewildered. All the fight seemed to go out of her.

"How dare you!" Mrs. Jaiswal hissed, as she pulled the strap back out of Mrs. Pathak's limp hand. "How *dare* you!" she repeated, and Mrs. Pathak flinched, as if expecting Mrs. Jaiswal to strike her with it. But all Mrs. Jaiswal did was to open her purse and fold the strap into one of the compartments.

"For your information, I have nothing to hide in my purse," Mrs. Jaiswal said, and held open the compartment for everyone to see. Mrs. Mirchandani extended a hand to feel inside, but was stopped by a withering look from Mrs. Jaiswal. Mrs. Ganesh was curious about the other compartments, but decided not to say anything.

"*Now* can we go?" Mrs. Jaiswal said, and the women nodded in unison. The ambulancewalla started to say again that he wouldn't let them pass, but sheepishly lowered his arms as Mrs. Jaiswal approached with her entourage.

"Why won't anyone pay me?" he moaned, as they filed past him down the steps.

Mrs. Pathak spotted a piece of cheese that had been flattened under Mrs. Jaiswal's sandal, and picked it up. She looked at it in her palm, as she would an injured bird that needed nursing back to health. "Pay him," she said tonelessly to Mr. Pathak, pressing the cheese with her fingers to coax it into a cube.

"Listen to your wife only, and pay me," the ambulancewalla chimed in.

Mr. Pathak looked sternly through his glasses at Mr. Asrani, who started shifting uncomfortably.

"Actually," Mr. Asrani mumbled, his face reddening as he stared at his wife's feet. "Actually, Mr. Pathak asked me to help him call the ambulance." He looked up to gauge her reaction, then quickly lowered his eyes. "How could I refuse only, he asked me when I was on my way to the temple. So I had to give my name, too." His voice choked, as if he had just discovered a remnant of biscuit lodged in his throat.

Wordlessly, Mrs. Asrani went back into her flat. She reemerged moments later, and put some bills and a fifty-paisa coin in the ambulancewalla's hand. "Here's our share of the money," she said, not looking at the Pathaks or her husband.

Mr. Pathak paid the ambulancewalla the other half. "Now go downstairs and take him away," he directed authoritatively.

"I will," the man said, "but you have to sign this first." He produced a printed form from his pocket, which Mr. Pathak looked at suspiciously.

"Well, either you or the lady there—someone has to sign it. *Someone* has to agree to pay the hospital charges when the patient gets admitted."

THE RED HAS returned, it surrounds him again. Behind it, he can hear voices, rising and falling, the color bulging as they try to push through. The red stretches like a balloon, then ruptures, and the voices flow in. Vishnu hears Mrs. Asrani and Mrs. Pathak—they are both very angry.

Floating above the others, he recognizes the voice of his mother. He tunes everything else out and focuses only on it.

"We all start as insects," she is saying, "every one of us. That's why there are so many more insects than people." He recognizes these words—it is the tale of the yogi, the yogi-spirit named Jeev, the yogi-spirit born nine hundred and ninety thousand times. A tale stretching all the way from Jeev's past through all his incarnations in the future.

"Jeev started from an insect so tiny, it was smaller than a banana seed. Of course, as an insect, he was not a yogi. But even then, some part of him knew there was more to be aspired to than just being an insect."

Mrs. Pathak starts screaming at Mrs. Asrani. The story of the yogi's ascent is in danger of getting lost. He wants to hear his favorite incarnations—the one where Jeev is born as a pig and saves a child, the one where he is a mistreated ox who sets a landlord on fire. "It took the yogi many lives to reach the level of a human," his mother says, "and he fell back several times to where he started. But finally, he got to the next level—he became human like you and me."

This is the part Vishnu likes best. The lives of wealth and indulgence that await Jeev. The feast where each grain of rice is dipped in silver, where the apricots have emeralds as pits. The marriage to the princess of Sonapur, with the procession of the thousand trumpeting elephants.

"Bit by bit, life by life, Jeev sated his soul with worldly pleasure. And only then, when he had slaked its thirst, and quelled its hunger; only then did his soul allow him to look upwards again. To a place beyond his own needs and his own self, where he could be of service to others." Vishnu recites the words along with his mother. He is proud he knows the story so well.

There is a crash, and the sound of more screaming. Noise has been pouring in steadily, cascading down the steps and flooding the landing. Waves of sound lap at his neck. The story starts dissolving, Jeev's years of service begin to break off, renunciation and enlighten-ment swirl away. He tries to reel in the thread of his mother's voice, but it snaps and comes back weightless through the surge of sound.

All the noise he has borne in his life, every shout, every insult, every curse, is roaring down on him. The pounding of feet on the steps, the crackling of songs from the radio, the squabbling of horns in the street—they are all there, and getting louder every second. Even the chimes of the ghungroos have turned into crashes—Vishnu wonders how such tiny bells can make so much noise.

He realizes he has to escape this noise. This noise that has tor-mented him for so long. Born at the moment of his own birth, it has swelled insidiously over the years. This noise that has been the price of every breath he has taken, of every action, every event in his life. This noise that is submerging him, taking over his brain and obliter-ating his senses. If there is anything to be left of him, he must escape this noise.

With all his will, Vishnu pushes on the ground. He feels his torso lifting up, feels the floor straighten under his feet. Part of him remains behind, sprawled under the sheet. Ahead rise the stone steps, spiraling into light.

Noise still surges down. Perhaps, Vishnu thinks, the best way to escape is to descend. He turns around, but cannot see the stairs that have always connected him to the street. The landing is suddenly immense, stretching in all directions into milky darkness.

A man comes down the stairs. There is a white band around his arm, with a red cross on it. The man doesn't notice Vishnu, but goes over to the figure stretched under the sheet. Vishnu sees him bend and feel a wrist, then straighten out and shake his head. He tries to follow the man, but loses him somewhere on the landing.

Vishnu stands before the steps, gauging the monument he must scale. He lifts a foot tentatively, then places it on the first step. The stone feels cold and smooth against his sole. He has not felt anything for some time now—the sensation is surprising, welcome. He presses down the toes, the arch, the heel, so that each part of his foot can feel the surface.

He wonders what to do next. He pushes down with the other foot, but nothing happens. He tries to recall the mechanics of climbing—is it his ankle he should bend? Then he remembers—he has to lean his weight forward and straighten out his knee.

Vishnu thrusts his body forward and up. The muscles in his leg flex. His foot relinquishes contact with the landing, it lifts into the air. The spell of gravity is broken, a sensation of buoyancy infuses him. He stands on the first step, and feels he can float up the rest.

Chapter Four

Mrs. Jalal stood on her second-floor balcony, watching the ambulance depart. Must be for Vishnu, she thought, not allowing herself to breathe—perhaps the Pathaks or Asranis downstairs were having him admitted to a hospital. When she was six, Nafeesa had terrified her with stories about the germs released into the air by ambulances, about people inhaling them and dying horrible, twisting deaths. Her sister's warnings still tightened around her lungs every time she heard the telltale siren. She waited until the van had reached the far intersection before cautiously sniffing a small sample of the air.

It was Short Ganga who had told her this morning about Vishnu lying unconscious on the landing. Mrs. Jalal had been skeptical at the report—could he again be feigning some illness, as he had done so many times in the past? "The last time that happened, Mr. Jalal revived him with a ten-rupee note," she told Short Ganga.

"Not everything can be cured that way, memsahib. Maybe Mr. Jalal can save his ten rupees this time," Short Ganga said without looking up, and without interrupting her ferocious scrubbing of the iron pot with rope.

Mrs. Jalal felt her cheeks burn red. She wanted to defend herself, to protest the unfairness of the comment. How many times had Vishnu come to their doorstep with some real or fabricated ailment, and hadn't they always sent him away with something? Even though he hardly did any errands for them, compared to all the work he did for the Pathaks and the Asranis. And the time he had stolen their car—what about that? They had not even reported him to the police, to get him the thrashing he deserved.

"When Mr. Jalal comes home, I'll send him down to see what can be done."

Short Ganga didn't reply. She rinsed the pot out, banging it around in the basin with unnecessary violence, her pigtail snaking angrily behind her. "Is there anything else you want me to do now?" she asked when she'd finished, wiping her brow with her forearm.

"No, nothing," Mrs. Jalal said. She felt guilty, without being certain why. "Wait—these bananas—Mr. Jalal isn't going to eat them. They're not going to last another day—here—for the children." She broke off two bananas from the bunch and thrust them into Short Ganga's hand.

A look of such contempt sprang into Short Ganga's eyes that Mrs. Jalal was appalled. For a moment, she wondered if Short Ganga was going to hand the fruit back to her. Then Short Ganga wrapped the edge of her sari around the bananas and left the room.

Mrs. Jalal took a series of tentative breaths, still alert to the possibility of pestilence in the air. What disease was going around these days that everyone was acting so bizarrely? Short Ganga storming off like that. Salim playing hide and seek with that Hindu girl from downstairs. Ahmed, her husband, whose behavior she couldn't even begin to comprehend. She took a professional-sized gulp of the air, and satisfied that the answer didn't lie in it, went back to the kitchen.

The remaining bananas sat on the table. She knew she never should have bought them. Salim was never around, Ahmed ate less and less every day, and she herself had always loathed their slimy feel. If they'd been less expensive, she'd have given the whole bunch to Short Ganga. But now there were three left, and she was the only one around to dispose of them. She peeled the darkest one, broke off the top section, and put it in her mouth. The ripeness made her gag, but stoically, she chewed on the mushy flesh.

Ahmed. She'd resolved to stop obsessing about him, but the banana fumes had for some reason sent her mind down that track again. She couldn't believe it had started all the way back with the fasts at Ramzan. How happy she'd been then, when instead of one or two half-kept rozas, Ahmed had decided to stick with them for the entire fasting period. She had always been distressed by his failure to assume the proper role in their family's religious activity. Month after month, year after year, it had been she who had written out the checks for the due to the poor, who had made all the arrangements for festivals, and taken Salim to the masjid on Fridays. Upon prodding, Ahmed would sometimes join her when it was time for namaz, but usually he simply left the room, still reading his book, whenever she unrolled the prayer mat. Her father had warned her, had almost turned the proposal down. "He seems to have read a lot of books, this Ahmed Jalal," he'd remarked. "Perhaps one of these days he'll even accidentally open the Koran."

She'd realized, quite quickly after their wedding, that her father had been wrong about Ahmed. Her husband *had* read the Koran, in fact, he had read it frighteningly well, and could recite several passages from memory. The problem was his interest in religion only seemed to extend to reading about it, not practicing it. "Thought control," he would call it, "something to keep busy the teeming masses." Then, without looking up from his book, he would add, "Not to exclude you, my love," and she would feel herself turn red at the blatancy with which he mocked her.

Some nights he would spout passages from the Bible or a Chinese religious book whose name she could never remember. He would compare these quotes to verses from the Koran, assessing the strengths and weaknesses of each text, unmindful of the fact that she was covering her ears to deflect any possible blasphemy. She especially dreaded the times he brought up the Din Ilahi, a sixteenth-century amalgam of Hinduism and Islam that the Mughal emperor Akbar had concocted to unify his subjects. "Religion revealed by man, not prophet," their school mullah had contemptuously asserted, "is religion fit for no one."

Ahmed, though, was all for it, and regarded Akbar as a personal hero. "He really put the mullahs in their place," he would say, as he looked for opportunities to taunt people. "Perhaps it's time to give the experiment another shot—force everyone to convert to it, Hindus and Muslims alike. Just think of it—instant peace, instant harmony—the mullahs might have to share their masjids, but so what?"

Statements like these made her wonder how many more she could afford to hear before being condemned to accompanying Ahmed into the fires of hell. An image from the Koran kept coming to her—that of Abu Lahab being consumed by flames, his wife bringing the firewood, a rope tied around her neck.

For the first few months of their marriage, she had meekly listened to everything Ahmed said, without comment. But she soon learned that her silence elicited increasingly outrageous pronouncements, which let up only when he had succeeded in provoking her into an argument. She had embarked then into the next phase, the one where she believed that she would be able to change him, that the intrinsic virtue of her beliefs would shine through and banish the shadows from Ahmed's mind. But she had found herself unequipped to match his prowess at debate—the keenness of his words, the onslaught of his ideas, the way he spun strands of her own arguments into webs around her and then watched in amusement as she flailed and struggled and tried to cut herself loose. She had felt the ground of her own faith begin to soften, and had realized the danger of allowing herself to be further engaged. That is when she had summoned up the courage to deliver an ultimatum—Ahmed was forbidden to talk about religion in her presence, or she would leave, taking Salim with her.

Of course, Ahmed wasted no time calling her bluff, carrying on as usual, ignoring her threat. Until one night, in the middle of a lecture on the equality of all religions, she grabbed Salim and rushed down the stairs to the taxi stand. Although she returned soon enough (she had forgotten to take money for the taxi), it got Ahmed's attention. At first, he was furious, railing at her for being unintellectual, calling her backward and brainwashed and bigoted. Then he tried appealing to her open-mindedness, her sense of fair play, arguing that a man should be able to discuss anything with his wife, that they were only words, not actions, so where was the harm? But she stood her ground, leaving the room whenever he brought up the subject, and for good measure, going to Salim's crib and pressing him to her bosom to reiterate her threat. Ahmed gave up soon after, and the nightly discourses came to an end.

It was several weeks before Ahmed's imposed stoniness thawed. But a trace of formality crept into all his dealings with her, a perceptible guardedness, that over the years hardened into something unbridgeable between them. He started lapsing into periods of secretive behavior—days, sometimes weeks, when he would keep to himself and hide things from her. She remembered one night in particular, not long ago, when he refused to let her look at his back, even though she could see a spot of blood soaking through his nightshirt.

Usually, though, the secrets he tried to keep were innocuous and easy enough to guess, and she would display just the right mixture of curiosity and consternation at his behavior to make him think he was getting away with them. What troubled her more, and what she blamed herself for, was the further deterioration in his observance of Islam. She watched in silent helplessness as his namaz-reciting dwindled month by month, as he started cheating at the one or two rozas he did keep and stopped going to the masjid altogether. Even more distressing was the fact that despite her best efforts, Salim was turning out more and more like his father. She reconciled herself to practicing her faith alone, and never being able to share this part of her existence with her family.

So when Ahmed started observing the rozas so diligently this Ramzan, Mrs. Jalal was startled, and quite pleased. Perhaps he had come around, maybe he was going to be like all the other husbands and fathers after all. Maybe there would even still be time to influence Salim. She had risen before dawn every morning to have turmeric potatoes and freshly fried puris ready for their breakfast, and stood on the balcony each evening with Ahmed, to wait for the sun to set. It had given her such a sense of fulfillment, doing the shopping herself every day, making all his favorite foods, feeding him the first bite of mutton kebab or chicken biryani with her own hands. And to her relief, he had not brought up the old discussions of other religions. Even Salim, persuaded by their joint example, had been moved to keep a fast or two.

But then the rozas were over, and Ahmed was still fasting daily. Sometimes he would keep them two days at a time, not eating from sunrise the first day to sunset the second. When questioned about it, he claimed it helped his digestion, or he needed to lose weight, or he was doing it in empathy with all the people starving in the world. Uncertain about how to respond to these assertions, and limited somewhat by the apparent absence of health side effects, Mrs. Jalal tried not to dwell on it.

But it got worse. He started wearing the same clothes day after day, ignoring the fresh white kurtas she laid out on his bed every morning. She would have to sneak out with his dirty clothes at night while he slept, and hide them in the dhobi hamper. Which didn't always work, since sometimes he would retrieve them the next day, and scold her for putting them there.

He stopped bathing for a while and only resumed when his body odor was so ripe that even the cigarettewalla was prompted to ask what was happening to the sahib. The radio suddenly started bothering him, making him irritable whenever it was playing in his presence. He would try to turn it off when he thought she was not looking, and if she objected, storm out of the room in a huff. One day she came back from the market to find it had disappeared altogether. That afternoon, a tearful Short Ganga demanded to know why the sahib had sold the radio for ten rupees to the paanwalla, when the opportunity to buy it should have been rightfully hers, given all the work she did for them, and who was the paanwalla to them anyway, when they hardly even ate two paans a month, if that? It had taken Mrs. Jalal an hour of standing on the pavement outside the paanwalla's stall and hurling accusations of thievery at him in front of his customers before he agreed to sell it back.

And then had come the night when Ahmed had thrown off the covers, turned on the light, and started rearranging the furniture in their bedroom. She had watched, frightened, as he deposited all the chairs in the corridor outside, moved the desk against the wall, and dragged the heavy metal trunk clear across the floor. Then he put his shoulder against the frame, and with her still perched on it, started pushing the bed towards the wall in short, grunting thrusts, like some overstimulated beast of burden.

"Ahmed, what are you *doing?*" she cried, not knowing whether to get up and assist him or sit there and allow her body to be jerked sideways with each thrust.

"Too soft," he mumbled through his exertion. "Bad for the back." He pulled a sheet out of the cupboard, and spread it out on the space cleared on the floor, then plucked his pillow off the bed and switched off the light.

"Ahmed, come back," she called to him in the dark, still sitting up in bed. "Why are you doing this?"

But he did not answer. She waited until she could hear his breathing grow soft and regular before lying down and trying to sleep herself. Sometime during the night, Ahmed tossed his pillow back on the bed, and she awoke in the morning to find him stretched out on the bare floor, the sheet draped over his body and his head.

The weeks went by, but he did not return. Although it had been years since they had done anything in bed but sleep, the presence of his body next to hers had always reassured her. She found now that if she happened to wake up at night (something that occurred more and more frequently as she grew older, or was it just her imagination?), she was unable to fall back asleep. Instead, she would lie in the dark for what seemed like hours, trying to lose herself in the sounds of his breathing, waiting for the dawn to paint its first strokes of pink across the ceiling.

She had been unable to solve the mystery of his behavior. She had tried reasoning with him and pleading with him, tried subjecting him to great big luxuriant blooms of tears (both silent and racking), and even threatened to leave him, but to no avail. He had stubbornly returned the same responses, insisting he was doing everything for his health, and accusing her of wanting to cripple him every time she asked him to start sleeping on the bed again. His answers had frustrated her, then made her despondent. These days, she was just plain exhausted—Ahmed's behavior had so sapped her that even a trip down the stairs seemed a major undertaking.

Mrs. Jalal looked at the remaining bananas. How many more would she be forced to eat in her life? How many times again would the slime coat her tongue, the ripeness fester in her mouth? Her throat constricted at the injustice of it all. She was tired, so tired, of being the one. The eating, the fasting, the aloneness, the silence. How much longer, how much further, how much more was she supposed to endure? Tears, thick and salty, started flowing down her cheeks.

It wasn't her fault this was happening. Perhaps she should let it out, tell her story, confide in someone. She had kept everything bottled up for too long. Maybe she would make a trip to her parents' house this very evening and reveal everything to Nafeesa. Let herself be ashamed no longer.

The door slammed, and Mrs. Jalal heard Salim's footsteps in the corridor. Quickly, she brushed off the tears with the back of her hand. There was no reason to get Salim involved in any of this—she would not let him find out.

Mrs. Jalal smoothed out her cheeks with her fingertips to capture the last traces of moisture. "Salim dear," she called out. "Come into the kitchen and have one of these bananas with your mother."

KAVITA ASRANI SLID the picture of Salim out from between the pages of the *Eve's Weekly* she was reading. "Tonight, my sweet," she said silently, and touched her finger to her lips, then to the picture. "Only a few hours left."

She had thought about taking some clothes, packing a bag. Now would have been a good time to do it, with both her mother and father on the landing outside, engaged in their weekly fight with the Pathaks. But she had decided against it. She wanted it to be just like it had been for Rishi Kapoor and Neetu Singh in *Zahreela Insaan*, for Rajesh Khanna and Sharmila Tagore in *Daag*. It was going to be a new world, a new life; why should her clothes be old? Besides, she had all the money from her savings account—the clerk had looked at her funny when she had given him the withdrawal slip, but she was eighteen now, and what could they do?

Kavita did not feel guilty about taking the money. After all, her mother had kept telling her over the years that it was for her dowry. While this was perhaps not (*definitely* not) the match her mother could have had in mind, they *were* going to get married, although they had not figured out yet how they would get a priest or mullah to perform the ceremony. Besides, there hadn't been so much money anyway—her mother should be thankful the family was getting off so cheap. She remembered the huge wedding and reception that Anita's parents had paid for last year, with the horse and the band and the dinner at Holiday Inn. A momentary wistfulness made her resolve waver, but then the prospect of romance won her over again.

Growing up, Salim had been one of the neighborhood boys, nothing more. She had seen him loitering around with the other teenagers, but had paid little attention to him. One day, the group had been particularly boisterous, and Kavita had complained to her mother about the catcalls and whistles they'd made. Mrs. Asrani had marched upstairs and accused the Jalals of harboring an eve-teaser. Salim's parents had sent him down to apologize—not to Kavita, but to her mother, who had met him at the door, arms crossed emphatically across her chest. He had stuttered at first, but then expressed such eloquent regret that Mrs. Asrani had melted—she had pulled him to her bosom and declared him to be her own son.

"From now on, Kavita is your sister," she said, and clasped their hands together. "If we can't all live in harmony in this building, what hope is there for the nation?"

"Sister," Salim said, with an expression so angelic that Kavita knew at once he was mocking her. She was going to pull her hand away, but stopped—there was some chemical reaction that had started between them. Electrons were being blown out of their orbits, atoms and molecules rearranged, heat was being generated, and she was suddenly afraid to interrupt. She stood there and felt the blood surge in her fingertips; she looked into his eyes, and saw the hint of green mixed in slyly with the brown, she noted the whiteness of his teeth and the fairness of his skin. She would not be his sister.

Mrs. Asrani's benevolence evaporated quite rapidly. "What all you keep doing to encourage this Salim character, I don't know—day after day he buzzes around like a flying cockroach."

"But he's my brother. You said so yourself."

"What brother-wrother? I pat him once on the head, and he becomes your brother? Who am I, the Queen of England?"

"But you said we all have to live in harmony."

"Yes yes. Everyone in the building has seen your harmony. Even Mrs. Pathak—the nerve of that woman. 'How broad-minded of you,' she tells me in the kitchen. 'He hardly even looks Muslim,' she says. I felt like slapping her."

"But it's not my fault if people think like that."

"Then whose fault is it? Parading up and down for everyone to see. Well, no more, I say. No more Master Cockroach Jalal. No more meeting him. Get rid of the bamboo, and the flute won't play."

"But that's so unfair."

"I'll talk with your father today only. We'll get your horoscope drawn. It's time to put henna on your hands, before you blacken your face too much for anyone to marry you."

Naturally, such proscriptions against seeing Salim charged their trysts with a new and delicious urgency. Whereas before Kavita had been content to just talk and spend time in his company, she now found herself consumed by the need for physical contact. She stroked his face with her fingers to feel the tingling rise up her hand, she brushed her lips against his mouth to experience the rush that raced through her body, she pressed her breasts against his shirt and fantasized about the thick dark hair on his chest rubbing against her uncovered nipples. And every time they met, she let Salim guide her hand closer and closer to places she had not thought about, before she pulled it away.

They began enlisting Vishnu's help. He had surprised them one day, as they were nuzzling in the dark on the stairs. "Watch out, your mother is coming up with the kerosenewalla," he had hissed at her, and Salim had just managed to make his getaway. For a while, they met on Vishnu's landing, bringing him little presents of money or food, for which he sat on the steps and warned them of danger. But it was impossible for him to keep watch both above and below them, so they started using him to communicate meeting places instead. And since they knew he couldn't read, Salim even sent Kavita a torrid letter or two through him. (The sight of the electrician downstairs reading out the newspaper aloud to a squatting audience that included Vishnu put an end to this.)

Mrs. Asrani, meanwhile, started pursuing the project of getting Kavita married with the zeal of a person whose true goal in life has just been revealed. She called the family astrologer and had Kavita's chart made ("three children, all boys" the astrologer promised, provided they matched things correctly, but "five girls, dark as coal" if they didn't watch out for Mars). Missives were sent to relatives far and wide (with the chart airmailed as far as Canada and Singapore) to scour the earth for a suitable match. A matrimonial ad was drafted for the Sunday *Times of India,* but was temporarily shelved when the next twelve Sundays were declared inauspicious by the astrologer.

It was when Mrs. Asrani's networking started producing results that Kavita realized she would have to leave.

"Mrs. Lalwani called last night," her mother announced one morning, beaming at everyone as she served them parathas at the breakfast table. "Her sister-in-law's cousin is an engineer. Just got a job with Voltas. Charts match so well that Mrs. Lalwani said they could have been Radha and Krishna."

Kavita nibbled at her paratha. She would just pretend not to listen. That always infuriated her mother. "Could I have the chutney?" she asked her father sweetly.

"Makes a good salary. Doesn't smoke or drink."

"I'll bet he's real ugly—must be, to want a fatso like her," Kavita's twelve-year old brother Shyamu snorted. "Mean, too—just what she deserves—someone mean and ugly."

"Shut up, Shyamu. The parents have a flat in Colaba. Own an Ambassador. He's the only son, so—"

"Maybe he'll beat her," Shyamu said, hopefully.

"How does the boy look?" Mr. Asrani asked.

"Look? Is that the only thing that occurs to you? What is she going to do—lick his good looks when they have nothing to eat?"

"I merely asked—"

"Mrs. Lalwani assures me he has a good height. Besides, he's an engineer. He must look like an engineer, what else? It's bad enough that I'm making all the effort—if you don't want to lift a finger, at least don't get in the way."

"She's barely eighteen. I just don't see why the hurry."

"Well, when *will* you see? When your darling takes wing with the flying cockroach upstairs? When we can't even show our face in public? *Then* will you see?"

"He's not a cockroach," Kavita shouted, unable to keep silent. "I'm going to marry him. I'm going to spend my life with him. Don't call him a cockroach."

"See? See your daughter's nine-yard-long tongue? This is how you've spoiled her. Day after day she gets more insolent, and I am the one who has to listen to it."

"All she needs is a good beating," Shyamu offered.

"If you to try to marry me to someone else, I'll throw myself in front of a train. Like that girl at Matunga station. I swear."

"How dare you talk like that. Don't think that just because you're eighteen you're too old to be slapped by your mother."

"Aruna, leave her alone."

"Slap her! Slap her!" Shyamu leaned across the table in excitement, overturning his glass and spilling Bournvita across the table. He yelped in surprise as his mother smacked his arm, then his face.

"Always causing trouble. Always. From morning to night, you just can't sit still." Slapping Shyamu felt so good that Mrs. Asrani did it again.

"But *she's* the one. *She's* the one who deserves it. You never hit her anymore, only me." Shyamu started sniveling, and this prompted Mrs. Asrani to slap him some more.

"Shut up, I say. And listen, everyone at the table. Mrs. Lalwani has invited us to come and meet the boy on Saturday. At her place. Says its more neutral that way. I've set it up for seven. I want everyone on their best behavior. You too, Kavita." Mrs. Asrani's voice suddenly took on a conciliatory tone. "He's a good boy. At least have a look at him. If nothing else, for your poor aging mother and father."

That was when Kavita decided. She would run away. Elope, they called it—the English word had such a voluptuous feel. All those movies, all those stories. She would be Laila, she would be Heer, she would be Juliet. "If that is what everyone wants, I'll do it."

The beam returned to her mother's face. "I knew you would," she said, putting her arms around Kavita and kissing her forehead. "Whose daughter are you, after all? Come now, after breakfast, I'll teach you to cook gulab jamuns so you can take some along on Saturday."

Originally, Kavita had planned to elope last night. But then curiosity had got the better of her, and she had postponed it a day. She wanted to see if she could pull it off. She wanted Mrs. Lalwani to be impressed. She wanted the poor engineer boy to fall madly for her, and have all his trite engineer dreams crushed when she ran away. She would cook to kill tonight, she would scent the gulab jamuns with the perfume of her own youth, sweeten them with the syrup of her own beauty. They would remember her, all of them—they would have her picture emblazoned on their minds, and pine for her return, but it would be in vain.

Kavita kissed Salim's photo and opened her purse to put it in. The smell of fresh hundred-rupee bills wafted out. A new life, Kavita thought, inhaling. The fragrance of a new future. She separated a note from the rest. Vishnu had not been well lately. This was for him—she'd leave it under his blanket as they left.

ON THE FIFTH step, he pauses. The stairs are curving round. The lower half of his figure has disappeared behind the stone. If he climbs another step, only the head will remain visible.

Vishnu looks at the torso outlined under the sheet. It lies there unmoving, mapping out the space he occupies in the world. He has worked so hard to stake out this space. Every inch his body has grown, every cell it has generated, every hair, every eyelash, has needed space. He has fought to claim it from the outside, gouged it out from the unyielding reserves around. He has guarded it, hoarded it, squeezed his body into its confines. He is loathe to give up this space.

His body, too—how will he leave it behind? It is his agency for experience, his intermediary to the world. This body that has borne him from infancy to manhood. Every imperfection in this body is his, every scar belongs to him—he can remember when it first appeared. He has cared for this body, fed it, cleaned it, nurtured it like a child. These lips that barely encircled his mother's nipple, this nose that has learnt to pick out Kavita's fragrance from a dozen others, these eyes that have watched the layers around Padmini's body peel away. He has tried to fulfill its longings, he has lain it down naked on the ground and felt the sperm surge out of this body.

Is it his perception, or is the stone under his feet beginning to fade? Are his limbs getting weightless, or was he always this light? Are his muscles losing their flex, are his bones turning to air, is his head threatening to float away? He can no longer feel his clothes, nor under them, his skin.

Vishnu mounts the next step. He wills the action, and it is done. There is no push against the ground, no thrust against the air, no activity at all. It is a strange sensation, vaguely unsatisfying.

He rises, and the stone slides across his view like a screen. Now, only his neck and head are visible, now only his face, now only his forehead, now only his hair. He closes his eyes. There he is, lying on the landing, the light cresting around him. He opens his eyes, then closes them again, making the image disappear, then reappear. He keeps them closed. He may have lost his sense of touch, he may have lost the comfort of weight, but he has gained, as well. He can see now, clearer, deeper, than he has ever seen before.

THE FIGHT HAD ended an hour ago—the landing had been cleaned up, the children beaten, the husbands berated, and both Mrs. Pathak and Mrs. Asrani were being borne towards their afternoon naps on carpets of satisfaction and inner peace, when Mrs. Jalal came down.

"Hello? Anyone home?" She knocked on the Pathaks' door, but there was no answer.

Salim had told her that the Asranis and Pathaks had been wrapping up their fight when he had passed their floor. "Looks like they couldn't agree who should pay for the hospital bed," he said. "So they sent the ambulance away without poor Vishnu."

Mrs. Jalal instantly felt the guilt, kindled that morning by Short Ganga. "You mean he's just lying there on the steps, dying?" she asked Salim. She paced her kitchen, worrying about it, and finally decided to go downstairs to see what could be done. "Mrs. Pathak?" she called now, wondering if she risked waking them if she rang their bell. "It's me, Mrs. Jalal."

There were shuffling sounds from behind the door. "What do you want?" It was Mrs. Pathak's voice, and muffled though it was by the door, the irritation it carried came through clearly.

"I was wondering if I may have a word with you. It's about Vishnu."

"What *about* Vishnu?"

"Well, Salim told me what happened—that you and Mrs. Asrani

had—had a problem getting him to a hospital—and—well, it's the whole building's responsibility, isn't it, not just yours, so I thought perhaps I should come down and help."

"What help now? The ambulancewalla has come and gone."

"Yes, Salim told me. So expensive. Hospitals, these days. But I have a suggestion. That's why I came down only. Perhaps we should call Hajrat Society."

"Hajrat Society?"

"They pick people up—people who're dying. To take care of them in their last moments. People who have no place to go. It's not a hospital, really, just somewhere a little more comfortable. And it's free."

"*What* society is this?"

"Hajrat. It's a charity organization. You can see their van pass by here sometimes. Some of the people from our mosque belong to it—even Mr. Jalal volunteered once. It's all free, of course."

"Oh. Related to your mosque."

"It's open to everyone—not just Muslims."

"Yes."

The irritation in Mrs. Pathak's voice was gone. In its place, Mrs. Jalal detected a careful tonelessness.

"I have their number. I could call them up."

"I see."

"They come quite quickly. I would just have to call them. You just need to let me know."

"Thank you."

Mrs. Jalal stood on the steps uncertainly. The tone of Mrs. Pathak's voice suggested she had been dismissed, but there had been no clear resolution to the conversation. Which was typical of her dealings with the Pathaks and Asranis. Why were these people so difficult? Why couldn't they be more like her upstairs neighbor, Mr. Taneja? She still remembered the weeks of antagonism that had followed when the main water pump had broken down, and the agonizing negotiations that had dragged on when the sewage pipes had to be replaced. Even something as harmless as giving Short Ganga five rupees for the new year had turned into a fight, with both Mrs. Pathak and Mrs. Asrani storming up and accusing her of spoiling Short Ganga, who now would expect the same from them as well.

At least Mrs. Pathak was still civil to her, unlike her abominable neighbor behind the adjacent door. Every time she encountered Mrs. Asrani on the steps, the woman made it a point to snort and rudely turn her face away. Which was quite rich, considering it was that fire-cracker daughter of Mrs. Asrani's who had ensnared her poor Salim. Mrs. Jalal stared at the black-and-white doorbell of the Asranis and wished she was agile enough to punch it and run up the stairs, like Salim used to, when he was younger.

For a moment, she contemplated going down to the landing to check on Vishnu. She still didn't believe he could be all that sick—perhaps she could trick him into recovery. But then Short Ganga's chastising words smoldered in her ears again, and she felt ashamed at her cynicism. The poor man was dying—*dying*—she herself had been talking of having his body carted away just a minute ago. No, there was no need to verify Vishnu's condition. Besides, if need be, she could always look into it later on her way to Nafeesa's.

There was nothing more to do. The trip had been a wasted effort. Mrs. Pathak, she knew, would not be calling. She never should have come down—it wasn't as if she didn't have enough problems of her own to worry about.

Mrs. Jalal turned around and, gripping the banister, began the climb back to her floor.

THE KNOCK ON the Pathaks' door had come just as Mrs. Asrani was about to fall asleep. At first, she had been too tired to get up and listen, but then the sound of Mrs. Jalal's voice had galvanized her to her own door. She stood behind it now, waiting for the footsteps to fade up the steps.

Mrs. Asrani looked at the Air India clock on the far wall. The maharaja's hands were both near the four, which meant it was too late to return to her nap. Besides, her heart was racing again—try as she might, she could never quite relax herself while she eavesdropped on Mrs. Pathak's conversations through the door. She had often wondered if she should see a doctor about this, if there was some little pill that he could prescribe for such occasions. But perhaps tea was all she needed, tea to soothe her mind and calm her heart. She opened her door a crack and peered out to make sure the landing was clear. She was about to enter the kitchen when the Pathaks' door opened and Mrs. Pathak stepped out as well.

In the kitchen, the two women did not look at each other, but kept their eyes fixed on their kettles. It was Mrs. Asrani who spoke first. "Hajrat Society. Never heard of it."

"It's a *Muslim* charity, she said."

"For what, though? To cart dead people away? What kind of charity is that?"

"She said to help them die. In comfort, she said."

Mrs. Asrani picked up her kettle and shook it vigorously to stimulate the water into boiling faster. "Forgive me, but if I were in that state I wouldn't be worrying about a pillow for my head," she said.

"I wonder what they do with the bodies."

"I'll tell you one thing they *don't* do. They don't cremate them."

"Of course. They probably just bury them."

"Who knows *what* they do with them."

"Especially the non-Muslims."

"They probably check the men, you know. Down in their private region. To see if they're Muslim or not."

"Poor Vishnu. I wonder what would happen to him."

"Nothing's going to happen to him. We aren't just going to hand him over like that."

"I'm sure the municipality does cremations if you contact them."

"If not, we'll take him to the ghat ourselves. Tell Mrs. Jalal we don't need her help."

"The nerve of that woman. Waving her charity in our face like that. As if we're incompetent. As if we can't take care of our own."

"Who knows what the real motive is. She and her crazy husband and that cockroach son of theirs."

"I'll call her up and tell her."

"Yes, give my name too. Tell her we have charities like that in our community also."

"Besides, I just put a new sheet on Vishnu. What does she think. I'll tell her he's quite comfortable, thank you."

THE NOISE HAS abated. Sprouting in its wake, like a field germinating after a flood, is a universe of sound he has never noticed before. Small sounds, tiny sounds—the footsteps of ants, the scurrying of beetles, the rustling of spiders, springing up from the ground. He hears the flight of a gnat across his face, he feels the rhythm of centipedes rippling the walls, he listens to the murmurs of cicadas rising from the trees outside. All the insects in the world are calling to him, he can hear their cries from forests and fields far away; they are calling his name, telling him their stories, asking him to track their progress as they crawl and creep and fly to their destinations.

A solitary ant crawls up the step before him. How high has this ant risen? he thinks. Has it ever been a bird, an animal, a human? Could this be a prince who has tumbled down, a Brahmin who has fallen astray? He listens for the voice of the ant, tries to hear its story. But the ant climbs on, steadily, and does not speak.

Vishnu watches the erratic path it traces. A step in one direction, two in the other, an intricate dance that slowly pulls it up. It reaches the top, and waves its feelers in the air, searching for the stone surface. Vishnu waits for it to push its body over the edge and start traversing the breadth of the step. But it turns instead and begins to move along the edge.

He looks at it inching its way towards the wall and wonders if he should correct its path. He places a fingertip on the edge to block it. But the ant crawls around the finger, without ever touching it, and continues along the edge. He tries again, and again, but each time, the ant circumvents his finger, single-mindedly continuing its course. Vishnu watches as the ant nears the wall and the hanging shadows slowly swallow its body.

There are other things alive in the stairs as well. Tiny bugs flit in the evening light filtering in through the window. A mosquito hums next to his ear. He feels he is in a forest, and there is life hiding everywhere.

He reaches the landing of the Asranis and Pathaks. There are more ants here, he sees them thread across the floor. Bits of food move along the line, like light along a string of bulbs. Vishnu follows the line to a corner of the landing, and sees a piece of cheese hidden there. The ants are swarming all over it with their black bodies, breaking off tiny chunks and carrying them away. As it becomes lighter, they try to move the whole piece; Vishnu sees it rock and twist a little. Then, like an enormous trophy being carried in a victory procession, it is hoisted off the ground, and borne unsteadily through the air.

Vishnu remembers his battles with the ants. How many times has he woken on his landing, to see the lines swarming over his blanket, his possessions, himself. He remembers the box of sweets he bought for Padmini. He has wrapped it in plastic, and buried it deep in his pile of belongings, hoping the ants will not discover it. But by morning, they are swarming all over it. He sets the box in the sun and waits for the light to drive them out, then presses their bodies one by one into the ground with his thumb. Before giving the box to

Padmini, he examines every sweet, and carefully pinches the remaining ants out.

The first thing he remembers Padmini saying upon opening the box is "Look, an ant." She pulls a piece of barfi out, and there, sprinting across the silver leaf coating, is the tiny black insect. Vishnu feels the guilt rise to his face, and waits for Padmini to throw the box down. But she is amused. She flips the barfi upside down as the ant reaches an edge, then watches it race across the top to the other side, before flipping it again. Finally, she tires of the ant and flicks its body into the air. She puts the piece into her mouth and takes out another. "Any more, my little darlings?" she says.

Vishnu wonders how many ants he has killed. All those bodies he has crushed, did they all have voices? He lifts his foot to clear the ants on the landing, then stops. His animosity has vanished, he will not bring it down. He watches the cheese move along the thread, it is almost at the door of the kitchen now.

Voices come through the door. Mrs. Asrani and Mrs. Pathak are discussing his body. How curious, he thinks, when he is right outside, listening to them. How surprised they will be when they see him standing there.

It is Mrs. Asrani who comes out first. She looks straight at him, but does not see him. Mrs. Pathak is right behind her, carrying her cup of tea as well. Her gaze falls upon the ants, her eyes widen at the sight of the cheese. "Damn ants," she cries, and kicks the cheese across the landing. She lifts her sandal and brings it down repeatedly on the convoy.

The screams are so loud that Vishnu covers his ears. He thinks of children run over by cars, families crushed by buildings, people burnt alive. He covers his ears to keep the agony out, but the screams claw them apart and burrow into his brain.

THE LAST RAYS of evening light are filtering through the window when Vishnu sees the image. A man is standing over his body on the landing down below. He kneels besides him, and pulls back the sheet. With one hand, the man touches Vishnu's cheek; with the other, he presses the forehead and brushes the wisps of hair off the eyes. Fingertips trace across Vishnu's lips, then down his chin, and to his chest, where they rub against his heart.

The man has his eyes closed. His neck is arched, head tilted upwards, lips reciting silent words. Vishnu has seen this silhouette before, he knows he should recognize the crouching figure.

The man's eyes open. Their whiteness reaches through the dark. They are large and milky, staring up through the air, through the ceiling, through the stone, at some point outside in the sky. Vishnu looks at them and is unsure if they are filled with reverence or fear.

The eyes blink, the fingers caress the tufts of chest hair, the lips open and close. Soft words float slowly up from the upturned face. Vishnu sees the gray hair, sees the bulbous nose, sees the pockmarks on the cheeks. Recognition floods in finally. He peers down at Mr. Jalal on the landing, crouching next to his body, staring up through the darkness towards heaven.

Chapter Five

Mr. Jalal read from his book.

The eyes. Surdas's eyes.

The two fountains of sight.

It would have to be the eyes, Surdas decided.

The eyes are the windows to the world, and to the soul.

The sin he had committed, through those eyes.

The sins we all commit. Not the same, but the gravity, the gravity of the sins.

Surdas looked at his eyes. His eyes in the mirror.

The sin, the hierarchy of sin, like roots and a trunk and branches and twigs, a network of sin.

He said, With these eyes have I sinned, and with these shall I cleanse myself.

Surdas the poet, the greatest poet in the court of Akbar, the greatest king. He had sinned. He had sinned with his eyes. His poetry would not be enough to save him.

These eyes shall be my freedom. These eyes shall be my penance. With these eyes shall I attain salvation.

Mr. Jalal paused. What had *he* sinned with? His hands, certainly. His mind. His body. His tongue, perhaps? His nose? Had he sinned with his nose? Perhaps by smelling something he shouldn't have? Mr. Jalal pondered this question, whether it was possible for a nose to be guilty of sin.

Surdas picked up the knife. It was a small ornamental knife, with a sharp, curved blade. It had a wooden handle, with three diagonal marks on it.

The handle with its marks pleased Mr. Jalal. Every account he had read said something different. In one, Surdas was said to have used a skewer, in another, a sword; still another had him pick up a razor, which Mr. Jalal considered the least attractive alternative, since who knew what beards the blade had scraped against? The ornamental knife in this book was much more deserving of the task. Mr. Jalal imagined it gleaming its purity, the mysterious marks on its handle transmitting a sense of ceremony to Surdas's fingers as they closed around.

He slashed his left eye first. He had not meant to scream, but the pain was so intense that he must have, since they came to the door. Surdas, let us in, they pleaded. He saw the blood spurt out, run down his nose, collect at his lips. All this he saw with his other eye.

Mr. Jalal touched his own eyes. Surdas had coveted a girl he shouldn't have. He had undressed her, drunk in her nudeness, made love to her, all with his eyes. Mr. Jalal tried to think—had he done anything to match that? There must have been something—his eyes couldn't be innocent. Mr. Jalal decided to be on the safe side, and add them to the inventory of parts of his body with which he had sinned.

Surdas picked up the knife again. This time, he knew he would not see anymore. He stared at the blade calmly, so calmly, with such elaboration, knowing it was the last thing he would see. He took his fill of the sight of the blade like a man taking his last drink of water, his last breath of air. And when he knew the memory would forever be with him, only then did he bring the blade up.

The pain was much worse this time, but he was not surprised by it, and he did not scream. The satisfying, cleansing pain, his mouth filling with blood, a red, peaceful, calming night descending over everything.

And Surdas went to the door and opened it. He turned his face to the horrified people assembled there.

And said to them, Now I am free.

Now I am free.

Mr. Jalal stared at the words. The brown print stood like dried blood against the yellow of the paper. He ran his fingers across the letters, half expecting the clotted ink to come off against his fingertips, red and rejuvenated.

He imagined if he could ever pierce his own eyes. Find a knife just like the one Surdas had used, and watch himself in the bathroom mirror as he raised it to his face. See the blade, feel it, know what the first whisper of contact meant. Or perhaps cut off some other part from the inventory. Maybe all of them. (Had he decided yet about the nose?) Not so much because he felt guilty, like Surdas, but for the sanctity that penance bestowed. "Happy are those who have purified themselves," the Koran said. Mr. Jalal wanted to be pure. He wanted to rise, to be enlightened, to be introduced to the rapture of faith. He yearned for it more than anything else.

Of late, he had been delving into the penance prescribed by different religions. The nuns and monks who flogged themselves to experience the trials of Jesus. The fakirs who lay on beds of ice in the Himalayas to overcome their attachment to the body. The flagellants who roamed the streets whipping their bare torsos with long, tapering ropes. Mr. Jalal would come to the balcony every time he heard the drums that announced their arrival. He would watch them as they danced with their ropes held high above their heads, and flinch every time they cracked them across their backs.

The tragedy was that he had no tolerance for pain. He was terrified of the slightest cut or bruise—had always been, ever since he was a child. The sight of blood made him heave. He had often toyed with the idea of going downstairs and asking one of the flagellants the secret of their endurance.

Recently he had seen a man recite several pages of the Koran while holding his palm over a gas flame. He had decided to try it himself at home, but the gas, when he had turned it on, had burnt with a blueness that had been too intimidating. He had rummaged around the kitchen drawers and found a packet of birthday candles, which had seemed perfect to start with instead. He had lit one and lowered his hand over the flame. Almost immediately, the sensation had been too much to bear. He had experimented with the different colors, hoping that one of them (pink, he had guessed) would be less hot. But the candles had all burnt his palm with equal efficiency. Finally he had decided to douse the candles with his fingertips—even that had sent him running to the medicine cabinet searching for the Burnol.

Much worse was what had happened at Muharram. For years, he had watched the processions, snaking through the streets of Bombay. The men cried and wept, whipping their backs bloody with ropes and chains to lament the treatment of the Prophet's grandson at Karbala. He would see people slash at their bodies with sharpened pieces of metal, see the blood well out of gashes on their chests and limbs. Sometimes they would fall to the ground, quivering in pain, but they always picked themselves up and continued again. He would marvel at the penitents' faith—the faith that was said to heal their wounds overnight, no matter how deep or grievous. He would wait until the procession had passed, then follow in its wake, stepping his way carefully through the fragments of rope and metal, staring in fascination at the smears of blood drying darkly on the road.

He had gone to see the procession as usual this year. Through the crowd, Mr. Jalal had seen a young boy, no more than sixteen, lashing himself with a belt studded with pieces of metal. Each time the boy brought the belt down, the sun reflected off the metal edges as they whistled through the air. The boy's back was bathed in a sea of cuts, but he kept whipping himself, his face contorting in pain, his lips never stopping repeating the name of Allah. The only concession Mr. Jalal heard was a sharp intake of breath after each stroke, the first syllable of "Allah" half swallowed, but still audible.

He did not know what happened next. He was moving along with the procession, staring at the bloody pattern on the boy's back, trying to hear the sound of each "Allah," when he found his fingers unbuttoning the shirt he wore and reaching for his own belt. He tied his shirt around his waist like some of the other men and stepped into the procession behind the boy. One end of his belt grasped firmly in his hand, the buckle end swinging by his side.

The mourners swelled around him, immersing him in their religious fervor. The metal-studded belt rose and fell in front of him. A streak of blood flew through the air and landed diagonally across his chest, like a challenge daring him to make his own mark. He lifted the belt into the air and swung it around, but the momentum was wrong, and the belt coiled itself around his arm. He tried it again, and once more the belt did not behave, flopping harmlessly against his shoulder. He wondered if the people around him were watching, if they had noticed his ineptitude, if they were whispering and pointing at the novice, the fake. Fresh droplets of blood rose from the boy's back and spattered his face. He let the belt straighten under the weight of the buckle. Then he swung it in a wide arc, saw the buckle rise through the air and disappear over his head, and waited for the contact that would initiate him into the crowd.

The first sensation he felt was a stinging blow, like that of a pellet, aimed just below his shoulder blade. He had meant to shout Allah's name like the boy, had the word at the tip of his tongue, waiting to be exhaled. But the pain that surged in at the next instant was so intense that all he could do was to scream out loud. He released the belt, and it swung from his back—the prong in the buckle had lodged in his flesh. He screamed again and again, and clawed at the belt, then fell backwards on the road, which pushed the metal further in. The procession pressed on, unmindful of his agony. He crawled through the tangle of legs into the bank of onlookers, to a man who pulled the buckle out.

"Wait, your belt!" the man cried, waving it in the air after him, as Mr. Jalal staggered away through the crowd.

He would never be able to inflict pain on himself. He would never experience its serenity, its sanctity, its purity. All he could do was read about it and fantasize. Mr. Jalal wondered wistfully why pain had to be so *painful*.

He had chosen the next best thing. Deprivation. It had occurred to him during Ramzan. He had never fasted much before, except once or twice each year to appease Arifa. Even then, he would usually end his fast before the proper time. This time, Arifa had persuaded him to keep the first roza all the way to sunset.

Perhaps it was the fact that he was in it for the full duration, but by midmorning, all he could think of was food and water. His mouth felt papery, his tongue dry and listless, and his throat scraped like leather when he swallowed. Hunger bored through the tissues of his stomach and spread like a fever to the far reaches of his body.

It was in the early evening that a strange clarity opened up to him. The hunger and thirst were purifying agents, cleansing his mind of unnecessary thought, fortifying his body against the laxness to which he had allowed it to become accustomed. He decided he would continue subjecting himself to them, making them part of his existence, fasting every day of the Ramzan period, and continuing after that as well.

He had been doing it now for three months. The problem was his body seemed to have become too used to hunger, and the exercise was in danger of not qualifying as deprivation anymore. He had tried fasting for longer stretches than the traditional sunrise to sunset, but the emptiness had made his head spin, forcing him to stop. The path to enlightenment for him, he had decided, could not be paved by pain *or* dizziness.

Instead, he had tried to find new ways to deprive himself. He had given up reading the newspaper, then stopped listening to music, but these had seemed like minor sacrifices. He had tried not washing, but people had complained too much about his odor. He had started sleeping on the floor. Arifa had called to him to get up and join her in the bed, but only for the first few days. Lately, he noticed with resentment, she had been spreading out quite comfortably on his side of the bed as well, and snoring even louder than she normally did.

In the past week, he had embarked on a new project. He would climb down the stairs late at night and sit in the dark next to Vishnu. Sometimes he would watch him for an hour before returning to his flat. Once, he fell asleep and only woke up at dawn, just in time to avoid Short Ganga on her morning milk run.

Sitting there, he would play with a curl of Vishnu's hair and reach out and touch Vishnu's face. His mind would wander across all the little deceptions he had allowed Vishnu to get away with over the years. The compensations for injuries supposedly sustained while running errands, the reimbursements for prices purportedly inflated by shopkeepers. Perhaps it had been his years of laxness that had encouraged Vishnu to steal their car that one time. What a shock that had been to him. But it all mattered so little now.

Mr. Jalal would move his fingers over Vishnu's nose, his eyelids, his lips. The skin would feel hot against his cool fingertips, and he would try and read Vishnu's expression using his sense of touch. Was the forehead furrowed in concentration, or was it from pain? Were the eyelids twitching from a fever, or was Vishnu experiencing a dream? Was it the sight of some fantastic vision that was making the lips tremble, the nearing of some profound unrevealed truth that fueled the urgent rasps of breath? Most important of all, was Vishnu still suffering, or had he transcended it, gathering momentum from its throes to launch himself to a higher, more tranquil plane?

Mr. Jalal was fascinated by Vishnu's current state. He felt there was something holy, something exalted, about being so close to death. He had almost died himself, when he was five. A case of smallpox had left him in a state of delirium for days. He had tried many times to recapture the memory of that experience, to feel again what it meant to be able to look over the edge.

Sitting next to Vishnu, he could sense it everywhere—a premonition of momentousness, a cognizance in the air, that floated through the dark and landed around his shoulders like a shawl. Mr. Jalal wanted to wrap himself tight within the feeling, he wanted to be irradiated by the energy spreading everywhere through the landing from Vishnu.

Tonight, he had decided, he would go one step further than before. He would spend the night with Vishnu. Stretch out on the landing next to him, and sleep right there beside him. He would be like Mother Teresa, like St. Francis, and embrace Vishnu as a brother. Not shrinking at the smell, the filth, or the possibility of infection. Perhaps someone would notice him, but he would not care.

Mr. Jalal returned to his book. His fingers trembled as they smoothed out the page in front of him. The time would soon be at hand. When he, too, would see.

IT HAD HAPPENED several years ago. It was not as if Vishnu had intended to *steal* the Jalals' Fiat. "Pick me up in a motor, and I will let you drive me anywhere," Padmini had promised. The only way to collect on the offer had been to *borrow* the car.

It had taken some effort, too.

"Sahib, I will be your driver from now on," he had announced to Mr. Jalal on the staircase one day.

Mr. Jalal was taken aback at the offer. "Since when did you learn to drive?"

"Me? Hah! So many years, I've been driving. Fiat, Ambassador, even imported, no problem. I can show you, now only, let's go to your car."

Mr. Jalal waved him away, saying he did not need a driver.

"Even Indira Gandhi I once or twice drove," Vishnu cried after Mr. Jalal, who did not look back.

When his badgering did not yield results, Vishnu tried another tactic. Mr. Jalal came downstairs one morning to find him polishing the car with a filthy piece of cotton.

"All clean and shiny, sahib," Vishnu said, saluting smartly. Then, noticing one of several oil stains he had missed, he spat robustly into the cloth and rubbed the moisture into the metal.

"There," Vishnu said, and Mr. Jalal noted that the stain was now evenly distributed over a larger area.

The morning came when, against his better judgment, Mr. Jalal caved in. After checking Vishnu's breath to make sure he hadn't started drinking already, he instructed Vishnu to drive them to the Binny showroom at Opera House. Relaxing in the backseat, Mr. Jalal noted that although Vishnu's chauffeuring was not anything Indira Gandhi could have possibly been accustomed to, it was a luxury, nevertheless, to be driven around.

"This was very nice, but we really can't afford to keep a driver," he told Vishnu afterwards, offering him a two-rupee note.

"Who said anything about money, sahib? I just want to do it to get a chance to drive again."

Perhaps Mr. Jalal should have listened to the warning bells beginning to peal so lustily in his head, but he didn't. Instead, he asked Vishnu to drive him the next day to Crawford Market. There, while he argued with the merchants about the price of a basket of mangoes, Vishnu stole away to the keysmith to have the car key duplicated. And that night, as Mr. Jalal fantasized about being driven to Juhu Beach or perhaps even Versova, Vishnu and Padmini were coasting in the Fiat along Marine Drive, enjoying the sound of the waves rolling in rhythmically from the Arabian Sea.

A BREEZE BLOWS down the staircase. Vishnu can suddenly smell the sea.

"I feel so light. Like I am floating," Padmini says, opening the car window and holding her head out.

Vishnu looks at her, her face framed against the yellow of the dupatta billowing up around her. He puts his hand on her thigh, and she does not push it off.

"Someday, I want to ride in an aeroplane," Padmini says, closing her eyes against the wind, and Vishnu's hand glides against her skin and meets no resistance.

"Will you take me on a plane?" she asks again later, searching his face, as he unbuttons her blouse in the backseat. They are parked just below the overlook of Hanging Gardens, in the darkness of a building under construction. Down below, curving next to the inkiness of the bay, each pearl of light glitters in its setting along Marine Drive. He lays his cheek against her breast, and feels the resilience of her flesh.

"We'll go together—we'll go to Agra, and see the Taj," he says, rubbing his nose against her nipple, and smelling the scent of her which attar cannot conceal.

"Promise?" she says, her eyes wide, wary, like those of a child trying to decide whether to believe an adult.

Vishnu looks from the bareness of her neck to the strand of lights stretching by the sea below. "I promise," he whispers.

His lips close around her nipple. She arches her back to put more of her breast in his mouth. He takes it in greedily, first the dark ring around the nipple, then the mound of flesh that follows. But part of her breast spills out. He feels it press against his chin, his cheek, and buries his nose in its warm attar-laden scent.

He moves down her torso. Her skin is silver in the light floating in from outside, smooth and glistening like the surface of a freshly caught pomfret. She undulates under his lips, pressing her chest, her abdomen, her pelvis against him, offering each in turn to be anointed by his tongue. He runs his fingers across the softness of her belly, then grazes the stubble on his chin against it. She tries to move away, but he grabs her breasts and holds down her body, then runs the bristles across her skin again. He feels her writhe beneath him as his chin descends down to her groin. Wisps of hair start curling against his face and he stops, but she clasps his head and drags it lower. She thrusts her pelvis towards his mouth, he feels her wetness smear against his lips.

He breaks himself free of her hands and hoists himself on his forearms. Tonight will be different. Tonight, she will not be the one in charge. He pins her hands above her shoulders. Her elbows strain against the air, they rise and fall like wings next to her head. Tonight, he will take what she reserves for the big sahibs, take what she has teased him with but never given. He looks at the surprise clearing her eyes, satisfied.

He caresses her lips with his cock. She turns away, but he follows her mouth and caresses it again. He plays along the line at which her lips meet, his dark brown skin stark against the redness of her lipstick. She does not turn away, but keeps her mouth closed.

He bears down on her wrists. Lipstick smudges her teeth as he coaxes apart her lips. He pushes against her mouth, presses his weight against her face. But there is no entry. She stares at him from the car seat, her head very still.

"Please," he whispers. "Just once," he says. He relaxes his grip.

She makes no move to free her hands. Her eyes are fixed upon his face, contemplating him with a composure he finds disconcerting. He sees a determination move into them, a self-assuredness that spills over and ripples down across her features. Slowly, deliberately, she parts her lips.

"Just this once," she says.

Gratefully, he eases himself into the admittance he has been granted. The snugness of her lips closes around his flesh and he feels her tongue explore the length of him. She takes him in deeper into her mouth and he sees the sureness mount in her face. As he is engulfed by the rhythm of her efforts, as he loses himself in sensation, he sees the sureness ignite in her eyes, until he can discern no iris, no white, no pupil, just an organic and unyielding resolve, that erupts from deep within her and exposes him to the core of her being.

"Let's run away," he says afterwards. "Just keep driving, and never come back."

"Where would we go?" she says, her eyes closed.

"Anywhere you want, anywhere the car will take us."

"Take me to Lonavala, then."

It is still dark as he drives down the winding road from Hanging Gardens. He looks at her, asleep on the seat next to him, her arms tucked tightly under her dupatta to keep them warm. Behind her, soft and unfocused, the lights near the sea blossom occasionally through the window. Above, the branches of mango trees stretch thickly across the road, their leaves reflecting whatever dabs of moonlight are to be found.

A gust of breeze, cool and salt-laden, blows in from Padmini's window. He reaches across her seat to roll up the glass. "No, leave it open," she says, stirring. "I like the cold." She turns back to sleep.

Vishnu follows the road curving into the darkness ahead. Soon he will pass the Towers of Silence, where even the vultures must be at peace at this time. Then he will see the lights of the flyover, guiding cars through the air all night. He will ascend high above Kemp's Corner, and try to glimpse the sea through the gaps in the skyscrapers. The sun will not rise for many hours, and it will be a long drive through the night. And all through the journey, he thinks to himself, Padmini will be asleep by his side.

MRS. LALWANI LIVED in Colaba, way up near Sassoon Docks.

The cab had barely passed Churchgate when Mrs. Asrani started to grumble.

"What kind of arrangement this is God only knows, that we have to drag our daughter halfway across the city. Everyone knows the boy is supposed to come to *our* place—not this neutral-veutral territory." She glared spitefully at the taxi meter, which, as if to mock her, made a "plink" and displayed a new number in the rupee slot.

"It's better this way, Aruna. Think how bad it would've been with Vishnu at home. Besides, we're already at Churchgate, so it won't be that much more."

"You think I care how much more it will cost? You think I would worry about a few rupees when my daughter's future happiness is at stake?" Mrs. Asrani inhaled several gulps of air and puffed up in outrage.

"All I said was the distance—the *distance* won't be that much more."

"Yes, yes—you don't have to give me geography lessons. I've lived in Bombay all my life. Shyamu, get back in from the window—do you want your head to get cut off by a BEST bus?"

The counter made another plink and Mrs. Asrani resisted the urge to accuse the taxiwalla of having tampered with the meter. These people were all robbers. She'd already had to shout at the driver twice about the route he'd tried to take them by. She *hated* taxis, thought they were a tremendous waste of money—it was better to wait for a bus and be late than flag a taxi down. She had tried, over the years, to impress this ideal upon Mr. Asrani, but suspected he remained secretly errant.

"Shyamu, didn't I say to put your head back in? Think of how foolish you'd look walking around without it—everyone saying that's the boy who stuck his head out and got it cut off by a bus."

She'd had to succumb today because of all the jewelry and silk Kavita was wearing. Mrs. Asrani looked at her daughter, sitting serenely between Shyamu and herself. How she glowed. It was as if a complete transformation had taken place—so stubborn one minute, and then so docile and agreeable. Kavita had even allowed herself to be led to the kitchen and taught how to make gulab jamuns. (The lesson had been a disaster, and they'd had to stop at the halwai to get a box, but that was beside the point.)

Mrs. Asrani supposed that was what the prospect of marriage did to young people. She tried to remember how she had been at that age. Had she gotten all dressed up, had she tried to make gulab jamuns as well? She looked at Mr. Asrani, sitting at the front window next to the driver, the wind from Queen's Road ruffling the few locks that still ringed his head. How much like a child he was, enjoying his window and his taxi ride, just like Shyamu at the window behind. An unexpected clutch of emotion appeared in her throat. How long ago had that been, how many years had passed by already. The feeling spread upwards from her throat, through her mouth, up her nose. So long they had traveled together, an endless cab ride with just the two of them. Like that saying about life being a journey that can only be shared with one person. Mrs. Asrani sat in the backseat of the cab, staring through the window, unaware of the tear that rolled down her cheek and wet the cover of the box of gulab jamuns in her lap.

She was still moist-eyed when Regal Cinema flashed by. Something about the sight didn't seem right. Suddenly, Mrs. Asrani realized what her momentary lapse had cost her. "Who told you you could bring us from here?" she shouted at the driver. "Everyone knows to go through Cooperage. Isn't your meter fast enough, that you have to take us the long way as well?"

The taxiwalla stared at the road and kept driving. Not satisfied that she had made her point, Mrs. Asrani continued, "Click, click, click— every time I blink there's a new number on the meter. You'd think we were being driven to Poona, looking at the fare."

The driver stopped the taxi and got out.

"He's leaving," Shyamu exclaimed. "Look, he's going to the chai-walla shop."

"What?" Mrs. Asrani tried to look past Kavita and Shyamu, but couldn't see anything. "What is he doing?"

"He's ordering tea," Shyamu said delightedly. This spectacle was an unexpected bonus to the luxury of a taxi ride. "Can we go, too?"

"The scoundrel. The cheat. *This* is the reason. This is the *exact* reason why I never go in a taxi." Mrs. Asrani emphasized the words as if they were the final moral of a tale, being underlined for the benefit of the listeners. She turned to her husband. "Well, don't just sit there, jee, ask him to come back."

"After what you said?"

"What *did* I say? What's wrong with the truth only? The meter is still on, you know. Go—you're the only one here who knows how to deal with these people—go—all the taxis you like to take."

So Mr. Asrani went and talked to the taxiwalla, who came back, once he had finished his tea. They proceeded to Mrs. Lalwani's building without incident, the taxiwalla, newly refreshed, ignoring Mrs. Asrani's mutterings from the backseat about reporting him to the authorities.

When it was time to pay, Shyamu, in the hope of coaxing out some last bit of entertainment from the drama, pointed to the meter and remarked loudly how high the fare seemed. For this effort he was roundly slapped, not only by Mrs. Asrani, but by Mr. Asrani as well, and yanked sniveling up the stairs to Mrs. Lalwani's apartment.

AT FIRST, KAVITA did not look at him. This was the way brides-to-be were supposed to behave. Their stories written by their parents and the boy and the boy's parents, but not by themselves. What was the use of looking, when they had no say in the matter anyway? If fate decided, they would see the boy soon enough when he pulled back the gunghat on the wedding bed. A face they would have to see for the rest of their days together on this earth.

She would be just like one of those brides-to-be who had gone before. Who had sat in countless rooms all over the country like this, and waited silently. Afterwards, she would dance like Nutan in *Saraswatichandra*. Hide her tears in her dupatta while singing that she loved her new life so much she had forgotten her father's house.

Kavita's heart fluttered with a feeling of oneness with her predecessors. What an injustice to have to go through this. She tried to latch on to the thought, to try and experience exactly what they must have felt. But Nutan kept distracting her. Nutan dancing with all the other women in her new household. Nutan singing about sending messages of happiness back to her mother. Nutan wearing that beautiful embroidered cream sari, though it was hard to tell on the VCR, especially in those older films that weren't in color.

"Kavita, dear, this is Pran."

Pran? She couldn't believe it. *Pran?* The villain who had terrorized so many leading ladies for so many years? Pran of the shifty eyes, Pran of the scheming mouth, Pran, who got soundly thrashed by the hero at the end of each movie. Who would ever name their son after *him?* Despite her resolve to keep looking downwards, her eyes wandered up to see what this Pran looked like.

He was standing there uncomfortably in front of her, like a boy who had been positioned just so by his parents, and told to wait. She tried to look at him, but he would not meet her eye. He kept looking down, as she had been, and when his mother, Mrs. Kotwani, instructed, "Pran, say hello to Kavita," a red bloom spread over his face.

"Hello," he said, still without looking up, and Kavita resisted the urge to act the groom and turn up his face with her thumb and forefinger.

She tried to say "Hello" back in a voice even meeker than his. But it came out sounding assertive in comparison, and she noticed her mother wince. It was going to be difficult to maintain the role of bashfulness she had written for herself. How perplexing that she had to compete for it with Pran.

Mrs. Lalwani and the two sets of parents stood around watching expectantly, as if Pran and she were a biology experiment that had just been set into motion. Even Shyamu was peering out with interest from behind their mother. Wasn't someone supposed to do something, say something, to propel the action on? She herself couldn't even decide whether to lower her eyes or keep them where they were, focused on Pran's chin. Again, she had to stop her fingers from reaching out and gently nudging up that chin.

It was Mrs. Lalwani who finally spoke. "Kavita is doing her B.A. at Elphinstone College," she said, as if this somehow explained it all, as if this was the reason they were all standing around and taking part in this exercise.

"She went to Villa Teresa," her mother added, in further clarification of the situation.

"Pran just got a job at Voltas," Mrs. Lalwani, ever the essence of even-handedness, announced.

There was a moment of silence, as everyone waited for the revelations to sink in.

"I hear you play the sitar very well, beti," Mrs. Kotwani said to Kavita.

Shyamu snorted and was dragged away to the bathroom by his father.

"Oh, just a little bit. As a hobby," Kavita said. She was finally getting into her role, lowering her eyes just so, and allowing the ends of her words to trail off, to impress upon everyone the debilitating quantities of shyness she was struggling to overcome.

"What about you, beta?" Mrs. Asrani addressed Pran. "Do you have any hobbies as well?"

Pran shook his head, at which Mrs. Kotwani tousled his hair. "Of course he does," she said. "Tell them about your stamp-collecting, Pran."

Pran did not speak. Mrs. Kotwani turned to everyone. "He's just so shy," she announced with a laugh. Kavita felt a stab of resentment at this further encroachment of her role.

Eventually, though, Pran was persuaded to speak. Haltingly, he explained the design of the new water pump that Voltas was developing. Mr. Asrani asked several perceptive questions and nodded with approval at each answer. Mrs. Asrani beamed happily at this test that her husband, at last good for something, was giving the boy. So far, he seemed to have demonstrated an excellent knowledge of the pumps, and final approval for being a son-in-law could certainly not be more than a few questions away.

At some point, the gulab jamuns were brought out, and Mrs. Kotwani remarked on their perfectly round shape, and Mrs. Lalwani bit into hers and pronounced them divine. Even Mr. Kotwani was moved to lay his hand on Kavita's head in blessing as he passed by on his way to get another one. Shyamu was brought his gulab jamun in the adjoining room.

"I think we should let them have a little time by themselves," Mrs. Lalwani whispered to Mrs. Asrani, and the elders filed out of the room, with Mr. Kotwani discreetly popping the last gulab jamun into his mouth on his way out.

They sat there in silence, just the two of them, Kavita on a chair and Pran on the sofa near the door. Kavita looked at Pran and tried appraising him as she would a vegetable or a piece of fruit at the market. Somewhat pimply—even his ears seemed to be red from acne. Or perhaps that was just the blush from his shyness again. His nose was too big for his face—perhaps a mustache would help, though then there might be the problem of a disappearing upper lip. She was surprised he did not wear glasses—she expected all engineer types to peer through thick, sturdy lenses. His eyes were a further surprise. The few times she had managed to look into them, they had been soft and brown—she hesitated to describe them as appealing, and settled on pleasant. He really looked scrawny hunched up in his chair like that—someone needed to grab his shoulders and straighten him up.

What would he do, she wondered, if she went over and sat next to him, and took his hand in hers? Or pressed her lips to his. Ran her hand down his stomach to his thigh as Salim had taught her to do. She captured the giggle in her throat before it could escape. She could have him stretched out helplessly next to her on the sofa in a minute. "No, let me go," she could cry to bring the adults running back in.

"Are you two talking to each other, or what?" Mrs. Asrani called from the other room. "Don't feel shy, now—*talk*."

Since Pran wasn't about to say anything, there was nothing to do but take the initiative herself. "I like the furniture in Lalwani aunty's drawing room. Especially the wall hangings. Is that from Kashmir, do you think?"

Again, she saw the blush spread from his cheeks down to his neck and up his ears. She got up to inspect the tapestry. "The border, especially, it's so intricately woven."

Pran mumbled something behind her, and she turned around.

"Hmm? What did you say?" Kavita asked, eager to hear something, anything, from him.

"I hope you say yes," Pran said, his brown eyes lifting to her face.

"What?"

"You're very beautiful," he said, just as Mrs. Asrani, unable to contain herself any more, burst through the door.

THEY ARE AT the outskirts of Lonavala. Vishnu sees himself at the wheel of the Fiat, sees Padmini beginning to stir by his side. By the time they reach the city center, she is wide awake and hungry. "Let's stop for some bhajia, hot-hot," she says, as they pass a halwai shop.

The bhajia are, indeed, hot—the halwai is ladling a fresh batch of the fritters out of an enormous cauldron of oil. He mixes them with salt and wraps a handful in newspaper for Vishnu.

"Did you get the chili ones?" Padmini asks, poking around in the newspaper. She pulls out a chili by the stem and takes a large bite. "Ah," she says, closing her eyes, "there's nothing like a chili bhajia. My mother had to fry up an extra batch every time, just for me, because otherwise nobody else would get any."

"Where is she now, your mother?" Vishnu asks, and Padmini looks up sharply. He realizes he has said the wrong thing.

"I haven't come here to relate my Ramayana to you," she says, her face tight.

But later, at the market, she volunteers matter-of-factly, "She lives near Ratnagiri. She thinks I make dresses for a living."

Padmini laughs. "Can you imagine? Me, a seamstress? I couldn't sew a diaper for an infant, much less a dress. But at least this way she doesn't expect any money from me. Let her sons support her."

There are so many questions in Vishnu's mind. He is hungry for information about Padmini. Every bit she opens up is a step towards the chance that she will love him. "Do you ever see your mother?" he asks.

But Padmini is not listening, distracted by a man selling toys. "Buy this for me," she commands, pointing to a doll made of cloth stuffed with cotton.

They drive to Sunset Point. The overlook is high enough that mist hovers in patches, even though sunlight sweeps down from the sky to dissipate it. Mountains stretch from east to west in a solid wall, their slopes lush with the green of jambul trees. Cutting through the vegetation are the fine white lines of waterfalls, emanating from springs high above. A koyal sings somewhere, its notes resonating clearly in the crispness of the air.

"Can you hear him? I wonder where he's hiding," Padmini says, running to the railing. "Koo-koo, koo-koo," she cries to the mountains, cupping her hands. She cocks her head to listen for an echo, an answer. "Koo-koo," she repeats, but there is no response. The only sound they hear is the rush of water spouting unseen from somewhere below.

She turns around and poses against the railing. "I wish you had a camera," she pouts, stretching out against the poles and rubbing her body against them.

The wind picks up and drapes her dupatta around her head. She looks up, the yellow silk veiling her face, and Vishnu thinks she might have just emerged from a temple.

"It's so nice that there's no one here," she says, and Vishnu moves to the railing next to her. All night, he has looked at her lying so close next to him, wanting to touch her, to taste her, to breathe her in.

"So beautiful," Padmini says, and stops, as Vishnu positions his lips next to hers. Before she can draw back, he kisses her through her veil. She looks down at the ground as he picks up the edges of the dupatta and raises it slowly up her face.

"Am I your bride?" she asks, as he kisses her on the forehead, then on the lips again.

"You ran away with me, remember," he says.

"Then how many of these would you like?" Padmini asks, holding up the cloth doll. She waves it in his face.

For a moment, Vishnu thinks that here they are, the two of them, or maybe a family of three. They have come up to Lonavala, like other people, for a long-awaited holiday. Back in Bombay, they are a real couple, and real lives await them. Not rich ones, necessarily, just ordinary lives. A flat or even only a room, with a cupboard and a bed. A toilet that is probably shared, a kerosene stove like the one his mother had. An address and a ration card, a postman who brings them mail. A job to go to every morning, a woman to whom he is wed.

Perhaps it shows in his face, because Padmini stops smiling. For an instant, he thinks he glimpses concern mixed in with the confusion in her expression.

Then the absurdity of the situation strikes him. The preposterousness of his images, the foolishness of his feelings, the comicality of chasing currents that skim across Padmini's face. He thinks how absurd this whole trip has been, how absurd is the presence of the two of them in Lonavala, how absurd is the scenery itself that stretches before them. He thinks of poor, ridiculous Mr. Jalal, waiting back in Bombay for his Fiat, and of how Padmini will react when he asks her to buy them petrol so they can get back. Relief comes pouring in, and he begins to laugh; laugh at the veil still covering Padmini's head, laugh at the doll dangling by her side, laugh at the reassurance his laughter brings to her eyes. Padmini begins to laugh as well, and from somewhere in the faraway trees, the koyal joins in with its mocking call, and as the peals of their mirth get louder, Vishnu hears them sound through the valley, echo across the mountains, and reverberate up into the sky.

CHAPTER SIX

IT WAS DARK by the time the taxi reached Dongri. The call to the evening prayer was echoing from the buildings, and Mrs. Jalal cocked her ear and listened to the familiar sound. She missed having the masjid with the peacock-green tiles just around the corner, missed the summons from the prayer tower that marked each day into regular segments. Down the road, she knew the women in their black burkhas would be haggling with the butcher from behind their veils at the Rahim Meat Shop, and next to it, old Anwar chacha might still be sitting at the register of the Allah Ijazat Hotel, calling out orders for fish fry and lamb's feet to the workers in the kitchen. She wondered if he would recognize her now, if he would offer her a sweet from the jar he kept at his elbow, as he did every time her mother sent her down to fetch cold drinks from him.

She walked down Jail Road and turned into the market street. The corridor was as crowded as ever, with throngs of people milling around and arguing with the vendors squatting on the ground. Everywhere were piles of fruits and vegetables, mounds of glossy black brinjals, pyramids of carefully stacked oranges, baskets of ripe red tomatoes, and most precious of all, crates filled with green and yellow mangoes, still partially wrapped in tissue to protect them from bruising. There was a man hawking kerosene stove parts, another with tubes of insect repellent (except the brand read Odomol, not Odomos), and outside the Indore Sweetmeat Store, a boy standing over dozens of identical plastic dolls spread out on a sheet, like babies arranged in orderly rows in an orphanage. "Two for three, two for three," the tout yelled out, and Mrs. Jalal felt a hundred eyes peering up at her from the ground, reproaching her for not saving them at such a bargain.

At the corner of Nawoji Hill Road, she paused. Down the street, next to the bus stop around the bend, used to be the chaatwalla stand where she had first met Ahmed. She wondered if it would still be there, if she should walk down and check for it. All those evenings that Nafeesa and she had succumbed to the promise of chili on their palates, the anticipation of tamarind tickling their throats, hooking them and reeling them in as surely as fish at the end of a line. The dark winter evenings, the hot and listless summers, even the rainiest days of the monsoons, when they huddled next to the chaatwalla under the bus stop shelter, and the wind tried to pluck away the leaves folded into cups from their hands.

And that one moonlit starry night—or perhaps it was cloudy and starless—when she crushed that first golgappa in her mouth, felt the crisp papdi shards and the soft yielding chickpeas between her teeth, tasted the sweet and fiery chutneys on her tongue, closed her eyes as the gush of tamarind water exploded down her throat. The initial dose of acid and spice always brought tears to her eyes. As she dabbed at them, she was dimly aware of Ahmed smiling at her from the other end of the semicircle of customers. He raised his leaf to her, and when the chaatwalla doled out a golgappa into it, scooped the papdi out and closed his mouth around it with an expression of such luxuriant satisfaction it could have only been for her benefit.

She looked away at once, not wanting to acknowledge his expression. Instead, she fixed her gaze on the large steel vessels and earthenware pots rising from the red cloth covering the stand. She watched intently as each golgappa was created: the tap to make the hole in the top of the papdi, the scoops to fill it with chickpeas and chutney, the final immersion into the pot of tamarind water, the chaatwalla's hand disappearing almost to the elbow. She had been determined to keep her attention thus occupied, but then her second golgappa developed a leak, and as she tilted her head to swallow the water spilt into the leaf, her vision got entangled in Ahmed's smile again.

She almost smiled back. But she caught herself in time, summoning up a glare instead. A glare, she hoped, that would burn with the same intensity as that of the kerosene lamp blazing at the center of the stand. It worked—not only did Ahmed look away, but he motioned to the chaatwalla that he had had enough, and was ready to pay.

As they searched for turnips in the market afterwards, she told Nafeesa what had happened.

"The nerve of these hooligans," her sister responded. "They grow more audacious day by day. Just imagine, while eating pani-puri, no less!" Nafeesa shook her head. "But tell me, Arifa, what did he look like—was he at least handsome, this Romeo of yours?"

"He wasn't my Romeo," Arifa snapped, "and I was only trying to eat my golgappas, not be a judge in some beauty contest."

"Of course you did the right thing. But such severity? He was only smiling at you after all, the bechara."

She had been about to berate her sister for being so naive when suddenly there was Ahmed, at the Ijazat Hotel counter.

"Oh my God, it's *him*," she whispered. "And he's talking to Anwar chacha."

What her sister did next was supposed to have been a prank. But it changed everything, it changed her life.

"Let's have some fun," Nafeesa said, and holding her by the wrist, pulled her to Ahmed.

She had never quite decided how much gratitude and how much resentment to feel towards her sister. Over the years, she had felt both, maybe even in equal measure. Ahmed turned out to be the son of a friend of Anwar chacha, and with his credentials thus established, acquired an immediate sheen of respectability—and eligibility. Nafeesa quickly pronounced him too ugly, and was surprised that the meeting developed into anything more. ("All those scars on his face—so unfortunate he had smallpox, but does that mean one has to marry him out of pity?") But Arifa looked beyond the face, beyond the scars, into the intensity burning in his eyes. She was fascinated by it, fascinated and a little frightened, because she could not tell from where it sprang, or how deep one would have to delve to find its source.

And she was flattered. Here was someone who was interested in *her*. Not Nafeesa, the glamorous one, but her, *Arifa,* the one with the awkward limbs and the gawky body, the one whose face, according to her aunt, so serenely radiated its plainness, the one with the personality, she had been advised, that could only aspire to pleasantness. A man, a *suitor,* who wanted to know what she thought, what she felt; who gave the promise, so recklessly professed, that he would carry her away and change her world. She had trembled in the little green tract near the masjid, as Ahmed had held her hand and said this. The buildings behind them had listened on in silence, the windows all around had borne witness.

She would always remember that pouring July afternoon, not too many days later, when they sneaked upstairs to the third-floor verandah. She had spent all morning experimenting with Nafeesa's make-up, and as Ahmed led her through the doorway, she wondered if the rain was going to wash it all off. He pulled her to him and embraced her, and she felt the heat of his skin through the wetness of his shirt.

The flower pots on the ledge began to fill, and she watched the water, red with earth, run over the rims and disappear down to the street below. Drops of rain splashed off his face onto hers, and she was surprised to find her mouth seeking his. Their lips, amazingly, made contact, and she stood there, riveted by the shock of the kiss.

Ahmed did keep his promise, taking her away from her world—from the masjid, the market, from her house, her family. She had felt so strange moving into his flat, sandwiched as it was between Hindu families both above and below. Instead of a masjid, there was a church across the street, the tip of its white cross visible when she lay down and stared through her bedroom window. She had missed the market the most, the fruitwalla here next to Variety Stores being overpriced and arrogant, the meat shop too far to walk to, and no Anwar chacha to greet her at the Irani hotel downstairs.

It had taken some time before she had learnt to listen for the vendors carrying meat and produce from house to house, shouting the names of their wares and looking at the balconies for customers. Mrs. Taneja, from upstairs, had shown her where the chaatwallas sat near Breach Candy, and she had found she could take the 81 bus all the way to the mosque near Metro. Downstairs, the paanwalla started greeting her with a "Namaste, Jalal memsahib," and the cigarettewalla started doing the same. And every time Vishnu saw her on the steps, he inquired if memsahib needed a taxi, and ran down ahead to flag one down if she nodded.

She had never been able to solve the puzzle of what Ahmed had seen in her, why he had married her in the first place. After all, he was from a family that had both wealth and culture, and she was not the person his parents would have picked for him (as his mother had assured her once). At first, she had obsessed about this question, and tried to force an answer out from him. But with time had come the realization that it might not be something she really wanted to learn.

She often wondered, though, if Ahmed had truly come to love her in those first few years. That crucial period, when love, if it catches, can be enough for a lifetime of memories, as the song went. She had almost made it there herself, reaching the stage where she could look into her heart, and view the room she was preparing for him. A little longer, and she would have ushered him in and captured him there forever. There might have still been doubts, and anguish even, but she would have been able to subsume anything into the thickness of those walls.

Mrs. Jalal sighed. This was not the time to worry about the empty chambers people carried around in their hearts. This was not the time to follow the call of tamarind back into the past. She was visiting Nafeesa to talk things through, not break down and wrest her pity. It was important she keep her composure, important she get her mind off such maudlin thoughts.

Mrs. Jalal peered one last time towards the invisible bus stop. Then she crossed the street and walked the remaining distance to Nafeesa's building.

KAVITA SAT AT the dining table, staring at the masala chicken on her plate. It was her favorite dish. Her mother had taken great care that morning to fry the masala until it was nice and red, and decorate the dish extravagantly with cashews before bringing it out. The accompanying rice was deep gold with turmeric, and generously laden with the tasty bits of fried onion that Kavita so loved picking out. "There's even mango kulfi for dessert," Shyamu excitedly whispered to her as they sat down. "You must let lots more boys look at you before saying yes."

Food was the last thing on Kavita's mind. All she had been able to think about, through the daze of the trip back from Lalwani aunty's house, were the words Pran had spoken to her.

"I hope you say yes."

She had just stood there and stared at him. His head lifting up, his eyes meeting her face, his cheeks, his neck, his ears turning red.

"You're very beautiful."

She could hardly believe it. Her charms had worked. She had ensnared herself an engineer, just as she had set out to do. What heights her beauty must have moved the poor bashful boy to, that he was able to summon up the courage to bring forth such words. Pran's eyes opened before her, like buds flowering reticently in the light—she could feel the breath catch in his throat and hear the blood pound in his ears.

What part of her, she wondered, had he found most irresistible? Had it been her hair? The locks that (people said) curled around her face so perfectly, the tresses that (they added) cascaded so luxuriantly down to her shoulders? Or was it her eyes—so round and wide (and eyeliner-accentuated today), against which Mrs. Kotwani had pressed her lips so lovingly in farewell. Or maybe her lips, painted with her new Revlon lipstick, the one so startlingly red that her mother had forbidden her to wear a red dress with it. She had kept her lips in a pout and glossed them over frequently with her tongue. Pran's eyes, she had noticed, had sneaked several times to their level before darting away.

It was certainly a call for elation, this success she'd achieved in her first try at being a temptress. Why then was a part of her so confused? The part that had noticed the smooth fine hairs glistening along Pran's upper lip. The part that had detected the quiver at his throat as he had strained to get the words out, the part that had looked deeper into his eyes than had probably been prudent. There had been a tenderness hiding there, an unexpected sensitivity, that had shyly communicated its presence from behind the fear. For an instant, her own breast had throbbed with his longing, and she had felt an urge to sweep him into her arms and squeeze his ache away. To reach through his timidity, to coax out the tenderness caged inside, and feel its warm presence nuzzle against her face.

"Look at her, can't even eat anything," her mother said, bringing out the ice cream. "What's the matter, can't stop thinking about you-know-who?" Mrs. Asrani beamed, radiating goodwill at everyone at the table.

Somewhere the lights were dimming, and a movie was starting up. Her parents and his parents hugging each other as she said yes. Anita and the rest of her girlfriends giggling as the henna was put on her hands. People lining up along the sands at Juhu to watch the wedding procession arrive. Trumpets and trombones gleaming as the band played a song from *Bobby*. No, *Sachcha Jhootha*. No, *Do Raaste*. No . . . she'd have to think about the music.

Pran arriving on a mare, just like the groom at Anita's wedding. Riding it all the way to the entrance of the Holiday Inn. Or maybe, the Kotwanis having insisted, it was the Oberoi instead, and Anita was green with envy. Shyamu eating too many laddoos and sadly having to be led away before the ceremony. The groom blushing even more than the bride as the priest started the prayers.

But just then, a reel from a different movie seemed to get mixed in. There she was again, all dressed up as a bride, but now it was Salim, not Pran, next to her. And they weren't at the Oberoi, or even the Holiday Inn—they were at Victoria Terminus, sitting in a train. The whistle blew, the train began to move, and slowly they drew out of the station. The streets started passing by, the houses illuminated silently by the mercury lights, the vendors rolling their carts through the empty markets, the stations deserted at this time of night. Salim's arms encircled her body, his face drew next to hers, and together they looked through the window, at the city they had lived in all their life.

Then suddenly it was the first movie again, and she was sitting on their petal-strewn bed in the bridal suite of the Oberoi. She felt her gunghat being lifted up, and looked down at her henna-stained feet, then allowed her vision to rise to Pran's face. Except it wasn't his eyes she saw, but Salim's. That mischievous, leering look she knew so well, those lips which always seemed ready to kiss. Salim's mouth pressed against hers, and she smelled the spicy fragrance of his skin, tasted the toothpaste freshness of his tongue. The petals floated away, the room trembled and dissolved around them, and the sky began to lighten through the window. She found herself snug against Salim in a railway berth, a blanket wrapped tightly around their bodies. Dawn raced along with them, breaking in a thin orange line across the fields outside. She closed her eyes against Salim's chest and let the train rock her back to sleep.

"So what did you think, beti?" her mother asked, interrupting her romantic-dawn-in-the-train scene. Kavita felt a hand stroke her hair lightly, questioningly. "Do you think we should go forward with it?"

"Really, Aruna, there should be some limit—give the poor child a chance to breathe at least," her father said.

"You stay out of this, jee. Lots of breathing you've let her do. Even the people down the street have been hearing her breathing." Then, seeing Kavita's expression, Mrs. Asrani quickly softened her tone. "All I'm saying is that if we like him, we shouldn't delay. What if tomorrow some other girl turns his head—engineers don't grow on trees, you know. Especially not Voltas."

"I say we show her around some more," Shyamu announced, licking the last of his ice cream. "And get pista flavor next time."

Should she say yes? Should she agree to marry Pran? What about Salim? What about the money she had withdrawn from the bank? Even if she were to put it back now, how would she explain it on the monthly statement? Besides, it was nine-thirty already, and Salim would be waiting for her on the terrace at midnight.

The movie had been rewound to their wedding night again. Except this time, as she and Pran were being wed, Salim was singing a sad song, alone, on the terrace. Looking across the bay, calling to his love, reminding her of the promises they had made to each other. His eyes, so full of playfulness usually, now so empty and far away.

No, this was too sad, she couldn't do this to Salim. She needed to find another way. But where was the time? Already her sari had been secured to the wedding cloth trailing behind Pran, and the seven circles around the fire were about to start.

Suddenly a voice rings out across the hall. It carries the authority of a thousand wedding scenes past, declaring the sentence that has been inescapable since talking movies began.

"This marriage cannot take place!"

Conversation stops, and people look up, shocked. The priest drops his holy spoon in the fire. Pran tries to get his headdress off, but can't.

It is Salim, astride the same white mare that carried Pran to the hotel earlier. He gallops through the ballroom of the Oberoi, vaulting over tables laden with food. Guests scatter in his wake, and he rides up to the very mandap itself.

With one stroke of his sword, he slices the knot binding Kavita to Pran. He scoops her up with his other arm, then waves at the speechless onlookers. He spurs his mare, and they stride up the stairs. They burst through the lobby, and into the night outside. They gallop past the Air India building, past the Oval Grounds, past Flora Fountain. In the distance, Kavita sees Queen Victoria standing above her railway station. Holding her beacon high above her head, lighting the way to escape, to victory, to freedom. The train waiting inside, steam rising from the nostrils of its rearing engine.

She would do it. She would elope with Salim. It was meant to be. She would try not to think of the forlorn figure removing his headdress in the empty Oberoi hall.

"Mummy," Kavita said, and Mrs. Asrani shushed at everyone for quiet. "Mummy, I think—I think I might like to say yes."

THE SUN HAS set. The stairs are dark again. The sounds have stopped. Below him, Vishnu can see the first-floor landing.

Music wafts down the stairs to him. *You did, oh yes you did, it was you who did, who stole my heart with a trick . . .* The words are muffled and faint.

Vishnu listens to the lyrics. *I don't know how you looked at me, but my heart started going tic, tic, tic . . .* They are coming from the next landing, the one between the first and the second floors. He follows them up.

. . . tic, tic, tic, tic . . .

It is Radiowalla, sitting hunched on his landing, a sheet draped around his shoulders. The radio is cradled in his lap, his head bent forward at an angle, as if trying to catch the sounds of an infant. The volume is turned so low that it is only Vishnu's new, heightened sense of hearing that makes it audible.

Perhaps Radiowalla senses Vishnu's presence, because he draws his arms around his knees, curtaining off the radio with his sheet. He turns his head this way and that, then dips his face into the chamber he has created, pulling the sheet to his neck to seal off the music. Vishnu can still hear an occasional *tic,* but the rest of the words remain trapped inside.

Radiowalla rears his head back from his chamber, like a dog looking up from a bowl. He scans the landing once more, then bends forward, pulling the sheet right over his head this time. He sits there in the dark, covered by the sheet, his body motionless underneath.

The first time Vishnu met Radiowalla was years ago, when Vishnu had just moved to the building. Back then, Radiowalla, having not yet acquired a radio, was still Nathuram. Nathuram, the cart pusher, whose single burning ambition in life, declared to Vishnu the day they met, was to own a transistor radio, the one sitting in its own glossy brown leather case in the Philips showroom window at Kemp's Corner.

Since Nathuram did not have his own cart, work was somewhat erratic, and he would sit for days on end at Gowallia Tank with the other cart pushers, waiting for his turn. But every time he was paid for a job, Nathuram would save something, even if it was only a two- or three-paisa coin, putting it in a large cloth bag strung around his neck, which jingled his arrival on the steps. And when the coins added up, he would exchange them for a rupee note at the cigarette-walla, who provided the service free of commission, as long as Nathuram bought a beedi in return (two beedis for exchanging one-rupee notes to a higher denomination).

"Eleven rupees today," Nathuram would say to Vishnu. "Fourteen rupees." "Eighteen." "Twenty-four." The tally went up month by month, year by year. Vishnu would sit with Nathuram at the bottom of the steps and listen to him talk about how wonderful it would be once he got his radio. The whole building would be filled with the sweet sounds of Naushad and Madan Mohan, and Lata's haunting voice would be like a creeper curling around the flights, its tendrils reaching out to caress every nook and corner. Everyone would be invited to gather in the evenings for special programs on film music, with a few nights of devotional bhajans and perhaps even western music thrown in.

The day finally came when Nathuram fulfilled his dream, and proudly carried the bright red cardboard box to his landing. Tall Ganga arranged to come back early from her cleaning jobs, and even the cigarettewalla clambered up the stairs to watch. It took Nathuram several minutes just to pry off the staples, so determined was he to preserve every last detail of the box. Each piece of packing material inside was carefully removed and passed around for the people gathered to marvel over. Short Ganga was particularly fascinated by the Styrofoam, and asked if she could keep a sample, but Nathuram was horrified at her request and quickly plucked away the piece from her hands.

When the last piece of plastic had been circulated and folded away, an expectant hush fell across the landing. Nathuram raised his hands and rotated them in the air, like a magician displaying his palms to an audience before a trick. Then he reached deep into the box and slowly pulled up the transistor. The knobs rose into view first, shining in a smart row across the top surface, the sleek black dial window emerged next, its numbers embedded in yellow against a blue background, and then came the silver front with the speaker holes arranged geometrically in a circle. Nathuram carried the transistor around the assembly like a baby in his arms, quickly retracting the instrument in case a hand got too close to it.

That first night, the transistor filled all the landings in the building with its sound. The cigarettewalla had shown Nathuram how to connect it into an old socket which hadn't been used since the time there had been bulbs illuminating each landing. People stayed until the last program on Vividh Bharati ended at 11:30 p.m. Nathuram tried to get something on the shortwave channels afterwards, but no matter how the antenna was adjusted, the signals that were captured were too weak. Vishnu came up after everyone had left, to find Nathuram fast asleep, the radio still on in his arms, waves of static whooshing through the landing like an ethereal tide.

The radio quickly became an integral part of life in the building. Every morning, Vishnu woke up with the Glycodin commercial on Radio Ceylon. When the K. L. Saigal song came on, he knew it was almost 8 a.m, almost time for the radio to be switched off. A few minutes later, Nathuram would come down the stairs, the transistor in its leather case, strapped around his neck. In the evenings, Nathuram greeted people who came up the stairs, showing them where to sit on the landing, like an usher at a movie theater. The most popular program was the 9:30 Listeners' Requests. Tall Ganga claimed to have mailed in a request herself, and listened eagerly each evening as the names were announced, but hers was never called out.

In time, everyone in the building, even Mr. Jalal and Mrs. Asrani, started calling Nathuram Radiowalla. Radiowalla never went anywhere without his radio—he played it on the rocks at Breach Candy while performing his morning business, carried it slung behind his back while pushing his cart, and even slept with it hugged tightly to his body under his sheet.

· It was not clear exactly when the changes started to occur, or what caused them. Everyone still gathered on Radiowalla's landing in the evenings for the new hits by Lata and Asha and Rafi. But whereas before Radiowalla walked around greeting people with an animated smile, he now sometimes just sat next to his radio and stared wordlessly at his audience. One Wednesday, he insisted on tuning in to devotional music even though Binaca Top Twenty was playing on Radio Ceylon; another evening he refused to move the dial from All India Radio, forcing people to listen to news programs, that too in English. The cigarettewalla, who had been entrusted with the care of the box the radio came in, was suddenly accused of using it to store cartons of matches. Radiowalla angrily took it back and spent several days airing the pieces of packing material on his landing to get rid of the smell of sulfur he claimed clung to everything.

His audience, reluctant to lose their evening gatherings, were ready to make allowances. "Oh, he's not feeling well these days," they would say. "What to do, the bechara hasn't been hired for two weeks now," they would postulate.

But things became impossible to ignore the night Tall Ganga's name was called out on Listeners' Requests. At first, she couldn't believe it, but then she yelped in delight and burst out clapping. Her song came on, and tucking her sari into her waist, Tall Ganga stood up to dance to the music. Someone asked Radiowalla to turn up the volume.

For a minute, Radiowalla did not move, but stared at the people who were clapping and shouting along with Tall Ganga. Then he reached over and switched off the radio.

"Tell her to get her own radio," he said, turning his back to Tall Ganga, who stood in mid-dance, her long limbs frozen by the silence.

After that, the evening assemblies rapidly came to a close. Radiowalla started turning his radio on only when people weren't present, switching the channel to something boring or even to just static when anyone came to join him. Vishnu was sent one day to talk to him, but Radiowalla greeted him with suspicion, and ordered him not to come close to his radio. To make matters worse, someone tore off the lid from the radio box in retaliation and ripped up the packing material inside. Radiowalla came back from work that evening to find the landing littered with plastic and Styrofoam and cardboard. He gathered up all the pieces he could find and put them back in the box. The next day, he chased Short Ganga down the steps, accusing her of having ripped open his box to get the Styrofoam inside. It was only the cigarettewalla's promise to give Radiowalla a thrashing that made Short Ganga feel safe entering the building again. Especially since she had not been able to resist carrying off the two most fascinating chunks of Styrofoam the day she had found the box vandalized.

Radiowalla stopped speaking to people in the building. He started playing his radio so softly that nobody could hear it except himself, lowering the volume even further when anyone was passing by. Every once in a while, he could be seen on his landing with the packing material all spread out in front of him, turning and examining the pieces as if he were trying to decipher his fortune in them.

As Vishnu passes by him now, Radiowalla's head again emerges from the sheet. A catch of music escapes, and Radiowalla quickly pulls his sheet around tighter. Vishnu imagines the notes bouncing around inside, imparting rhythm and energy as they break against Radiowalla's skin. The faintest drafts of melody follow him up as he continues past on the stairs.

BY THE TIME they reached the shrine of Amira Ma, Mrs. Jalal was feeling light-headed with relief. A nazar, that's what it was, and this was the place to counteract it. Nafeesa had diagnosed it with an air of clinical certainty, and that too before they had even finished their tea. "Someone's put an evil eye on your Ahmed," she'd declared, "and until it's lifted, his condition can only grow worse."

Mrs. Jalal's mind had reeled. Why would anyone hate Ahmed? Who would do such a thing to him?

"Are you serious?" Nafeesa said. "The way my dear jija carries on about religion, I wouldn't be surprised if Maulvi sahib himself didn't put a curse on him. But who knows how these nazars can happen—praise someone too much, and they get a nazar, don't put a soot mark on your baby's cheek, and he'll get a nazar, say something nice about your spouse, and he'll catch a nazar—they're easier to catch than the flu."

Mrs. Jalal felt the color drain out of her face. "You aren't saying *I* could have done it, are you? Oh my God, what if it *was* me?"

"It hardly matters how it happened. The important thing now is to counteract it. We'll go right now—to Amira Ma's. Tie a thread at the shrine, and that should do it."

A beggar limped up to them as they waited for a taxi. Nafeesa started to shoo him away, but Mrs. Jalal pulled out a one-rupee note from her purse and handed it to him, under her sister's disapproving look. She felt she needed all the luck she could get, and giving alms couldn't hurt. In the taxi, they passed a marriage procession, surely another good omen, and Mrs. Jalal began to relax. She even managed to convince herself that nothing she had done could have caused the nazar—after all, when *was* the last time she had praised Ahmed?

The taxi left them at the mouth of a passageway lined with stalls. As they made their way through, dozens of hands reached out, offering to sell them coconuts and flowers and incense. "All we need is thread," Nafeesa said impatiently, brushing off the hands.

The gates were already closed at the shrine entrance, and only visitors who had a relative being treated inside were being admitted. "We're here to see our mother," Nafeesa told the scowling attendant,

"to see if you've managed to beat the ghosts out of her yet."
Reluctantly, the gate was opened a crack to let them in.

The gateman was still watching, so they mounted the steps to the women's dormitory, as directed. They passed a series of closed doors, and Arifa tried not to listen to the sounds of scratching and flailing. The last door was ajar, and as they neared it, a scream emerged, so full of despair that it stabbed right into Arifa's heart. Arifa looked inside and made out a body, naked from the waist up, glistening through the loban smoke. The woman screamed again, and Nafeesa pulled her away from the door, but not before Arifa noticed the woman's hands tied to a beam near the ceiling.

"This way," Nafeesa said, and they descended a narrow staircase that brought them back to the courtyard.

There were several people here, and Nafeesa hissed to Arifa to act as if they belonged. "The shrine is through the door, there," Nafeesa said, and Arifa saw an opening cut into the stone on the far side, next to the neem tree.

Amira Ma had been a holy woman, widely reputed for her powers of exorcism, who had lived there several decades back. Arifa remembered her stone grave, and the marble grate that surrounded it, from the time Nafeesa had brought her there once before. Pilgrims traveled from as far as Pakistan to tie threads to the grate, and it was said that those who came with pure hearts had their wishes fulfilled. The tradition of exorcism continued to this day, with people possessed by spirits being brought there to inhale the holy loban smoke, or in more serious cases, to be left behind for treatment.

They passed into the inner sanctum and Arifa saw the fire in front of the grave. Flames leapt up from a square hole cut in the stone floor, shooting into the air in flares of blue and green and yellow. It was the strangest fire she had ever seen, smokeless, but accompanied by loud crackling and popping sounds, as if the ground itself was being consumed. A woman stood over the hole, drawing her hands over the flames, beckoning them to come to her. Her eyes seemed strangely blank behind the colors that danced in them, and her hair, uncombed and knotted, hung in black tangles around her shoulders. As Arifa neared, the woman turned to face her, rubbing her palms over her chest, as if to transfer the heat from her hands to her bosom.

"The thread," Nafeesa reminded her, and Arifa tore her eyes away from the woman and stumbled after her sister.

The grate looked molten in the light of the fire, like something just disgorged from the earth's magma. Arifa drew up to it and touched it cautiously, half expecting it to sear her skin. But the marble was cool against her fingertips, and she ran them over the carved stone, feeling the threads that others had tied. Thousands and thousands of them, white ones and red ones, fine black sewing string and sturdy brown twine, a few already unraveling against the marble.

She pulled out the thread Nafeesa had bought her from one of the stalls outside. It felt so light in her fingers. Would it be strong enough to save Ahmed, to bring him back from wherever he had gone? What if the good omens had not been enough? What if the unthinkable happened, and the thread broke while she was tying it? But she was being ridiculous.

"This knot I tie for Ahmed," she whispered to herself, as she tied the thread to the marble. "Set him free from his nazar, Amira Ma." The thread did not break.

Arifa felt her sister's hand on her shoulder, and brought it to her face to kiss it. Her eyes felt wet, but when she dabbed at them, there were no tears. Perhaps she had cried enough. It was now up to Amira Ma. She would just wait and see.

The woman by the fire had disappeared. The flames were still flaring into the night. A man was rolling a giant drum into place for the morning ceremony.

"All those colors," Nafeesa said. "It's the spirits, being purified in the flames. The blue is for evil, the yellow for mischief. People carry them here from all over in their bodies, and when they stand close enough, the spirits can't help diving in. The green you see—those are the spirits that have reemerged, all purified again."

Out of the corner of her eye, Arifa saw a movement near the grate. A black shape, whirling and turning, and coming towards her. For an instant, she thought it was a spirit, headed for the flames, and she was directly in its path. Then she realized it was the woman who had been dancing next to the fire. Her hand was outstretched, and she was coming to give Arifa something.

The woman smiled, and Arifa noticed the teeth, stained orange and brown from years of paan-chewing. The blankness had disappeared from her eyes, and in it now was a knowing shrewdness. The woman was saying something to her, which Arifa could not understand.

Arifa leaned forward to catch the words. "This is for you," the woman said, and pressed something into her palm. The smell of ash and charred hair lingered where the woman had been an instant ago.

Even without looking, Arifa could feel it. It can't be, she thought to herself, not wanting to open her palm. As her fingers unfurled, the thread came into view, Ahmed's knot still in it, as sturdy and secure as when she had tied it. But the thread itself had been broken, the frayed ends where it had been pulled apart curling against her skin. She tried to speak but couldn't, her lips parting helplessly, her hand rising and falling mechanically with the thread. Her voice came back to her, and she tried to expunge the horror, tried to clear it from her throat and expel it from her lungs. She screamed, and the sound was so rending that it stopped Nafeesa as if she had been stricken, made the man by the fire lose control of his drum. She held up the thread in the light of the fire and screamed again and again. And beyond the courtyard, beyond the gate, in the kerosene-lit corridor of stalls, the shopkeepers at their ledgers stopped counting their money and looked for a moment towards the shrine of Amira Ma.

SOMEWHERE IN THE darkness is a bevy of scents. It hovers beyond his reach. Perfumes perch along the periphery of his perception, flitting away at his approach. He follows a riddle of spice—cumin, or turmeric, perhaps—it flashes through the air and escapes without being caught. There are flowers here, and fruits, too, and the smell of mud and oil and rain.

When the gods descend, Vishnu knows, it is by their scents that he will recognize them. Ganesh will smell of the fruits he loves, Varuna will smell of the sea. River breezes will herald the arrival of Saraswati, Indra will bring the rain. Krishna will smell of all that's sweet, of milk and gur and tulsi. Of sandalwood and kevda flowers, of saffron, of ghee, of honey.

And Lakshmi. Lotuses will flower beneath her feet, scenting each step with their fragrance. Mangoes will turn the color of the sun, filling the world with their ripeness. Tulsi plants will wave in the wind, whispering their secrets to the air. The earth will stretch out, rich and fragrant, and await her touch against its skin.

Vishnu inhales, and the air is sweet with lotus. He thinks his senses are deceiving him, and inhales again. The scent is overpowering, as if thousands of flowers have opened, as if the steps, the walls, the ceiling, are all awash with blossoms. Mixed in with their sweetness is the spiciness of basil, barely detectable at first, but becoming more intense by the second, until that is all he smells, and he thinks that a million tulsi leaves are being rubbed between invisible fingers. And then come wafts of mango, waves that begin to wash over the tulsi, each swelling stronger than the one before, and redolent of all the different varieties he knows. Vishnu recognizes the wildness of Gola mangoes, the tartness of Langda, the cloying sweetness of Pyree, the perfect refinement of Alphonso. The perfume is so thick and potent that he can feel it press against his face. Except that now it is the earth his nostrils are pressed against, earth that is wet and aromatic, earth that smells sweet and loamy, with the pungency of dung mixed in. Vishnu inhales this new fragrance. It is the scent of the land, the scent of fertility, the scent that has existed since civilization began, and Vishnu marvels at its immutability.

And then all the scents he has smelled are upon him, blending together to form a new aroma, an aroma fruitful and flowerful and profound, that conveys unmistakable femininity. It is an aroma he has never before smelled, but recognizes instantly.

Vishnu looks up at the stairs leading into the darkness. Tonight is the night he will see his beloved. Tonight is the night that Lakshmi will descend.

CHAPTER SEVEN

It was a little past midnight when Kavita made it to the terrace. Salim was waiting by the television antennas, looking over the inky waters of the bay, like a captain at his prow, surveying the sea. Seeing him silhouetted so masculinely against the sky, Kavita was overcome by the affection, the passion, the deep attachment, that she felt for this, her true love. She had made the right decision.

"Did you leave your luggage downstairs?" Salim asked her, after they had kissed.

"Luggage? Why would I need *anything* when I have you?" Kavita extended her hands to frame Salim's face, but he caught them in his own, and brought them down.

"You *will* need clothes, darling. And other things as well. Perhaps you could go and pack something up—we still have time."

"Oh don't be such a bore, *darling*." Kavita had meant to mock Salim gently with the last word, but was surprised by the intensity with which it emerged. She softened her tone immediately. "All I need is love. Love, love, love. The old Beatles song, remember?"

Salim didn't reply, but looked at her worriedly, so she dangled her purse in front of him. "Besides, guess what I have here. It's my dowry. It's *our* dowry. Thanks to Mummy and Daddy."

"How much is it?" Salim wanted to know.

Kavita's face darkened. "Only fourteen thousand. What did they expect, that they would marry me off on Chowpatty Beach?" She shook the hair off her face. "But anyway, it's enough for me to buy a lot of clothes, so let's go, before we get caught or something."

"I really think that—" Salim began, but Kavita cut him off.

"You really think *what?* That I'll spend it all on clothes?" Again, her words came out more severe than she had intended, and she tried to cover them up. "I don't need much, darling. There's nothing to worry about."

She had to watch herself. She wondered why she was snapping so much at poor Salim. Perhaps she was on edge. Well, *of course* she was on edge—she was *eloping,* after all, not going around the corner to eat golgappas. But maybe there was more to it, maybe the trip to Lalwani aunty's was still playing in her head. No, that was ridiculous, that was all over, a little dream sequence she'd had, a side plot in the story of her life. By now, the audience didn't even remember the name of that unfortunate boy she'd met. Well, okay, *she* did—it was Pran, but that was only because of the film connection. This was *not* the time to think of Pran.

"Could you go a little slower?" she whispered irritatedly to Salim as they went down the steps. "It's not as if they've started chasing us already."

How silly of her to have even made the comparison. Pran, whom she had seen just once today, and that too in a meeting where, one had to admit, he had come off as a bit of a pumpkin. And Salim, whom she had known all this time, her one, her only, her *true* love.

Well, he *had* to be her true love, didn't he, if she was following him God knows where?

"Where are you carrying your Juliet off to anyway, my Romeo?"

"Romeo would have to be a lot stronger to carry a Juliet like you, my little potato chop."

Kavita stopped. "Whom are you calling a potato chop? Do I look like a potato to you? Do I?" Her voice rose well above a whisper. "Don't suppose there aren't others who would be glad to have me, if you think that I'm too fat."

Salim turned around. "You know I was just joking. You know I don't think you're fat." He put his bags down and hugged her. "Is something the matter? Is everything okay?"

"Everything's fine. Why wouldn't it be? But don't think you're doing me a favor, taking me away like this—Pran would never do such a thing!"

Of course, she didn't really speak the last sentence, though the thought came so vividly into her mind that it almost felt like she had blurted it out. She supposed she was being unfair. After all, it had been she herself who had initiated the scheme to elope. But on the other hand, Salim had been the one to agree. She couldn't imagine someone as decent as Pran—an engineer, a *stamp-collector* no less—agreeing to such an escapade.

Where would she be twenty years from now? Kavita closed her eyes and imagined herself married to Pran. They'd have two children—the elder, a boy, good in mathematics like his father. They would go to a top school—a Catholic one, naturally—Campion or St. Mary's or (if one was a girl) to Villa Teresa. Every summer, the four of them would pile into the family car and drive to Matheran. Her friends might tease her about Pran—good old dependable engineer sahib. But she would be the only one who would know that special look he had, the blush that came over his face, that spread up his cheeks and into his eyes as she began to unwrap her sari for him.

But no, she would be with Salim. Salim and herself, twenty years hence. Nothing came to her mind. Their future was an unknown, a blank. No, blank was too harsh a word to describe it—it was a *mys-*

tery—yes, that was it—for when one embarks on adventure, one can hardly be expected to know the end.

The truth growled at her suddenly, like a cheetah surprising its prey. *She was not sure.* She did not know if she wanted to accompany Salim down that stairway, into the city waiting below. She needed more time—more time to breathe, more time to think, more time to understand. But it was too late, already too, too late. The money from the bank burned in her purse, and only Vishnu's landing separated them from the street.

How peaceful Vishnu looked. She could see him stretched out below, and in the dark, there seemed to glow an aura of tranquillity around him. She followed Salim down the steps to his landing, snapping open her purse and taking out the currency note she had reserved for him. As she bent down to tuck it under his head, an image from her childhood sprang into her mind—Vishnu playing hide and seek with her on the steps.

"He's not going to need money where he's going," Salim said. "You might as well keep that."

"What?"

"Even the ambulance came and went yesterday. It's too late for the bechara."

"What lies. He's going to be fine. It's only a hundred rupees that I'm giving him—you don't have to get hunger in your eyes for that even."

"Is that what you think of me? That I'm eyeing your hundred rupees? That I'm running away with you for your money?"

This was the moment. She could either take it, and goad Salim on, to make a clean break of it, or leave it, and follow him into the life he was leading her into. Years later, when she was old and her life was spent, perhaps she would look back to this juncture, and feel relief or maybe regret, but one thing would be clear. This would have been her chance to act.

What should she do? Whom should she choose? There was so little time to think. It was so unfair—in the movies, there would be a song right now, and the good and bad points of each suitor would be clearly spelled out to music. The kind of song with the long, soothing notes in the background, the kind Lata would sing, with multiple flashbacks of each of the prospects superimposed on the heroine's face. (Though this would be a little difficult with Pran, since she'd only met him today.) But no, she would have to choose herself, without the benefit of such a summary.

"I'm sorry," Kavita said finally. "I'm all nervous, you know, and what you said about Vishnu—that just made me—" She broke off.

At this, Salim came to her, and took her in his arms. "It'll be okay. They don't really know how he is. He'll be fine. You don't have to worry."

"But how can we leave him like this? When he's so sick? When we don't even know? How can I leave my Vishnu?"

Kavita went up to the recumbent body. "Vishnu, talk to me. Please, open your eyes, say something, it's your Kavita."

She put her hand to his cheek. "I wonder if he's feeling cold," she said. Unwinding her dupatta from around her neck, she spread it over the top half of his body. "Maybe that will help a little." She stood up.

"Take care of yourself," Kavita said. Then she turned, and with her hand covering her mouth, and the background music welling up in her ears, ran down the stairs with all the drama the scene demanded.

Salim went over to Vishnu and bent down to retrieve the money Kavita had left. "Goodbye, my friend," he said, pocketing the bill, then followed Kavita down the steps.

OH, THE SCENTS she has left behind, the leaves and fruits and flowers. The beauty she has carried to earth, the pleasure it has brought. The dupatta that I can feel on me, with the perfume of her skin.

Come back, Lakshmi, come back. Don't you see your place is here with me? Don't you know you were meant for Vishnu, don't you know you are his strength? Come back so I can touch your face, come back so I can caress your feet. Come back, and keep me eternal company, O Lakshmi of mine.

What will happen to the flowers, now that you are gone? The earth that clings to the steps, the tulsi that begins to sprout. The colors that brighten the darkness of the stairs, the scents that perfume the air. Must I climb alone the petal-strewn trail of your descent?

But wait. Who is this, who emerges from the Jalals' door? Is this another god, who dares match your step with his own? He grasps onto the banister, and climbs so stealthily down. His shadow moves noiselessly against the walls, his footsteps sound quietly on stone.

The flowers so red and vivid seconds ago succumb under his tread. Petals wither where they lie, their scent fades into the ground. Stamens are crushed under his feet, their pollen blows all around.

The shadow falls thickly across the landing. This is man, not god, not yet. This is Mr. Jalal, his shoes still firm upon the stairs, his weight still heavy upon this earth, his grasp still reaching for the air.

AT FIRST, MR. Jalal thought he would bring a sheet with him. But then he decided not to—he was, after all, there to lie next to Vishnu, body and flesh, and a sheet would only insulate against the connection. He did, however, retain his sleeping suit, the one with the red cord around the collar and the matching cord lining the cuffs of the striped pajamas.

It had not been easy tonight. For some reason, Arifa had been very agitated. "Don't leave me, please," she said, as Mr. Jalal was spreading out his sheet on the floor. "Not tonight, you mustn't."

Mr. Jalal paused, the sheet billowing out from the two corners he was holding in his hands. "You know I like to sleep on the hard floor. I thought we understood that by now. My back—"

"No, Ahmed, not tonight. Not tonight of all nights. Come back to bed, please, I beg you to."

There was something suffocating about his wife's pleading. Since this evening, when she had come back from her sister's, Arifa's demeanor had been one that foreboded great tragedy. Her wavering voice and plaintive urgency further contributed to this effect. Mr. Jalal had been looking forward for some time to stealing away downstairs.

"What's so different tonight from other nights?"

Mrs. Jalal did not speak. Instead, she got up from her bed and started pulling off the sheet from her mattress as well.

"If you won't come back, I'm going to join you on the floor."

And so it was that Arifa set up her bed right next to his, and lay down by his side. "There, I'm sure it will be good for my back as well."

Apparently, however, it wasn't. After tossing and turning for an hour, and after a number of grunts of "Hai," Arifa (once Mr. Jalal pretended to have fallen asleep) stole back to her mattressed bed. Within minutes, her loud and rhythmic snores told Mr. Jalal it was time to make his move.

It had been years since Mr. Jalal had come down the stairs at so late an hour. He groped around for the light switch, before remembering that the lights had not worked in at least a decade. Some sort of fight with the downstairs neighbors about how to divide the bill between different floors. Cautiously, Mr. Jalal made his way past Radiowalla, past the Asranis and Pathaks, down towards Vishnu's landing.

He wondered why Arifa had been so insistent this evening about sleeping with him. The first few nights he had spent on the floor, her sighs had filled him with guilt. Was he depriving her of his presence? he had wondered. Was he shirking his spousal duty? Should he be confiding in her, explaining to her the journey on which he had embarked?

He had decided against it. Arifa would not understand. She would be suspicious of his motives and raise doubts and objections about everything. Besides, when was the last time they had even hugged in bed, much less made love? No, it must be something else—one of those generic unhappinesses that women suffered from, that had been unfortunately, unfairly, triggered off by his efforts. He had to be firm, he had to be unwavering—what he was striving after was much too important to lose in the shadows of her gloom. Besides, she was the one always complaining about his lack of faith. This was his chance to do something about it, not only for himself, but also for the two of them.

How different Arifa had been when he had first met her. Or perhaps it was he, Mr. Jalal thought, *his* opinion, that had changed. Could he have really found her neediness so reassuring back then, her insecurity so endearing? And the naiveté with which she stumbled through life—was there really a time when he had been charmed by it?

Those had been the days he was going around with his intellectual friends—the bearded, bespectacled group with whom he met every night to discuss philosophy and the fate of the world. "Every leaf has its story" was his favorite saying, and Arifa had been a leaf that had fallen his way. How touched he had been by her plainness, her lack of a story, when he had smiled his encouraging smile at her that first day. Wasn't she, too, worthy of a story—didn't she, too, deserve to have someone write one for her? Why not undertake the task himself, he had thought, perhaps even write himself into the plot? Didn't he pride himself as being unswayed by wealth or position, didn't he profess such faith in the innate potential of every

135

human? This was his chance to prove it, prove it once and for all, by marrying this plain person. This person, whose only recommendation so far was the eloquence with which her features had communicated their gratification in the light of the chaatwalla's lamp.

It was an idea that had quickly taken root, an idea that had flourished and ripened in the idealism of those youthful days. "Are you sure," his father had asked, "about this Dongri girl?" And Ahmed's chest had puffed with assurance when he had said yes.

His conceit had been that he would transform Arifa, Pygmalion-like, that he would introduce her to art and literature and pure thought. That he would scrape and scrub away at her Dongriness, until she emerged, polished and precious, like a multifaceted jewel, able to hold her own with razor wit and glittering personality. He had dived into this project with great gusto, talking to her about Kant and Plato, reciting to her works by Shaw and Tagore, shaking her up, baiting her, challenging her to *think*. She had displayed a particular softness for religion, so he had tried to introduce her to the ideas, sometimes foreign, sometimes contradictory, that formed the essence of other faiths, to show her that these were all man-made inventions, and one could not be preferred over the other. He had especially tried to impress upon her the story of his favorite Mughal emperor, Akbar, who had come to power in India after a long history of Muslim invaders, but followed a completely different course—not only encouraging other religions, but even marrying Hindu princesses, inviting Christian missionaries to educate his son, and eventually renouncing so much in the pursuit of his own Din Ilahi religion that people said he was no longer a Muslim.

"Think of it, Arifa. An emperor who gave up Islam to unify the subjects in his land, a ruler who said all men were equal, no matter to which religion they were born."

His wife chose *not* to think about it. "Isn't it enough to lecture me from morning to night about every topic under the sun? What need is there to push this further rubbish down my throat?"

Arifa's resistance only made his resolve grow stronger. He would not rest until he had forced her to confront the irrationality of her beliefs. The harder he labored, though, the more stubbornly she resisted. Eventually, it was she who won—a victory that appalled him, since it represented the defeat of everything he championed—rationality and reason—to so primitive a force as faith.

That was when the absurdity of his situation struck Mr. Jalal. He had knowingly pursued and tied himself to a woman with whom he had little in common. Now she turned out to not even be the blank slate he had expected to fill. Instead, she came programmed with ideas of her own, convictions he had not been able to dislodge, beliefs he might never exorcise.

What was it about Arifa's faith that had such tenacity in the face of his efforts? How could he have underestimated it so disastrously? He had always been proud of his conversance with not only Islam, but all the major religions of the world. He could explain how different beliefs arose and melded with their parent philosophies, detail obscure rituals from Africa to the Amazon practiced in the name of worship. Why, then, did he not understand the mechanism of faith? What did religion do to people, to provoke such obstinacy, such hysteria—how did it push people to the stage of torturing themselves and killing each other?

He had always assumed it was a flaw in people, a human failing, that created this need to believe in something beyond the ordinary. Religion existed to control society, to monitor those without the capacity to think things through for themselves, to provide promises and shimmering images in the sky, so that the urges of the masses could be calmed and regulated. What, after all, did the word 'faith' connote, except a willing blindness to the lack of actual proof? It was only natural that Arifa, with her untended intellect, had to lean on this crutch of faith to negotiate the inscrutability of life. Whereas he did not, in fact *could not*, have any use for the same.

But then an unexpected doubt arose in Mr. Jalal's mind. What if he was being too arrogant? What if there was another dimension to faith, another way of understanding it, of experiencing it, of which he was simply not capable? What if the shortcoming lay not with Arifa's outlook, but his own—if it was he who was limited, closed-minded? After all, wasn't he constantly amazed at the number of very smart people who were believers—hadn't even Einstein professed the existence of God?

The question began to gnaw at Mr. Jalal. The possibility that it was his intellect that might be wanting jabbed at his ego. He brooded for weeks on end about being less complete than Arifa, about being somehow inferior to the hordes of people thronging through the mosques and temples and churches of the city. Every time he saw a sadhu or a mullah, or even a group of worshipers with red temple marks on their foreheads, Mr. Jalal was confronted with the question: was it they who were flawed, or was it he?

Gradually, it dawned on him that there was only one way to find out. He would have to try and personally experience this thing they called faith. Perhaps by switching off his intellect and inviting religion to come and seek him out. Offering himself to be swept away like the mourners in the Muharram procession, like the Krishna devotees dancing through the streets on Fridays. So far, his interest in religion had always been clinical—never possessing his spirit, never penetrating the caul of his intellect. He would prove that he was just as complete as the next person, just as capable of having his spirit moved. The difference would be that for him it would be an experiment, one that would afford him an insider's view on faith. Afterwards, when he had returned to his normal self, he would sift through the experience to see if it contained anything of substance. Who knew, perhaps he might even encounter Arifa on his journey to the other side, and persuade her to accompany him back.

The more Mr. Jalal thought about this project, the more he was filled with enthusiasm. The idea of being an interloper among those of faith fascinated him. But how should he go about curbing his intellect? Where did one find the recipe to lure religion to one's doorstep?

Mr. Jalal pulled out his books on the Buddha and Mahavira Jain and the Hindu sadhus and fakirs. He pored over the accounts about sitting under trees, roaming in forests, subsisting on whatever food and water could be found. Wasn't renunciation the key to what all these people had achieved? Hadn't they succeeded in focusing their minds by denying the needs of their bodies? Could this be the prescription he was himself seeking?

That very week, he took the local train to Borivili, to wander around barefoot in the wilderness of the national park there. It was difficult to avoid all the families on picnics, but Mr. Jalal persevered, walking across the rocky soil until his feet were well blistered. He was astonished, and quite pleased, to come upon a magnificent banyan tree, right in the middle of the park. Surely this was a sign, he thought, a little guiltily, since he forbade himself from believing in signs. He cleared a site among the gnarled roots of the tree and sat down on the ground self-consciously. He tried crossing his legs into the lotus position, but gave up, and just closed his eyes instead.

He had been sitting there for some time, refusing to be disturbed by the footsteps, the voices, the occasional giggles, even the roar of a jet passing overhead, when it happened. Suddenly, he felt light surge into his face, a momentary flash which turned the insides of his eyelids a vivid red. He kept his eyes shut, and wondered if he was imagining things. Seconds later, he felt the flash again, and this time, his heart began pounding. Something was occurring, something unexpected, something extraordinary, and he was the medium through which it was being manifested. His mind raced through the books he had read—had the Buddha spoken of a flash, had Mahavira? What did it mean, what did it signify? The flash returned, lingering a little longer this time, and for an instant he wondered if this could be the first step towards enlightenment. A feeling of warmth began to permeate his shoulders, and he suddenly started feeling very light. Then

139

he heard a laugh, his eyes flickered open, and he was greeted by the sight of a group of schoolchildren gathered around him. One of them flashed the mirror a final time into his eyes, another kicked dirt into his face, and then they all ran away laughing.

Wearily, Mr. Jalal got up and shook the mud out of his hair. As he limped bleary-eyed towards the taxi-stand, he decided the world had become too overpopulated a place to recreate the conditions for renunciation from the Buddha's time.

Even though he had been tricked, one thing about the experience stayed with him. It was the memory of those last few instants, when the exhilaration had spread like a drug through his body, when his mind had surged with optimism, and he had felt himself floating, as weightless as a balloon. Mr. Jalal wanted to relive that feeling, he wanted to be able to recreate the conditions that produced it. He found himself diving into his quest with a new urgency, and starting to hope, against the grain of his nature, that he would find something. That the trials he was putting himself through, the pain, the deprivation, would yield a more authentic sign—one that he would not be able to refute, one that would blaze its energy through every cell and fiber of his body. With each new attempt he made, this longing only grew, and soon Mr. Jalal had to periodically remind himself of the skepticism that had always been such an essential part of him.

Tonight, as he edged his way down the dark and moonless steps, it was not skepticism but excitement that hummed in Mr. Jalal's mind. He had been waiting for this all day, he had a feeling about this experiment—perhaps this would be the stop on his journey when he finally arrived somewhere.

He eased himself into the calm that hung over Vishnu's landing. It was like entering a different dimension, one where the nature of every object had been softened, the sharpness of every corner rounded away. Vishnu's form lay covered by a bedsheet, and the bright orange floral pattern on the cloth gleamed in the dark around his feet. Mr. Jalal noted that the sheet had changed since the last night, as had Vishnu's position on the floor. Even the smell was different—mixed in with the odor of excretion was the astringency of phenol, hanging over the landing like the air in a hospital. He wondered who had cleaned Vishnu up. The changes worried Mr. Jalal, since he had counted on the filth to make it more of a test than it might turn out to be now.

As Mr. Jalal prepared to join Vishnu, he tried to imagine what the Buddha might have done before lying down. Surely there must have been some prayer uttered before settling into meditation. And what about Mother Teresa and St. Francis? For a second, Mr. Jalal toyed with the idea of crossing himself, but then decided not to. Using his sense of touch, he aligned himself with Vishnu's body in the darkness. He stretched out on the ground, thankful that it felt harder, somehow, than the floor of his bedroom.

The edge of Vishnu's sheet brushed against Mr. Jalal's pajamas. Body and flesh, he had promised. He eased out some of the sheet from under Vishnu and arranged it over his nightshirt. Then, reaching in with his arm, Mr. Jalal felt around under the sheet until his fingers came into contact with Vishnu's.

LET ME TELL you, my little Vishnu, of a yogi-spirit named Jeev. A yogi-spirit named Jeev born nine hundred and ninety thousand times.

Vishnu stops on the stairway to listen. Which one of Jeev's stories is his mother going to relate?

Many, many centuries ago, during the days that the Pandavas and Kauravas were living the Mahabharata, Jeev had just risen from being an insect. Sometimes he would be born a bird, and a few times even a small animal. Brahma had awoken from his sleep and breathed out the universe only recently. The air was still new, the streams had cool, clear water; there were enchanted forests in the land, and even the trees had spirits living in them. The lives Jeev led were easy ones—he hopped and flew and ran, using the tiny quantities of pure air and water that he needed for his existence. He went through many deaths and rebirths, it is true, but when one is so small, it is not too painful to be born again.

It was during one of his lifetimes as a bird that Jeev found himself being carried to the Pandavas' house. He had been about to alight in a tree when an arrow came flying through the leaves and grazed his skin. A puff of feathers flew into the air, the sight of which caused him to fall to the ground in shock.

"Open your eyes, little sparrow," a voice said, and Jeev found himself cradled in a palm. "The arrow was not meant for you. I was practicing hitting that branch without looking, and you had not appeared when I put on the blindfold."

The voice belonged to Arjun, the greatest archer who ever lived. Jeev saw Arjun's handsome face, saw the rippling chest made strong by archery, and felt a surge in his little feathered breast.

"Such a pretty bird you are," Arjun said, stroking Jeev's beak. "Come, I will take you home—you can stay with us till you feel better."

Arjun wrapped Jeev in a handkerchief and tucked him into his vest. As they made their way home, Jeev lost himself in the scent of Arjun's body. Even in the time it took to be carried to the Pandavas' hut, Jeev found himself helplessly in love.

They reached the hut, and Arjun called out, "Look, Mother, come and see what I have found."

His mother answered from inside, "Whatever it is, you must share with your brothers."

Being a Rajput, Arjun was bound by his mother's words, words that once spoken could not be retracted. So it was that Jeev became a mascot for all five of the Pandava brothers. They took care of him day by day in turn, feeding him from their palms, letting him alight on their shoulders, petting his tiny head with a finger. And when they traveled, they took him along wherever they went, carrying him in a golden cage when his wings could not flap fast enough to keep up.

At first, Jeev tried to live with this arrangement. But he was not happy. He wanted to eat only from Arjun's palm, nestle only against his body, sing only in his ear. He lived for that fifth day in every cycle, when everything felt and smelled and looked perfect, when he was with the only brother out of the five he truly cared for.

Eventually, Jeev could not hide his feelings. He started becoming ill-tempered the four days he was not with Arjun. He refused to eat anything, and pecked at fingers if Arjun's brothers tried to stroke him. His greatest ire was reserved for Arjun's mother, whose directive had been a curse for him, and could never be taken back. He began leaving droppings on her bed and pecking at her head while she was asleep. The brothers tried mollifying Jeev, but the rage he felt would not be controlled.

The day came when Arjun put Jeev in his cage and started out for the forest. They journeyed for many hours, past unfamiliar trees and streams. As they traveled, Jeev kept his eyes on Arjun's face, and tried to understand the sadness in it.

They reached a clearing, and Arjun opened the door of the cage. Jeev hopped onto the finger Arjun offered, and felt himself buoyed through the air.

"Each creature has its own karma to follow, little sparrow," Arjun said, and kissed him lightly on the side of his head. "Today, it is time for you to find yours."

For a moment, Jeev saw the face he loved so much right next to his, gazed at the mouth, the lips, that had just pressed into his feathers. Then it all disappeared in a blur as Arjun whisked his finger into the air. Despite himself, Jeev found his feet letting go of their perch, found his wings unfurling, found the muscles in his breast begin to pump. He found himself rising, rising above Arjun, rising above the plants and the trees, rising above the forest, until he could look down and see a sea of green, and in the distance rivers cutting through, and further beyond, the mountains, and beyond them even, the trinity, with Brahma reclining in the chariot of the seven swans, and Vishnu rising in all his brilliance into the sky, and Shiva at the edge of the world, getting ready to do his dance.

DURING THE NIGHT, Mr. Jalal had a vision. A vision that seemed much too intense to Mr. Jalal to have been a dream—a vision he was convinced was a revelation, a visitation. Mr. Jalal spent part of the night tossing and thrashing in its throes, and as he rolled about, the sheet and dupatta covering Vishnu's body were pulled off and wrapped around Mr. Jalal instead.

In his vision, Mr. Jalal was sitting on the step above the landing, still dressed in his pajama suit. Vishnu, looking quite recovered, was seated next to him. Between them was a bowl of walnuts.

Vishnu picked up a walnut from the bowl and set it on the landing. He brought his fist down and smashed the shell, then sifted through the pieces to extract the kernel.

Mr. Jalal tried the same, but his walnut did not break, and his fist bounced back painfully from the shell.

"It's not so easy," Vishnu said, laughing. "Only I can do it." He thrust some of his walnut bits into Mr. Jalal's hand, who stared at them uncertainly. "Don't worry, they're safe. I'm quite well now—you won't catch anything from me."

Mr. Jalal put the pieces in his mouth. They tasted very nutty, as if fried in oil to bring out their flavor. He looked at the bowl and hoped Vishnu would break open some more, even though it probably wasn't a good idea to eat walnuts so close to bedtime.

"I see you've come to sleep down here tonight," Vishnu said, smashing open another nut and handing over the entire kernel to Mr. Jalal. "Tell me, what do you hope to find? Besides walnuts."

Mr. Jalal felt the soft crispness of the kernel under his teeth. Thick walnut juice oozed out and coated his tongue. He tried to recall why he had come.

"Enlightenment," he said, remembering. "I've come for a sign."

Vishnu laughed. "And what do you think—this enlightenment that you're seeking—it comes in a nut? That it's waiting for you in one of these shells—for me to crack open, and you to swallow?"

Mr. Jalal bristled. "I'll have you know I've been sleeping on the ground for months now."

"And look, you even came down tonight without a pillow. Surely that merits something." Vishnu broke open another walnut and offered it on his outstretched palm. "Here, maybe this is the one you've made your pilgrimage for."

Mr. Jalal's face turned red. "I've starved myself. I've beaten myself. I may not be the Buddha, but that should count for something." He pushed away Vishnu's hand. "All I'm asking for is a sign, not an entry into heaven."

"If signs were so easy, people would be lining up and down the stairs for these nuts. I would be selling each one for a fortune."

"You don't understand," Mr. Jalal said. "You don't know. How long I've been trying. I'm not just any person, you know—all this time, I've thought of nothing but this." Mr. Jalal's voice rose to a whine. "If anyone deserves enlightenment, it should be me."

"You and a million others. It's not so simple. I've already told you. Maybe you should come back some other time. Perhaps in a few more years. Yes, come in a few years. Maybe you'll be more ready then." Vishnu brushed the nut residue off his hands.

Something flared inside Mr. Jalal. "And who do you think you are? Who are you to decide? I didn't come here tonight to listen to you, you drunken fool. Who even asked you anything?"

"Such anger. You know it will only cloud your vision. Not that it makes any difference to me." Vishnu started humming. "Though what a shame that would be, if you were too angry to notice." He

145

began examining the walnuts in the bowl, flipping several over, like a fruit vendor arranging his wares to bring the most unblemished specimens up to display.

"Notice what? Are you going to show me something? A sign, perhaps? You're from heaven, is it? Come to distribute magic walnuts?"

"Calm down," Vishnu said. "Calm down and pay attention. Or you may miss what you've come for."

"I will *not* calm down. I will *not* keep quiet." Mr. Jalal stood up. "*This* is what I think of your sign." He kicked the bowl of nuts, sending it flying into the air. "What I think of you and your walnuts." The bowl struck the wall and overturned, emptying its contents on the landing. Walnuts spun across the floor and clattered down the steps.

"No more signs," Mr. Jalal shouted. "No more religion. No more nonsense. It's all a hoax. One big giant hoax." He raised a fist above his head and shook it in the air. "I've been at this for months, and I've seen nothing. One big giant hoax against all of mankind, I say."

"*Ahmed.*"

For an instant, Mr. Jalal did not know where the voice came from. Then he realized that Vishnu had risen as well, and now stood face to face with him.

"Look, Ahmed," Vishnu said, holding up a walnut in his hand. "A final one. That I'm going to break open. For you."

It was strange, very strange, to hear Vishnu use his first name. Had he completely forgotten his place? Surely such familiarity should not be allowed to pass unreprimanded. Mr. Jalal was debating what to say when Vishnu brought the walnut closer, until it was touching the center of his forehead. *What does the fool think he's doing now?* Mr. Jalal wondered. He could feel the individual bumps on the shell press against his skin. "Take that away at once," he began to say, but before he could get the words out, there was a blur of motion, and Vishnu's fist swung up through the air and smashed the walnut into his skull.

"Now look at me and see who I really am."

The first thought that occurred to Mr. Jalal was that Vishnu had gone insane. What kind of person would drive pieces of walnut shell into someone else's brain? Then Mr. Jalal realized that the walnut had opened up a hole in his forehead, a hole that was like a third eye, through which he was seeing intense light. Mr. Jalal saw a sun emerge from behind Vishnu, and was surprised he could look straight into its molten white center. As he watched, he saw two suns, then four, then eight, and sixteen. The suns kept multiplying, and rising into the air, until the sky was covered with suns, and there was no more blue to be seen, just the brightness of incandescent discs stretching from horizon to horizon and pouring their brilliance down on him.

When Mr. Jalal looked back down from the sky, Vishnu's body was metamorphosing. Into something liquid and luminous, that sucked the light from the air and released it back with a concentrated intensity. Limbs started appearing from all around Vishnu's perimeter, and at their ends Mr. Jalal saw exquisitely carved conches and fabulous jewel-encrusted maces. Some of the hands that emerged held lotuses, which opened to reveal enormous anthers poised over their centers. Limbs kept emerging and Vishnu kept expanding, until he was touching the suns above and Mr. Jalal couldn't tell where he started and where he ended. A sweet fragrance, like that of incense, but with a perfume that smelled of no flower Mr. Jalal knew, began filling the air.

At each point of contact with the suns, heads now appeared, wearing the suns as crowns and stretching down for many miles. Giant eyes opened in the heads, and Mr. Jalal drew back in fear, as they blinked in unison and looked down at him. The mouths flew open, and in them were visible teeth and fangs and long lines of spurting flame, some of which leapt out and scorched the ground at Mr. Jalal's feet. There were serpents in the mouths, and skulls too, and Mr. Jalal saw human bodies being crushed and popped between the teeth.

As Mr. Jalal looked on, Vishnu kept expanding, with new heads and appendages being generated in his insides and bubbling up to the surface. Smaller forms detached and reattached themselves along his periphery, like tongues of flame at the edges of a fire.

"Who are you?" Mr. Jalal stammered. "Tell me, who are you in this terrible form?"

"I am what you taste in water, I am what you see in air. I am the breath in every flower, I am the life in every creature. I am all living things, I am creation itself. Look at me and see in my body the whole universe."

A huge mouth opened up and snapped at the air near Mr. Jalal's head. Giant fangs snaked out to blow fire at his face, and Mr. Jalal felt the hairs in both his eyebrows become crisp.

"I encompass the sun gods and the moon gods, the wind gods and the fire-eating gods of the world. I am the aging of time, the beginning and the end of the universe. As each day ends, all creatures are destroyed and renewed in me."

Mr. Jalal saw demons take shape and break free from Vishnu's boundary. The demons bared their teeth at Mr. Jalal before being obscured by the vapors issuing from their nostrils.

"Where did you come from?" Mr. Jalal asked, his voice trembling.

"Forever have I been here, and forever shall I remain—I am everywhere and everything all at once. In every living cell of every living thing shall you find me. Lucky are those to whom I show myself, for it is not through penance or rituals that you will see me."

The heads had multiplied, and were now craning their long necks to surround Mr. Jalal and stare at him from all directions. A steady stream of gods and ghosts and demons were passing from mouth to open mouth, undaunted by the skulls and mangled bodies dangling between the teeth. The air was so heavy with heat that Mr. Jalal felt the inside of his chest was on fire.

"What do you want from me?" he wheezed.

"Fortunate are those who recognize my presence. Blessed are those who acknowledge me, worship me. Tell them down there to recognize me for who I am. I can wait only so long. Before it is too late, too late for all. For I have come to save and destroy the universe."

And then, as Mr. Jalal looked, Vishnu began to expand even more, until he filled all of space, and suffused all of time. Mr. Jalal felt himself becoming one with Vishnu, not only in this, but in all his previous existences as well. The last thought he had was about the splinters of walnut shell still embedded in his forehead, and then he was overcome with a sense of oneness, all touch and feeling subsiding, all thought and emotion fading, the intensity of the vision engulfing him in all its splendor, and once fully encapsulated, an unexpected peace descending, a quiet, a solitude, a meditative calm, and then, finally, sleep, pure and silent, unusually deep, from which Mr. Jalal was awoken a few hours later.

CHAPTER EIGHT

SHORT GANGA SET the bottles of milk down. Although she could manage to carry all eight of them from the milk booth to the building without pause, climbing the stairs with them was a different thing, and she always took a break, both before starting and at the Jalals' landing. She was careful not to wake up Man Who Slept on the Lowest Step. Not so much because she was concerned about his sleep, about which she couldn't care less, but because he unfailingly tried to look up her sari if he was awake when she went past. Even though she wore her sari in the Maharashtrian fashion, which made looking up it impossible, she still felt uneasy at his attempts. She almost wished he was improper with her in some other, more tangible way, so she could approach the cigarettewalla about giving him a beating.

The morning milk run was the most hectic part of the day. First she had to stand in line to get the milk from the ration booth, using the cards that each family gave her. Then it was a race to distribute all the milk to the buildings before it soured in the heat. April was one of the hottest months, second only to May, and already this week two of her customers had complained about spoiled milk. When this happened, the loss was quite staggering, since the cost of a bottle was roughly what she made per household for a week's delivery. Often, when people demanded she pay them for the spoiled milk, she just stopped delivering to that address—if enough gangas did that, then the housewives would no longer be able to wield such tyranny over them.

Her break over, Short Ganga picked up the two wire holders and started climbing the steps. All she had been able to get today was the bottles with the red foil caps, the ones with reconstituted milk. Which meant there was bound to be a fuss. Especially with the Asranis and the Pathaks. Short Ganga knew they would accuse her of selling their good milk to nonration customers and substituting the cheaper variety for them. Which she did do occasionally, but the point was that today was not such a day.

Let them just try it, Short Ganga thought to herself. The heat was making her bellicose. She'd accuse them of poisoning Vishnu. That would shut them up. It wasn't so far from the truth anyway—the cigarettewalla had told her that neither family had offered to pay for the hospital even though the ambulance had come to pick Vishnu up. "All those years he has worked for you, and this is what you give him?" she practiced to herself. "A death worse than a dog's?"

Short Ganga had reached the stage where she had stopped caring so much about losing a few households. It made so little difference anyway, the amount of money she made from one place. If anyone wanted to get rid of her for speaking her mind, let them. She'd show them—she'd blacklist them in the books of all the gangas she knew. Then they'd see the result of firing her, of underestimating her. *Short* Ganga, indeed! If it hadn't been for Mr. Taneja on the third floor, she would have struck this building off her list a long time ago.

Poor Mr. Taneja. The man never seemed to leave his flat—he depended on her not only for the milk, but for the food she delivered to him every afternoon. The paanwalla had told her the sad story about Mrs. Taneja's death, many years ago. "What a woman she was," the paanwalla would say, stroking his mustache. "Every day, she had to have her sweet paan, come rain or shine." After his wife's death, Mr. Taneja had gradually become a recluse, and the people in the building now regarded him as something of a mystery figure. "Tell Mr. Taneja he is rarer than the new moon of Eid," Mr. Jalal would say to Short Ganga, who was the only one who still had regular contact with him, and in whose hands the paanwalla, still sentimental about the memory of Mrs. Taneja, sometimes sent up a complimentary paan.

Perhaps she should tell Mr. Taneja about Vishnu, to see if he could be the one to help. Since the man never came out, he probably didn't even know about Vishnu's illness.

She had almost made it to Vishnu's landing when a sudden thought startled her. What if she was the one to find Vishnu dead? That would be terrible—there might even be a police report to fill out, an interview to give. She would check if he was alive, and even if he wasn't, tell Mrs. Pathak he was still breathing. No sense in getting involved in unnecessary complications. Besides, it was Vishnu's fault anyway—never eating, always drinking, not taking any medicines, even though he knew he was getting worse.

The tip of Vishnu's sheet came into view, then the rest of it, then the shape of the body underneath it. Short Ganga gasped when she saw it move. He was still alive—maybe he was even improving. She left the milk bottles on the side of the stairs and ascended the remaining two steps to the landing. Then she stopped.

There were *two* bodies there. One was Vishnu, who was lying against the wall, his body uncovered and still. The sheet was wrapped around the *second* body, which was also that of a man, but very much alive, since it was snoring quite audibly under the cloth. Bunched up with the sheet and coiling around the head was a red-and-green dupatta.

What should she do? Her first instinct was to try and see who it

152

was, and even arouse the person. But then she wondered—what if it was Radiowalla? He might suddenly wake up even if she was only trying to peek under the dupatta. The man was quite deranged and had never quite forgiven her for the Styrofoam—what if he killed her then and there? No, it was safer to go upstairs and get Mr. Pathak.

The milk forgotten two steps below, Short Ganga ran up to the first-floor landing and pressed the Pathaks' doorbell. Mrs. Pathak answered the door.

There was no time to waste on her, Short Ganga decided, this was a job for a man. "Is Mr. Pathak there?" she asked importantly.

ALTHOUGH HE CERTAINLY knew the way down to Vishnu's landing, Mr. Pathak followed Short Ganga down the stairs, as if she were leading them on some recently discovered treasure path. Mrs. Pathak brought up the rear of the procession, prepared, it seemed, to use her husband's body as a shield in case of trouble, but making quick darting movements outside the realm of protection to offer advice or spur them on.

"Stranger and stranger this thing gets," Mrs. Pathak announced unnecessarily. "Now we will go see who is this Mr. Mystery Man who has dropped by to take a nap."

Short Ganga shushed Mrs. Pathak, who put a finger on her own mouth in obedience, even though this was a needless exercise since they were, after all, descending to awaken the Mystery Man.

They stood over the sheet-and-dupatta-covered figure. "Look, he's stolen my sheet from poor Vishnu—what a Mystery Man and a half, to steal the covering from a dying person," Mrs. Pathak exclaimed. She bent down to take a closer look. "And this dupatta—I've seen it before—who wears this color dress? Is it Mrs. Asrani or Mrs. Jalal?"

Short Ganga turned to Mr. Pathak, who cleared his throat. "You can take off the sheet and see who it is," he instructed her, loath to do the task himself.

Short Ganga thought about protesting, but a part of her was excited at the prospect of being the one to unmask the Mystery Man. Besides, if it did turn out to be Radiowalla, and he attacked her, she would have evidence against him to take to the cigarettewalla, with both the Pathaks present as witnesses. She extended a hand to the edge of the sheet, but just before she could touch it, the figure underneath stirred, then sat bolt upright, its face still obscured.

Short Ganga drew back, and Mrs. Pathak let out a squeal of fright. Even Mr. Pathak's voice wavered, as he mustered all the sternness he could. "Who are you?" he asked.

"Vishnu? Is that you? Who is it? Why can't I see anyone? What is this over my head?"

"Jalal sahib? What are you doing here? Ganga, help Mr. Jalal to get the cloth off, will you?" Mr. Pathak said, still hesitant to touch anything himself. "What happened, did you fall in the dark?"

Short Ganga pulled the dupatta off, to reveal Mr. Jalal blinking in the landing light, looking as disoriented as an insect emerging from its pupa.

"Did I fall?" he repeated dully, as if asking the question to himself. Then, suddenly remembering, he sat up straight. "Vishnu!" he said. "You won't believe what I saw. He came to me. As a god."

"Maybe he did fall," Short Ganga suggested. She wrinkled her nose at the smell of refuse and phenol emanating from Vishnu and now lingering like a cloud over Mr. Jalal as well.

"You can't imagine what he looks like. It's scary even now to think of it."

"Mr. Jalal, what are you talking about?"

"He showed me. I saw him. Hundreds of eyes and arms and legs. Flames as long as rivers spurting from his mouth. Corpses crushed between his teeth. He's a god, he said, and he won't wait around much longer, unless you acknowledge him. Unless we all acknowledge him. That's what he directed me to tell you. Not to make him angry."

Mr. Pathak looked at his wife.

"Mr. Jalal," Mrs. Pathak said. "Can you see me?"

"Yes, of course, I can see you."

"Do you recognize me, Mr. Jalal?"

"Yes, yes, of course I do, look, I don't have time for this."

"*Who* told you Vishnu is a god?"

"He did, of course. Vishnu did. Is it so hard to believe?"

"But Vishnu hasn't spoken for days," Mrs. Pathak declared, pleased at the simplicity of her logic. "He may even be dead by now—have you checked his pulse?"

"I don't have to. I just talked to him. Haven't you been listening? Go ahead, one of you, check his pulse if you don't believe me."

Mrs. Pathak turned to Mr. Pathak, who turned to Short Ganga, who looked back defiantly. There was nothing that was going to persuade her to search Vishnu's limbs for a pulse.

"He's not dead, I tell you. He just spoke to me. Not spoke, really—he *revealed*. That's what gods do when they want to say something. They reveal."

"What did he reveal exactly?"

"I told you. His real self. He looks just like those gods in the religious calendars—the ones the cigarettewalla has hanging in his shop. Even more mouths and arms and feet, if you can imagine."

Mr. Jalal paused, examining the air, as if Vishnu's apparition might still be floating around. "He was standing here, in front of me, before he swallowed everyone and everything."

Short Ganga and Mrs. Pathak exchanged a look. Mr. Pathak sighed. "Come, Mr. Jalal, you've had a difficult night. Perhaps you should go upstairs."

"Yes," Mrs. Pathak added. "Mrs. Jalal must be worrying."

"A ghost has mounted him," Short Ganga whispered. "Entered

through some orifice he left open and climbed up to his head. Definitely a ghost." She examined Mr. Jalal suspiciously, letting her gaze linger at his ears, his mouth, even his buttocks. "Through some orifice."

Mrs. Pathak shushed her. "Come, Mr. Jalal, we'll help you up to your flat. Ganga, could you unwrap the sheet from his legs?"

Mr. Jalal watched distractedly as Short Ganga pulled the sheet down to disentangle first his left foot, then his right. The pattern on the cloth caught his eye. The flowers which had looked orange in the landing light last night were actually yellow. He felt elated at this—yellow was an auspicious color, yellow flowers were like little suns, signifying light, signifying energy. Leaning forward, he plucked the sheet out of Short Ganga's hands, just as she was beginning to fold it up.

"This is Vishnu's," he announced, and arranged the sheet over Vishnu's body. "We really have to get a pillow for his head."

As the Pathaks were helping him up the first of the stairs, Mr. Jalal suddenly clasped each of them by the forearm. "It's finally happened, hasn't it?" he said, pulling them closer to him and looking from one to the other.

Mrs. Pathak's bangles jingled in protest as she tried to free herself, but Mr. Jalal's grip was too insistent.

"Even to me it's happened. I can't believe it," Mr. Jalal said, scanning first Mr. Pathak's face for confirmation, then Mrs. Pathak's, and failing entirely to notice her agitation at having her arm seized by a man not her husband.

"It's so amazing. I've received my sign," continued Mr. Jalal, still oblivious to Mrs. Pathak, and to the alarm now spreading across Short Ganga's face as well. Fortunately, just at the point when Mrs. Pathak's scream seemed imminent (with Short Ganga getting ready to run for the cigarettewalla and Mr. Pathak still wondering how to intervene), Mr. Jalal released his grip and allowed himself to be led up to his flat.

THE LANDING IS deserted again. Mr. Jalal's revelation drifts silently over the steps.

Could it be true?

He is Vishnu.

Can Mr. Jalal's vision be trusted? Does he know what he is saying?

He is a god.

Could that be why he has become weightless? Is that how he can will himself from step to step?

He is Vishnu.

Yes, it must be true. How else could his hearing be so sharp that he catches Radiowalla's music, his vision so acute that he sees through brick and stone?

He is the god Vishnu.

Isn't that what his mother always told him? Isn't that why she gave him his name? How did that saying go, the one she used to make him repeat?

I am Vishnu, he says. He hasn't said it since he was a child.

I am Vishnu, he practices saying. It sounds right to him.

But what, suddenly, has made him a god? What has changed, after all these years as a mortal? Or was he a god all along, just did not know his power? Was it there within him, waiting all this time to be set free if he tried?

I am Vishnu. Keeper of the universe, keeper of the sun.

If he is a god, shouldn't he consort from now on only with other gods? Isn't he above ordinary humans—people in this building, people on the street? He has heard Mr. Jalal tell them they should submit to him, venerate him. What if they don't—how is he to punish them? How will he deal with those who have wronged him in the past, those who dare deny him in the future?

There is only darkness without me.

Can he take away the sun and the moon? Can he plunge the universe into night? Everything that lives, does it live in his light? Must every desire of his be accommodated, every whim obeyed?

But what is it he wants? What are gods supposed to desire?

I am Vishnu, he says to himself. He is eager to learn the new ways and powers.

IT WAS NINE o'clock in the morning before Mrs. Asrani entered Kavita's room. Ordinarily, she would have allowed her daughter to sleep much longer on a Sunday, even until noon, but in light of the "I think I would like to say yes" answer from last night, Mrs. Asrani wasn't sure she could hold it in herself any longer not to seek a confirmation. She had been so excited all morning that she had hardly paid attention to Short Ganga's gossip about Mr. Jalal being found asleep on Vishnu's landing, and of his attempted assault on Mrs. Pathak. She was surprised now to find Kavita's bed all made up, since her daughter almost never did that, and more surprised to find that the bathroom was empty, since Kavita spent what seemed like hours there every morning.

"Have you seen Kavita?" Mrs. Asrani asked. Shyamu and Mr. Asrani looked up from the breakfast table. "Did she go outside?"

Mr. Asrani shook his head. "No one's been outside since I got the newspaper."

"I'll find her for you," Shyamu offered. "Kavita," he called out. "Kaveeetaaaaaaaa . . ."

There was no reply. "She's not there," he said. "I guess she ran away with the Jalals' son after all, so we can all live happily ever after."

It was definitely the wrong thing to say. Mrs. Asrani's inaugural slap of the day was so energetic that Shyamu burst out crying. "Go

158

inside to your room," Mrs. Asrani commanded, taking away his half-eaten jam sandwich.

Shyamu kept crying at the table, so Mr. Asrani returned his sandwich to him. Between sobs, Shyamu started putting pieces of jam-spread bread in his mouth.

"God help you if she's run away with that cockroach. God help you if you have a black tongue," Mrs. Asrani thundered. "And you, jee?" she said, turning her attention on Mr. Asrani. "Are you going to just sit there and sip tea, or are you going to try and find your promising young daughter?"

"I'll go look in her room, to see if everything is still there," Mr. Asrani said, glad for a chance to be out of range of his wife.

He came back a few minutes later. "Everything is intact," he said. "There's nothing missing, and even her suitcase is still in the cupboard. She must have gone out while I was not looking—she should be back soon."

"I knew it was too good to be true," Mrs. Asrani lamented, her anger temporarily diffused by despair. "Her saying yes and everything. What are we going to do? What will I say to Mrs. Lalwani?"

"Calm down, Aruna. Nothing's happened. She'll be back—"

"You," Mrs. Asrani snarled, replugging into the socket of her anger. "This is all your fault. From when I have been predicting this, and all you can say is 'Calm down, Aruna. Calm down, Aruna.' *Now* do you see the result of letting your daughter climb on top of your head?"

Mr. Asrani was silent. He knew, from experience, that the safest course of action when things reached this stage was one of abject contrition, like that expected from an errant schoolboy. He sat at the table and tried to look as wretched as Shyamu.

"What are you so silent about now? Is some magic genie going to pop out of your tea cup and tell you where she is?"

Mr. Asrani did not look up. Shyamu, still sniveling, but tired of his sandwich, started breaking the bread into crumbs and mashing them on his plate.

Mrs. Asrani looked from her husband to her son, and back to her husband again. She was suddenly uncertain about what point she had been trying to make. But it was apparent she had gotten it across. She took a deep breath.

"Now listen everyone, and this means especially you, Shyamu. If she comes back in a little while, good. But until she does, I don't want either of you telling anyone—and I do mean *anyone*—that she's gone. Especially not the next-door neighbors. Who knows, maybe they're the ones who even put some sort of nazar on her." Mrs. Asrani cast a baleful eye towards the Pathaks' apartment.

"And if, God forbid, our Kavita actually has run away with that cockroach, then we just have to wait. Wait till she comes to her senses, wait till she comes back, and not breathe a word about it until then. It would be ruinous if people came to know what has happened.

"Understood?"

Shyamu flattened the remainder of his sandwich and watched the jam squeeze out.

"Shyamu, I'm talking to you. *Understood?*"

With a look dripping with misery and remorse, Shyamu nodded that he had understood.

MR. JALAL LAY on his bed and tried to make the cricks in his back disappear. He had several months' worth of them to work on. Now that his travails had paid off, now that he had received his sign, there seemed no reason to deny himself small luxuries, such as returning to his bed. He pressed his neck muscles into the mattress, then the ones in his back, feeling the cotton stuffing yield to fit the contours of his body. Ah, the softness—so pleasurable, so decadent—no wonder people didn't get revelations every night as they slept on their pillowed and padded beds. Something in Mr. Jalal's spine released with an audible pop, and the relief that flooded into his brain almost made him swoon.

As he had waited for Arifa to let him in, there had been only one thought burning in his head. The directive that Vishnu had given him. He had to spread the word, inform people, impress on them that Vishnu was a god. He had braced himself at the door like an athlete at the start of a race. He would sprint in straight to the telephone, call all the people he knew, even contact the *Times of India*.

But a peculiar incoherence had possessed him. His words had not seemed to convey their message. "Enlightenment *does* come in a walnut," he had insisted, and the Pathaks had discreetly taken their leave. "Thousands of hands and feet," he had said, waving his arms around to simulate Vishnu's many limbs, and Arifa's expression had changed from confusion to dismay. Eventually, he had allowed himself to be ushered into their bedroom for a rest.

It was not going to be easy, Mr. Jalal realized. First the Pathaks and Short Ganga, now Arifa—nobody had believed him. He supposed he couldn't really blame them—what he'd seen was so fantastic, and he'd been too excited to be articulate. But if he couldn't even convince his wife, what chance did he have with the rest?

How had the Buddha done it? And Jesus and Muhammad and the other prophets? Even the present-day godmen. He remembered seeing the Satya Sai Baba on TV, descending from his podium onto a platform that swept through a sea of adoring disciples. Waves of devotees surged towards the platform, screaming and crying as they tried to touch his saffron robes. The Baba walked along unperturbed, with his arms raised in blessing, a beatific smile fixed on his face. It had been hard to see the Baba's feet on TV, and the effect had been of someone gliding across water.

Mr. Jalal imagined himself standing on his balcony, clad in robes of saffron himself. The road below choked with people assembled there to receive his message. Taxis and buses honking their horns as they tried in vain to negotiate the throngs. Silence descending suddenly and completely, as he raised both his hands just like the Baba had done. He would gaze individually at as many of the thousands of upturned faces as he could—the sea, *his* sea of followers. All those eyes focused on him, all those ears waiting to hear the compelling words issue from his mouth.

But what, exactly, would those words be? The ones that would crackle down through the air, like lightning, like electricity, and energize the entire crowd? From where would he summon the power to seize the attention of such an enormous congregation? To inspire them, to incite them, to make them forever his followers?

Mr. Jalal felt his back begin to stiffen again and willed himself to relax. He was getting ahead of himself. Right now, the important thing was that he was in, he had been initiated. He had opened his mind wide enough to receive the vision. The giant mouths, the tongues of fire, the steam and smoke, all these he had witnessed. The sign he had been waiting for had finally been granted. He tried pressing his spine into the mattress again, and heard several small crackles, but nothing as satisfying as the previous pop.

Or had it? What tangible evidence did he have? Wasn't he being absurdly credulous? Couldn't the whole thing—heads, tongues, fire—just have been a dream? He had, after all, dreamt before—had he forgotten how real some dreams could appear? Wasn't this explanation a more rational one, not involving signs and visitations and other fanciful notions? Wasn't it, in fact, the *only* logical explanation, the one that *demanded* his immediate and complete acceptance?

Mr. Jalal recognized his old friend, Reason. Revived and hungry to reclaim its rightful place. Perhaps it had wakened from its hibernation the instant he had lain down again in this bed. Perhaps it had sniffed out the torpor into which the mattress was lulling his body. Already, he could feel it nipping here and there tentatively, testing the durability of what he had witnessed.

He had to get off the mattress immediately. There could not be a second's delay. Mr. Jalal rocked himself on the bed, then rolled off the edge. A dull crack jarred through his spine as the back of his head hit the floor. That was good, he thought, it would discourage his prowling friend. He lifted his head and let it thud several times to the floor. Maybe *that* would send Reason whimpering back into its cave.

He lay on the floor and closed his eyes. He could feel the familiar hardness of the tile against his back. Pain throbbed into his forehead from the base of his skull. He had to concentrate, concentrate to make things as they were before.

The image came slowly, like a painting raised to the surface of a murky pool. The swords were the first to be visible, edges glinting as they sliced through the air. Then came the arms that brandished them, and the mouths and the eyes and the faces. Then there was Vishnu towering above him, in all his hideousness and splendor.

"Why have you not done what I commanded?" Vishnu roared, and Mr. Jalal smelled the sweet fragrance of his own burning flesh.

He opened his eyes. He was alone on the floor of his bedroom. Street noise and sunlight streamed in through the door leading to the balcony. Arifa was talking to someone on the phone in the next room. Somewhere in the building a meat curry was being cooked.

What was real, he wondered, and what was a dream? Didn't the Hindus hold that reality was just an illusion? That everything was *maya* as they called it—all existence a temporary delusion—hadn't even the Buddha accepted that? And the westerners, too—wasn't there something about the world not existing, only mental representations of it? Was it Kant who had said that? Or Nietzsche? No, someone else, someone less well-known—who was it, Berkeley, perhaps? For an instant, Mr. Jalal worried about where all his books on philosophy had gone. He hoped Arifa hadn't thrown them out.

Perhaps there were some things that could only be experienced, not explained. Perhaps logic was not the answer to bolster every truth in the universe. Last night's vision had felt as accurate as a shirt against his skin. But surely its fabric could be scrutinized to yield

163

flaws, its fibers worried until they unraveled. And yet, he had felt it clothe the center of his self, transform the way he felt about the world. He would not, *could* not, dismiss the reality of his experience.

But how was he to convey this reality to others? How, without the benefit of logic or argument, was he supposed to capture people's minds? All he had been given was a sign. With this he had to arm himself, and go out and change the world. He supposed this was the essence of faith. There was no science that governed it, no calculus that propelled it, just the raw strength of his own conviction. Whether he succeeded or not depended on how well he could combat doubt, both his own and in others.

And succeed he had to. Vishnu's words came back, his promise to save, to destroy the universe. He had to be recognized, recognized before it was "too late for all." They could not afford to ignore his warning. Mr. Jalal saw Short Ganga being consigned screaming into Vishnu's giant maws. Then the cigarettewalla and the paanwalla, the Pathaks and Asranis. Their bodies masticated together into one bloody mass, their shocked faces popping and exploding, torrents of fire reducing them to instant ash. And from somewhere, barely audible, Arifa's plaintive voice, begging to be spared.

Mr. Jalal sat up on the floor. He was the only one who could save them. He would have to use what little he had, and hope it was enough to connect people to the urgency of what he had witnessed. The rest would be up to them.

But first, he had to return to Vishnu's landing. With a sweet, a fruit, or other offering. This was the proper way, he knew, that one asked for blessing from a Hindu god.

MRS. JALAL STARED at the letter Salim had written. What had the world come to today? First Ahmed, babbling about walnuts and gods, led upstairs by the Pathaks and Short Ganga of all people. How would she live the shame down? Being found next to Vishnu in such a condition—with a dupatta wrapped around his head, as Mrs. Pathak had pointed out—not once but three times—the cheek of that woman. At least Mr. Pathak had had the decency to conjecture that Ahmed might have fallen and knocked himself unconscious. Thankfully, she'd had the presence of mind to say that she had often warned Ahmed about taking his night walk down the dark steps.

And now this. Salim writing simply that he was going away for a few weeks. Why wouldn't he have told anyone? What possible place could he have gone to, that he couldn't have let her know in advance? She was surprised at all the clothes missing—which told her it was a planned decision. But planned for what? Nothing was making sense—nothing on this inauspicious day.

There was no point telling Ahmed about the letter—not until he had returned to his senses. She had thought about calling the doctor, but had been scared at the prospect that he would recommend psychiatric evaluation, or even hospitalization. She didn't want to have Ahmed committed to a mental asylum, or worse, end up in a place like Amira Ma's. Once such news spread, it was difficult to contain, so she had to be very careful about what she was doing.

Just then, Ahmed walked into the room.

"How do you feel?" Mrs. Jalal asked, trying to put on a cheerful face. She suddenly noticed how awful he smelled. "Should I get the water ready for your bath?"

Mr. Jalal shook his head. There was something he was holding behind his back. His eyes circled the room, estimating distances and angles from where he stood to Mrs. Jalal and the front door.

Mrs. Jalal tried to see what he held in his hand, but he used his body to screen it from her. "What's that, Ahmed," she finally asked, "behind your back?"

Reluctantly, Mr. Jalal showed her. It was one of the mangoes she had put in the refrigerator last night. It looked nicely chilled, the moisture glistening against its golden skin. Why had Ahmed been concealing it?

"Should I cut it open for you?"

"It's not for me," Mr. Jalal said, sheepishly. "I was taking it downstairs. As an offering for Vishnu."

"An offering? What do you mean, offering?"

"One has to offer gods things to eat. That's what they do in the temples."

The light suddenly left the room. Mrs. Jalal watched as the gloom began to scale the walls. Ahmed had not recovered. He was still ailing from the delusion he had experienced last night. She had known, since that omen at the shrine, that she should not have let him out of her sight. Couldn't she have kept awake on the floor for just one night to watch over him?

"I don't think Vishnu is well enough to eat a mango," she said, keeping her voice steady. "They're very heating—it might upset his stomach."

"I would've taken a banana, but I couldn't find any. There were so many lying on the dining table yesterday—I'm surprised you ate them all."

Mrs. Jalal's throat constricted. Somehow, she had forced down the last banana last night, even though it had been well past ripe. She tried to stop the tears flooding her eyes, but couldn't.

"Don't cry, Arifa. Why are you crying? Is it the mango? Here, you can put it back—I'll find something else."

Mrs. Jalal looked at the mango her husband was offering, his face innocent of guile. As if it were an enchanted fruit that would arrest her tears, as if a bite of its magic flesh would carry her away from her problems. What had gone wrong, she wondered, who had made this happen to him? She felt so powerless—what could she do to make him right again? "I don't care about the mango," she said, averting her face.

"Then come with me," Mr. Jalal said, grabbing her hand. "Come, let's go make this offering together. Ask his blessing, both of us."

"Ask whom for blessing? Not *Vishnu*. Are you crazy?" Mrs. Jalal pulled her hand away. Instantly, she missed the reassurance, however slight, that Ahmed's touch had transmitted.

"It'll be much more effective if we both go. I can't do this alone, Arifa. Come, be my partner."

"What are you saying, Ahmed? Stop—just stop all this, please."

"Listen to me, Arifa. I've changed. *You've* made me change. All the arguments we had about religion. I'm now like you. I've let myself be touched. By something—by a sign, by faith." Mr. Jalal took his wife's hand again, and squeezed it, as if his newly acquired faith would flow through in proof.

"You don't know how much I worked, to open my mind, to free it. All the fasting and the sleeping on the ground. You saw last night how hard the floor of our bedroom is. Try it for a month, *then* you'll see."

So this was the explanation. She had known, of course, that he had been lying, but that didn't stop the blood from burning in her cheeks. All those nights she had spent alone in her bed, all those times she had called out to Ahmed, pleaded with him to tell her what was going on. And this? *This* was what it was about?

"Last night it finally happened. I saw a hundred suns fill the sky. Flowers so unusual, I can't describe them, jewels so fantastic, you wouldn't believe existed. Then *he* appeared. Vishnu. *Our* Vishnu. Yes, I couldn't believe it either. But fifty—no, *five hundred* feet tall. With fire and smoke, and more heads than I could count. It was terrifying. Yet beautiful, too."

Mrs. Jalal opened her mouth, but her husband started speaking faster, to prevent her from saying anything. "He told me I was to be his messenger. That he would destroy us all, if we didn't recognize him. I know what you're thinking,—why would he ever choose me? But it's hardly surprising, is it? After all the effort I've been putting in. Who are we to argue anyway, Arifa? If Vishnu wants me to be his prophet, that's what I must be."

Mrs. Jalal felt a chill in her shoulders. What was Ahmed saying? This talk of Vishnu being a god, this talk of Ahmed being a prophet. It was one thing to ramble on about these things in the incoherent state he was in this morning. But looking into his eyes now, she saw an alertness that frightened her. Did he not understand this was blasphemy?

"I need your support, Arifa. Just give it a chance. Even if you don't accept everything I witnessed. Even if that is too much to hope for."

"Stop what you are saying, Ahmed. Stop, and listen to me. What you saw was a dream. A nightmare. More vivid than most, but nothing more. Understand? Vishnu is *not* a god. You are *not* his messenger. You are *not* to call yourself prophet. There *are* no more prophets. It's written in the Koran."

"It wasn't a dream. No matter what you or anyone says, it wasn't a dream." Stubbornness settled at the corners of Mr. Jalal's mouth. "No one can tell me I didn't see what I saw. As for the Koran, doesn't it also say a wife is supposed to obey her husband?"

"Just listen to yourself. You, the pillar of rationality. This is the best you can come up with? *This* is what you preach? That we all sit down and pay homage to your dream?"

"A vision, it was a vision, didn't I just tell you? I know it must be hard for you to accept, but what's the point if you don't even try?"

"You're right, it *is* hard for me to accept. That my husband's lost his mind. That he's lost all sense, all logic. That he's calling some drunkard a god. Have some sense, Ahmed, have some shame."

"I thought you'd be happy. That I've finally found something in common with you. Faith, religion, call it what you may. Don't you see? It's a sign that I've received. Or all of a sudden do you not care?"

"You want me to rejoice? That you're declaring yourself prophet? That you're hailing some mortal as god? All these years of begging you to come to the masjid with me, and this is what you offer?

Blasphemy? You've found nothing, Ahmed—you've only lost. You've lost my respect. You've lost your religion. You've turned your back on everything it stands for."

"But I haven't given up anything. We all discover our own god. I've just begun to define mine. Think of the people I can lead to Vishnu. Think of all the people who might find their god in him."

"There is no God but God," Mrs. Jalal screamed. "Don't you understand? Say no more, Ahmed, for I cannot hear you speak."

LISTEN TO WHAT *the man says, I am Vishnu. Listen to what he says, yes, I have come to save or destroy you. See me descend to earth in my different avatars. Matsya and Kurma and Varaha and more.*

She is sitting by the shrine in the hut. It is raining outside. Flashes of lightning play with the features of her face. She waves incense over the idol as he watches from his mat and waits. "When will I be in heaven, O Krishna, to hear the sweetness of your magic flute," she sings.

She is next to him now, shaking her hair loose over her shoulders. He can smell the coconut oil as her fingers run through the strands. She reaches back to tie it up again, and he sees the sweat darkening the armpits of her blouse. It is her essence that he knows so well, the sweat mixed with the coconut oil.

"Little Vishnu," his mother says. "What avatar has my Vishnu come down as today?"

The rain outside is a quickening drumbeat. Gusts of wind blow through the hut and the flame in the oil lamp flickers.

He giggles and hides his face in the mat. He pretends to answer, mumbling something he knows she cannot hear.

"Let's see. What is he? Hmmm—burying his head like that—all curled up—he looks like a tortoise, perhaps, hiding in his shell."

He shakes his head. He is not a tortoise tonight.

"Not a tortoise. But yet so bunched up. Could he be a dwarf, then—little Vamana, waiting to confront Bali?"

He shakes his head again. He moves his arms over the mat, as if he is is swimming. Tonight, he is in the mood for an aquatic incarnation.

"Aha, the rain. Of course. It's Matsya the fish. Is there going to be a flood, then?"

He nods. "So you must put me in the sea where I belong."

"And if I don't?"

"Then I will grow and grow and grow before your eyes, and become so big you won't know what to do with me." He puffs up his cheeks as he says this, and stretches himself out from his balled-up position.

"No, no, Matsyaji, I will do as you say and carry you to the sea. Will Juhu Beach do, or will it have to be Chowpatty?"

"The Gateway of India. And hurry, I'm already twice your size, and soon you won't be able to carry me anymore."

His mother scoops him up into her lap. "Oh, my—you are a big fish. How happy you might make some fisherman if he caught such a big fish in his net."

"How dare you joke with me. The net has not yet been sewn that can catch Matsya. Now put me in the sea and do as I say, unless you want to be washed away with the rest. For it is Vishnu you are talking to, Vishnu who has descended personally from the heavens, to save you from the flood."

"Forgive me, Vishnuji, for I did not know. Tell me what I should do."

"First you must build an ark. Then go to the forest and gather seeds from every plant and tree you see. Tie the ark to my horn when the flood comes and I will tow you to safety."

"Which horn, O great Matsya? All I see is this." His mother tweaks his nose, and he giggles.

"When the flood comes, my horn will grow," he says. He is getting sleepy.

"When the flood comes," he hears his mother whisper, as she pulls the blanket over his falling body.

Outside, the rain spills over from the gutters and forms a stream. Streams that course through unlit passageways and coalesce cunningly in the night. Stealthily, the water rises, burrowing under tin walls, seeping through cardboard sides, silently lifting objects off the ground. It creeps up and encircles his mat, then gently laps against his body.

"Vishnu," his mother calls, but he has found his fins. Through the open door he swims, into the river waiting outside. Bubbles rise from upturned faces, still asleep on the riverbed. Huts pass by underneath, then houses, then buildings, as he rises with the water. The glow of streetlights floats up silently from submerged lampposts.

"Vishnu," he hears his mother call again. She is standing on the top of the Gateway of India, surrounded by the four carved turrets. Beneath her feet, the stone plunges in giant arches to the plaza far down below. Children run on the plaza, couples linger in front of the monument. They do not see the wall of water that rises behind in the bay.

He feels his horn grow. He feels the skin on his forehead erupt, and the appendage push out. He can see it curve through the water, thickening and hardening as it emerges.

The water begins its descent. The sea rushes in to embrace the land. Children fly into the air, then vanish in the foam. Buildings rock and sway, then acquiesce majestically. "Vishnu," his mother cries as the water surges over her feet.

He submerges his head. Ahead are the arches of the Gateway, fish dart in and out of them. Already, his body is too big to pass through the side arches. He swims halfway through the main arch, centering his body under it. Then he begins to rise, to rise and to push upwards.

His horn breaks the surface first, then his head. The Gateway comes off its foundation, and rises on his back. He turns his head around and looks at his mother, still standing on the top. She throws a rope around his horn, and nods at him.

With the chariot on his back, he turns to the sea. Through the waves he rides, towards the sun, leaving behind the ruined city.

CHAPTER NINE

MR. JALAL CRANED his head around the stairway to make sure there was no one on the landing. Vishnu lay just as he had been left this morning, the suns on his sheet beaming in the light filtering in from outside. Seeing his inert body, Mr. Jalal had the strange feeling of being a murderer stealing back to the scene of a crime. He shook his head to expel this thought—what if Vishnu was able to read it in his mind?

How frail Vishnu looked. It was hard to imagine that this body before him could have metamorphosed into something so terrifying. Had it all been a mistake? Was it simply a dream, after all? But wait, wasn't that a grin Vishnu's face was twisted into? Could he be smirking at the folly of mortals, whose flaw it was to always go on appearance, whose fate it was to never comprehend what lay underneath?

"Give me strength," Mr. Jalal whispered, looking around furtively, "to be your messenger." It had been so many years—decades, perhaps—since he had uttered any kind of prayer that he felt self-conscious saying these words, even though no one was there. He laid the mango next to Vishnu's head and wondered if there were other steps he should perform. Scattering flowers, lighting incense—what ceremonies were needed to make the offering complete?

Mr. Jalal tried to remember how they had done it at the temple at Mahalakshmi. That one time he had visited a Hindu temple—it had been while he was reading all those books on Akbar. Akbar, who might be the only Muslim ruler to set foot in a temple—who, in fact, frequented all sorts of places of worship to mingle with his subjects, always in disguise.

As he had followed the throng of people up the steps to Mahalakshmi temple, Mr. Jalal had felt like a masquerader himself. His heart had pounded as he walked barefoot across the stone to the shrine. This is the way Akbar would do it, he told himself, and boldly sounded one of the brass bells suspended from the carved ceiling. Then he waited, fidgeting, in the line to walk past the idols. He seemed to be dressed like, to look like, the other people. But he worried nevertheless—could they tell he was a Muslim, were they able to sense his ignorance, his unease?

The woman in front of him was carrying an elaborate offering on a polished metal thali. Several bananas, a coconut, strings of marigold, and to crown it, a large lotus flower. Mr. Jalal stared at the vermilion splashed over the whole arrangement and mounded generously around the edge. What was the significance of this bright red powder? he wondered. Was it the same powder with which married Hindu women lined the parting in their hair, so that their skulls looked freshly cracked open in neat red lines? Could the red be related to blood, like the blood from animal sacrifices, like the blood of Christ? Even though they didn't sacrifice animals anymore—perhaps this was a remnant from a more ancient ritual?

He was pondering which of his books at home might contain the answer when he saw the woman hand over her thali. He realized they were inside the shrine already, and he was standing empty-handed in front of the idols. Panic gripped him as the priest turned and extended a hand towards him. From behind the priest, the three incarnations of Lakshmi regarded him dubiously with their six questioning eyes. He was beginning to stutter some excuse, some apology, when the priest thrust a disc into his palm, the line moved along, and he found himself outside, blinking and free in the sunlight. He opened his palm and looked at the peda nestling there, round and golden like some forbidden fruit. The other worshipers were reverentially putting their pedas into their mouths, but Mr. Jalal hesitated. Although he regarded all religions to be equally irrelevant, he had never actually participated in a rite from another faith. What would Arifa say if she saw him now, with this Lakshmi-blessed food poised in his fingers, ready to be brought to his lips? But he could already smell the flowery scent of the peda in his nostrils, then feel it crumbling between his teeth, then taste its intense milky sweetness against his tongue. A sweetness, an incriminating sugariness, that spread purposefully down his throat, and insinuated itself through his entire body.

Mr. Jalal made his way to the rocks behind the temple, climbing down to the water's edge. The tide was coming in, and he had to retrace his steps to a higher rock, to avoid being sprayed. He looked across to the middle of the bay, where the masjid of Haji Ali rose from the water. As a child, he had often accompanied his mother across the stone path that made the masjid accessible during low tide. Now he watched the waves break over the stones and submerge the bases of the lampposts that lined the way. It would be some hours before the path was traversable again. He imagined Akbar, sitting where he was sitting, surveying the religious landscape of his kingdom. The temple on the hill behind him and the mosque surrounded by water in front.

Hadn't Akbar experienced a vision of some sort as well? Mr. Jalal found himself back in the shadows of Vishnu's landing, trying to recall the accounts he had read. Akbar had been riding in the forest, hunting for tigers, when it had happened. His soldiers had come upon him laughing and dancing among the trees and shearing off locks of his hair. Could that have been the catalyst for the new religion he had created? His Din Ilahi, his grand, doomed experiment, to reconcile opposing philosophies and unite his Hindu subjects with their Muslim brethren?

The hairs on Mr. Jalal's arms suddenly stood up. Could it be possible that he, Ahmed Jalal, was poised on the brink of something equally grand? What if he was going to be the next great unifier, the one whose destiny it was to change the land? Was that the sign he had just received, the message he had just been given, the one that would bring people together across the country? After all, wasn't he born a Muslim, just like Akbar—could that be why he had been chosen by Vishnu?

Mr. Jalal peered at Vishnu. Yes, that was a smile of acknowledgment on his face, a smile of encouragement, a smile that indicated great things were in store. Vishnu was giving him the blessing he had come for, telling him to go forth and heal the world. Perhaps he should descend this very minute, go downstairs and convert the cigarettewalla, the paanwalla. Knock on every door he could find, stop at the shops in the adjacent building, go to the church across the street, to Mahalakshmi, to Haji Ali.

But first he would try once more with Arifa. She was his wife, Salim was his son. Before he saved anyone else, it was his duty to save them.

Mr. Jalal looked at the mango next to Vishnu's head. The offering had pleased Vishnu. There was no need for flowers or incense.

MANGOES. SO FULL, so sweet, so scented, the oranges and yellows of sunlight. So this is the food gods get offered, Vishnu thinks. Ah, mangoes.

From the orchard mist she emerges. The mango goddess. Her figure lush with mango leaves as she makes her way across the shadows of trees. She stands in front of Vishnu and lets her cloak of leaves drop. Her body is bountiful with fruit underneath. Mangoes, ripe and perfumed, grow from her bosom, they swing from her arms, hang heavily from her thighs.

Vishnu brings his face to her neck and breathes her fragrance in. He touches a mango attached to her breast, and traces the curve of its smooth skin. His fingers linger at the node at the base, swollen, and yielding to his touch. He closes his hand over the mango, she quivers as he plucks it off her skin. Sap oozes out of the rupture, he puts his lips on her breast to stem the flow. She presses her arms around his head and lets him taste her essence.

She directs him to another mango, growing between her thighs. He touches it and pulls on it, anticipation plays on her lips. He detaches it with a snap, and sees pain twinge across her face. Sap flows out again, more abundant, more fertile this time, filling his mouth with her feminine nectar.

One by one, he plucks all the mangoes from her body. When he is done, she stands before him naked, clothed only in the scars of her harvest. He spreads her cloak of mango leaves on the ground and she lays herself down upon it. He kneels between her legs, and kisses a scar still wet with sap.

She guides his body into hers. Tears moisten her eyes. As he fills her with seed, she arches back her neck to face the dying sun.

Afterwards, he drapes the cloak around her. He watches her tread to her orchard through the twilight. Underneath the leaves, he knows, her scars are already beginning to sprout. With buds of fruits barely visible, fruits that will grow and ripen in the next day's sun.

He looks at the mangoes she has left behind, scattered on the ground. They will sustain all his creatures, they will sustain the universe until she returns.

THIS GODLY WAY with mangoes. Vishnu is not impressed. What about the act of eating to which mortals are accustomed? The essence of mangoes, their taste, their feel. The satisfaction of separating pulp from peel by scraping slices between the teeth. He wonders if gods are allowed only heavenly bliss, if earthly pleasure is beyond their reach.

He sees himself lying naked with Padmini under the sheets. It is the summer his brother has sent him a mango basket. He has brought it to Padmini, she has invited him in.

Padmini turns over on her stomach and drags the basket to the bed. "So many mangoes," she says, gazing at the basket. She looks up. "Are you sure they're all for me?"

"Every one of them," he says, exhilarated by the greed he glimpses in her eyes. He feels the pang of a familiar longing. How many baskets would he need to make her forever his own?

She rolls a mango between her palms to soften the insides. "Lajjo says the foreign mems eat mangoes with spoons, can you imagine?" She laughs. "Maybe that's what I should do—be your English memsahib." She bats her eyelids and puckers her mouth into an exaggerated kiss.

"Maybe you should," he says. He wills the longing to disappear. He has given up the idea of possessing her, he reminds himself, he has resolved to be satisfied with what she gives.

"Why, is my skin not fair enough for you?" she pouts, lying back on her pillow and bringing the mango to her lips. She peels the skin off the top with her teeth. "I used to have so many mangoes, growing up in Ratnagiri." Juice dribbles out as she sucks at the mango, it trickles down her chin and pools beneath her throat.

Vishnu wants to follow the trail of juice, blot it drop by drop off her skin with his tongue. This is what he has taught himself to be content with—the pleasure of her body, when she allows it, and nothing more. He believes then that his visits will continue forever, a string of lightbulbs glittering through the reaches of his future.

Padmini squeezes the mango to push out more pulp. But she presses too hard, and the whole seed slips out—it lands on her chin and slides down to her chest. She shrieks and tries to grab the seed, but it is covered with pulp and slips out of her grasp. She laughs as she chases the seed over her body, catching it finally at the base of her abdomen.

"Give me that," Vishnu says, and rubs it over her belly, as if it were a bar of soap. A swath of pulp glistens on her skin.

"Everywhere," she instructs, so he scrubs her waist, and lathers her between her legs.

"My mango queen," he says, when the mango is spent. Her skin is wet, pieces of yellow pulp stick to her breasts, her stomach, the hair between her thighs.

He tastes her neck first. It is sweet with mango, salty with sweat. He moves downwards, capturing the dabs of pulp with his mouth, lingering at each nipple, stopping to sip the liquid collected in her navel. She gets saltier as he descends, and more aromatic, as if the mango is mixed with something pungent in the earth from which it has sprung. As he enters her, his tongue encounters a sweetness not encountered before in these folds. Lured by the sweetness, he dives in deeper, and then deeper still. Probing, caressing, tasting, but never retrieving, the tiny nugget of mango he knows is nestling there.

So many earthly ways to enjoy mangoes. Vishnu is loath to give them up.

AT FIRST, WHEN Short Ganga saw the mango, she was tempted to pick it up. It looked so ripe and delicious, and was one of those refined varieties, not the half-wild types that she occasionally was able to afford.

But then she wondered who had left it there, right next to Vishnu,

and why. She knew of all sorts of spells and nazars that people plant-
ed in pieces of fruit, nazars that could spring out and seize you if you
even touched the piece. Lemons were particularly dangerous, and
Short Ganga always made a detour when she saw one in her path,
but mangoes might be even more hazardous, and it was probably not
a good idea to gaze at this one for too long.

Her skin began to crawl as she stood on the landing. First the
ghost that had possessed Mr. Jalal, and now this. There was something unnatural lurking on this landing—perhaps it was the spirit
that was waiting to take Vishnu away. Short Ganga shivered under
her sari, then grabbed the tiffin box and ran up the steps.

The final flights were always the hardest. Short Ganga wiped her
brow as she clambered past the second-floor landing. She tried not
to think about Vishnu or the mango. Instead, she concentrated on
Mr. Taneja's tiffin box, hanging by her side, growing heavier with each
step she rose, absorbing weight from the air like a sponge drawn
through liquid. It was to be expected, of course—it was normal—a law
of nature, a physical principle, that she had figured out all by herself.

Things grew heavier the higher they were lifted.

It was a discovery she was proud of, a finding that had obsessed
her for the past several weeks. It had struck her one day as she was
huffing her way up the Makhijanis' building—the one with the lift
that servants were not allowed to use. On the ground floor, the tiffin
box felt so light she wondered if the compartments had all been
filled, if the food would be enough for both Mr. and Mrs. Makhijani.
By the third floor, however, the box was heavy enough that she started cursing the Makhijanis' appetites, cursing the gluttony of all the
rich, whose swollen tiffin boxes left daily red marks where the han-
dles cut into her fingers. It was as she was shifting the box from one
hand to the other that the realization struck her. *The box had put on
weight.* The lid, the containers, the handle, the food—everything had
become heavier.

And was becoming heavier still.

A shiver ran through Short Ganga's body as she felt the first thrill of scientific discovery. How could she have not noticed it before? All those years of carrying things, all those times she had panted and strained and barely made it to the top floor. She had always blamed herself, thought it was she who was tiring out. But how much more obvious was this new explanation, how much more intuitive and logical. It was the height that was to blame, not she, the height that added kilo after kilo to her load, as she trudged up the floors.

An intense curiosity awakened in Short Ganga. She found herself driven to perform experiments. Each day, she assessed the weight of her tiffin boxes, both on the ground and the top floor of every building she climbed. She did the same with her bottles of milk. One day, she even borrowed a ten-kilo measuring weight from the bania merchant and struggled with it up several flights of stairs, all for the sake of her science.

Every result confirmed her conjecture. Every object she experimented with became heavier—the higher she went, the more weight things gained. But her experiments left her dissatisfied, thirsting for more. She wanted more precision, she wanted to quantify the weight gain. She tried to borrow the weighing scales from the bania, but he refused.

It was then that she was confronted by an exception to her theory: her treasured pieces of Styrofoam. She retrieved them from between the saris in her iron trunk one day and carried them to the second floor of the Makhijani building. They did not feel any heavier. She went up to the third floor, then the fourth and the fifth, but the pieces did not feel different. No matter to what height she took them, they refused to put on weight.

For a while, Short Ganga lapsed into depression at this setback. But then she put things in perspective. On the one hand was the mountain of evidence she had assembled, on the other a solitary aberration. Why not just ignore the Styrofoam? It was stolen, anyway—perhaps that was what jinxed it.

She decided it was time to reveal her results. She would leave out the part about the Styrofoam. But whom should she talk to? The other gangas could hardly be expected to appreciate such sophisticated concepts. Besides, what if one of them decided to steal her discovery, to claim all credit for it? She had to be very careful. There might even be some money due to her for having made her scientific advance. Perhaps there was a government bureau to which she should be submitting a claim. It would not do to trust one of the gangas. No, it had to be someone else, someone knowledgeable and trustworthy, who would not take advantage. Someone like—Mr. Taneja, perhaps.

It had not taken long to decide on him. He was the most likable customer she had. One customer like him made up for a building full of Asranis and Pathaks. Short Ganga looked at the steps in front of her, cut so high she could barely mount them. Three floors of these she climbed every day, just to make sure Mr. Taneja got his lunch. She pulled herself up the last few steps and paused outside his door, waiting to catch her breath.

Would this be a good day to approach Mr. Taneja? She could tell him first about Vishnu being sick, then casually break her theory to him. Even offer to let him carry the tiffin box to the terrace so that he could have a demonstration. What would his reaction be?

Short Ganga's hand hovered near his doorbell. Her instructions were simply to leave the tiffin box on the landing, but she sometimes rang the bell, just to catch a word with him, and make sure not too many days went by without anyone seeing him. Mr. Taneja was never upset when he was summoned this way to the door. Rather, it was she who felt guilty at the intrusion. His wife's death had occurred years before she had come to the building. But people still behaved as if Mr. Taneja's tragedy was fresh, as if his name had to be spoken in a whisper, and he still needed to be handled like someone fragile. Short Ganga often wondered about this—what was it about Mr. Taneja that prompted such a reaction? Perhaps it was the feeling one got even as one looked into his eyes and conversed with him that he was not wholly present, that a part of him was afloat somewhere else, lost in a private sea of contemplation. She herself could not stop treating him with the care reserved for the very elderly, or the very sick.

She was still debating about the doorbell when the song started. The music welled up in waves, and riding the crests came the first of the lyrics. Short Ganga imagined Mr. Taneja standing over the gramophone, alone in his room. She knew this song, knew for whom it was played. Today, she decided, would not be the day after all.

Short Ganga left the tiffin box next to the door and walked back silently to the steps.

VINOD TANEJA LISTENED to the words.

> The night will come and cool our bodies, the rain will come and
> sprinkle our skin;
> You and I will become just one, on this, the first night of our
> union.

For years after Sheetal had gone, he had played the song at the same time, day after day. He still remembered to play the record at least once a week. Sometimes he stood next to the gramophone, but often he went to the balcony and let the music waft out to him as he looked at the cars and the buses three floors below.

> The flowers will open and sing to us, cats will purr and meow in
> our ears;
> You and I will be forever just one, from this, the first night of our
> union.

Little had he known, when he had first listened to the banal lyrics, that over the years, every note on the record, every word, every sound, would become an indelible part of him. It had been Sheetal's favorite song from the last movie they had seen together, and he had wandered into a music store a few weeks after her death to buy it. He watched it now, the red label in the center a little faded with age, but the dog-and-gramophone logo still clearly visible, the surface of the disc almost as unscratched as the day he had first played it twenty years ago. Of course, the grooves had dulled over the years, but the sound was still so surprisingly clear.

> The sun will dip into the ocean from the sky, the owl will hoot from
> its branch on the tree,
> Together on the sands of time we will run, on this, the first day of
> our union.

The record had been a journal that had charted his recovery after Sheetal. Day after day, year after year, he had taken his emotional pulse as he had listened to it. In the beginning, there had been no pulse. He had performed each task dutifully: cranking the handle, placing the record on the turntable, setting the needle down, receiving the notes transmitted. But these had not added up to the experience of listening to the song. It had been some weeks before he had actually sensed the music, and even more time before he had heard the lyrics. Then, one day, it had happened—suddenly, he could see Dilip Kumar and Meena Kumari on the CinemaScope screen, feel Sheetal's hand resting under his own in the cool darkness of the movie theater. That's when he had begun to cry, his tears so big and splashy that he had shut the gramophone lid, afraid of getting them over the record. For months, he had been able to listen to only part of the song before breaking down.

A year later, it was only anguish he felt when he heard the song. A deep, penetrating, physical anguish, the kind that comes when a

dentist drills too deep into a tooth. Over time, this anguish had gradually dulled, leaving behind only the memory of pain; a quiet, almost
sweet numbness which lingered in the hollow where the ache had
been rooted. Now, even that numbness was fading.

> *Look at the moon, see how he smiles from the sky; see the stars,*
> *how they wink from up high;*
> *We'll wave at them from here on the ground, on this, the first night*
> *of our union.*

This was the part, the part near the end, that always took him
back. Back across the fading nights and days, filled with dimly remembered happiness and pain; back through all the doorways traversed,
both alone and hand in hand with Sheetal; back through the ravaged
map of his existence, with the stars that drew it burning triumphantly above. Vinod looks at the record and waits to see her, he looks at
the rotating blackness of the disc, and waits for her image to emerge.

ON THE DAY Vinod passed his Bachelor of Commerce exam, his
father announced they had found a suitable match for him. Would
he have any objection to marrying Sheetal, the niece of his uncle's
wife, who had been at Paplu's birthday party last week?

Vinod remembered seeing her there. He hadn't paid her any special attention, nor had he tried to talk to her, although he was sure he
had said hello once at a previous family function. She was not the
most beautiful woman he had laid eyes on, but on the other hand, he
couldn't remember any obvious physical defects either. Thinking
about it overnight, he could come up with no particular reason to
either reject or endorse the match. The wedding was negotiated that
very week.

A few days later, he found himself at the house of his future in-laws. Sheetal's mother brought out the sets of jewelry that were to be given with the bride and laid them out for his family's inspection. His mother put on her reading glasses, and lifting the pieces from their red velvet boxes, started examining them one by one. Vinod watched the proceedings for a while, and then, with nothing to do, picked up a necklace himself, and held it up against his palm.

He was trying to follow a point of light as it skittered from stone to stone when his eyes met Sheetal's. He was startled by the disdain in them, a disdain so keen he had to look away. He put the necklace down immediately, then tried to catch Sheetal's eye again. But she did not look up, keeping her face properly lowered through the rest of the meeting.

He saw her next a few weeks after that, at their engagement. He wanted to talk to Sheetal then, but their eyes did not meet once during the entire ceremony. Even when he offered her the laddoo, Sheetal did not raise her head, but waited for him to bring it to her mouth, so she could take a delicate bite.

The period between the engagement and wedding passed by in a haze. Vinod spent the days at his new job in the bank, and his evenings as before, gathering with friends at the café near Churchgate. There were many jokes about his impending union, but somehow he managed not to think about how his life was going to change. The wedding always seemed to be at least a few days away, and Vinod occupied his hours without letting himself worry about it.

It was only when he saw his garments being tied to Sheetal's that the enormity and irreversibility of the situation hit him. He was getting married, and he did not know why, or to whom. He looked up at the guests and relatives all around and heard them whispering and saw them smiling at him. He suddenly felt like protesting—there had been a mistake, it hadn't sunk in, he hadn't had the time to think about it, it had all been too hastily arranged. He saw the fire at the center of the gathering, the priest chanting and spooning ghee into the flames. The vapors were so strong he could taste them. He felt a gentle tug on his clothing, and realized that the seven circles had started. The fire always to his left, a hush spreading over the crowd, the priest reaching out to throw camphor into the flames, Sheetal behind him, tied to his body by her sari, destined to follow him forever. The fire seemed to grow more intense with each round, the flames jumped into the night air, and he wondered if they might leap out and set the knot that tied him to Sheetal aflame. Buds of white swayed and dissolved before his eyes as the curtain of flowers hanging in strings from his turban swung in front of his face. He wished the curtain was more impermeable, so that he could shut out the sights in front of him, so that he would not feel the heat of the fire he imagined on his face, or hear the priest's stream of Sanskrit, growing steadily unbearable in his ears. On and on the circles went—three, four, five, six—and he wondered if he could quit before completing the seventh one, run through the guests and vault over the walls of the mandap to freedom. But then his feet had crossed the threshold for the seventh time, and then Sheetal's feet, the edges stained orange with henna, were crossing it too.

And then he was entering their wedding-night room and closing the door; the sounds of giggling were left outside, and his bride was sitting on the petal-strewn bed. He had seen this scene so many times before—Raj Kapoor and Nargis, Guru Dutt and Waheeda Rehman, Dilip Kumar and Madhubala, the heroine always in embroidered silk, the groom in impeccable white, and when the hero pulled back the heroine's ghunghat, she kept her eyes closed. He reached out to lift the cloth, and his hand wavered. What if Sheetal's eyes were staring at his, defiant, with the look of that first day? But his wife must have seen the same films he had, because when he looked under the cloth, her eyes were closed, the dots painted in ceremonial white forming a serene arch over her eyebrows. For a second, he wondered if he should break into song as they did in the movies. Instead, he lifted her head slowly, and asked her to open her eyes.

In that first clear look into the eyes of the person with whom he was supposed to spend the rest of his life, he was relieved to find not defiance but curiosity, not disdain but unfamiliarity, not love but not dislike, either.

We will produce a new and soulful tune; the flute will play, the guitar will strum;
Now we are two, but soon we'll be three, from this, the first night of our union.

They sat there next to each other, the layers of clothing and ornaments they were wearing too intimidating to allow conversation, let alone intimacy. More daunting was the fact that they had met only twice since the engagement, that too under the supervision of a caucus of chaperons. The silence pressed around them, as oppressive as the heat and the humidity in the air.

Vinod cleared his throat, preparing to say something. But no topic of conversation suggested itself. He gazed at the new ring banding his finger. How were they going to fill all the minutes, all the hours, between now and the end of their time together?

Whispers came from the other side of the door, then the sound of muffled giggles. Suddenly, a radio was turned on, at full volume. The soaring chorus of the national anthem filled the room, and Sheetal looked up, confused. For a moment, he thought she was going to stand to attention beside the bed. There was laughter from the corridor outside, then the sound of running feet, and his mother's scolding voice. The radio was switched off just in the middle of the final "Jaya he."

Vinod heard his mother tiptoe away from the door.

"Do you know all the words?" he asked Sheetal.

"Of course," she replied. "Everyone learns it in school. Didn't you?"

"I did. But I could never memorize the whole thing."

Sheetal did not respond.

"They must have waited," he said. "Waited till eleven-thirty, for the station to shut down and the anthem to come on. I should have run to the door and grabbed their radio from them. We could have had a little music."

"But the station has shut down, you said."

"The foreign stations run all night. We could have heard jazz. Do you ever listen to jazz?"

"No."

"Well, I don't much, either. Except late at night. Otherwise, I listen to Radio Ceylon. They have the songs from all the new films. Months before they get them on Vividh Bharati. Do you like seeing films?"

Sheetal nodded.

"Did you see *Mughal-e-Azam*?"

"Yes, and I *hated* it. I *hate* Madhubala."

"How can you possibly hate Madhubala?"

"She has the face of an elephant."

"She's not even fat."

"Not her body. Just her face. Her nose, especially."

"You don't know what you're saying. She has a beautiful nose."

"An elephant. I'm not going to any Madhubala films with you."

They argued about Raj Kapoor and Dilip Kumar, Meena Kumari and Vyjayanthimala. They talked about their favorite films. Sheetal shyly revealed that she often liked to memorize not only songs but also pieces of dialogue that moved her. As an illustration, she recited her favorite lines from *Love in Rome*.

"Remember that scene in the restaurant, when they eat all that Italian food?" Vinod said, laughing. "What does it turn out to be—octopus or something?"

Sheetal's face darkened. "Don't expect me to cook any non-veg for you," she suddenly declared.

Vinod was taken aback.

"But your family isn't vegetarian," he protested. "You yourself were eating tandoori chicken tonight at the reception."

"I like to eat it, but I'm not going to cook it. It's a hundred times more sinful to cook it than eat it."

"But nobody said anything before the wedding. How will we eat meat when we start living by ourselves if you won't cook it?"

"What if I teach you to cook it?"

"But I'm the husband. I'm not supposed to cook. And also, if I did, then all the sins would come on my head."

Sheetal's brow furrowed. "And since you're my husband, they'd be on my head too." She fell silent. "I guess we won't be able to have meat after all," she said.

They looked at each other gloomily. Married life had barely begun, and already abstinence was the forecast for the future.

The talk about cooking had made Vinod hungry, so he suggested sneaking out to locate the wedding sweets. Sheetal demurred at first, but then gave in—she, too, was hungry. They took off all the ornaments they could, Sheetal being especially careful to remove her noisy ankle bracelets. Vinod got out of the stiff wedding jacket that had been choking him all evening, and Sheetal wrapped her long ceremonial sari around her shoulders and stuffed the end into her waistband. Then, in bare feet, they crept to the door.

Vinod opened it a crack. A multitude of snores streamed in. He stuck his head out. Starting at the door and stretching out all along the floor were dozens of recumbent wedding guests. It looked as if a cyclone had blasted through the corridor.

They made their way to the kitchen through the maze of bodies. Sheetal accidentally stepped on one of her cousins, and they both held their breaths, but the girl muttered something and went back to sleep.

In the kitchen, they were unable to locate the sweets, but came across a large platter of the tandoori chicken in the refrigerator. They looked at each other. "Let's find some pickle and onions to go with it," Sheetal whispered.

The kitchen floor had been cleared to accommodate more of the sleeping guests, and Vinod and Sheetal crept around them to the dining table, which had been pushed to the far side. The chairs had been stacked up in another corner, so they sat cross-legged on the table itself, the platter of chicken between them.

"What do you like," Vinod asked, "breast or leg?"

"I like the little leg attached to the breast. It's my favorite part."

"But it's so little."

"I always get both of them. It's the only part I really like. Though I can eat the big leg if necessary."

Vinod tore off the wing portions from two of the breasts and handed them to her. "Here. You can have the little legs every time we have chicken."

"Thanks," Sheetal said, smiling shyly as she accepted the pieces from him. "Here's some onion—I couldn't find the mango pickle."

They sat in the dark and ate their chicken. The only light came from a streetlamp outside, through a small window on the opposite wall. It was quite hot, and Vinod could hear a mosquito whining around near his ear. He looked at Sheetal. His wife. She was gnawing at the cartilage in a wingjoint, red specks of tandoori spice stuck to her lips. In the dim light, Sheetal looked even younger than her nineteen years. He imagined her hair braided in pigtails, looped around and tied behind her ears, like a schoolgirl's. Who was this person? What did she want from life? Sheetal selected a red pickled onion from a bowl and bit off a chunk of it.

Clumsily, Vinod leaned over with his face next to hers and tried to kiss her. Sheetal drew back. "What are you doing? Are you crazy—with all these people here?"

"But they're asleep," Vinod protested.

"That doesn't matter. They're still here." Sheetal resumed munching on her onion.

Vinod looked at the sleeping people. There was Pramod uncle and his wife, lying next to each other. How long had they been together? He wondered when his uncle had first kissed Manisha aunty, and whether her mouth had been redolent of cumin and onion when he had done so. He looked again at Sheetal. She had finished her chicken. Her tongue was wiping her lips clean, leaving behind a thin glisten of saliva that outlined her mouth in the silvery light. He had never kissed a girl before. He was determined to do so tonight, in this kitchen, on this table.

Vinod eased the platter out of the way and moved closer to Sheetal. He could feel her stiffen, could almost hear her heart start beating faster. He slowly put his arm around her neck, then tensed his muscles, ready to resist in case she tried to escape. She sat there, rooted to the wood, looking straight ahead. Quickly, he pressed his mouth over hers. He sensed the back of her neck go slack. Her saliva felt wet and sticky and strangely exciting on his lips. He held them there for a moment, inhaling the spicy meatiness of her mouth. Then, not sure how to proceed, he released her mouth and drew his head back.

She looked away from his eyes. Her hand went up to wipe her lips, but she stopped and self-consciously brought it down. She sat on the table next to the platter and the onions, the bone of a chicken wing still in her hand.

They went back to their bedroom. Nervously, Sheetal unwound her sari, and quickly got into bed. She shivered, even though the room was unbearably warm, and pulled the sheet up to her blouse. Vinod took off his shirt but not his pants, and got in next to her.

They stared at the wedding decorations festooned over the bed. The sound of the mosquitoes diving among the streamers mingled with the snores that trickled in from under the door. A balloon rested listlessly against the ceiling, its thread dangling all the way to the floor. Down the street, a dog barked, and further away somewhere, they heard a car start up.

Vinod could feel Sheetal's body breathing next to him in the dark. He thought of her bosom beneath its blouse, the red cloth rising and falling with each breath. In the sixth standard, a friend had shown him his first photo of a naked woman. He tried to picture that image under Sheetal's blouse, tried to imagine the contour of each breast, the fleshiness of each nipple. He saw himself kissing her neck, bringing his mouth down and wetting the material of her blouse and, when the nipple was clearly outlined, taking it in his mouth through the cloth.

"Are you asleep?" he whispered to Sheetal.

"No," she replied. "I was thinking."

"About what?" Vinod's voice was hoarse.

"I was thinking," Sheetal said, turning around to face him, her expression troubled. "I was thinking perhaps it wouldn't be such a big sin to once in a while cook chicken?"

CHAPTER TEN

THE THRASHING ADMINISTERED to Shyamu by his mother that afternoon was earned fair and square by him in the half hour that preceded it. Even Mr. Asrani, when confronted with the evidence, would have had to agree that it was fully deserved, not that he was given a chance to arbitrate. Shyamu, of course, tried to deny everything, which was not the wise thing to do, since it enraged Mrs. Asrani even further. But then, Shyamu was never one given to wise choices, as evidenced by his behavior.

What happened was this. Shyamu had been playing aeroplane with Rajan, the Pathaks' younger son. The two children had brought several empty ghee and cooking-oil tins from the kitchen and arranged them to form the central corridor of seats in the inside of the plane. They were taking turns being the pilot and crash-landing the plane. First, Rajan crashed the plane, the impact sending the tins helter-skelter, and killing all the passengers. Then it was Shyamu's turn, and he killed not only all the people on board but several unfortunate bystanders on the ground as well. Then it was Rajan's turn, with Shyamu being a hijacker, and once again the loss of life was total, with several of the deaths being gruesomely enacted among flying cooking-fat tins.

Short Ganga had left behind the dupatta found that morning, draped prominently over the grinding stone outside the kitchen. Mrs. Pathak, not wanting to handle it herself in case it had been infected by Vishnu, had asked Short Ganga to place it there. Mrs. Pathak had a hunch that the key to the mystery of Mr. Jalal lay in the dupatta, and she was keeping close tabs on it to try and catch either Mrs. Asrani or Mrs. Jalal picking it up.

The game had by now shifted to dacoit pilots chasing terrorized villagers through mountain ravines. And killing them. The score was roughly a dozen villagers each, though Rajan had scored extra for decimating a herd of cows as well. It was Shyamu's turn, and he had an idea. They would drape the dupatta over some tins to represent a buxom village belle (the kind Reshma played in the movies) and then riddle her body with bullets.

Since there were no more empty tins left, they dragged two containers of rice and stacked them one on top of the other. These were covered with the dupatta to produce a passable belle. Shyamu got into his cockpit and started spraying everything with his imaginary machine gun, and Rajan toppled the belle over after she had been hit what seemed like a sufficient number of times.

This was not enough fun, so Shyamu decided to make it more realistic. The belle would be Kavita, since it was her dupatta anyway. And Rajan could be Salim, though he would have to kiss the belle first, for realism's sake. They would be running away from home, and Shyamu would be the police chasing them from the aeroplane, with orders to bring them back alive, or preferably, dead.

The game started, but Rajan didn't want to kiss Kavita, even the rice-container-and-dupatta version of her. Eventually, he was persuaded to, and just as he was locked in embrace, Shyamu's plane zoomed in, and he said, "Run, Salim, run, Kavita, or the police will catch you." Mrs. Pathak, who looked out that instant to see if the dupatta was still there, was horrified to see her son kissing it, and absorbing God knew what type of germs into his mouth. She came running out, just as Shyamu, still shouting, "Run, Salim, run, Kavita," deployed his newly acquired grenade launcher at his sister, and blew her up into bits by smashing two of the empty ghee tins into her. Perhaps he underestimated the force of the grenades, because Kavita the belle literally did fly to pieces, losing her head and showering rice all over Rajan, Shyamu, Mrs. Pathak, and the landing.

When Mrs. Asrani was awoken from her already troubled unscheduled morning nap, she found first of all that her best Basmati rice was lying scattered all over the floor outside the kitchen. She also found that Shyamu had, in an effort to explain his game to Mrs. Pathak, told her not only that the dupatta belonged to Kavita, but also that his sister was missing, and had probably run away with Salim.

"Did you get any news yet?" Mrs. Pathak asked, her voice oozing with sympathy that barely concealed the titillation.

"What news? There's no need for news. Don't believe everything Shyamu is saying. Kavita's just gone to visit a friend."

"Yes, it must be. Mr. Jalal says that Salim too has gone to visit a friend. I wonder what it all means." Mrs. Pathak slipped in her little lie to see what Mrs. Asrani's reaction would be. She was not disappointed.

"Mr. Jalal told you that? When did he say it?" Mrs. Asrani's jaw was set in a grim line.

"Well, Mr. Jalal was saying all sorts of things this morning. Something about a walnut, and that Vishnu was an incarnation of God come down to earth. Who knows what all he said—he was quite incoherent. And then wearing that dupatta—do you know he even tried to attack me?"

"Yes, yes, but what did he say about Salim?"

"Something about visiting a friend," Mrs. Pathak said vaguely. "He was saying two hundred things, though—you should have heard him.

It's as if he'd *really* seen something. We led him upstairs, and my husband asked him, Mr. Jalal, you're a Muslim, how strange that you are talking to us about our Hindu gods. And you know what he said—he said if people like us didn't realize when a god came down, they needed someone like him to open their eyes. Imagine—Mr. Jalal, a prophet."

"And you said he was *wearing* Kavita's dupatta?"

"He had it wrapped around his head."

"How strange, how very strange."

"If there's anything I can do, I know what a difficult time this must be for you, if there's *anything* . . ."

But Mrs. Asrani was already turning back towards her flat, trying to decide which she would do first, gather up the rice or give Shyamu his beating.

Years later, when you are still young, when this union has produced
  a little one,
Together we'll look back and sing, about this, the first night of our
  union.

The actual night only came a week later. By then, Vinod had reconciled himself to the fact that his wife clacked her teeth in her sleep. When he mentioned this to her, she complained that he snored every night, and that that was much worse than her clacking, which was due to a misalignment in her mouth, and which only occurred on some nights, and which wasn't as loud or as hard to adjust to as snoring, anyway.

The monsoons had been delayed again that year, and the heat had been building up night after night in their room. Vinod took off his shirt, hesitated, then took off his pants as well. "It's so hot," he explained apologetically, as he got into bed. "Too hot for my pajama suit." Sheetal, who was wearing a nightie, didn't say anything. "Why don't you take your nightie off as well," Vinod suggested.

"What, and be naked?"

"You'll be much cooler."

Sheetal was quiet for a moment. "Okay, but don't look," she whispered.

Vinod felt her get out of bed. She returned in a moment, and drew the sheet up to her neck.

"What's the point if you're going to cover yourself with a sheet? You'll sweat even more than in a nightie."

"I have to put something on. I'm completely naked otherwise. *You* have your underclothes on."

"Okay, I'll take them off."

Vinod took off his undershirt as Sheetal watched. He rubbed the cotton cloth over the hair on his chest to soak up the sweat, then threw it into a corner of the room.

"You're still not naked. What about those?" Sheetal pointed her chin at his briefs.

"Look the other way, and I'll do it."

"See, you're embarrassed, too."

"It's not the same. It's different for men."

"You expect me to take off my sheet, yet you won't take off your underwear."

"Oh yes? Well, here." With one quick sweep, Vinod tried to pull his briefs off, and got them all the way to his feet, where they became entangled in his toes.

A cry escaped Sheetal's mouth, and she covered her eyes with her hands. She looked through her fingers and began to laugh as she saw Vinod try to cover himself by crossing one leg over the other.

"What do you have there?" Sheetal said, pointing at his nakedness and laughing.

Vinod uncovered himself to show her. "Why don't you see for your-self?"

Sheetal screamed as he placed her hand on his cock and closed his thighs over it.

He held it there. "It feels so good," he said, and Sheetal's face turned a dark crimson.

Still holding her hand in his crotch, so that she couldn't move away, Vinod sidled next to Sheetal. He slipped his leg under the sheet and rubbed it against hers, feeling the coarseness of his hairs against her smooth skin. Hooking his foot around hers, he slid closer, until his chest was touching hers. Carefully, he peeled the sheet off her body, as if uncovering a sleeping child.

Sheetal pressed her arms over her breasts. She crossed her legs just as he had done a minute ago, keeping her gaze focused on the pillow next to her head. She bore his kisses silently, in her hair, at her brow, on her lips. As his mouth left hers, she turned to face him. Visible beyond the reticence, Vinod was surprised to see, was the unmistakable glint of curiosity.

He couldn't remember the instructions his brother had given him. Something about kissing, something about caressing, something about pressing their bodies together until they fit correctly. He kissed Sheetal's cheeks, her nose, her lips, but that didn't seem enough. He tried rubbing himself against her body, but stopped, because it was bringing him too close to the edge. He suddenly became terrified that he would ejaculate all over her body. He imagined his white semen squirting uncontrolled over her abdomen, like some pubes-cent emission, pooling in her navel, running down her thighs.

Apparently, Sheetal had received some advice as well, because she took him in her hand and guided him into her body. He felt the warm compactness of her, and smelled her odor, like freshly cut yams, that he would forever associate with sex. He came almost immediately, his body twitching, eyes rolling back in his head, Sheetal holding him tight in her arms, so tight he could hardly breathe. He pulled out and managed to focus on her, and was embarrassed at the confusion flushing her face.

"Next time will be better," he said, unable to bring himself to watch if the confusion was giving way to understanding, to disappointment.

"It's okay," Sheetal said, as she wiped herself clean. She got out of bed and put on her nightie.

"Good night," she said, as she got into bed and turned to face the window.

"Good night," he replied, looking at the small of her back, unable to reach out to comfort her. As the minutes ticked away, he stared at the motionless contour of her body and waited for a dog, a car, a mosquito, anything, to break the silence that hung over the room.

WHEN MRS. JALAL opened the door and saw the expression on Mrs. Asrani's face, she knew it was not going to be a pleasant conversation.

"Could I speak to Salim?" Mrs. Asrani asked, in a tone that was polite, but as primed as a sitar string.

"Uh, he's not in right now."

"Oh, where is he, may I ask?"

"I don't know. He's gone away for a little while."

"Do your children often go away without telling you where they're going?"

"My son is an adult. He can come and go where he wants. I don't insist on keeping tabs on his every move like some people."

"Well, maybe you should. Unless you think being an adult means he can carry away other people's daughters."

"I have no idea what you are talking about."

"You heard me. Carry them away in the middle of the night. Like a dacoit, in the darkness, when everyone is asleep."

"Keep your voice down, please. My husband is not feeling well."

"And maybe your husband would like to explain what he was doing with my daughter's dupatta wrapped around his head?"

"I don't know what you mean."

"Yes you do. You know what you've done. Taken my Kavita from me. As soon as you learnt she had accepted a good proposal, a proposal from a proper, decent family. You've kidnapped her. Father and son and mother together. Is this what you people came here to do, steal our daughters from under our noses?"

Mrs. Jalal slammed the door in Mrs. Asrani's face.

The doorbell sounded angrily, as angrily as its tinkling sound would allow. Then there was the sound of fists pounding on the door. "Open this, you coward. Come out, daughter of a swine, and answer my questions."

Mrs. Jalal looked at the door, backing away from it as if it would burst any moment. What should she do? Ahmed was still quite useless. What if Mrs. Asrani managed to break down the door? The woman seemed deranged. Who knew what these Hindus were capable of? She remembered all those nights in Dongri during Partition, cowering under the bed with Nafeesa as Hindu gangs roamed the streets outside. Just yesterday there had been a news item in the paper about an entire Muslim village in Bihar being massacred. Perhaps she should call the police.

Abruptly, the banging on the door stopped. Mrs. Jalal heard the sound of footsteps descending the stairs.

So the worst had happened. Salim *had* run away with Kavita. All those trips to the mosque over the years, all those lectures on what was right and what was wrong, and this is what it had amounted to. Her only child doing a thing like this. Where had she gone wrong?

And what was the business about the dupatta? What had Ahmed been up to? Why had he been wearing Kavita's dupatta over his head? Mrs. Jalal had not known what to make of it when they'd told her this morning. She could make out even less now that the dupatta had turned out to be Kavita's.

She had to speak to Ahmed. Coherent or not. Find out what had been going on. She had seen him come back upstairs and go back to their bedroom.

Mrs. Jalal knocked on the door, then opened it and went inside.

THE FIRST MORNING Vinod headed back to work after the wedding, Sheetal was waiting at the door, his tiffin box packed and ready. Vinod felt like kissing her goodbye, but didn't, because his mother was watching. That evening, he hurried home to be with Sheetal, even though he hadn't seen his friends at the café for two weeks. It was not long before he began to resent this routine, however, and had to remind himself that Sheetal remained cooped up at home with his mother all day. Living under one roof did not seem to be fostering the loving relationship he had envisioned between the two of them. Few days passed without his mother grinding in a subtle pinch of criticism about Sheetal to flavor the evening meal.

They were finishing breakfast one morning when Vinod noticed the untouched omelette on his mother's plate. He asked if something was wrong.

"She's put onion in it," his mother said sadly, in a whisper loud enough for Sheetal to hear. "She knows I'm not allowed onion on Wednesday because of my fast."

"Why didn't she remind me?" Sheetal asked from the sink, without turning around. "What kind of fast is this, anyway, that one can eat meat and egg but no onion?"

"See the way she talks to me? This is how I'm treated day after day while you're away." His mother's eyes had misted, and a tear was threatening to roll down one cheek.

"Tell her not to pretend so much. It's all for your benefit. We've all seen what her tongue is like—it could cut holes through cloth."

"Sheetal!" Vinod exclaimed, getting up from his chair, as his mother dissolved into sobs.

"I'm tired of trying to satisfy her. She's never happy with anything I do. Tell me why she can't make her own eggs, if she doesn't like the ones I cook for her."

His mother's sobs rose to a wail, and Vinod found himself striding to where Sheetal stood. He felt a sting in the fingers of his right hand, saw a flash of disbelief light up his wife's eyes. Then, head lowered, hand pressed against her reddening cheek, Sheetal left the room. Behind him, his mother blew her nose into a handkerchief.

Afterwards, Vinod went to work as usual. He sat at his desk the whole morning, his head burning as if ravaged by some disease. He returned home early, bringing along two cups of ice cream in the flavors Sheetal liked best, choconut and pista. His mother was taking a nap in the living room, and he crept past without waking her. Sheetal was not in the bedroom. A stack of his clothes, neatly ironed and folded, lay on the bed.

He put the cups on the dressing table and went to the kitchen to look for Sheetal.

"She's gone," his mother said. She had awoken, and was sitting on the couch, preparing herself a paan. "She went to her mother's, I expect."

"But why didn't you stop her?"

"What am I, crazy, to stick my nose between husband and wife? Don't worry, she'll be back when she cools off—she only took a few clothes." His mother cracked some betel nut between the blades of her nutcracker. "Today's girls. Such temper. Such arrogance. We were taught to touch our husbands' feet and thank them whenever they saw fit to teach us a lesson."

His mother folded up her paan and popped it into her mouth.

Sometime that evening, he remembered the ice cream he had bought. It had all melted, so he put it in the freezer.

Sheetal did not return for seven days. His mother kept assuring him that she would come back, and that he had done the right thing.

"It's best to make things clear from the beginning only," she said. "That way, they don't get out of hand." He nodded in agreement, but every night his spirit grew wearier as he made his way to the empty bedroom.

One week after the slap, Sheetal's father escorted her back in the evening. His mother received them in the living room, as she would any guests, and his father talked to Sheetal's father about the price of petrol. Her father did not stay for dinner but hugged Sheetal and left at about eight o'clock. No mention was made of the slap.

Dinner was quiet and tense. Sheetal didn't look up once, eating everything with her eyes lowered towards her plate. His mother started to say something once or twice, but caught the warning glance in Vinod's eyes and kept silent. Afterwards, his parents cleared out of the room more quickly than usual. Sheetal took the dishes to the sink and started wiping the food off them.

"You don't have to do that," Vinod said, coming up behind her. "The ganga will do it in the morning."

Sheetal did not turn around. She turned on the tap and started washing a plate.

"Leave them and come with me," Vinod said, wrapping his arms around hers.

"Let me do the dishes first. After all, isn't this why you married me?" Sheetal turned around. The accusation was so strong in her eyes that Vinod had to look away.

"Isn't it?" she said.

"I'm sorry," he mumbled, then said it again. "I'm really sorry. I've missed you. I'll never let it happen again. Please forgive me.

"Please forgive me," he repeated. His voice felt so weak that he wondered if he was going to cry. "This has been the worst week of my life."

She softened but didn't forgive him, not quite then. When he brought out the two cups of ice cream, she ate the pista one first, then the choconut one as well, not offering him any, and not smiling when he joked about the crystals formed because of refreezing. That night in bed, she maintained a gap between their bodies, shifting away with a start whenever he touched her, even accidentally.

The period of probation lasted for a month. One day, soon after that, she came into his arms. "Let's look for a place of our own," she said.

ONCE THEY MOVED into the flat above the Jalals, Vinod noticed a new softness begin to flower in Sheetal's personality. Day after day, night after night, she became more relaxed, even more receptive in bed. Some evenings she even allowed herself to be led into the bedroom before they had eaten dinner. A trace of color began to show in her cheeks, and she put on some weight, though Vinod still worried that she looked too thin. Her relationship with his mother became cordial, almost loving, except when his mother raised pointed questions about why it was taking so long for them to produce a grandson.

Sheetal adored the flat, despite the three flights of stairs that had to be walked up to get there, and despite the church in front of their building that cut off the view of the sea that could have otherwise been theirs. It was close enough to Vinod's bank that he could come home for lunch every day. On some afternoons Sheetal would pack the food in his tiffin box and they would carry it downstairs to eat in the shadow of the pipal tree spreading over the church courtyard. They both looked forward to Wednesdays, when Tall Ganga arrived earlier than usual, bringing along a freshly killed chicken, which she cooked into a curry under Sheetal's supervision.

Sometimes Vinod wondered about Sheetal's days. She shopped and cooked, he knew; she talked to Mrs. Jalal from downstairs and listened to Vividh Bharati in the afternoon; she hung up curtains and changed the sheets and watered the flowerpots on the balcony. But was that enough? Was that enough to occupy her, to make her happy, even, dared he ask, to fulfill her?

"It's not so trivial," Sheetal said, when he brought the question up one evening. "I'm a woman with a flat to run, not some girl playing house."

They had seven happy years there. Then, at the insistence of his mother, they went to the hospital near the income-tax building to find out why Sheetal had not become pregnant yet. By then, as the specialist from Bangalore explained to them, the cancer had already spread beyond the uterus. A hysterectomy was performed, and Sheetal underwent various other treatments and therapies. When the doctors were finished with her, she was allowed to come back to spend her last six months at home.

Sheetal's illness was so unexpected that for a while Vinod felt as if he were in one of those melodramatic tearjerkers, the ones that always completed silver jubilees at theaters like Roxy or Opera House. Suddenly his life became one long undulation of visits to the chemist and the temple, of hours spent blankly at work, of nights passed watching his wife's face as she rested. Then, before he could prepare himself, the routine ended—the dressing table was cleared of prescriptions, the extra blankets were packed away, and all that was left of Sheetal was a photograph on the wall, its frame adorned with a single strand of marigolds.

For a long time after she died, it seemed as if she was still around. As if she had been in the room with him a minute ago, and just gone downstairs to the store. She hated doing that, and would often wait until he came home from work rather than shop herself, even if all she needed was some coriander to complete the night's dinner. "And get me a paan, too," she would say, "if you're going down anyway."

Sheetal loved paan. Not the plain kind, but the sweet ones, with lots of coconut and candied betel nut and all the minty pastes and mixtures that the paanwalla kept in silver boxes around the circumference of his tray. "You missed that one," she would say sternly, when she went down to get the paan herself. "At least don't cheat your most regular customer." And she would watch to make sure he did not shortchange her on the tiny silver candy pills which were her favorite ingredient. The paanwalla adored her, and asked after her every day when she fell ill. Even in the last few days, when she could barely chew or swallow, she insisted on having her paan. "It helps me relax," she would say, as Vinod put the paan gently between her teeth, and for a moment, the familiar orange paan stain on her lips would be a blossom that brightened her face.

"Remember what you need to do after I'm gone, Vinod. Remember your promise to me, whatever you do, don't forget," Sheetal would gasp, as she tried to chew her paan, and Vinod would be by her side, kissing her hand, assuring her he would keep his promise, and wondering how he would.

For what Sheetal wanted, what she had become obsessed with in the last half year of her life, was to get into *The Guinness Book of World Records*.

It was Vinod who had bought the book, as a present to celebrate her return from the hospital. Sheetal read it immediately and by that evening she had made up her mind—her name was going to be listed. She had never been truly exceptional at any activity. Now she would prove to the world that she, Sheetal Taneja, was in fact the best at something. The question was, what?

She read and reread the categories in the book, but there was nothing in which she could remotely hope to win. Her only chance would be to create a new category. One morning, she announced that she had decided on it: dialogue. She had always had a knack for memorizing it. "What if I memorize the dialogue of an entire movie? Surely they will have to put me in the book for that."

She asked Vinod to fetch her the newspaper to see what was playing. There was so little time to lose. They would go the very next day.

She chose *Jeevan*. Life. There was irony in the title, since it starred Meena Kumari, who, as in many of her best movies, died in the end. What could be a better selection? Sheetal asked Vinod to borrow the new cassette recorder his brother had bought, the kind that could run on batteries. Vinod could record the whole soundtrack while he sat next to her.

It took her a full hour to dress. She wrapped her thin frame in the most cheerful sari she owned, and tried to cover the hollows in her face with makeup. Somehow, she steadied her hand enough to put on the lipstick, both on her lips and for the dot on her forehead. She asked Vinod to thread the earrings through her ears, and wore a necklace and gold bangles, even though they were only going to a matinee.

When the time came to go downstairs, she was unable to negotiate the steps. Eventually, she sat on one of the dining-room chairs, and Vishnu and the paanwalla carried her down, like a queen on a palanquin. Vinod took the two of them along to see the movie as well, so they could carry Sheetal upstairs to the balcony of the theater, where she had insisted on sitting.

They sat in the first row, right behind the railing. Sheetal watched most of the movie, though a few times when Vinod glanced over, her eyes were closed, as if she had lapsed into deep thought. Neither Vishnu nor the paanwalla had ever seen a movie from the balcony, and the paanwalla claimed several times that not only was the sound better up there but also the picture, because the screen was designed to send more light up to the expensive seats. It took three of the cassettes to record the two-and-a-half-hour soundtrack—Vinod was careful to reload the recorder during the songs, so that none of the dialogue would be lost.

The next day, Sheetal dictated a petition for Guinness, telling them what she proposed to do. Vinod took it to be typed by one of the professional typists in Tardeo, then mailed the letter himself at the post office, making sure the clerk canceled the stamps in front of him, as per Sheetal's instructions, so nobody would take them off for reuse.

For the next two months, Sheetal lay next to the cassette recorder and memorized. Sometimes when the different roles on the soundtrack became too confusing, she recruited Tall Ganga to help her. "Don't you have any shame, teasing girls like that," she would berate Tall Ganga, who would slowly, awkwardly, mouth the hero's response. Vinod would come home from work and hear Sheetal repeating "When I'm with you, my heart starts going *dhuk dhuk*—why do you think that is?" He would kiss her good night, and she would say, "Even if God forgives me, I won't be able to forgive myself for what I have done." Sometimes she would have a fever but still she would persevere, even if it meant memorizing only a few words that day.

Two months after seeing the movie, Sheetal made her first attempt. Vinod's brother and sister-in-law were called in to act as witnesses, and everyone gathered around Sheetal's bed to hear the recitation.

It was a disaster. Sheetal confused lines, forgot entire scenes, and became too emotional to continue when Dilip Kumar consigned his beloved's ashes to the Ganges and watched them float away in the water. "This, the first night of our union," Mohammed Rafi sang sadly on the tape as Vinod ushered everyone out of the room.

Sheetal grieved for days over her failure. She did not try again for almost three months. By then, she had deteriorated to a point where it was easy to convince her that she had done it, that she had managed to go through the entire movie. She went to sleep that afternoon already able to imagine her name in the book.

Three weeks before Sheetal died, the postman delivered a letter with a big blue-and-orange stamp from the United Kingdom. Sheetal got so excited that she forced herself to sit up in bed as Vinod opened the letter.

"Dear Mrs. Taneja," Vinod read aloud, "Thank you for your recent petition regarding the creation of a new category for memorization of the dialogue of a movie. We regret to inform you that we do not anticipate adding this category at this time. We would, however, like to congratulate you on your most interesting achievement in this regard."

It was signed "William Warby, Associate Editor, *Guinness Book of World Records*." Accompanying it was a flyer for the new edition of the book.

Sheetal was devastated for the rest of the day. But the next morning, she had Vinod reread the letter, making him go over the actual wording of the rejection several times.

"Aha," she said, interrupting him. "They've written that they can't do it *at this time*. Which means they are planning to keep it in mind for the future. Plus, who knows how long this Warby character will last, especially if he is turning down such good proposals? Once he goes, the new person will have a fresh chance to look at this."

That's when she extracted the promise from Vinod. "Keep trying until they put me in. Tell them that I died of cancer even, then they'll have to relent. Especially once the new person comes in." Meanwhile, the letter she had received was matted and framed, and hung over her bed. Every day, she reached out to touch the part which complimented her on her "most interesting achievement."

The year after Sheetal died, Vinod re-sent the petition to Guinness. A few months later, he got an almost identical reply, complimenting him on his wife's interesting achievement, and signed once more by William Warby.

CHAPTER ELEVEN

THE JAMADARNI IS squatting on the landing, eating the mango. *His* mango. Her mouth is smeared with yellow, visceral pleasure gleams in her eyes. She scrapes the pit clean, then runs her teeth over the peel for bits of pulp she may have missed.

Is this what it means to be a god? The first offering made to him, and he isn't even the one to enjoy it? Vishnu looks at the jamadarni— she is working on the pit one more time, trying to suck out some more flavor.

What else will he have to forsake? All the tastes and smells of his life? He has already lost his ability of touch—will he lose all power to experience as well? Could he choose *not* to be a god?

The jamadarni gives a contented sigh, then throws the pit and the peel into her rubbish basket.

He thinks of his final time with Padmini. "What if one day you came, and I was no longer here?" she says, sitting up in bed. "Would you try to find me?"

"Of course I would. Why do you say that?" he says.

"No reason. But you know, you'd never be able find me if I decided to leave."

Then, seeing his expression, she laughs. "Don't worry, I'm not going anywhere." She looks through the window. "No, Padmini will always be here."

He follows her gaze past the veil of red silk over the window. There are women standing on the balcony of the facing building, laughing and calling to the people down below. He wants to press his face into Padmini's neck, he wants to squeeze her body against his chest, he wants to hear her promise again and again that she will never abandon him, she will never go. How little of her he has learnt to live with—the minutes he steals from her are so precious, she will never know. The sound of a hawker selling bhajia rises from the street—onion and pepper and brinjal and potato.

But leave she does. The brothel owner does not know where she has gone, but offers him Lajjo instead, or Gulabi, or even Reena, who normally commands a higher price. Vishnu is distraught. Padmini, he cries, he wants Padmini. He roams for days looking for her but her prediction is true, he does not find her.

But he is a god now. He can bring her back. He need only gaze across the lay of the city, and pinch her out of the cranny in which she hides. Kiss her, hug her, love her, splay her on the floor if he pleases. Never let her out of his sight again.

Why does the thought no longer compel? Why have the pleasures of Padmini's body faded to such a subdued fragrance in his memory? A fragrance incorporating the perfume of mangoes, the wetness of water, the flavorings in tea. Has he lost his desire, has he been rinsed of his experience, has all the physical cognition acquired through his existence been suddenly rendered irrelevant, obsolete?

A warm indifference spreads through him to the cravings of his body. He is not sated, no, yet he can partake no more.

The jamadarni picks up her basket and starts up the steps. Vishnu is glad she has eaten the mango, he does not begrudge it to her.

THE NEWS TRAVELED fast down the core of the building, raging through the ground floor like an out-of-control conflagration. Short Ganga told the cigarettewalla, who told the paanwalla, who told the electrician. Mr. Jalal had been found sleeping on the steps, and when he awoke, had tried to molest Mrs. Pathak in front of her husband. Man Who Slept on the Lowest Step heard about it from the cigarettewalla, who added his own fictitious update about how Mr. Jalal's eyes had been rolling uncoordinated in his head when he came down just now to buy cigarettes. In turn, Lowest Step told the jamadarni that a mental asylum ambulance had taken Mr. Jalal away. This was refuted later by the jamadarni, who heard from Mrs. Pathak about Kavita's elopement with Salim, and Mr. Jalal's mysterious part in it. The elopement quickly turned into an involuntary one, because of the illegitimate child Kavita was expecting, and then into a full-fledged abduction perpetrated by the Jalals. Mr. Jalal was said to have had a fight with Vishnu, who had recovered miraculously to try and save Kavita, but was then mercilessly beaten by father and son. A supporting version claimed Vishnu managed to knock Mr. Jalal unconscious before he was overpowered himself, and Kavita left behind her dupatta to implicate the true wrongdoers. Another theory had it that the dupatta was ripped off in an attempted rape, and that Kavita had been kidnapped to be part of a famous Muslim smuggler's private harem. Nobody seemed clear about exactly what Mr. Jalal had said about Vishnu himself, though the jamadarni alleged he had called him a Hindu devil who deserved to die.

MRS. JALAL LOOKED at her husband, asleep on their bed. At the angle at which he was lying, the light from the window reflected off his cheeks, obscuring all the pockmarks, so his face shone unblemished as a child's. She lay down next to him and cradled his head in the crook of her elbow. Her poor Ahmed, how hard he had tried, how hard he still tried, to transcend himself. She had never seen a person with such aspirations, such ideals. She reached out to brush the hair off his forehead. Was there anything she could say, anything she could do, that would stop him in his bizarre pursuit?

Ahmed snuggled closer to her. "Arifa," he murmured, his eyes still closed. He wrapped an arm around her and stroked her neck with the back of his fingers. "I feel so sleepy. But so much work to do."

"Shhhh," Mrs. Jalal said. "Later." She raised a hand around his face to block the sunlight that was dappling his eyelids. Instantly, the marks rose back to view on the surface of his skin. She looked at them and traced their unevenness with the tips of her fingers. She wondered what he thought about them, what he had felt growing up with his face all cratered like that. She had asked him once long ago, but he had not answered. Had people called him names in school? Had he been shunned by classmates who might have otherwise been his friends? Had he gone through life always conscious of this handicap, which captured attention with such cruel clarity at first meeting?

She herself had never minded the marks. If anything, she was glad for them in her selfish way, because they balanced her own feelings of inadequacy. Ahmed's skin was Ahmed's skin, and these were just variations—variations in texture and color, that she was sure could be explained in terms of biological factors like nerves and blood vessels and pigment cells.

It was what lay beneath the skin, inside his head, that she had difficulty with. Why couldn't she learn to think of those differences too as biological variations? She had heard somewhere that all thought, and with it, feeling and belief, arose from a series of chemical and electrical impulses. How could something so unemotional, so scientific, be responsible for causing so much turmoil? Why had the paths in Ahmed's brain arranged themselves in such perverse ways, so diametrically opposite to what she had been taught?

Lying there now on the bed with him made these things seem less important. She drew her head next to his, and brushed his cheek with her lips. He kept his eyes closed, and continued rubbing his fingers against the nape of her neck. Nuzzling with him like this reminded her of the times she would lie next to the goat her father brought home every Bakr-Eid. She would wrap her arms around its body and pet its head, and bury her face in its fur. Sometimes she would lay her head against its chest and listen to its beating heart.

The goat would be housed right outside the kitchen, where it could be fattened a little more with a steady stream of vegetable scraps. She loved feeding it herself, watching it nibble delicately at carrot tops and cauliflower leaves. Always, though, would be the thought in her mind that the day of Bakr-Eid was arriving. The night before Eid, she would lie in bed, knowing it was the last time she would fall asleep to the sound of the goat bleating on the verandah. She would fantasize about setting it free to sprint down the wide stone steps. It would race down Jail Road, loping past milkwallas on their bicycles, dodging taxis and BEST buses, to freedom.

One year she stumbled upon the actual sacrifice. She had followed the cadence of her uncle's voice, and come upon her father and cousins crowded around a doorway. The white cotton kurtas felt soft and smelled of attar as she squeezed through between the men. She saw her uncle standing in his embroidered robe next to the butcher, the cloth streaming down from arms raised at right angles to his body. He lowered them, and she looked past and saw the head of the goat. Its neck lolled against the curved blade, the eyelids twitched, as if awakening from deep slumber. There was a trough on the ground, with blood so black and viscous it looked like tar. The tiles around were stained in red, and she noticed that her uncle's own shoes were spattered as well. She screamed and tried to squirm back through the men, but got caught in the suffocating folds of white cloth. She screamed and screamed, surrounded by the white, until her father's arms found her and lifted her away.

Her uncle came to see her afterwards. She was unable to look at him at first, terrified that she would find drops of blood in his beard. Once she stared into his eyes, she was pulled into the deep calm in them.

"Do you know why we do this, Arifa? Why we sacrifice a goat?"

She looked at his shoes in silence. The blood had dried to a dark brown along their edges.

"It's to remind us how precious life is. To remind us that anyone who sacrifices a goat must be prepared to sacrifice themselves in the same way, for God."

The words did not make sense to her, but she nodded in agreement, nodded to let him know that she had understood, nodded to escape the incriminating calmness that emanated from his eyes.

Now, so many years later, her uncle's words had an immediacy for her that she found frightening. Ahmed had already crossed the line, and the Koran was clear on blasphemy. Would she be called upon to repudiate him? The Koran recommended divorce, it prescribed death. Would she be able to banish him from her life?

Ahmed opened his eyes, and she looked into them. No, she was not strong enough. She could not abandon Ahmed. She could not draw a knife across his throat. She would stay by his side, and carry him through, come what may. There would be time later to atone, to settle her debts with God.

"Tell me again, Ahmed," she said, "what Vishnu told you last night."

216

THE CLAMORING DOWNSTAIRS was getting louder. "We can't let these Muslims carry away our daughters." "Who do they think they are? They should be put back in their place." "We have to teach them a lesson, before they get out of hand."

When Mr. Pathak came down for cigarettes, a group of people congregated around him, as if he were a film star. "What did Mr. Jalal tell you?" they asked. "Did he reveal where Salim is hiding?"

Mr. Pathak was overwhelmed by all this attention. "I'll answer all your questions, just let me get my cigarettes." As he paid for his packet of Charminar, he imagined reporters milling around and flash-bulbs popping in his face. He gestured to the questioners to follow him, and sat down on the third step of the building stairway.

Mr. Pathak pulled out a Charminar and tapped it on the packet. He put it in his mouth and searched for his matches, but a lighter miraculously appeared to light his cigarette. He inhaled deeply, then blew out the smoke while looking skyward, as he had seen important film people do while talking about their work. "Mr. Jalal is apparent-ly a very complex man," he began.

Unfortunately, Mr. Pathak had overestimated the gathering's appetite for analysis. What they were hungry for was facts—or, if those were not available, then the next best thing, rumors. "Did Mr. Jalal confess?" "Was Vishnu badly hurt in the fight?" "Did you see blood on the dupatta?" they pressed.

Anxious to retain his grip on his audience, Mr. Pathak began answering all their questions, some with half-truths, some with a ran-dom yes or no, taking care to lubricate things with adequate amounts of embellishment.

"Yes, there was blood on the dupatta, but at this point it's impossi-ble to tell whether it was Mr. Jalal's or Vishnu's when they got into a fight, or perhaps it could even be Kavita's if God knows who tried to outrage her modesty."

"Yes, Vishnu was hurt in the fight, which is so bad because he was doing quite well yesterday—even the ambulance people said he didn't need to go to the hospital, but now he's lying there near death.

"No, Mr. Jalal didn't confess, not exactly, though he did say that if Hindus aren't prepared to give their daughters in marriage, then Muslims have no alternative but to take them by force."

These answers seemed to be the right ones, since they suitably roiled the congregation. There were shouts to protect the honor of the Hindu bride pool, and to beat a confession out of Mr. Jalal. "Nobody should be able to get away like this with impunity."

At the idea of violence, Mr. Pathak started getting nervous. Perhaps the Hindu-Muslim bit had been too much, perhaps he should take it back. But he was loath to relinquish the position of leadership the people had bestowed on him. He tried to search for a middle way. "Let's go inform the police," he said, pushing his glasses back up the bridge of his nose. "Let's go ask them to search for Kavita."

But the gathering was having none of it. "The Jalals must pay for what they have done. Who do they think they are, doing this in a Hindu country?"

By now, Mr. Pathak was perspiring. The situation was getting quite out of hand, and he hadn't even mentioned to his wife that he was going downstairs. The assembly was becoming nastier before his eyes—already, he could see one or two bamboo lathis being wielded at the periphery. What would his wife say if she heard he had incited a lathi-armed mob up the stairs to beat up poor Mr. Jalal? "Let's just calm down for a moment," he tried saying, but a chorus of voices drowned him out. Sensing his weakness, the congregation turned instead to the cigarettewalla, who had emerged from his shop, a lathi held expertly in one hand.

"All we want is justice for Kavita," the cigarettewalla said, and there were cries of approval. The cigarettewalla slapped a palm on his forearm and thigh, and then held his lathi up. "Let's go get some more lathis and some more people," he said.

"Wait," Mr. Pathak cried, as people started filing past him.

"Wait," he said once more, his face ashen behind the harsh black frame of his glasses, as the cigarettewalla led the gathering into the courtyard at the back of the building.

AT FIRST, VISHNU does not notice them. The tiny flames at his feet. He is standing before the Jalals' door, stopped by a single thought. If he is Vishnu come to life on earth, which one of the ten avatars is he?

His mind races through the names his mother has taught him. All the times that Vishnu has descended to earth to battle evil. He wonders if he could be Narasimha, the man-lion, who sprang out of a pillar to slay a demon. Or Vamana, the dwarf, who taught the tyrant Bali a lesson. Or one of the later avatars, like Krishna or Buddha, the ones who came down as humans. But then he thinks that Narasimha has already come and gone, as have Vamana and Rama and Krishna. How could he be an incarnation that has already been lived? The flames begin to grow a little, they raise their heads and glance curiously around.

There is only one avatar yet to descend. The last avatar of Vishnu. The one they call Kalki. Destined to cut the thread of time and purify all of mankind.

The flames have discovered their mobility. They spread over the floor and lick the walls. They spiral up the handrail and race down the steps.

Kalki. Riding in on the white horse that carries his name. Wielding his burning sword. Striking it on the ground and setting the world aflame.

Through the smoke he sees his mother. She is on the floor of the hut, on all fours. He is seated on her back, with a stick in his hand, which he waves about like a sword.

"Tell me who you are," he demands, as his mother bears him across the floor.

"I am your horse, O great Vishnu," she replies. "Kalki is also my name. Together we will descend to earth to battle the wicked—come, hold on fast to my mane."

He smells the coconut in his mother's sweat. Her body rocks and sways. He feels its leanness beneath him, and hugs it as tight as he can. They fly down from the heavens and alight on the spreading plains.

"I am Kalki," he says, brandishing his stick. "I have come on my horse to end this age. I will gallop across the land to save the good and set the wicked aflame."

The walls have come alive. The ceiling has begun to dance. The Jalals' door starts to buckle, plaster begins to fall.

His stick becomes a sword. He looks at it in amazement. From behind the burning walls come the sounds of screams. The flames leap higher and higher.

Suddenly he is astride a real horse. Its body is pristine white. Its back feels strong against his seat, its flanks bulge against his legs.

He wonders from where the horse has come. What does it want from him? He looks around for his mother. But her scent has swirled away in the smoke, and she is nowhere in sight.

The horse is raring to go. It gives an eager snort. It strikes its hoof impatiently on the step and strains against his thighs.

The wall in front of them crumbles. The church across the street ignites. They stand together at the landing's edge and watch the buildings burn below.

The horse prepares to jump. He feels its muscles tense. He wants to pull it back from the edge, but it wears neither bridle nor restraint.

They leap into the air, leaving behind the blazing frame of his building. The white of the horse's mane gleams against the blackness of the night around. A cool wind begins to blow over his head. As he hugs the animal's body, as he holds on tightly to its neck, he wonders: Who is this horse, and where is it taking him?

I AM KALKI, the white horse of Vishnu. His final avatar is known by my name. From the heavens I descend with Vishnu to gallop across the waning days.

For so many miles do I bear him. His legs pressing into my flanks. The dampness of his sweat anointing my skin, his body sliding against my back.

Sometimes, when I smell his scent mixed in with mine, when he pets my mane and whispers in my ear, when I see him donning his battle gear, I wish I had wings. I wish I had wings to fly away with him, to some heavenly paradise, before time comes to an end.

Then I remember the work we have come down to do. The work that may never get done if I am not strong. For the country has been overrun by barbarians. Infidels rule the land. They have buried the teachings of the Vedas, they have poisoned the air with their alien ways.

Vishnu seems less outraged at this invasion. "Evil is evil," he says. "It springs up from inside the hearts of people, it needs no external source to appear. The land is impure because the people are impure, they have grown careless and allowed the seeds of evil to sprout."

"Yes," I say, "but who is nourishing these seeds? From where are the winds blowing in the clouds to water the sprouts? From lands far away, bearing not only moisture, but also the seeds themselves."

"The seeds are always there, my friend," Vishnu tells me, patting my head. "Embedded in the human condition. Constant vigilance is what is needed to keep them in their dormant state."

"My lord, it is written in the Puranas," I remind him. "That the barbarians are to blame. That you will get rid of them to restore the Vedic order to the land."

Vishnu smiles but does not answer. The problem, I sometimes think, is he is too full of charity. Is this a virtue, I wonder, or a weakness in him?

For I have seen what the barbarians have done. I have seen them set farmers afire in their fields. Cut the throats of priests in their temples. Behead every sacred idol, even the ones of Vishnu himself.

Fortunately, I am here to make sure that justice is done. That law and order are restored. For I am the one who decides where our campaign will take us. A rider can only journey where his horse conveys him. I look at the sky and listen to the wind. I follow them to where the barbarians are. Fire and the sword are the only purifiers they understand. And sometimes, if Vishnu falters, if he leaves a job half done, a barbarian half alive, I finish things off myself. For Kalki, remember, is not only Vishnu's name, but also mine.

Today we ride along the bank of the Ganges. Across plains that rise from the water's edge and carpet the earth. Here and there, the green is interrupted by the torn huts of abandoned villages. Behind us recede the remains of a city we have razed, smoke rises from it and blots the sun. A thin trickle of blood drips down my side from Vishnu's sword—he will wait until this evening to dip it in the Ganges and wash it clean.

We come to a village. Colored flags flutter against the sky. The adults are all in the fields somewhere. Only the children remain, playing in the central square.

"Barbarians," I say, looking at the flags. "Barbarian children," I gesture, pointing with my head.

"They are young," he says, and I know he will waver again.

"You do not kill," I remind him. "You just send them to a less ignoble rebirth. Sweep down your sword, and let them be borne away."

"I can't," he says. "To kill someone that young? How can it be in my lot to perform such cruel acts?"

"It would be more cruel to let them live. To grow and become barbarians as well. Why not give them another chance? These acts before you are not dishonorable, Vishnu. Free them from the existence to which they have been condemned."

But he does not unsheathe his sword. In his face, I can see the stain of pity, discoloring his judgment.

"It is your sacred duty," I urge him. "Your dharma, as foretold in the Agni Purana. To cleanse the barbarians from this land. The earth is parched, it has been insulted enough. Quench it, irrigate it, fill its barren furrows with red. Accept the dharma you must perform, O Vishnu. For there is nothing more dishonorable than failing in your sacred duty."

Finally, he raises his sword.

"This land of the Vedas, this land of the holy Ganges—purify it to make it great again. Proudly, O great lord, proudly. Proudly perform your duty today."

In his heart, he knows I am right. That is why he does what I say. His sword flashes in the sun, once, twice, and more. I watch, as silence descends on the playground.

I gaze past the huts, past the fields, to the blue line of the Ganges. Beyond it, I see the plains sweeping all the way to the edge of the sky. This is the land of the ancients, I think, these are its browns, its blues, its greens. I see a country that shimmers its purity under the sun. I see a civilization restored to the greatness to which it was born. I see villages and towns and cities where rites and rituals are preserved, where children respect their elders, and wives obey their husbands, where castes do not intermarry, and people are honest and moral and upstanding. Somewhere far away, I hear the verses of the Rig Veda begin to be chanted.

Vishnu sits weeping on the ground. The sun shines off his armor, his hair. I am wrenched by his beauty, I wonder how a god can look so vulnerable.

"Arise, O great warrior," I say, allowing myself to betray no emotion. "Arise, and let us be on our way."

Chapter Twelve

The doorbell rang, and Mrs. Jalal looked through the mail slot to make sure it wasn't Mrs. Asrani again. She was surprised to see the cigarettewalla's face trying to peer inside. Perhaps Ahmed had ordered something, perhaps the cigarettewalla had come upstairs to deliver it. She opened the door.

Mrs. Jalal was nonplussed by what she saw. For next to the cigarettewalla stood the paanwalla, and behind them were more people, most of whom she recognized from downstairs. Sprinkled among the gathering, Mrs. Jalal counted at least a half-dozen lathis, the blunt ends where the bamboo had been cut rising ominously into the air.

"What have you come here for?" Mrs. Jalal asked, trying to retain normalcy in her voice.

"Is Salim baba here? We'd like a word with him," the cigarettewalla said.

"He's gone away to see a friend. What did you want to talk to him about?"

"We have some questions we'd like him to answer."

"Why don't you just ask me? I'll answer whatever I can. Does he owe you some money?"

The paanwalla stepped forward. "Don't pretend to be so ignorant. You know why we have come. You can't do dacoity in someone's house like this and then act so innocent."

"I don't know what you mean. We haven't done dacoity in anyone's house."

"Tell us where you have hidden the Asranis' daughter," a voice shouted from the back, and there was a chorus of "Yes, tell us."

The cigarettewalla held up his hand. "We don't have any fight with you, Jalal memsahib. If your son is visiting a friend, could we speak to your husband? Surely he isn't visiting a friend also?"

"Actually, he's not here either. He's gone to the doctor. He hasn't been feeling well."

"Liar," the paanwalla shouted, banging his lathi on the ground for emphasis, but the cigarettewalla held up his hand again.

"If he's gone as you say, then you won't mind if we come inside and look around, will you? He may have come back without you knowing."

At this, Mrs. Jalal drew in a breath. "Since when did you get so big, Romu?" she said, addressing the cigarettewalla by his first name. "To demand to come in and search *my* house? All this time that I've seen you grow up. If your father were still alive, he would hang his head in shame to hear your words."

Mrs. Jalal pulled her sari firmly around her shoulders. "I've already told you we don't know where the Asranis' daughter is. If you're so interested in knowing, go ask *them,* ask them where they've hidden her. Now go away, and don't come back."

Mrs. Jalal tried to close the door, but the paanwalla stuck his lathi in between the door and doorjamb. "We're not going anywhere, Jalal memsahib, till we speak to your husband or your son. Now bring them out, unless you want us to come inside and drag them out ourselves."

"Get your lathi out. Get it out this very instant, or I will call the police."

"Giving us the threat of the police? Think we're scared of them? Go ahead and call them," the paanwalla said, though he took the bamboo out. Then, as if to compensate for this retreat, he feinted threateningly with it.

The cigarettewalla spoke again, this time in a very reasonable tone. "Look, nobody wants a fight. We're just very concerned about Kavita memsahib. We want to ask Jalal sahib a few questions to solve the mystery, that's all. There's no need to call the police."

"People who want to ask a few questions don't knock on their neighbors' doors with lathis. Now please leave—I've already said Mr. Jalal is not here."

Mrs. Jalal was just about to close the door when from the bedroom came Mr. Jalal's voice. "Who is it, Arifa, and what do they want?"

THE IMAGE OF the horse is still with Vishnu. The full implications of being Kalki, the last avatar, are beginning to dawn on him. All the power he has, all the people for whose fate he is responsible. How will he decide whom to cut down, whom to let stand? A vision of the burnt-out shell of the building comes to his mind.

Mrs. Pathak, for instance. For years she has wrapped her stale chapatis in newspaper and left them on the floor next to his head. Did she act nobly, save him from starvation? Or were her offerings so old, so unwanted, they were an insult, especially to a god? What should be her fate? It is not an easy question, not even for Kalki.

Perhaps he should first practice his power on something small, something less significant. That way, if he errs, the scheme of the universe will not be disturbed too much. He notices there is a line of ants meandering along the edge of the landing. There are so many

227

ants in the building. Surely a few will not be missed if delivered from their ants' lives. If anything, it will be a boon to them, being promoted to a higher existence.

Vishnu wills the line to be immobilized where it stands. He imagines the ants curling up one by one. He pictures all the freed souls flying to their next appointments. Perhaps he will rid the entire building of ants.

But nothing happens. The ants go on with their industry, unheedful of his efforts to liberate them.

Angered, he tries stepping on them, as Mrs. Pathak had done. But he has forgotten his weightlessness.

It is then the thought comes to his brain. What sense does it make that he is Kalki, if he cannot even dispatch an ant?

WHEN MR. JALAL called from the bedroom, Mrs. Jalal seized the opportunity, and slammed the door while people were still reacting. She went immediately to her husband. "Quick, call the police, before they come in."

"Nonsense. Let me talk to them."

"Ahmed, don't be crazy. They're armed with lathis and God knows what else. They want blood, they'll tear you to pieces."

As if to emphasize Mrs. Jalal's words, the doorbell rang, first in short musical tinkles, then in a medley of chimes that would have been a pleasing background tune had the situation been different.

"Open the door, Mrs. Jalal," the cigarettewalla's muffled voice came through the door. "We only want to talk to him, not hurt him."

"See?" Mr. Jalal said to his wife. "They just have some questions— I can go and clear things up."

"If you won't call the police, I will—I'm calling them right now."

"It'll really look foolish when they come and find us all chatting. But you do what you want. I'm going to the door."

"Ahmed!" Mrs. Jalal grabbed her husband's arm. "Don't do it."

Mr. Jalal turned around and held his wife with both hands. "Tell me, what would the Buddha have done at a time like this? What would Akbar have done? Would they have turned their backs and run? Would they have been too afraid to face whatever lay ahead?" Mr. Jalal shook his head. "No, they would have been grateful. That's right, grateful at the sight of such a crowd, grateful so many people had been led to them."

"Ahmed, don't start that again. We just went over all that. You aren't the Buddha. You aren't a prophet. That was a *dream*, do you understand? A *dream*."

"Call it what you will, Arifa, but look how everything is suddenly making sense. Everything I've been trying, and now all these people being led here to hear me. It's all bubbling up inside, it's all coming together. I feel like Akbar must have in the jungle all those years ago."

"Ahmed, listen to me." Mrs. Jalal tried not to let the panic crack her voice. "Listen to me. You just stay in this room. Read one of your books. Just stay here till the police come."

"Take my hand, Arifa. Be by my side. I want to share it with you. You come before all these other people. You and Salim." Mr. Jalal took her hand urgently. "Call Salim. Let's all hold hands, here, in this room. Let's all concentrate and try to see."

"Yes, Ahmed, I'll go call him." Holding his hand, Mrs. Jalal led her husband to a chair, and sat him down.

Mr. Jalal seemed lost in thought for a moment. Then the doorbell chimed again, and he jumped up. "No. I can't keep them waiting. They might go away. Let me answer that. This is such an opportunity. You and Salim and I can talk right afterwards."

"Ahmed," his wife shouted. "Don't go. If not for your own sake, then mine. Answer the door and something awful will happen."

"Don't be silly, Arifa. Nothing's going to happen." Mr. Jalal patted his wife's hand as if reassuring a child. "You know I have to talk to them. They've come here all confused. I'm the only one who knows about Vishnu. I can tell them about him. Think of how rewarding it is. To set someone's mind free."

"Stop, Ahmed, stop. For the sake of Allah, have some fear. Don't open the door. Don't let my hand go, just stay here." Mrs. Jalal started sobbing.

"Come now, go call Salim, and you can both listen as well."

Before Mrs. Jalal could protest further, Mr. Jalal strode to the door and threw it open.

VISHNU IS UNEASY about his powers. The riddle of the ants haunts him. What if he is not a god after all? He reminds himself again of the evidence. Willing himself up the stairs, gazing through walls as if they were glass. Surely only gods can do that.

But could he have squandered too much of his power on such acts? Drained it before he was fully infused? Should he return to climbing once more like a mortal?

Climb he must. The answer, he is convinced, is waiting at the top. He does not know exactly what he will find there. Perhaps the white horse, who will thunder away somewhere with him. Perhaps Lakshmi, who will transfer to him the energy that he needs from her own body. Perhaps Krishna, whose flute-playing will invigorate him. There is not so much further to go—soon he will have the strength, soon he will have Kalki's power to kill the ants.

There is a commotion below. It is the mob at Mr. Jalal's door. Vishnu realizes he need not concern himself with it anymore. He has risen above it, risen to the landing between the second and the third floor.

He looks around. This is the landing of Thanu Lal. The one they say can sleep for days on end. In fact, he is here now, curled up and snoring on his mat. When he is not asleep, Thanu Lal stands by the pipal tree in the courtyard of the church and chews paan. Nobody has ever seen him work, no one knows where he gets any money. All people know about him is the story. About the day his forehead was brushed by the fingers of God.

It happened, the cigarettewalla says, when Thanu Lal still had a wife and daughter, when he was living in a hut in the Ghatkopar slum. He awoke one morning to find his forehead covered with ash. "A miracle," his wife, Jamuna Bai, declared, getting him a mirror, "just like those pictures of Sai Baba."

By the time he came out of the hut, the news had already spread, and a crowd had gathered in front of his door. Thanu Lal sat down cross-legged on his rope charpoy and turned his face to his audience. On his forehead, his cheeks, his neck, and even his arms was the ash—chalky raised patches of it, that looked like the mounds left behind when insects bore through wood. As people watched, the ash above his brow started welling up and dropping to the ground in clumps, where it lay in powdery contrast to the dark earth.

One of the onlookers broke from the rest and advanced to the bed. He ran his fingers through the ash on the ground and smeared it on his forehead, then scurried back. A second person was about to do the same when Jamuna Bai charged at him. "Stay away, you hear? Don't touch the ash. Do you think he is doing this for your sake, so you can come here and loot us like this?"

Jamuna Bai instructed her daughter, Vasanti, to hold a stainless-steel thali under Thanu Lal's face. She carefully harvested the ash onto the plate. "I don't want it flying away or falling to the ground. The newspaperwalla is on his way—he'll want to see it."

By the time the *Loksatta* reporter came, however, Thanu Lal had stopped producing ash. In her zeal to conserve it, Jamuna Bai had brushed too much off onto the plate, and the reporter, disappointed by the faded patches on Thanu Lal's face, asked his photographer to take only one photograph.

"Come tomorrow," Jamuna Bai said. "He will bring forth even more ash. Fresh for you. It will happen every day."

The next morning, an even bigger crowd gathered to witness the miracle. At ten o'clock, Thanu Lal came out of the hut and had his wife and daughter wash his feet in a large thali. Jamuna Bai announced that those who had brought offerings of flowers and coconuts should put them in another platter, which she placed at the foot of his charpoy. They began the wait for the newspaper man to come. At eleven, when he still hadn't shown up, Jamuna Bai asked for silence from the crowd. She announced the ash would be produced anyway.

Thanu Lal closed his eyes and concentrated. But nothing happened. His skin remained clear. There were whispers in the audience, which became louder as Thanu Lal's forehead contorted, as his cheeks turned dark with effort. Finally, he burst out in tears and ran inside the hut.

For many mornings after that, Thanu Lal sat on his bed outside and tried to produce ash. The crowds came to watch at first, but gradually thinned, until it was mainly a gaggle of children who gathered in front of the hut. In an effort to attract an audience, Jamuna Bai brought out the thali of ash she had saved, and allowed onlookers to mark their foreheads with a fingertip's worth. One day, when the ash failed to materialize again, Thanu Lal took the thali from her hand and beat her unconscious with it.

The cigarettewalla says that Thanu Lal actually killed Jamuna Bai, and spent many years in prison for the murder. But according to the paanwalla, once Jamuna Bai had been beaten, *she* was the one who started producing ash, and became very rich after she opened a shrine to herself. Vishnu does not know which version, if any, to believe.

He feels the urge to wake Thanu Lal now, and ask him. Talk to him about God and ash, about looking through walls, and being able to kill ants. *Thanu Lal, wake up,* Vishnu says, but the man does not stir.

Wake up, wake up, it's Vishnu. I have something to ask you. Thanu Ram keeps sleeping.

Vishnu goes over to shake him awake. But of course he can't, not without his sense of touch. Thanu Lal turns over on his side, and remains asleep. Vishnu notices another line of ants, taunting him from the wall behind.

The questions descend again to torment Vishnu. How can he be a god if he has no power? Could he just be a man, the man he has been his whole life? If this isn't divinity he is looking at, if it isn't immortality, then what is it?

This is not the time to think of answers, Vishnu tells himself. His task, for now, is to keep ascending, and not waver until he reaches the top.

Chapter Thirteen

When he was first told the seriousness of Sheetal's illness, Vinod was devastated. Not only by what the news meant for Sheetal, but also for him. The future he had constructed so painstakingly over the past few years in his mind would crumble, now that the person around whom he had built it was to be taken away. He sat in the hospital waiting room and felt the resentment grow underneath the sorrow—why had he been treated so unfairly by fate? He found his mind wandering to thoughts of what his life might have been had his parents married him to someone else.

By the time he started caring for Sheetal at home, Vinod's inital shock had subsided. As the weeks went by, he found he was able to look deeper into Sheetal than ever before, to glimpse into her very soul, and see the strength that, even as she wasted away, held up the spirits of everyone else. "When I get well, I want to go to Kashmir," she would say. Or, "We'll go to Nepal for our second honeymoon." It was always some place in the north, some place cold, some place far away from the Bombay where she knew she would be spending her remaining days.

The month she died, Vinod felt his love for his wife had become so strong that a part, maybe all, of him would die with her. He wondered if he would want to live after Sheetal. What if he decided not to? How would he kill himself? He started appropriating some of the sleeping pills the doctor had prescribed for Sheetal, taking one or two at a time, and storing them in an opaque brown bottle that he hid in the dressing table.

A few days before her death, Sheetal saw him take one of her pills. "I know what you are doing," she whispered, her eyes half closed. "But it's not your turn yet. Wait until your turn comes." She fell asleep.

That evening, he flushed all the pills down the toilet. He went down to the rocks at Breach Candy and threw the empty brown bottle into the sea. In the days that followed Sheetal's death, he often regretted his decision. But he did not try to reverse it. Sheetal's command had been one of the last things she had said to him, and he would obey it.

His mother tried several times to get him remarried. But he had closed the door to this possibility. He felt he had already experienced whatever there was to be experienced between a husband and a wife, that he had shared a part of himself with another person in a way too profound to be duplicated. There was a reason fate had brought him to this spot. It would be up to fate now to lead him somewhere else.

With nothing else to do, Vinod immersed himself in his work. Over the next fifteen years, he was promoted to manager and then senior supervisor. The flat had already been paid for by his father, and with the simple needs of his single life, he didn't need much. Then, one after the other, his parents died, leaving him their old apartment, which by now was worth a large amount of money. At the age of forty-five, Vinod found he had enough wealth to last him his whole life. He resigned from his job.

AT FIRST, VINOD stayed home. He found it a relief to stop pretending he was really interested in his work, that his job was anything more than activity with which to fill his day. Colleagues from the bank called in the beginning, but the phone soon stopped ringing. He began spending his days in bed, getting up for food, or to play his record.

What would happen, he started thinking, if he just remained in his flat? Ate less and less, and waited for his existence to end? Who would find his body, how long would it take? Probably Tall Ganga, he decided—she still stopped by occasionally to ask if there was something he needed. He wondered if this was what had been ordained for him—if tired of forging the corridor that was his life, the stars had simply decided to seal it off.

He was surprised to feel guilt at these thoughts, guilt at the listlessness in which he had allowed himself to be enveloped. All around him were reminders of activity—the knock of Tall Ganga at his door, the smell of tar from the resurfaced street outside, the call of vegetable hawkers, the dust and din of traffic. What gave him the right to stop, to surrender his existence to such self-indulgent rumination?

On the other hand, what did he have left to pursue? What goal could he conjure up to validate the rest of his life? Perhaps it was outside himself that he should seek the answer—some external cause, a good and noble one, in which he could discover meaning again. He had never thought of himself as an altruist, a social worker, but the idea began intriguing him. Surely a city like Bombay must be teeming with unmet needs, waiting to bestow well-being on the person who filled them. He contacted Mr. Wazir, an old philanthropist friend of his father's. Upon Mr. Wazir's recommendation, Vinod was invited to join the board of the Greater Bombay Social Cooperative.

The motto of the GBSC was "Through united hands we uplift the life of the slum-dweller." The first meeting Vinod attended turned out to be a field trip to the Dharavi slum, where a project had been underway for several years to improve the water supply. Several of the residents were presented shiny brass taps, and Mr. Kailash, the GBSC president, promised pipes to attach them to, very soon. The slum children went around and garlanded each of the board members (including Vinod), after which the board retired to the bus for cold drinks.

"The beers are in the icebox in the back," Mr. Kailash explained, as Vinod was trying to decide between a Limca and a Gold Spot. "We can't take them outside because of the alcoholism project we're sponsoring here." Mr. Kailash introduced Vinod around the bus to the other board members, most of whom were industrialists. A few looked puzzled when Vinod said he had been a bank manager.

"But that's why Wazir sahib recommended you," Mr. Kailash said, pouring himself a Kingfisher beer. "We need someone we can trust. These bloody contractors are all thieves. They deserve a good thrashing, every last one of them."

It seemed natural for Vinod to volunteer for the task of dealing with the contractors. With the nose he had developed at the bank for detecting irregularities, he was able to intercept and put an end to some of their tricks. But detective work was not enough. Vinod was eager to do more, to experience the satisfaction of labor, to distance himself as much as possible from the inertia of his month at home. He started spending his days at the construction site, busying himself with checks and inventories, offering assistance where needed, even helping to lay pipes once in a while. Night after night, he returned exhausted to his flat and put on a pot of water to boil for his bath. As he watched the grime from his body swirl across the tile and vanish into the drain, he tried to think of the day when water would flow just as freely for the residents of Dharavi.

One of the women on the board was Mrs. Bhagwati, who had taken over her husband's seat after he had suddenly died of a stroke. When the weather got cooler, Mrs. Bhagwati started accompanying Vinod to Dharavi once a week. Vinod was pleased to have someone help with the contractors. Of late, they had grown very resentful of his presence, and they were staging regular slowdowns to embarrass him. Mrs. Bhagwati, with the vast soap-making fortune her husband had left behind, was quickly able to lubricate the gears and move things along.

A few months after her deepened interest in the slum-dwellers' welfare, Mrs. Bhagwati invited Vinod, along with the other board members, to a party at her house. By now, everyone knew Vinod as the person who was going to turn the Dharavi project around, and Mr. Kailash even proposed a toast to "bank manager sahib." Vinod was polite to the other guests, and to their conversation about factories and unions, but it was the buffet table which dominated his interest. It had been years since he had eaten so well, and when the servants carried in the main course of stuffed pomfret, he was quick to excuse himself and make his way to the table.

"Basmati with cashews," Mrs. Bhagwati said from behind him as Vinod helped himself to the stuffing spilling out delicately from the pomfret's belly. "I had a hunch you might like it."

Towards the end of the party, Mrs. Bhagwati asked Vinod if he would mind staying until after all the guests had left, since she wanted to go over some questions about next week's site visit. So as Mrs. Bhagwati bade her guests goodbye, Vinod sat by himself in the TV room, and a servant put on the video of a new movie, *Romeo in Bombay*.

Vinod had not seen a movie for many years, not since *Jeevan*. He found this one quite interesting, since it had Reshma and Amitabh Bachchan in it, two actors he had heard about, but never seen.

A half hour into the movie, Mrs. Bhagwati came into the TV room. Vinod noticed she had changed into a salwar kameez, which was a lot less formal than the saris she always wore. He was surprised at how tightly the kameez clung to her body, how it pulled at the contours of her figure and thrust her bosom forward. He tried not to look at Mrs. Bhagwati's breasts.

"Would you like a Scotch?" Mrs. Bhagwati offered "Black Label—I picked it up myself at the Singapore duty-free." Vinod politely declined.

"Shall we discuss the visit now?" Mrs. Bhagwati asked, and Vinod had to make an effort to give up the movie, which had suddenly become very riveting. Reshma had been kidnapped by Shatrughan Sinha, who was a villain Vinod had also never seen before, and the hero was about to burst into the den where she was being held.

"Let's go into the other room," Mrs. Bhagwati said, and reluctantly, Vinod followed.

The other room turned out to be a bedroom, and suddenly it struck Vinod that the questions Mrs. Bhagwati was interested in discussing might not involve slum-dwellers. He started feeling very uncomfortable, and Mrs. Bhagwati, being an industrialist's wife, picked up on this discomfort at once.

"I'll get to the point, Vinod—it's one thing my husband taught me to do. It's hard to look at twenty-five, thirty, or however many years we have left, hard to look at them and see only solitude. Fate may have decided we sleep in an empty bed night after night, but we don't have to listen to fate."

Vinod wished he had eaten less of Mrs. Bhagwati's pomfret. Somehow, in spite of all the site visits on which Mrs. Bhagwati had accompanied him, he had not seen this coming. In retrospect, he supposed it had been quite naive of him to think she *enjoyed* going to slums, when she had such a nice bedroom and all the new actors to watch with a click of her TV.

"Here's my proposal, Vinod. I've seen you on the board. I've worked with you, side by side, in the dirt and disease of Dharavi. I know you're an honest person. I know you want to improve the lives of the slum people."

Vinod tried, but could not recall having worked in dirt or disease with Mrs. Bhagwati. As for the rest, he supposed it was true, though of late he had wondered whether his motives were purely unselfish.

"Marry me, Vinod. We will make each other happy. All my wealth will be at your disposal, to spend on whatever little slums you want to improve. It's not a small amount, Vinod—together, we can clean up the filth with our own four hands, clean up the whole city of Bombay."

Vinod had a vision of Mrs. Bhagwati, dirt-streaked and sweating, digging canals and ditches all over the city. To bring water to the teeming residents and clear away the sewage from their homes. He looked at her, standing in the tight kameez, her hair unraveled from its customary bun, the silence broken only by the sound of Reshma singing faintly in the adjoining room. Mrs. Bhagwati was not an unattractive woman. He had not been with anyone for more than sixteen years.

Vinod went up and kissed Mrs. Bhagwati on the cheek. Mrs. Bhagwati made a small sound in her throat, and closed her eyes. He looked at her mouth and noticed that her lipstick made her lips look quite moist. They were slightly parted, and past them, Vinod could just make out the gleam of her front incisors.

He was about to kiss her on the mouth when behind her he noticed Mrs. Bhagwati's dressing table. It was covered with jars and vials, and had a large mirror attached, just like Sheetal's used to. He remembered the slots for lipstick, the compartments for makeup and jewelry, and at the bottom, the drawer where he had hidden the brown bottle with the pills. How long ago had he carried the bottle to Breach Candy? It had bobbed in the water for a while, and almost smashed against a rock, but then a receding wave had borne it out to sea. He wondered if it had ever washed ashore again, perhaps at Chowpatty or Juhu, where an urchin might have found it and added it to his bag of salvaged glass to sell to the recycler.

Vinod wondered if that day he had done the right thing. Had his life been worth living since then? He thought about this question as he walked home all the way from Colaba, where Mrs. Bhagwati lived. He had abruptly said his goodbye to her, leaving her standing in her bedroom with the TV room attached, where the Amitabh Bachchan–Reshma movie was still playing. He walked past the Gateway, and looked at the boats in the distance, their lights like oil lamps floating in the still, dark water.

He took the long way home, past Regal Cinema, past Nariman Point, down Marine Drive, past Chowpatty, staying next to the sea as far as possible. Looking for the occasional seagull that still flew by, wondering if the fish were still swimming about in the water. At Kemp's Corner, he paused, and stared at the Air India billboard. The Air India maharaja was advertising flights to New York City. "Uncle Shyam wants you!" the sign said, with the maharaja wearing a hat with stars and stripes on it and pointing a finger at passersby. For a moment, he wondered if he should keep walking until he reached the airport at Santa Cruz, get on a plane there, and go to the United States. Leave Mrs. Bhagwati and the board behind, leave the slums where they stood, leave his life and just go away. Then he remembered he didn't have a passport, or visa, or, for that matter, money with him to buy a ticket. He looked once more at the glint in the maharaja's eyes, the expression that said it wouldn't take no for an answer. Then, thinking about the sea behind his building, the water that stretched past the horizon, the lands, the countries, the continents, that lay beyond, and above them all, the sky, with its unexplored worlds, its planets, its moons, its sun, and its endless constellations of stars, Vinod continued his homeward journey.

VISHNU STANDS IN front of Vinod Taneja's door. He has checked the entire landing, looked into every nook and cranny, searching for ants. He is glad he hasn't found any, glad they have not made it to this level, glad he has risen above them.

He wonders who has been running Mr. Taneja's errands while he has been ill. Who has been buying the toothpaste Mr. Taneja likes, the biscuits he eats with his tea?

Vishnu remembers the first time he went shopping for Mr. Taneja. It was for soap and a packet of blades, and Vishnu inflated the price by a good half rupee. He expected to be challenged, but Mr. Taneja just gave him what he asked for. Soon he was overcharging Mr. Taneja two or three rupees each time, and still, Mr. Taneja did not say anything.

Then the unexpected happened. Vishnu started feeling guilty. He tried telling himself that Mr. Taneja had enough money and would hardly miss a few rupees. Or that Mr. Taneja had certainly caught on by now, and must knowingly be paying the inflated prices. But the feeling persisted, and Vishnu was forced to roll back his add-on, first to a rupee, and then to half of that. Which did not eliminate his guilt, but made it recede to a tolerable level.

Now he feels ashamed of what he has done. Especially for a god, to act like that. Even if that was in his more forgivable human state. Perhaps he will come back down the stairs to apologize to Mr. Taneja. Surely this is someone that Kalki will save.

Only the last flight of stairs, the one to the terrace, remains. Vishnu takes the first step.

THE CROWD WAS silent. Mr. Jalal stood at the door. Behind him was Mrs. Jalal, poised to pull him in if there was trouble. She wondered if she could risk leaving him alone for a few minutes to call the police. The phone, unfortunately, was in the front room, in full view of the door, and she was afraid that if she attempted to make the call, someone would try to stop her.

Mrs. Jalal stared at the faces of the people assembled. They were the same faces she had seen for years, yet they seemed so different now. The eyes, especially—all those years she had looked into them and seen only good-naturedness. Where had this brazenness come from, when had they filled with such contempt? Had it always been there, hiding behind all those greetings of "Namaste, memsahib," watching, growing, until an excuse like this presented itself? How would she ever look at these people again, how would she ever walk past their shops, without a shudder running through her body?

For a while, nobody said anything. The cigarettewalla and paan-walla had not expected to actually confront Mr. Jalal and were unprepared to interrogate him. They stared at each other, and at the floor, shuffling their feet, and secretly wishing they were in the back of the crowd. Finally, the electrician asked, "Where is the Asranis' daughter?"

"I have no idea," Mr. Jalal replied, his brow unfurrowed, his voice calm. "I haven't seen her in ages."

"What did your son do with her?" the paanwalla asked, getting his voice back.

"What did *you* do with her?" the cigarettewalla demanded in a louder voice, spurred out of silence by the paanwalla.

"My son is visiting a friend. When he gets back, I'll ask him. And I've already said I haven't seen Miss Asrani for a long time."

"Liar," someone shouted from behind the cigarettewalla. "What were you doing with her dupatta around your face, then?"

"Yes, how did her dupatta leave her shoulders and find its way to your head?" the cigarettewalla added, determined not to let anyone hijack his leadership.

"That's what I've come to talk to you about," Mr. Jalal said, and murmurs of surprise rippled through the crowd. "I spent last night sleeping on the landing. With Vishnu." There were more murmurs, and Mrs. Jalal put her sari worriedly to her face. "The dupatta was already on him when I came. I have no idea how it got there."

Mr. Jalal paused to scan the crowd. The cigarettewalla, the paan-walla, the electrician—everyone was looking at him intently. How quickly fate had operated to bring him his audience. Surely this was another sign urging him to assume the role for which he had been chosen. He would make the most of it—he would try to win over the entire assembly, with this, his first sermon.

"This has been a long and difficult journey for me," he began, "and last night my quest brought me to Vishnu."

Mr. Jalal related his story. "A walnut, a walnut this big," he exclaimed, holding up his fingers in front of the cigarettewalla and paanwalla's faces, "right into my forehead." He made his hand into a fist and slammed it into his head, noting with satisfaction the way their eyes widened. "That's what allowed me to see."

He recounted the vision. "Imagine a body with so many arms that it could pluck every one of you from where you stand. Imagine a being with so many mouths that it could crush you all between its jaws." The cigarettewalla took a step back as Mr. Jalal grimaced and flung his arms into the air. "With smoke in its nostrils and flame in every breath."

He was keeping their attention—they were hanging on his every word. A few of them had even set down their lathis and were squatting on their haunches, rapt in what he was saying. Why had he never recognized before this talent he had? This power to convince, this ability to hold an audience? As Mr. Jalal spoke, the crowd before his eyes began to multiply, until it was thronging down the steps and through the streets, all the way to Haji Ali.

"And I am convinced, absolutely convinced, that there is only one course of action that can save us all—to follow the directive that Vishnu has asked me to convey to you. Wake up and recognize him, before it's too late."

Mr. Jalal ended his account with a flourish. He beamed roundly at the assembly, like a politician finishing the speech that will get him reelected.

Silence hung over the crowd. The cigarettewalla rubbed his chin thoughtfully.

Then the electrician hissed, "You bastard."

People turned to look at him. The triumph on Mr. Jalal's face gave way to confusion.

"You damn bastard," the electrician hissed again. "How dare you."

"Yes, how dare you," the cigarettewalla hissed as well.

"That was no dream. That was the Gita. The eleventh chapter. Did you think no one would recognize it? You made it all up about your dream, didn't you? To save your own skin."

Mr. Jalal gaped at the electrician. He had no idea what the man was talking about.

"How dare you make fun of poor Vishnu. How dare you throw our own Gita in our faces like that. What have you come here to do, you Muslim bastard, reveal Krishna to us?"

A seed of recollection blew into Mr. Jalal's brain. Yes, there was something in the Bhagavad Gita—something about Krishna revealing himself—to Arjun, was it? It had been so long since he had read it—but yes, there was a familiar aspect to the dream, now that he thought about it. "But I *did* dream it," he said, "even if it *is* in the Gita. This just proves my point—it had to be Vishnu speaking, not me."

"Liar." "Blasphemer." "Cheat."

The voices from the back were getting louder, so the cigarettewalla decided he had better assert himself. "How dare you even think of quoting our holy book to us, you unbeliever," he said, even though he had little personal knowledge of the Gita, having never had it read out to him. "What kind of fools do you make of us? We'll take you to the police."

"Take him to the police?" the paanwalla said. "What rubbish— we'll deal with him ourselves, right here, right now. What are you, too scared to punish this scoundrel yourself? If you can't use that lathi, give it to someone who's less of a coward." With this, the paanwalla snatched the cigarettewalla's lathi from his hands and gave it to a lathi-less person standing behind.

The cigarettewalla, angered by this abrupt usurpation of his authority, lunged for the paanwalla's lathi, managing to catch one end of it. As the two were fighting over the bamboo, Mrs. Jalal, taking advantage of the diversion, pulled Mr. Jalal inside, and whispered to him to call the police.

Mr. Jalal was still trying to sort out the hostile reaction to his account. It was a reaction that had been completely unexpected. He had imagined his words would inspire the crowd to lay down their lathis, inspire them to rush downstairs and prostrate themselves at Vishnu's feet. The preparations of the crowd to assault him were bewildering. Now, as his wife whisked him into the flat and pushed him towards the phone, he tried to recover his equilibrium and make sense of what was happening.

Obviously, the crowd had rejected his message. But why? He couldn't see what the objection was, why having a dream about the Bhagavad Gita should disqualify the directive he was conveying. If anything, this should prove that his vision was grounded in ancient revelation, that it was authentic, and more than just a dream. What more evidence could they require?

It was then that Mr. Jalal looked through the living-room window, at the church across the street. A big white cement cross formed the front of the building. That was the answer, Mr. Jalal realized. He had not suffered. Prophets had to pay to be believed. They had to be tortured, they had to be flayed, they had to be crucified, and only then would people accept their message. Blood was the only watermark of revelation, suffering its only currency.

Mr. Jalal stood by the phone. He was close enough to pick it up, to dial a one, a zero, a zero. It would take five seconds, ten at the most. He saw his wife gesticulating to him, her eyes widening as she urged him to hurry up. He saw the paanwalla and the cigarettewalla stop their fighting and look up, the paanwalla's nose flaring as he caught sight of the telephone within Mr. Jalal's reach.

Surdas picked up the knife.

246

Mr. Jalal saw words form in his wife's mouth, and did not hear anything.

It was a small ornamental knife, with a sharp, curved blade.

The paanwalla had come in through the door, and Arifa was screaming at him.

It had a wooden handle, with three diagonal marks on it.

The paanwalla was revolving his lathi above his head. As Mr. Jalal looked, the lathi seemed to move slower and slower, until it hardly seemed to be moving at all.

Now the crowd would witness the payment he was prepared to make, Mr. Jalal thought. The initiation he was willing to suffer for their sake. There would be pain, for sure, but the infliction of it would not be under his control. He would finally feel its beauty, the sheer experience of it. And he would not have to worry about when it would start, how it would be administered, or when it would stop.

The paanwalla was drawing within striking distance of him. The lathi had stopped rotating, and was now rising, ever so slowly, into the air. The paanwalla's eyes were flickering, calculating—judging the speed of the lathi, estimating its distance from his body, adjusting for the amount of force with which he wanted it to land.

And Surdas went to the door and opened it. He turned his face to the horrified people assembled there.

The lathi had reached its apex, and was swinging down now, still in slow motion.

And said to them, Now I am free.

Mr. Jalal could hear the lathi whistling through the air. He braced his chest for its impact.

Now I am free, Mr. Jalal thought, as he saw the wood make contact with his body and waited for the pain to register in his brain.

Chapter Fourteen

When mr. jalal's nerves signaled to his mind the impact of the blow, he was transported once more to a familiar place. It was the same place he had visited when he had tried to read the Koran with his hand on the flame, the same place he had found himself the time he had joined the Muharram procession. Mr. Jalal was surprised, he was shocked, he was amazed, at the sheer painfulness of pain.

But this time was different, Mr. Jalal thought to himself, this time he really did not have control over it. Everyone who does penance must have to go through with this. It would be good for him, he would bear it, he simply had no choice, no escape.

The second blow landed. Thoughts about penance and martyrdom dissipated quite briskly with it, and were fully beaten out with the third. All Mr. Jalal could think of by now, all that every cell in his brain screamed, was ESCAPE. Mr. Jalal flailed around in the living room for the telephone, toppling the delicate table on which it was perched.

By the fourth blow, Arifa had come to his rescue, and was grappling with the paanwalla, holding his lathi-wielding arm and trying to bite it. Mr. Jalal was dimly aware of the paanwalla screaming out an epithet, and his wife saying through blood-stained teeth, "Run, Ahmed, run—to the bedroom." He saw the electrician swing his lathi behind Arifa, and tried to warn her, but his mouth seemed filled with wool. As Mr. Jalal turned around to flee, he had a glimpse of Arifa sinking to the floor, a thin red line forming at her temple.

He was about to enter their bedroom when he remembered there was no latch on the door. So he swerved into Salim's room instead, and slid the heavy metal bolt across—the one Salim had insisted on having installed for privacy. Almost immediately, there was the sound of pounding. Mr. Jalal heard the paanwalla say, "Let us in," in a very reasonable tone.

The door seemed to strain and bulge. Mr. Jalal backed away from it, but the bolt held fast. He looked around the room, and found a chair to put under the doorknob. There was no other door in the room, only two windows and the balcony. Unlike the one in the other bedroom, this balcony did not open onto the street, but onto the courtyard at the back of the building. He wondered if someone in the courtyard would hear his cries and come up if he shouted for help. Then Mr. Jalal remembered that everyone from downstairs was already in his living room, and they were, in fact, the ones trying to break down the door.

The door heaved. How much time did he have before it gave? There was only one thing to do. Mr. Jalal went to the balcony and looked down.

The first floor had no balconies. He would have to jump all the way to the ground to escape. He studied the courtyard two floors below. The cement looked extremely hard, and Mr. Jalal wondered whether cracks would form in the surface when his body hit the ground.

Perhaps he should go up, instead of down. Mr. Taneja's balcony overhung his own, perhaps he could pull himself up to it. Mr. Taneja, he was sure, would protect him—he had a phone, and they could call the police. That seemed to make more sense than to risk being injured in a jump to the ground. And then, as he was lying there, having the mob descend on him to finish him off.

Mr. Jalal hoisted himself onto the railing of the balcony. With one hand on the wall of the building, he balanced himself with both feet set on the railing. He called Mr. Taneja's name several times for help, but there was no response. Then, trying not to look down, and amazed he was doing this, Mr. Jalal advanced along the railing and reached towards the overhang of Mr. Taneja's balcony with his free hand.

LET ME TELL you, my little Vishnu, let me tell you a tale. A tale about the yogi-spirit Jeev born again and again and again. About how one can rise to be a Brahmin, and then fall down to the level of a monkey again.

His mother's words come down the remaining spiral of steps. Vishnu always feels sorry for Jeev in this story. He wonders if he should be careful himself, not to fall, now that he has climbed so high.

It was bad luck, really, that brought Jeev tumbling down. Though the problem also lay with the village in which he was born. A village where the castes were still very separate—not like today, here in Bombay—and Brahmins, especially, were expected to enforce all the old rules. The lowest castes were not to let their shadows fall over the path of a Brahmin, they were to carry a broom everywhere to sweep the ground clean after their feet contaminated it, and they were punished for the slightest mistake.

Jeev might not have found himself agreeing with all the rules, had he stopped to weigh their fairness or lack of it. But he followed them like everyone else in the village. They had, after all, been around for centuries—who was he, a newly realized Brahmin, to argue with such wisdom? He was expected to treat the lowest castes with rigor, to contribute to the squalor of their days. Didn't this, in fact, help them grow, prod their souls through a painful but necessary phase? A phase he must have endured himself to have reached this station, so where was the unfairness, where was the harm?

One day the village jamadarni happened to straighten herself from the gutter she was cleaning just as Jeev was walking by. Without thinking, she looked right into his face, even began to wish him good morning, before realizing what she was doing. But it was too late—several villagers had witnessed her error, and the remedy was clear—she had to be beaten. Jeev could have had her pardoned, but a beating was no great penalty, and since there had been such a clear violation, it didn't even occur to him to meddle with the established rules.

The first few blows the jamadarni bore well. But then the stick fell against her backbone in a way that made her scream out loud. And here was where luck stepped in—who should be looking down that very instant, and hear the jamadarni's cry, but the king of heaven, Indra himself.

Of course, Indra didn't intervene—the king of heaven can hardly be expected to waste his time on such trivialities. In fact, all he did was observe aloud, "Is a stick really necessary, wouldn't words have been enough?" before turning his attention to other matters. But a lesser god, hearing this, decided to try and please Indra, in the hope of being promoted. He arranged for Jeev to be reborn as a monkey, and sent to earth with the memory of his Brahminhood intact.

That's how Jeev ended up in a forest. Swinging through the trees, subsisting on whatever nuts and fruits he could find, whiling his days away in contemplation of his dramatic fall. There wasn't a breath he was able to take without being reminded of the position that had been snatched away so unfairly from him.

One morning, Jeev opened his eyes to see a mesh floating down through the air towards him. Before he could react, he was surrounded by the net. He felt his body swing through the air, and turned around to see the tree trunk just before his head smashed into it.

When he awoke, there was a leather collar around his neck, so tight he could barely breathe. Running from a loop in the collar to a peg in the ground was a rope. All around were huts and small buildings—the trees of the forest were nowhere to be seen. Jeev struggled with the clamp around his throat, but it would not come off.

"No, my little bandar. The collar is here to stay." It was Mittal, Jeev's new owner, holding one of those tiny drums that bandarwallas play. "Your only worry now is to learn to dance. Come, let me teach you."

Mittal raised the drum into the air. Ta-rap ta-rap came the sound, as the stones tied to the periphery blurred through the air and struck the drum at the ends of their strings. "Dance, bandar," Mittal commanded, and pulled forcefully on the rope, so that Jeev fell headfirst to the ground.

Jeev felt himself jerked upright repeatedly, hard enough to almost snap his neck, and then dragged to the ground again. As he tasted the mud in his mouth, resistance began to spark up within him. He was a Brahmin, not a monkey. He would not be humiliated. He would not dance. There was no other choice, really—to succumb was to accept his new lot in life and forever abandon his claim to his rightful Brahminhood.

Now Mittal was not a cruel man. But if he couldn't train Jeev to dance, to go around and beg for money from the people who stopped to watch, then neither of them would eat. So he started feeding Jeev less and less, and training him with a stick. Striking him lightly at first, but with increasing force as Jeev's obstinacy refused to soften.

As one week passed, and then another, the welts grew on Jeev's body. The sound of the drum hammered into his brain so persistently he began hearing it even when Mittal was not around. He would awake terrified at night, the sweat cold on his starved body, and the

252

sound would be there, as predictable and enclasping as the collar around his neck.

"Don't fight it, little bandar," Mittal said to him one day. "Learn to accept it." The words filtered in as if through a fog, and Jeev looked up. He trembled as he ate the banana Mittal offered him, then fell into an exhausted sleep.

He awoke to the drum rapping as usual inside his head. But the notes seemed less harsh. Their stridency was tempered now by a tunefulness he had not noticed before. Had this underlying pattern always been there, he wondered, and if so, how could he have missed it?

The sound stopped, and Jeev looked up. Mittal was staring at him, arm suspended in the air, stones still twirling around the stationary drum in his hand. Slowly, Mittal resumed rotating the drum, not taking his eyes off Jeev's face. The ta-rap ta-rap started up, and Jeev found his limbs unfurling. He felt his shoulders begin to move, his hands wave through the air, his feet slide across the ground. The rhythm tugged at his body like the strings of a puppeteer.

Once he began to dance, nothing seemed more natural. The ta-rap ta-rap awakened some primeval response in his body, some ancient consciousness in his brain. As long as the drum sounded, there was no room for thought, only motion. Under its spell, he forgot who he had been, and what he aspired to become.

The days went by, and the welts on his body began healing, then disappeared one by one. He started traveling with Mittal through villages and cities, dancing and begging for money wherever an audience could be found.

Once in a while on their journeys they would stop outside a temple. Jeev would notice a knot of priests in the audience. He would stare at the holy marks on their foreheads. Their Brahmin's threads would shimmer in the afternoon sun.

That's when Jeev would come to a halt. A gentle tug on his collar would remind him of the dance that still had to be done.

He would gaze an instant more, at the sky beyond the temple. Then the sounds would restart. His tail would loosen, his feet would begin to move. He would raise his arms and feel the rush of air through his fingers. The audience would clap, and whistle their appreciation. The priests would blend into the ribbon of faces around. Jeev would dance, oblivious to everything but the rapture of the drum.

TWO DAYS AFTER the party, Vinod mailed in his resignation from the board. He was frustrated by the continuing problem of the contractors, who by now had arrived at a coordinated strategy to slow things down whenever they wanted more money from Mrs. Bhagwati. The project had been dragging on for years before he joined, and there seemed neither doubt nor concern on the board that it would continue for another decade. He was troubled, also, by questions of his own involvement: Why was he doing this? Who were the slum-dwellers to him? Did he really feel empathy for them, or was this just activity to fill his time? Mrs. Bhagwati's offer, to which he wrote a very cordial (and separate) letter of declination, only hastened his decision to leave.

Once he was back at home, Vinod felt the loom of inertia again. There in the corner was the bed in which he lay; up above, the ceiling at which he stared; on the table, the record he would play every day. Had he done the right thing in resigning? Should he have considered Mrs. Bhagwati's offer more seriously? What did he want the remainder of his life to be?

He tried to look inward through meditation, which he had learnt in college, but never practiced since. Sitting cross-legged on the floor, he closed his eyes and concentrated on the bridge of his nose, as the guru had taught him so many years ago. He pictured the syllable *om,* and waited for its vibrations to sound silently through the passages of his body. But *om* proved elusive, flitting about unrestrained in his mind, discovering twigs and nubbles of thought on which to alight. Thoughts of Dharavi, thoughts of Mrs. Bhagwati, but mostly thoughts about Sheetal, which Vinod felt he should have long been over by now.

He decided he could no longer spend his days in the flat. He started walking to Breach Candy in the mornings, and sitting on one of the wooden benches there. There were no vendors hawking sugarcane or children riding ponies at that time. He would sit there undisturbed and if the time of the month was right, watch the tide go out in the sea behind. When the rocks were all uncovered and the water was a distant green, he would rise and walk back home. On some days, he went to the beach at Chowpatty instead, but the benches there were not as comfortable and he found the stretches of sand less interesting than the rocks at Breach Candy.

The paanwalla told him of an ashram run by a holy man in the distant suburb of Kandivili. One day, when the sun was too hot to sit outside, Vinod took the train there. A group of barefoot women clad in the white saris of widowhood were getting out of a taxi when he arrived. He followed them in through the open gate, past some gardens, to a large bungalow surrounded by mango trees. The sound of a devotional bhajan being sung came through the open door.

The women seated themselves on the floor at the edge of the gathering inside. He was about to sit behind them when someone came up and ushered him to the men's side of the room. For a while, he was thankful to be immersed in the anonymity of the singing, thankful that the people around were too engrossed to pay attention to his presence. He did not sing himself, partly because he did not know the words, but also because he felt awkward participating in such public worship. As the rhythm of the bhajan began to relax him, though, he remembered his childhood visits to Mahalakshmi, remembered the marble floor of the temple, where he would sit and sing along with his mother. Then the congregation came to their last song, and suddenly Vinod realized he knew the lyrics. *Om Jai Jagdish Hare*, he began to sing, unable to keep the words trapped inside.

Vinod started taking the train there daily, in the late morning, once the office crowds had subsided. He would sit at the back of the assembly, observing the other devotees, singing bhajans with them, but never conversing with anybody. Sometimes he spent the afternoon sitting in the verandah, watching the parrots in the mango trees lunge at the unripe fruit with their hooked red beaks. On other afternoons he remained in the bungalow after the bhajans, listening to the inspirational programs that followed. Occasionally he spent the entire day there, taking the train back only after partaking of the simple dinner of lentils and rice that was offered to all who came.

The first time Vinod had come to the ashram, he had worried about the exposés of godmen and gurus that had been appearing in the newspapers. He had read about the outrageous demands for donations, the bizarre religious philosophies preached, and the sensational rituals, even orgies, forced upon devotees. To his relief, Swamiji, as the holy man was called, did not fit the image suggested by the articles. Swamiji was a small man, perched on tiny toy legs, with a long gray beard, and a saffron-colored sheet wrapped around his loins and upper body. The overall impression projected, as he stood on the large white dais, like a candy figure decorating the top of a cake, was not of potency or stature, but comicality.

When the Swamiji spoke, however, his voice carried a calm authority that radiated from the dais and spread persuasively through the room. He began every sermon by talking about the stages of man.

"How long can man live for himself?" he would ask his audience. "How long can he allow the rule of the jungle to govern him? Plundering the pleasures he fancies, acting on every pinprick of desire, a slave to the promise of wealth, a puppet to the callings of the flesh?

"And yet. If he doesn't sate himself at this stage, he will never graduate to the next. He must drink from the pool of selfish gratification until he is sure he will be thirsty no more. Until he realizes that his body and all it desires is just maya—no more real than the reflection that stares back from that very pool from which he is drinking. It can take many lifetimes, but I have seen it done in a single existence, or even half an existence."

Vinod would watch the other followers rapt in the Swamiji's message. He himself was content just to be there, to be someone faceless in the crowd, surrounded by the tranquillity of the ashram. Swamiji's words floated in and out of his attention. He had heard this message so many times before—the maya, the illusion, that was the medium of all existence, like an endless movie in which all their lives were embedded; the journey the soul was supposed to embark on, to break free of the constraints of maya, rising through gratification, through selflessness, to the final goal which all creatures lived and died again and again for.

"And there will come a day, when all attachment is relinquished, when there is no memory of desire, of hunger, of pain, and then, only then, will he know what true freedom is."

Vinod wondered if people still went into the forest to renounce the world. He wondered if that was what the Swamiji would recommend for him. He never felt bold enough to go up to the dais. As the line of devotees filed past to touch Swamiji's small, perfectly formed feet, Vinod would stay where he was and try to make himself as inconspicuous as possible.

One day, Swamiji came up to Vinod and asked his name. "I've been seeing you day after day, sitting in the back. What have you come here for?"

Up close, the Swamiji looked much younger than the gray of his beard suggested. Vinod was flustered by the intensity in his eyes, an intensity that belied the serenity with which he spoke, and seemed to make transparent the most sheltered enclaves in Vinod's mind.

"I'm just an observer," Vinod said. "It's more peaceful than sitting at home." Then, seeing that the Swamiji's gaze was still boring into him questioningly, he added, "You don't have to worry about me. There's nothing that ails me, really, nothing that needs curing."

Swamiji did not press the matter. "I like what your name stands for. Happiness. Come sit closer to me tomorrow."

The next morning, Vinod found a place on the floor right near the dais. After his sermon, the Swamiji came up to him. "Last night, I prayed for the person you have lost," he said, as he handed Vinod his peda.

Vinod was stunned. "Do you have supernatural perception?" he asked.

Swamiji laughed. "There are no gods in this ashram. I am a man, just like you and everyone else. I do, however, notice, when someone your age comes alone so many times, and each time so sad, so empty of vinod. Though I think it is not sadness that brings you here, but anger."

"My wife passed away seventeen years ago, Swamiji. I don't think I'm sad about her any longer, and I'm certainly not angry."

"If you're not sad, and you're not angry, then you must be at peace. Are you at peace? Is that why you come here, because you're so at peace with yourself?"

Vinod was silent. The Swamiji shook his head.

"No, it's anger—anger hidden so deep you don't even recognize it. Anger that your wife has been taken away. Anger that you have been forced into this path that is not of your choosing. Anger that you were not asked to choose, though you know in your heart that if you had been, you would have chosen the easier way, not this way, my son, not this way, so full of pain, and yet reaching such heights that you have yet to see.

"Lucky are those that have no choice but to go on this path, but don't tell me you are not angry."

Vinod found the Swamiji too presumptuous. He got up and left.

FOR MANY DAYS afterwards, Vinod thought about the Swamiji's words. He looked into his heart, his mind, but could not find the anger the Swamiji had predicted would be hiding there. There was no doubt the man was very holy, but how could one single person be expected to administer to everybody, to be always right?

Then one morning, while he was listening to the record, something happened. He found he could not bear to listen to the words anymore. He lifted off the needle and set the speaker in its stand, then took the record off the spindle. He held it between the thumb and forefingers of each hand. The contact was precarious—a slight wrong movement, and the record would most certainly break on the tiled floor below. He wished a strong gust of wind would come and do the job. Perhaps he should smash the record on purpose, fling it across the room—maybe that would be the solution that would liberate him, set him free. Set him free from Sheetal.

He was surprised at this sudden thought—this idea that he still needed to be set free from Sheetal. It had been so long since he had lost her. Surely he had progressed enough since his years of grief.

Vinod twirled the record by twisting his forefinger and thumb. He felt a thrill as it spun around, as he wondered if it was going to fall. It didn't. He twirled it again. And again. And again. The record fell.

But it did not break. It wobbled around on the floor, like a giant coin spinning to rest, and stopped with the logo side up. Vinod looked down and saw the familiar red label, the dog still peering with curiosity into the gramophone horn.

He picked up the record. It did not seem to have been damaged. He rubbed it on his shirt and blew on it, then set it down on the turntable. The sound had not changed, the words came out as clearly as before. But now, with each lyric, he sensed something move inside him, some strange and alien force, like a wind changing course, or a gear shifting in machinery. He felt a void opening up where flesh and feeling had been packed in before. He felt anger, a steady, even-tempered fury, aimed at something just beyond his cognition. He felt like screaming, and did, several times, only stopping because he did not want to alarm the Jalals downstairs.

Then his rage subsided and Vinod collapsed into the chair by the gramophone. . . . *this, the night of our first union,* came the refrain as the song ended.

LATER THAT DAY, Vinod made his way down Warden Road, past the tall mute buildings facing the sea. It had been months since he had been to Breach Candy. He thought that watching the tide recede would soothe him. When he got there, however, he found that the benches had been ripped out, and a sign announcing the construction of a new park had been erected on the pavement. The water was still visible in the distance, but only through a wire fence in between.

He was about to turn back when he noticed there was a gate in the fence, and it was open. There was nobody around, so he entered through the gate and descended down the stones leading to the sea. The stones turned to rocks, and he picked his way across the slippery surfaces and the moss-green pools until he was at the water's edge, and the tide was gurgling at his feet.

Vinod squatted on his haunches and leaned his face forward over the sea. He waited for a wave to spray him with moisture. How many times, he thought, licking the salt off his lips, how many times had he and Sheetal . . .

He remembered the time they had clambered over the rocks to the furthest point they could reach on land. Sheetal put her head on his

260

shoulder and they shared a paper cone of roasted gram bought from a hawker on the shore. When the cone was empty, she smoothed out the paper and showed him how to fold it into a boat. He set it on the water and they watched it bob away on the waves.

Vinod wondered if he still remembered what Sheetal had taught him, if he could still make a boat. He searched his pockets for paper, and came up with a used envelope that had contained a bill. On the back was a shopping list he had scribbled. He tried folding the envelope into a boat, but it was too thick, and in addition, he realized he was no longer sure how to do it. His eye fell on the canceled stamps stuck to the paper—they were all quite colorful—a bird, a butterfly, and a fish.

He gazed at the water spreading into the distance, at the clouds gathering melodramatically at the horizon. He thought of Dilip Kumar standing at the banks of the Ganges, of Mohammed Rafi singing his sad song. A wave of emotion swept over him. He needed something that would float, something that wouldn't sink when he consigned it to the sea. If not a boat, perhaps just the envelope itself.

Vinod pressed the envelope against the surface of a rock and tried to smooth out as many crinkles as possible. He repeated this several times over until he was satisfied the envelope was flat enough. Then he reached down and set it on the surface of the water. The moisture crept up the paper and colored it a darker white, and Vinod shivered, as if it were his own skin against which the sea was advancing.

He watched the envelope twirl around lazily where he had released it, and then be pulled away by a retreating wave. It stopped at a rock rising out of the water, its edges catching the afternoon sun as they nudged and pushed against the outcrop. Then it cleared the obstacle and spun towards the open sea.

Vinod tracked its whiteness as it bobbed through the waves. Occasionally it would catch a crest and come closer to shore, but mostly it floated away further in the receding tide. He watched it until it was a speck in the distance, indistinguishable from the countless other specks that danced and glittered across the surface of the Arabian Sea. As he made his way home, as he climbed the steps to his flat, as he lay down that night in his bed, he imagined the envelope continuing its journey towards the horizon. The water dissolving the glue on the stamps, so that the menagerie detached itself upon arriving at the line between sky and sea. The envelope embarking on its voyage across the oceans, the fish and the bird and the butterfly floating free.

As TIME WENT by, Vinod found his anger spent. He felt a tranquillity he could not remember having experienced before. He wondered about returning to the Swamiji, but was embarrassed to do so, in light of the abrupt way he had walked off almost three years ago. He suspected, though, that he might have attained what the Swamiji had challenged him about, so he did not think it crucial to return.

Now, when Vinod tried to clear his mind, he found he could. He would concentrate on the syllable *om,* and feel the force that it embraced. He would feel the energy from the trinity that flowed through to fill all of him. He would see the universe being created in a single exhalation of Brahma's breath. He would understand the delicacy with which Vishnu balanced everything between creation and death. The physical would subside as Vishnu's cycle came to an end. The lasting resonance of the syllable would sound inside him as Shiva's sphere began to ascend.

During the day, he sat on the balcony facing the street. Sometimes he saw the bullock-pulled watermelon cart roll by. He remembered how Sheetal would whistle at the melonwalla from the balcony and haggle with him using sign language. He remembered how he ran down the stairs to get the watermelon if the transaction was successful. The cart would turn the corner, and with it, the memory would fade from his mind.

When it became dark, he ate the vegetables and three chapatis the ganga brought him for his evening meal. Sometimes he still felt hungry afterwards. When that happened, he took a biscuit from the tin he kept next to the tea things. He chewed it slowly on the balcony and listened to the sounds of the traffic at the signal downstairs.

On Sundays, he watched the worshipers congregate for mass at the church across the street. Once in a while he noticed Mr. Asrani among them. There were weddings on some days, and he looked at the young couples, so fresh and bright and innocent-looking, posing on the steps for photographs afterwards.

Mostly, though, like this afternoon, he just sat there and tried to hear the sea. Even though at fifty he was not yet an old man, he rarely left his flat anymore. He had not seen the sea for months now, not since the last time he had gone downstairs and decided to walk to Breach Candy. Instead, he would sit on the balcony, and try to remember the rocks there, remember the waves at high tide crashing along the shore, and the seagulls hovering above the foam. He would try to imagine that the occasional raindrop on his face was the spatter of sea spray, that the voice calling his name from somewhere today was the wind sweeping through the bay. Then he would close his eyes, and let the water seep out of his mind. In its place he would wait for the calmness of the sound to descend. Soon the cells in his brain would begin to light up or switch off, to form the familiar pattern, and he would transcend the limitations of the finite, of the physical and the perishable, as he lost himself in the vibrations, as he lost himself in the harmony and the eternal resonance of the beautiful sound *om*.

IT WAS ONE thing to grasp the base of Vinod Taneja's balcony. It was quite another, as Mr. Jalal learnt, to get a grip good enough to pull himself up. He tried to prod himself on by imagining the bed-room door breaking open and the crowd rushing in with their lathis. He would make quite a target, suspended between balcony and railing, every inch of his body exposed. There was only one chance he had, and that involved edging his way along the railing to the front. From there he might be able to reach up beyond the base to the bars that formed the grille of Mr. Taneja's balcony.

Mr. Jalal started inching along the metal bar, turning his feet this way and that, as if doing the twist. His hips swiveled and his buttocks swung, to give his body the momentum it needed. He danced his way along the railing, like a guest inebriated at a party responding to some particularly foolhardy dare. Once he reached the front of the balcony, he stood there panting, at the mercy of the wind. Feet perched on the railing, fingers scraping towards the overhanging balcony, body curving outwards, like a diver now, striking a pose before a jump.

He was at the moment of truth. He could not see the metal grille of the balcony above, but of course it had to be there. All he had to do was reach up on his toes and grasp it. The stone abraded his skin as he stretched up and grabbed around for the bars. He felt the tips of his fingers brush against metal. He managed to curl one index finger around a bar, but that was it. No matter how he strained, he could not get a more trustworthy grip.

Then a thought occurred to him. If he could wrap his index finger around, surely he should be able to do the same with his longer middle finger. And with the next finger as well, which was the same length as his index finger. Inspired by this logic, Mr. Jalal tried again, and was able to get not only the two extra fingers around, but the thumb and then the little finger as well.

Now that he had a grip with one hand, there was only one way to extend it to the other. Closing his eyes, Mr. Jalal propelled himself off his support, reaching up to grab the bar with his other hand. It worked—he opened his eyes to see his feet dangling over the courtyard below. Like those of a freshly hung prisoner swinging from a tree, he thought morbidly.

Only the final step remained, to pull himself up. Mr. Jalal hadn't done pull-ups since he had been in the eighth standard. He had never got very good at them, his adolescent body always flopping against the walls of the gym as he strained to drag it up. The PT master, Mr. Kola, used to go around and strike the back of the students' legs with a switch if they couldn't perform the exercise. Mr. Jalal's calves would be red and welted at the end of every PT period.

He remembered all the notes his father wrote out for him requesting he be exempted from PT. On some days, Mr. Kola would accept the notes, but on others, he would force Ahmed to run an extra lap around the field as punishment for trying to get out of PT. Mr. Jalal wished now he had not skipped any of the classes, and that Mr. Kola was there with his switch, to prompt him on to the next floor.

He struggled to bring his eyes up to the level of his hands. But he couldn't accomplish even that. He tried calling out to Mr. Taneja again, but his upstairs neighbor still did not come. Mr. Taneja, he knew, liked to sit in the other balcony, the one that faced the street. He had often seen him there from downstairs, head tilted back against his chair, eyes closed, lost either to sleep or to thought. He imagined his cries reaching through the upstairs flat and rousing his neighbor. Mr. Taneja's hands appearing like miracles from the air above, to powerfully grab hold of his own, and pull him effortlessly to safety. Perhaps Mr. Taneja would insist they have tea together on his balcony, while they waited for the police. They would chat about this and that, and Mr. Jalal would nibble on a biscuit, waiting for the opportunity to slip in some detail of the message he was trying to spread. Surely Mr. Taneja, with his superior education and background, would be easier to convince than the people from downstairs clamoring so irrationally for his blood.

But no magical hands appeared in front of Mr. Jalal. Perhaps, if he couldn't lift himself up, he should go back to his other option, of jumping down. But to do that, he should be hanging from the railing of his own balcony, not Mr. Taneja's, since the current position just added another floor to his fall. Now that he had launched himself off, how would he reverse the maneuvers that had left him suspended here? Mr. Jalal tried swinging his feet to reestablish contact with the railing, but all they touched was air.

He was stuck. It would just be a matter of time before they broke down the door and found him there, like some insect stretched out in a web. Maybe he could plead with them. The cigarettewalla seemed a little more level-headed than the others, maybe he was the one to appeal to.

What had happened to Arifa? He hoped she was not badly hurt, that they had not directed their anger on her when they couldn't get him. How attentively she had listened to everything he'd said earlier when they had lain together in bed. He had thought he was converting her, not realizing her attentiveness had been driven by skepticism, by guile. She had tried to find inconsistencies in his story, to listen for discrepancies that would prove him wrong. He had been surprised, but heartened at this reversal of roles. Arifa, his wife, finally learning to use his own weapons against him.

She had gone through so much at his hands. He was suddenly overcome with guilt—he had not been a good husband. Or perhaps he had just not been the *right* husband. Someone suitably matched, who could appreciate—who *deserved*—her innocence, her unspoiledness.

And what about Salim? Had he failed him as well? Had he been inadequate as a husband *and* a father? Mr. Jalal hung from the balcony and took stock of his parenting years. There had been a distance he had felt from the start, a removal from the day-to-day upbringing of his son. Why couldn't he have involved himself more? Learnt the names of Salim's friends, gone to his cricket and soccer games, sat with him when he did his homework, not let all the years go by? Why had he allowed aloofness to become the hallmark of their interaction? He supposed he could always lay the blame on his own relationship with his father. That would be the traditional Freudian theory, wouldn't it—a bit crude in this day and age, but surely still valid. There must have been so many other theories proposed over the years—but was there anything really startlingly new, anything that wasn't just a refinement of the original idea? Mr. Jalal resolved to try and keep better abreast of things.

Getting back to Salim, though, what was the mystery of the dupatta, and why did the people outside insist on linking his son with the Asranis' daughter?

And even more bewildering, how could they possibly imagine that he, Ahmed, was somehow involved, and what exactly was he supposed to have done?

A sparrow tried to alight on his hair, and Mr. Jalal bobbed his head instinctively to prevent it from landing.

It was all so sad. He was sure that in a less agitated setting, they could have all sat down and led themselves, step by step, to the answers that would have explained everything. The electrician's outburst about the Gita was particularly unfortunate. Mr. Jalal tried to remember what he could from the book. Didn't it teach that it was impossible to kill someone? That one was just reincarnated into another life, the choice of which depended on the deeds one performed in this existence? He wondered how that would apply to his situation. It was obvious the mob wanted him dead. Which in a way might be good, since martyrdom seemed the most reliable way to amass a following. He could plunge to his death below, and still come back. Surely his sacrifice would assure him rebirth in at least a comparable situation. He might even be able to take up his message where he had left it. Though there would be the problem of age— who would keep his following alive while he was growing up?

The sparrow returned, and Mr. Jalal shook his head again, more emphatically this time, to scare it away.

Perhaps that was what he should do. Allow himself to be killed by the mob, so that he could prove his integrity. It didn't appear he was going to have much of a say in the matter anyway. He imagined the door finally bursting open, to reveal the crazed faces on the other side. "There he is," the paanwalla says, and the crowd streams in and packs the balcony. He actually manages to dodge the first blow, but the second one knocks out both his arms. He hangs for an instant suspended in midair, looking up one last time for Mr. Taneja. Then the floors begin to pass before his eyes, Mrs. Asrani and Mrs. Pathak wave at him as he sails by, and he hears himself hit the courtyard on his back. Even as the faces two stories above fade out of focus, he makes out with satisfaction the guilt that begins to bloom across them.

Yes, that should be his strategy. All he had to do was hold on until they finally tore down the door. When they saw what they had done, saw his blood reddening the cement for their benefit, realization would strike them. He would be no more, but his message would ring accusingly in their ears. They would be forced to follow it, if only out of guilt. Perhaps they would even build a shrine for him, to mark the very spot where he would take his last breath.

The thought buoyed Mr. Jalal's spirits. Why was it taking them so long? he wondered. He could hear shouts and thuds, but the door was still unbreached. What kind of mob was this anyway, that it couldn't defeat a simple bolt?

Suddenly Mr. Jalal felt a sharp nip between the thumb and index finger of his right hand, a nip that almost made him let go his hold. He looked up and saw a flutter of brown feathers. It was the sparrow, its tail sticking out above the overhang. Was this a conspiracy—first people, now birds—was he to be attacked by locusts next? Didn't the sparrow have anything better to do than go after him?

The feathers jerked upwards, and he braced himself for another bite. The pain pierced all the way to the bone this time. Mr. Jalal screamed, a scream made more intense with a rage-filled desire to drive the bird away. But the sparrow remained unmoved. It resumed its exploration, pecking at the knuckles, jabbing at the fingers, savaging the skin and the fleshy parts, as if the back of his hand was a treasure field that had to be plowed up with its beak.

In a fit of fury, Mr. Jalal grabbed at the bird, actually managing to pluck out some of its feathers as it took to the air. But on their way down, his fingers clawed past the bar and were unable to regain their grasp. Suddenly the ground appeared where the sky had been, and a clump of feathers floated by his face. Then, as he swung one-handedly above the courtyard, the sparrow dove defiantly past his forehead and flew away.

Mr. Jalal steadied himself as best as he could. He tried not to think of the metal digging into his fingers, or the stone overhang scraping the skin off his wrist. It was fortunate he had been fasting so long, and was thus better able to support his weight. There was not much longer he would have to wait anyway, they should be coming through the door any minute. Surely his destiny was to hang long enough to attain martyrdom at the hands of the crowd. Wasn't that the reason he had ended up on this balcony, alone and at their mercy? Instead of choosing the one in the other bedroom, the one with people available below and Mr. Taneja waiting above to rescue him? Faith, as they said, could move mountains, and now he himself had acquired a share. His fingers would maintain their grasp, his body would remain aloft, as long as he held on to his faith.

It was so ironic. The reason all these people were after him was that he had experienced a vision from the Gita. From *their* holy book. What perverse pattern of logic could possibly have equated this with blasphemy in their minds? Mr. Jalal swayed in solemn contemplation from his bar. How long ago had it been since he had last read the Gita? Ten years? Maybe more? Wasn't it amazing that something he had read so many years ago should remain buried in his subconscious, to emerge suddenly in a dream?

Mr. Jalal stopped swaying. What was he thinking? It hadn't been a dream at all. It was a vision, a revelation, from Vishnu himself. His perusal of the book had nothing to do with it.

Or did it? Wasn't it true that once something entered the brain, it always remained there? Dormant, perhaps, but never without the possibility of being rejuvenated? Wasn't it well known that people had memories that cropped up from nowhere, spoke languages they had only heard, never learned, had nightmares of long-forgotten incidents that had occurred when they were children? Had he completely forgotten *The Interpretation of Dreams*? What would be so unusual about such a vivid scene tucking itself away in some secluded crevice of his brain, biding its time cozily until an opportunity to spring out presented itself?

No, he was getting it wrong again. Images floating up from the subconscious were never as pointed, as purposeful, as his vision had been. He had to be vigilant now, not to revert to his former self. One could tear apart any experience, no matter how insistent or inspiring, if one unleashed the ravenous hounds of skepticism. He would not let them out again, not this time. He had come to this juncture based on his experience, based on the faith he had felt budding inside. That same faith that protected his grip on the bar, that was preventing him this very second from hurtling to the ground below. This was his destiny in life, to be a leader, a prophet. He would not allow his destiny to be subverted by his skepticism.

But did this destiny make any sense? To sacrifice his life in the hope he could have another? What kind of insane gamble was that? It was one thing to believe, to have an open mind, but had he gone completely crazy? Why was he so eager to abandon everything he had ever absorbed, to repudiate his years of scholarship, of scrutiny? What good was his faith anyway, if it was only supporting him long enough to see him struck down to his death? Wouldn't he be better served hanging on to his life, rather than hanging on to such faith?

Mr. Jalal felt his grip begin to falter. It was the doubt, of course, lubricating his fingers insidiously, so they began to slip. There seemed no way out—the courtyard waited patiently below in either case, whether he chose to bolster his faith or ignore it. At least if he chose the first path, he could be a martyr, rather than just an outline on the cement below. But perhaps his choice no longer mattered. Perhaps he had gone too far, perhaps gravity had grown tired of being tempted by his dangling body. He felt his fingers begin to unravel. One by one, they started losing their contact with the bar, and he found himself grasping at the metal, then at the stone, then just at air.

There was a crash, as the door in the bedroom finally gave. Then Mr. Jalal felt his body fall, as voluptuously as a jackfruit from a tree, and the ground came up with astonishing speed to greet him.

VISHNU CLIMBS THE steps as he has climbed steps all his life. Even though he cannot feel the stone underneath. He raises one leg, then the other, mounting the stairs one by one, as if gravity still had a hold on him. This is the last flight he will mount before he becomes a god, he thinks, so he will perform the act as a human would. As an exorcism of his mortality, a farewell to his physical being.

He can feel his expectation rising as he approaches the top. What will he find? Will there be a cluster of gods behind the terrace door? All gathered there already, monitoring each stair he ascends, waiting to celebrate his arrival in their midst? He hears them applaud as he mounts the final step. Is that Shiva taking off his crown and polishing it on his sleeve? Brahma placing it on Vishnu's head and slapping him on the back? He feels an elephant trunk wrap around and lift his body high above the cheering gods—it is Ganesh, twirling him into the air. There are monkeys swiveling by their tails around the antennas, Hanuman swings from pole to pole in their midst. And that tune he hears above the clapping and the dancing—could that be Krishna, playing his solitary flute somewhere?

Only one god does not take part in the festivity—Vishnu sees him all dressed in red and green, standing apart from the rest. The god nods gravely, and raises his mace in greeting, but Vishnu does not recognize him.

But enough, he thinks, enough of these gods. Surely Lakshmi must be here in their midst as well. His eyes scan the crowd with excitement, impatience. Where is his Radha, he wonders, his Ambika, his Rukmini? His everlasting love, his eternal other half, who gives him sustenance, without whom he is not complete?

One by one the divine bodies separate, and he sees her features emerge. Like the moon from behind parting clouds, like the stars after a rain. She walks towards him, her body wet from the Ganges, flowers garlanding her bosom, perfumes rising from her skin. She reaches all four of her hands out—he finds, magically, that he can take each one of hers in one of his own.

He feels her fingers rub against his. Not the human sense of feeling, that he no longer possesses, but a deeper, more profound contact—what souls would experience when they caressed, were they composed of skin and flesh. Her arms draw his body close to hers, and the feeling spreads down his chest, his stomach, his groin, to wherever they make contact. Buds open and turn into fruit between them, rivulets of milk slide over their skin. He sees fields of mustard sprouting from the ground around, their yellow heads rising towards the sun. She touches her lips to his: he tastes the lushness of forests, the sweetness of springs. He looks into the face with which he has journeyed through so many lives—he is part of her, and she is part of him.

His body enters hers. It is like the earth opening to admit him. He finds himself carried away, up snowy Himalayan slopes, through valleys of teak and pine, down streams of ice-clear water that surge into the Ganges. Onward and inward he plunges, his thoughts overcome by sensation, his feeling and emotion coalescing, until only a single knot of energy remains. Energy trapped between their bodies, energy that dances and crackles, like electricity arcing through a filament, like sun rays trapped in crystal. He feels himself pulled in further, feels the energy seal him in, his body becoming one with hers, united with a cohesion so strong it is painful. For an instant, he has a clear look at her face: lips together in a half-smile, dew adorning the corners of closed eyes. Then the explosion arrives, their bodies fly apart into stars, stars that streak through the heavens, and populate the furthest reaches of the universe.

"In every life they live," he hears his mother say, "in every avatar they assume, they will find each other and be united, again and again."

But he is still on the steps. His Lakshmi is up there somewhere, waiting to ignite with him, but only if he is a god, not if he is a man.

God or man, god or man, the question strikes up in his mind with each step he takes. He has already been through this over and over again. All the magic of his ascent—what will possibly explain his powers if it turns out he is a man?

Suddenly, an answer comes to him, an answer that stops him in midstep. What if he is dying? What if these new abilities are not powers, but symptoms—symptoms of death? What if he is climbing, not to immortality, but to nothingness? The steps spiraling out in front of him—so few that he can almost count them—what if this is all that remains between him and the end? He imagines reaching the top and opening the door, stepping out to the terrace, and finding all the gods have vanished. All except the solitary red-and-green-decked figure, standing by the parapet. The figure turns around and beckons to him with its mace. Recognition comes with a shock—it is Yama, the god of death.

Vishnu stares up at the terrace door. It is open a crack—is there someone behind it, peering down at him? He wonders if he should try to go back, descend to his landing, try to reclaim his body, rewind the movie of his life. Or should he keep climbing, throw open the terrace door, boldly deal with whatever lies behind? He looks down the stairs he has just ascended—they seem strangely disorienting, listing before his eyes, rolling into the dark. He has climbed too far, he has worked too hard—there can be no return.

Perhaps the answer is to not let his mind waver, to fix it on the immortality he has been promised. Even if it does turn out to be Yama behind the door, what, really, has he lost? Does he enjoy his current existence so much that he cannot bear to give it up? Is the plot of this life so compelling that he will not exchange it for another?

He resumes his ascent. Shutting out the sound of "God or man, god or man," that still echoes with each step. Instead, he lets his mother's words fill his mind.

"One day my Vishnu will find his Lakshmi, and Garuda the eagle will appear to fly them to Vaikuntha."

He imagines opening the terrace door just as Garuda is alighting from the sky. The sun's rays splash like liquid gold off Garuda's head, they glance off his neck and sluice across his feathers. On his back, attached with strands of velvet, is the chariot in which they will be carried away.

Garuda nuzzles Lakshmi's head with his own, then bends so she can climb into the chariot. Lakshmi waves to Vishnu from the chariot, and he runs across the terrace to join her. But before he can get there, his path is blocked by Yama's mace.

"Not so fast, my friend," Yama says, and thrusts his mace at Vishnu. Vishnu feints, he dodges, but Yama seems to be everywhere.

"Time to rest," Yama says, and waves the mace in Vishnu's face. All at once, Vishnu feels his alertness begin to wane.

"Sleep, my friend," Yama says, his voice sounding far away.

Vishnu knows he must keep awake, he must not fall to Yama. He looks around for the chariot, but Lakshmi and Garuda have flown away. What did his mother say, how can he bring them back, how will he get to the paradise of Vaikuntha? He concentrates on her voice again, but the words she says are not the same.

"When the age of Kaliyuga is drawing to a close, then my little Vishnu will take a rest."

This is not the message he wants. He tries to retune his mother's voice, but the signals he receives remain the same.

"Ananta the snake will rise from the sea, and on his endless coils will my Vishnu rest his head."

Vishnu takes another step. He imagines the walls getting covered with scales around him, the stone turning soft and fleshy under his feet, as if it is the body of a living thing. He looks at the staircase. It is rising and dipping before him, like the coils of some fantastic being.

"The sun will go down and the seas will die as Vishnu closes his eyes."

He tries to negotiate the rearing segments, but loses his balance and falls. Drowsiness moves in swiftly to overcome him.

"Sleep will engulf my Vishnu, as time comes to an end."

The buckling has stopped, the stairs are uncoiling smoothly under him. His body is rocked gently by the undulations passing beneath. He turns around and looks with half-closed eyes at the door looming ahead. He tries to drag his body to it, up the three or four steps that are left.

"For eons will he sleep on Ananta, regaining all his strength. Only opening his eyes when it is time to begin the cycle again."

Vishnu knows the time for the great sleep is here. He is almost at the door, separated only by two steps. He can still crawl up, he thinks, he can still look through. All he has to do is cross the threshold to attain all the powers that await. But he is so tired. The last thing he notices is an ant emerge from a crack in front of his face and begin to crawl up the step leading to the terrace. Then all sound dies down, the lights dim, and as his eyes close, he thinks that a movie is about to start.

CHAPTER FIFTEEN

"FINALLY HERE, SEE it now," the man is saying. "So many decades in the making, *The Death of Vishnu.*" The man is standing on a chair in front of the ticket booth at Metro Cinema, next to the large "House Full" sign. Moviegoers are milling all over the place. Lines of people are stretching from the advance booking booth, they are snaking as far as the train station at Marine Lines.

"Better than *Bobby,* bigger than *Sholay,* see it now, *The Death of Vishnu.*" Touts are black-marketing balcony tickets. Already the price has climbed to twenty-five rupees. Someone has extra tickets, and a fight breaks out as the crowd surges to get them.

"Amitabh Bachchan as Vishnu, Reshma as Padmini, see it now, *The Death of Vishnu.*"

Vishnu takes the tickets out of his pocket. Where is Padmini? He told her to be here at 6:30 P.M. Now they're going to miss the advertisements, which Vishnu likes so much.

"Hear the music by Laxmikant Pyarelal. See the killer dance by Helen. Snap your fingers to the number one hit 'I am Vishnu, king of the universe.' See it now or wait till you can get the tickets, *The Death of Vishnu.*"

Padmini pushes through the people. She is breathless. Vishnu watches the gold-colored necklace resting on her bosom rise and fall as she inhales and exhales.

"Sorry I'm late." She brushes off the dress she's wearing, as if it were covered with dust. "Mai, what a crowd. How did you ever get the tickets?"

As they go through the entrance of the theater, she puts her hand on his. "Finally, a proper theater," she says.

Vishnu buys her a cold drink and a samosa. She eats the crisp part first, then the potatoes. "Ooo, nice and spicy," she says, pulling out a whole chili from the filling and putting it in her mouth.

The movie starts. Vishnu's mother comes on the screen. They are in their hut together, and she is singing a song to him, about the games he will play when he meets the baby Krishna. Suddenly, a storm breaks out, and lightning and thunder and rain start lashing the hut. The door opens, and lightning crackles as Vishnu's father walks in. It is Pran, the villain, his eyes red and bloodshot, the muscles in his jaw twitching, his lips set in a thin, cruel line.

"Oh, ma," Padmini says, and draws closer to Vishnu in her seat.

Vishnu can feel her hands gripping his arm as the Holi scene appears on the screen. He sees himself singing and dancing as he plays Holi with his mother. The screen fills with color, and then shifts to his father drinking bhang. Padmini's leg rests next to his, and he detects a tremble running through it.

Slowly, Vishnu puts an arm around her chair, then raises it so that it barely brushes the nape of her neck. She is too absorbed in the movie and does not notice. He lets his arm ease around her neck. Her cheek brushes against his shoulder. She nibbles the last of her samosa, the empty wrapper clutched between her fingers in her lap.

Kavita is played by a newcomer, Usha Bahaduri. Vishnu likes her very much. During the Divali song on the staircase, when Usha climbs up and down with phuljadis in her hands, he starts clapping his hands along with the music, as others are doing in the audience. Padmini looks at him disapprovingly.

But then Reshma, playing Padmini, comes on the screen, and Padmini sits back in her seat. "She should have lost some weight for the role," she sniffs to Vishnu, "though her acting, thank God, has improved." There are several songs that Reshma sings, and this makes Padmini happy.

"Do you think she's doing me justice?" she asks with concern during the interval, and Vishnu assures her she is.

"She'll get a *Filmfare* award, you just wait and see," he says.

Padmini asks Vishnu to buy her an ice cream, so they go to the lobby. He leaves her by the cardboard cutout of Reshma and Amitabh, but when he comes back with an orange bar, she is no longer there. She returns a few minutes later, her face flushed. "I went to see what the ladies' room looks like. Do you know they have those English-type seats there?"

Padmini takes the wrapper off her orange bar. "Let's go see the balcony," she says. Vishnu follows her up the stairs, into the dress circle. Padmini looks down at the screen, then turns to look up at the rows stretching all the way to the top. "It's so nice up here," she says. "These seats must cost a lot more." She licks her bar wistfully.

The movie starts again, and Vishnu is engrossed by the love triangle Kavita finds herself in. Tears come to his eyes as Kavita bends down next to him on the landing and bids him farewell. He tries not to let Padmini see that he is crying.

There is another song, in a flashback sequence of Padmini and him in Mr. Jalal's car, driving along Marine Drive. They go to Hanging Gardens and the love scene in the car follows. "Chhee!" Padmini says, averting her head, as Vishnu appears entwined with her on the screen.

The story progresses and Vishnu sees himself ascending the steps.

He wishes the movie would be more clear about what he is climbing towards. Whether he is the god Vishnu, or just an ordinary man. He is almost at the terrace door when Padmini gets up suddenly, excusing herself to go to the ladies' room. Vishnu feels like warning her to wait, they are near the climax, the movie is almost over.

The terrace door opens. Vishnu leans forward in his seat. He has not seen this part, he does not know what comes next. He wishes Padmini was watching with him. But her seat is empty. He looks at the seat on the other side, and that is unoccupied as well. He looks around, and row after row stares emptily at the screen.

Vishnu gets up. He is the only one left in the theater. The light from the projector strikes the top of his head and creates a void that stretches all the way down the picture. He walks towards the screen, and the shadow gets lower and smaller, until it is just a thumbprint at the bottom. He climbs the steps leading up to the stage. The movie continues in the empty auditorium, a succession of unseen images flashing through the dark.

Vishnu walks across to the center of the stage, then turns to face the projector. The screen is a giant lit field extending above and around him. He tries to see the seats, but the light from the projector is too strong. For all he knows, they may be filled again, Padmini and the rest of the audience getting ready to applaud as he takes his final bow.

He looks hard at the light. For an instant, he imagines the screen stretching out across the sky above the terrace. Then the image vaporizes in the blaze of the projector. He wonders what makes the light so strong. Why can he just see white when he looks into it? Where are the greens and reds that dance across his clothes? He looks at his body—it is drenched in color. His arms, his hands, his legs, are luminous, brilliant. He feels the brilliance being absorbed through his skin, saturating his flesh, flowing through his blood all the way to his fingertips. He starts radiating brilliance himself. Brilliance that illuminates each row of empty seats, brilliance that paints each wall a blinding white, brilliance that turns the curtains into sheets of light. As Vishnu watches, the entire theater becomes incandescent. He looks down at himself, but he can no longer tell where the light ends and his body begins.

THE FIRST THING that struck him about heaven was the whiteness of it all. The ceiling was white, the walls were white, there were white curtains that shimmered in the breeze. It made sense, of course—white was the color of unbroken light—it symbolized a purity, a wholeness, an unblemishedness, and wasn't that what heaven was supposed to be all about? Even the sunlight streaming in seemed so much whiter now—could this be because heaven was situated somewhere closer to the sun?

So he had done it, Mr. Jalal thought. He had attained martyrdom, attained sainthood. He wondered what they must be doing down on earth. Had they rallied yet around his message, around Vishnu? Or were they still gathered around the corpse he had left behind, cursing their blindness, praying for redemption, straining to touch his face, his feet, any part of his holy body? Perhaps the cigarettewalla, or even the paanwalla, would take up his baton, be the new leader, spread the word. Mr. Jalal felt he should forgive all his tormentors, harbor no animosity in his heart. This was the proper attitude to adopt, now that he was in heaven.

How relieved he felt to have made the right choice. For even though he had not managed to hang on, even though he hadn't actually been *beaten* off the balcony as planned, he *had* made the effort. What counted was that at the instant he fell, the correct thought had been dominant in his brain.

Or had it? Hadn't he wavered, hadn't doubt clouded up in his mind at the end? It was so hard to remember. Surrounded as he was now by this whiteness, this serenity, though, could things have really not worked out well?

He wondered if he should get up and explore heaven. On earth, he had never allowed himself to believe in it, but had heard people make all sorts of claims about it. It would be interesting to see if any of them were true—the pearly gates, the gold spires, the rivers of milk—probably none of these existed. What would be nice, though, would be a TV room, through which residents could monitor the progress of things on earth.

He sat up and took a deep breath of the fresh heavenly air. Why did it smell of disinfectant? And was that the sound of car horns he heard through the window? And what were those casts doing on his legs? Suddenly Mr. Jalal started noticing a number of incongruities—the cupboard filled with jars and bottles, the blood pressure gauge on the table, the bedpan by the door. And the white apparitions gliding through the corridor outside—the ones he had thought might be ghosts—weren't those nurses' uniforms they were wearing?

"How do you feel?" One of the apparitions had walked in the door and was taking his pulse. "You were quite lucky—jumping like that and breaking so little."

"Where am I?" Mr. Jalal managed to say.

"Bhatia Hospital. Your wife's on the next floor."

"My wife?"

"They're trying to do the best they can." The apparition's eyes narrowed and it looked at him with a hardness he found flustering. "Someone hit her quite hard, you know."

"What do you mean?"

"She may have bled inside."

The apparition put a pill in his mouth and a glass of water in his hand. "The police are waiting to record your statement, once the doctor has seen you," it said, swishing briskly out the door.

Mr. Jalal sat on the bed with the glass in his hand. The insistent note of a truck horn blared from the road below. He noticed the tat-

281

tered border of the curtain, the dust on the windowpane, the buildings lined up stolidly against the cloudless sky beyond. He had not died. He was not a martyr. This was not heaven. He tried to make sense out of what the nurse had said. Why had all this happened? Was it all a result of undertaking his quest? Could this all be part of a test, part of the penance expected from him? Was this the price tag that accompanied faith?

But Arifa? What had she ever done—why was she the one being made to pay? He wondered what was going to happen to her, what he was going to say to the police, what they would do to him. Would he tell them about Vishnu? Would he tell them about his vision? Was his faith strong enough to convince them? To convince himself?

The pill began to dissolve in his mouth, and Mr. Jalal tasted the bitterness seeping into his tongue. Wasn't medicine, ultimately, a matter of faith? Faith that the doctors knew what they were diagnosing, faith that their prescriptions would make you whole, faith that the tablet dissolving in your mouth would cure you, not kill you. Weren't entire hospitals built on faith? The floors that supported the beds, the walls that held up the floors, the bricks and mortar and cement that composed the walls. And the patients sitting on the beds, clutching at their sheets and their blankets, shivering as the medicines entered their bodies, wondering what the pills were supposed to cure.

For the second time that day, Mr. Jalal felt himself falling. But this time, there was no courtyard to break his fall, no ground to separate him from the blackness that opened below.

This is the house she grew up in, this is the house she has returned to now.
Who will dry the tears as her feet carry her back over the threshold?

Kavita tried to remember the lines of the song. Was it Nutan or Meena Kumari who sang it? She could see the film now, the young widow turned out of her dead husband's house, forced to make her lonely way back to the village where she was born.

Of course, Salim wasn't dead. Just incompatible. This much was clear after the night she'd spent with him. What a place to take her to, the waiting room at Victoria Terminus. At three o'clock in the morning, when the first train out to Jhansi wasn't until six. Couldn't they have just left later, she had asked, trying to make herself comfortable amidst the crowd of humanity. Especially the crying babies. Kavita had looked at their mother, a young Muslim girl in a burkha, not much older than herself, and shuddered.

And Jhansi? What kind of destination was that to elope to? *Jhansi?* All it was famous for was the Rani of Jhansi, but that had been in the previous century—or had it been the century before that even? Here she had been having visions of Kulu or Simla or Darjeeling, all places she'd dreamt about going, and to campaign for which she'd certainly dropped enough hints the last few weeks. But Salim had called these choices impractical, saying Jhansi was where he had a good friend, with whom he could start a car repair business.

Didn't people drive cars in other parts of the country, she had felt like pointing out. And a *car repair* business? All that grime and that grease and that oil—is that what she'd be looking forward to smelling every evening?

"But I love cars," Salim had said, and Kavita had tried to console herself with the idea that cars were bigger and more important machines than Voltas pumps.

The girl in the burkha was having trouble feeding her infant, with a second child sleeping in her lap and another crying loudly next to her. She looked at Kavita helplessly, but Kavita looked away, staring instead at the announcement board with the names of the trains. But then the girl leaned forward and tapped Kavita on the knee, requesting her to take the sleeping baby from her while she fed the youngest one, and Kavita had no choice but to agree. She accepted the baby with a forced smile, and held its body awkwardly in her lap, wondering if it was sufficiently well insulated against leaks. Imagine traveling in a second-class compartment, that too, to *Jhansi*, in a soiled dress.

Meanwhile, the oldest child was still crying, so the mother asked him to go stand next to aunty. Kavita felt her face turn red. She had never been called that before. She felt like protesting—she wasn't old enough, thank you, to be *anyone's* aunty. The boy came over, sniveling, and with the fingers of one hand in his mouth. He brushed up right next to her, and Kavita felt herself surrounded by an overpowering baby smell, tinged with traces of urine and vomit. The boy suddenly took the fingers out of his mouth and draped that arm around her neck, and Kavita tried not to imagine the saliva dripping down her dupatta.

"He likes you," the mother said. "See, he's stopped crying already. Say hello to aunty, Ijaaz." The baby suckling at her breast made a gurgling sound. "Newly wedded, aren't you? You'll learn soon enough how to hold a baby properly, don't worry."

The girl smiled, and Kavita noticed the two chipped teeth in the front row of her mouth.

"Where are you going?" the girl asked.

"Jhansi," Kavita replied.

"Jhansi? But that's where we're headed. It's a wonderful town. Not so big and noisy like Bombay, no big buildings and film industry. Much more quiet.

"I was born here, but I had all three of them once I moved to Jhansi. One after another, phut-phut. You'll see." The girl giggled.

"Maybe we can sit together on the train—my husband doesn't like me to travel by myself."

Just then, Salim came back from the ticket station. "You look so motherly with them," he said, seeing Kavita with the baby in her lap and the boy clinging to her side.

First auntyhood, now motherhood. This was too much to bear for one night. "Here, you hold them," she said, thrusting the children at Salim. "I need to go to the ladies' room."

They made it as far as Nasik. The girl with the children found seats with them and Kavita fumed the entire way at having to suffer the ignominy of an *unreserved* second-class compartment. At Nasik, she issued Salim an ultimatum. Either they traveled in first class or she was getting off and taking the next train back to Bombay.

"And of course, whatever Daddy's spoilt little brat wants, Daddy's spoilt little brat gets," Salim said.

"You're crazy if you think I'm going to live with a car mechanic the rest of my life."

"Don't talk to your husband that way," the girl, wide-eyed, admonished her.

"He's not my husband," she replied. That shut the girl up.

As Kavita stepped out of the train, she hoped Salim would relent and follow her. She hoped, as the whistle blew and the engine started up, that he would come to the door at the last minute and throw himself onto the platform for her love. Then she would consider taking him back—but only under some conditions—no Jhansi and no mechanic business. But the engine gathered speed, and the compartments started whizzing by, and she wasn't even able to tell which compartment had been theirs. For a second, she was struck with panic at having left her luggage in the train, before remembering she wasn't traveling with any. Then thick, dark smoke started billowing out of the engine, the compartments disappeared one by one into a tunnel, and the only sign remaining of the train was the acrid taste left behind in the air.

Now here she was, back at her building again. She couldn't believe it had been only fourteen hours since she had left. The question was, how was she going to explain that absence to her parents?

And more important, how was she going to explain her decision to them? Her decision not to marry Salim *or* Pran.

No, she was going to become a film star. A heroine. A glamour queen. No one man could hope to possess her, only long after her on the screen. Her life would be one of the fabulous ones she read about in *Stardust*, in *Filmfare*.

"Kavita memsahib? You?" she suddenly heard. She looked up to see the cigarettewalla gaping at her as she passed by his shop.

"Of course it's me. Whom were you expecting? Meena Kumari?" Kavita said, as she began mounting the steps.

THE POLICE INSPECTOR stared at Mrs. Asrani.

"You mean you've been here all day, and you haven't heard a thing?"

"No," Mrs. Asrani said, and winced because it came out more forcefully than she had wanted. The trick was to just say it without any sign of nervousness. "No," she said again, more calmly this time, "I've been watching the cricket test match on TV since morning."

"So you don't know, for instance, that Mrs. Jalal was taken to the hospital in a coma, or that Mr. Jalal broke both legs from a fall into your courtyard?" The inspector emphasized the word "your."

"Are they okay?" Now Mrs. Asrani's voice carried neighborly concern, the precise amount that would behoove someone living one floor down.

"Mr. Jalal—he'll live," the inspector said. "But his wife—we don't know yet how serious it is."

"That's terrible." Mrs. Asrani felt guilty about all the ill will she had directed towards Mrs. Jalal. She hoped none of this would boomerang back on her. She had not asked for this, she silently reminded whoever or whatever might be listening—even a bruise here or there would have sufficed as far as she had been concerned.

"Where is your daughter, Mrs. Asrani?"

"She's asleep. Why?"

"Not a cricket fan, I see."

"Only when certain cricketers are playing."

"Could you wake her up, please?"

"Is that really necessary? She's only a child."

"I understand she's—" The inspector consulted his notes. "I understand she's eighteen and a half. Do you consider that a child?"

Mrs. Asrani tried to peer into the inspector's notebook, to see what else was written there, but the inspector shielded his book and looked at her sternly.

"I'll go get my daughter."

Kavita was sitting in her room, her face ashen, when Mrs. Asrani unlocked the door and walked in.

"You can't keep me prisoner here. I'm an adult now. I'll tell the inspector. I won't be forced into marrying Pran. I've already told you I want to become a film star. Why don't you listen to me? Why don't you ever let me do what I want?"

"Now look here, you disobedient girl. You're in a lot of trouble already. Mr. Jalal tried to kill Mrs. Jalal because you ran away with his son. Then he tried to commit suicide himself. Almost succeeded. And all because of *you*. Whom are you going to kill next with your waywardness, your mother and father?"

Kavita started sobbing.

"You listen to me now. If you don't want to end up in jail. If you ever want to be able to show your face outside again. You tell the inspector you were here last night. *All* of last night. It's what the cigarettewalla and the paanwalla have already said. They're doing their best to stop the scandal from spreading. For *our* sake. For *your* sake. And remember, you don't know anything about the Jalals. Understand?"

"But I *wasn't* here. I was with *Salim*. He'll tell them that when he comes back, when they ask him. We'll be in trouble—the police will come and arrest us."

"What will they do, arrest the whole building? What is the word of one Salim-valim, compared to all of us put together? Whom do you think they're going to believe?"

"But the truth will come out."

"What truth? I just told you, the truth is you've been here all along. And you don't know anything else. Now you get that into your head, if you ever want to show your face in public again. Sneaking out God knows where in the middle of the night." Mrs. Asrani checked herself. She took a deep breath.

"I told the inspector you were asleep." Mrs. Asrani wiped Kavita's eyes dry. "Try to look as if you've got up from sleeping, not from crying."

When Mrs. Asrani returned to the door with Kavita, she found the inspector at the entrance to the Pathaks' flat, interviewing Mrs. Pathak. Who, coincidentally, had also been watching the test match since morning.

"And your husband?" the inspector asked.

"Oh, he's a complete fanatic," Mrs. Pathak said, fingering the necklace she had hastily put on over her house clothes when she had seen the inspector through the keyhole. "He hasn't even gone downstairs since the match started—not even to the cigarettewalla, believe it or not—that's why we have no idea what happened. It's impossible to pry him away from the TV, even though ordinarily on Sunday mornings he goes to the temple. Cricket before God, I guess." Mrs. Pathak raised her shoulders helplessly to the inspector, who did not smile.

"Should I get him for you?"

"No, that won't be necessary."

The inspector turned to Kavita. "And you, miss, have you been watching cricket as well?"

This was it. It was her chance to *act*. She would prove to her mother that she was a natural, a born actress, who should not be kept from her calling.

Kavita yawned. She stretched her neck, and languorously brushed her fingers against her lashes. "I've been asleep," she said, running her fingers through her hair and yawning again, giving a picture-perfect performance of One Who Has Just Awoken.

"And why are you so sleepy, miss?, Were you away doing something last night?"

"No, I've been here, at home. Where would I go?"

"Mr. Jalal says your dupatta was left behind on the landing last night."

Now it was time for One Who Has Just Experienced Shock. Kavita's eyes expanded in astonishment, until they were the size of four-anna coins. Her mouth opened to the perfect aperture of surprise mixed in with dismay. Her hands fluttered agitatedly, but uselessly, by her side.

"Why in the world would he say that?"

"That's not all," the inspector said, looking hard at Kavita, then Mrs. Asrani, then Mrs. Pathak. He had been saving the mention of Mr. Jalal's version of events until now. "Mr. Jalal also says that a mob including the cigarettewalla and the paanwalla and the electrician broke into his flat to question him about *your* whereabouts. They hit his wife on the head with a lathi, then threw him off the balcony."

Kavita was trying to decide on the next vignette in her performance when her mother burst in. "See this? See how they lie? Forever their son has been an eve-teaser after my daughter, and now these stories. I ask you, inspector, is it fair? Is it fair to ruin my poor girl's name, to implicate her in this mud?"

Encouraged by the inspector's silence, Mrs. Asrani continued.

"Day by day that man has been getting worse, and nobody did anything. 'Take him to a hospital, before he does something,' I told Mrs. Jalal, but who is she to listen? Now that the fruit they have got is rotten, look how they're trying to dump it in other people's plate. Look how they're trying to drag us all in. And the poor cigarettewalla and

289

paanwalla—if they hadn't responded to Mrs. Jalal's screams, if it hadn't been for them bursting in, I'm sure he would have finished her off."

Kavita began to say something, but her mother still wasn't finished. "Just one thing I want now, and that is not to let my daughter's name get mixed in with all this. Just now only the proposal has come for her marriage—and now this. Do you have daughters, inspector sahib, that you know how easily their reputations can be ruined?"

The inspector said he was unmarried. He had written down everything Mrs. Asrani had related. "And you, Mrs. Pathak, do you also think Mr. Jalal has been acting crazy?"

"The ganga woke us up this morning. Told us to come downstairs. It was Mr. Jalal. Sleeping next to Vishnu, can you believe it? All night he must have spent there, instead of in his flat. When he wakes up, he claims we should worship Vishnu because he's the real Lord Vishnu descended to earth. Then he grabs my arm as if he's going to molest me. With my husband watching, no less. If that's not crazy, I don't know what is."

"This Vishnu person—is he the one lying dead on your steps?"

"Dead?"

"We've radioed for the morgue van to come take him away. How long has he been dead, do you think?"

"He was alive yesterday . . ." Mrs. Asrani ventured.

"And today, when we went down and Mr. Jalal was sleeping there. I thought he must have been alive then," Mrs. Pathak said. "Though I didn't check his pulse."

"Yesterday evening when we returned—he must have been alive then, wasn't he, beti?" Mrs. Asrani asked her daughter.

Kavita did not reply. So it had happened. He had died, as she had worried he would. She wanted to grieve, she wanted to cry, but why were her eyes suddenly so dry?

"Did you know him well?" the inspector asked.

"Very well." Mrs. Asrani shook her head mournfully. "I used to bring him tea every morning. My family depended on him, we really did—in fact, Kavita grew up playing with him. We're going to miss him—a lot. In fact—"

"Actually, inspector, we knew him better," Mrs. Pathak interjected. "I used to feed him chapatis every day. He was like a family member to us. The same food I used to cook for my own family, I used to feed him also—"

"Yes, yes, but three days late. When they were hard as rocks, were her chapatis. In fact, I'm sure if you ask a doctor to do a postmortem, he would say that's what made him sick—he'd find a big undigested chapati piece stuck in his bowel—"

"Excuse me, but we *did* bring in a doctor. And we were the ones who paid for him, too, I will have you know. Not anyone else who is claiming to be so close and dear to Vishnu now, just to impress the inspector—"

"You liar. Didn't we pay half of that useless ambulancewalla your husband insisted be called? More than a hundred rupees we paid for that, and for what, I ask?"

The inspector held up his hand. "Do either of you know who his next of kin might be?"

"Maybe the ganga does. She'll be here tomorrow morning."

"Then tell her she's to come to the police station. Any other information you can give me?" the inspector asked.

No one said anything, so he examined the notes in his book. "There's a lot of discrepancy here with what Mr. Jalal says," he said, looking up thoughtfully. "Which could become quite important," he paused and eyed everyone in turn, "in the event his wife dies."

He shut his notebook with a snap, as if he had just trapped an insect between its covers. "Well, your statements have all been recorded—I'll have them typed and ready to sign by tomorrow." He put an elastic band around the notebook. "Of course, we'll locate the son and see if he has any more relevant information." He slid the notebook into his shirt pocket. "Now if there's nothing else—"

"Wait," Kavita said, "I have something to add. About Vishnu." This was it. The Sad Scene. It was her chance to prove herself. She had to produce a tear, it was the least she could do for poor Vishnu. "When I was little," she said, trying to think of the games they used to play.

Her mother recovered from her look of alarm, and bulged her eyes warningly. Kavita ignored her.

"When I was little," she tried again, and the inspector put his pencil to his lips and regarded her gravely. Why was it so hard to conjure up those images of firecrackers, of phuljadis?

"When I was little," she began a third time, and this time, she felt it. The moisture welling up in the corner of her eye. Growing, coalescing, trembling—and then, when her lashes could support it no more, rolling. Rolling from the cup of her eyelid, rolling over the rise of her cheek, rolling across the lush sweep of her face, like condensation tracing down the skin of an apple, like a rivulet of morning dew. Each drop radiant with the glow of her youth, each tear a pearl around a grain of her sorrow.

Kavita raised her face to her mother, she raised it to Mrs. Pathak, to the inspector; and as the sun shone in over the landing, she felt its energy glistening in her cheeks, its warmth caressing her face.

CHAPTER SIXTEEN

AFTER THE LIGHT comes darkness. Someone is playing a flute. It is so sweet, it makes Vishnu want to cry. He follows the strands of sound, they guide him like a rope through the darkness.

He feels the trees before he sees them. Twigs brush against his face, fallen leaves rustle under his feet. The branches above sweep over his head as he walks past, like giant hands reaching down unseen to bless him.

The darkness fades, and he sees the mist of a forest. Gradually, that clears as well, and the trees, green and stately, come into focus.

Through the trees, he sees the boy. Beyond lies the meadow, a hut in the forefront, cows grazing on the grass behind. The boy is hiding behind a tree, watching a woman churn milk. As Vishnu comes up behind him, the boy turns.

"Shhh!" he whispers, a finger to his lips, and Vishnu sees that the color of his skin is tinged blue. Vishnu creeps up beside him and they watch the woman together. She is singing a song, as she pulls the rope attached to the churn, first with the left hand, then with the right, in a rhythm that matches the tune.

The boy looks at Vishnu. "Are you ready?" he asks. Before Vishnu can answer, the boy is off, running towards the woman. In one speedy bound, he reaches her, and knocks over the churn. Milk splashes onto the grass, a white sheet that spreads over the green. The woman screams as the milk cascades over her feet. The boy dips his hand into the churn, and runs back to the trees as fast as he went.

"Wait till I tell Yashoda!" the woman calls out after him.

Vishnu sees something white and creamy in the boy's palm. The boy holds it out to him. Vishnu looks at it, but doesn't move.

"Don't you want any?" the boy asks, plunging a finger across his palm and licking it clean. Vishnu does the same—it is butter. But butter so smooth and rich, such as he has never tasted before. They eat the butter, fingerful by fingerful, and then the boy licks his palm clean.

"Would you like to play with me in the forest?" the boy asks. Then he frolics into the trees. Vishnu looks after him for an instant, then runs in behind.

VISHNU HAS BEEN sleeping in the forest, tired from all the play with the boy. A melody awakens him—it is the flute again, as agonizing as before. He rises and follows the sound—it leads him deeper and deeper into the forest.

He comes to a clearing. There stands the boy with the blue skin, his eyes closed, one leg bent at the knee, so that the tip of one foot touches the heel of the other. He is the one playing the flute, on his face is a look of rapture, so intense that Vishnu wonders if he is in pain.

He stands near the boy and listens to him play. The notes continue for a while, then stop. The boy opens his eyes.

"Who are you?" Vishnu asks, but the boy does not reply.

"Are you Krishna?"

The boy smiles. "You know who I am," he says.

The boy raises the flute. "You must be tired. Tonight I will play for you. Tonight, you can rest." He puts the flute to his mouth.

"And tomorrow?" Vishnu asks.

"Tomorrow, you go back," the boy says, and Vishnu hears the notes start up again.

Acknowledgments

There are several people I wish to thank. My family and friends for their support and encouragement and their comments on various drafts of the manuscript. Richard McCann, Matthew Specktor, and Rosemary Zurlo-Cuva for the interest they took and the guidance they provided at crucial junctures. Michael Cunningham for a life-changing workshop at the Fine Arts Work Center in Provincetown. S. Siddarth and Devdutt Pattanaik for sharing with me their knowledge of Hinduism and Hindu mythology. My editor, Jill Bialosky, for all her feedback and her support of the book (and its author). My agent, Nicole Aragi, for being the best agent a writer could hope for. Larry Cole, above all, for making everything possible in so many fundamental ways.

Sections of this book were written during residencies at the Virgina Center for the Creative Arts and the MacDowell Colony. Their support is gratefully acknowledged, as is that of the Jenny McKean Moore Fund at George Washington University.

Notes and Glossary

amavas: day with a moonless night, considered inauspicious by many

Ambassador: traditional Indian automobile

Ambika: goddess of mangoes, one of Lakshmi's forms

Ananta: "the endless one," the snake on whose coils Vishnu rests and goes to sleep as the universe comes to an end

anna: coin, one-sixteenth the value of a rupee

Arjun: one of the Pandava brothers, a key figure in the Mahabharata and the *Bhagavad-Gita*

attar: perfume

avatar: an incarnation of a god or goddess

Bakr-Eid: Muslim festival with a goat being traditionally sacrificed

bandar: monkey

banyan: large, spreading fig-like tree

barfi: diamond-shaped sweet dessert, with an ultra-thin layer of silver foil on the top

bechara: poor fellow

beedi: type of inexpensive Indian cigarette

Benarisi sari: one of the most expensive types of saris, from Benares

beta: son (also used to address boys who are not necessarily one's own child)

beti: daughter (also used to address girls who are not necessarily one's own child)

Bhagavad-Gita: one of the holiest Hindu texts, where Krishna, disguised as a charioteer, explains the goals of human existence to Arjun

bhajan: Hindu devotional song

bhajia: vegetable fritters (same as pakoras)

bhang: intoxicant, sometimes mixed with milk for consumption

Brahma: part of the primary Hindu trinity of gods, the creator, who breathes out the universe to make it come into existence

Brahmin: highest (priestly) caste

brinjal: eggplant

burkha: full-cover robe or dress worn by Muslim women who maintain purda, the screening of women's bodies from public observation

chaat: spicy-sweet snacks, usually flavored with tamarind chutney

chameli: jasmine

chapati: tortilla-like whole wheat bread

charpoy: cot

dacoit: bandit

dacoity: criminal activities of dacoits

dharma: sacred duty

dhobi: person who washes clothes

Divali: Hindu festival of lights celebrated with fireworks; the start of the Hindu new year, and the night the goddess Lakshmi descends to earth

dupatta: a woman's long scarf, usually worn with a salwar kameez

fakir: holy man

Ganesh: elephant god

ganga: female servant who performs domestic chores for several households

Garuda: gold-colored mythical eagle who carries Vishnu and Lakshmi to Vaikuntha, their heaven in the sky

ghat: flat area like a river bank; also a place where cremations are performed

ghee: clarified butter, used as a cooking medium

ghungroo: anklet festooned with bells

golgappa: popular snack item, bought from street vendors—a kind of chaat

gulab jamun: dessert of fried cheese balls in golden syrup

gunghat: veil, often the end of a sari draped over the head

gur: soft, unrefined sugar

halwai: maker and vendor of sweet desserts and snacks

Hanuman: monkey god

Holi: Hindu festival during which people are playfully doused with brightly colored powders

Indra: god of the heavens, comparable to Zeus

Irani hotels: old-fashioned tea shops started by Iranis who immigrated to Bombay in the 1920s and 1930s

jackfruit: large, heavy, intensely sweet tropical fruit

jamadarni: sweeper, cleaner of toilets

jambul: tree with small purple fruit

jee or ji: suffix added to a name to show respect, sometimes used by itself

kadai: wok-like cooking vessel

Kaliyuga: the current age we live in, which is the last of the four eras of this universe; this is the age when goodness disappears from the world and the universe is slowly inhaled back into Brahma's nostrils (before the cycle can begin again)

Kalki: Vishnu's final incarnation, and also the name of the white horse he will ride when he descends to earth to eradicate evil and end the current cycle of existence

karma: actions and deeds that will lead to consequences in this or future lifetimes

Krishna: one of the most revered of Hindu deities, celebrated both for his mischievous love of life and his divine power and wisdom; an incarnation of Vishnu, who as Arjun's charioteer in the *Bhagavad-Gita* reveals himself as God

kulfi: ice cream made with boiled milk

kurta: tunic-like man's shirt

laddoo: round, yellow walnut-sized confection, used as a ceremonial dessert

Lakshmi: goddess of fortune, consort of Vishnu, who accompanies him from incarnation to incarnation in her many forms

lathi: long piece of bamboo, usually used as a weapon

loban: a type of aromatic resinous wood

maharaja: provincial king; also the cartoon mascot of Air India

mandap: wedding platform

masala: spice mixture

masjid: mosque

Matsya: Vishnu's first incarnation, a fish that instructed Manu to save humanity by building a ship; Matsya towed the ship to safety when the deluge came

maya: the illusion that characterizes all transitory existence in Hindu philosophy, with only the spirit being permanent

mela: a fair

mem: a white memsahib

memsahib: a form of address used for higher-ranking or higher-class women; also, a general reference to such a woman

Muharram: Muslim holy day to commemorate the martyrdom of Prophet Muhammad's grandson Hussain in the battle of Karbala

mullah: Muslim religious man

namaste: greeting performed with folded hands, a hello

namaz: prayer performed by Muslims five times each day

nazar: curse or spell, evil eye

om: sacred syllable used in meditation, which combines the spiritual energy of Brahma, Vishnu, and Shiva

paan: chew made of betel leaf wrapped around spices and other ingredients

paisa (plural: paise): coin, one-hundredth the value of a rupee

pakoras: deep-fried fritters made with gram flour

paneer: homemade Indian cheese

papdi: puffy wafer used to make golgappa

paratha: pita-like bread, but without a pocket

pataka: firecracker

peda: a milk-and-sugar sweet, usually in the form of a yellow disc

phuljadi: sparkler

pista: pistachio

pomfret: flat diamond-shaped fish, prized for its texture and taste

Radha: incarnation of Lakshmi as Krishna's beloved milkmaid

Rama: an incarnation of Vishnu; the leading character in the Ramayana

Ramzan: the Muslim fasting month (Ramadan)

roza: daily fast during Ramzan

Rukhmini: incarnation of Lakshmi as Krishna's wife

rupee: primary unit of Indian currency

sadhu: Hindu holy man

sahib: a form of address used for higher-ranking or higher-class men; also, a general reference to such a man

salaam: formal salutation

salwar kameez: long tunic (kameez) and loose pants (salwar) worn by women of north Indian origin

samosa: deep-fried triangular Indian snack of dough stuffed with spiced vegetables

Saraswati: goddess of the arts, consort of Brahma

Shiva: part of the primary Hindu trinity of gods, the destroyer. Unlike Vishnu, Shiva (being an ascetic) prefers to distance himself from the world, and it is this lack of action that causes the universe's cycle to wind down

shrimati: wife

tamasha: fuss, spectacle

thali: round metal tray used to serve food

tiffin: stacking containers used to carry prepared food

trinity: Brahma, Vishnu, and Shiva. These are not separate gods but three faces of the same god, which is why the Hindu trinity is called "Trimurti" (three forms)

tulsi: basil

Varuna: god of the ocean

Vishnu: part of the primary Hindu trinity of gods, the preserver or caretaker of the universe, who must balance everything that exists, and whose constant action (karma) keeps everything running; worshipped in many forms all over India, especially as Rama and Krishna

walla: suffix meaning "one associated with," as in paanwalla (one who sells paan) or radiowalla (the one with the radio)

yogi: one who practices prolonged yoga or asceticism to gain control over the body and mind

About the author

About the book

Insights,
Interviews
& More . . .

Read on

About the author

Meet Manil Suri

Marion Ettlinger

MANIL SURI, a native of Mumbai (formerly Bombay), has lived in the United States since 1979. He is a professor of mathematics at the University of Maryland, Baltimore County. His fiction has appeared in *The New Yorker*. *The Death of Vishnu*, a nominee for the PEN/Faulkner Award, is his first novel.

Journal
Adventures of a Mathematician on a Book Tour

BOMBAY, DECEMBER 9, 2000

I sit on a dirty ledge and gesticulate as instructed at the Kemp's Corner flyover behind. Cars whiz by inches from my dangling legs. "Smile," the photographer from *India Today* magazine instructs, and I smile. "Wider," he says, and I break into a full-toothed grin. "Like you're having fun," he adds, "like you really mean it."

Unfortunately, I have not yet learned the art of smiling. I try to conjure up images of film stars and Colgate commercials, but all I can focus on are the contortions I have been forced to pose through in the last hour. I think of the string of photographers I have already disappointed. Perhaps they should give smiling lessons to prospective authors.

"A little more naturally," the photographer suggests, as a truck rumbles by and spews black smoke into my eyes and smiling mouth.

NEW DELHI, JANUARY 5, 2001

The first official day of my Indian book tour. Penguin India has set me up in a room at the Ambassador Hotel. I have seven interviews scheduled today, each lasting about an hour.

My cousin Sheena bustles in to say hello before the interviews start. She has been head housekeeper at other hotels for many years, and the room immediately meets with her disapproval. She terrorizes a passing maid into making my bed and refilling the complimentary bar. "Don't you know you have a famous author staying here?" she shouts into the phone as she bullies the front desk into sending up a "complimentary" fruit basket. I wonder how I will be able to show my face at checkout.

The reporter from *The Telegraph* comes in first. "I hope you don't mind, but I brought a photographer along." Almost all the interviewers do. By the end of the day, I am so used to smiling I have to remind myself not to do so at strangers in the street.

The questions begin to repeat themselves very quickly. I try pretending that I'm helping a succession of students during office hours. "Why did a mathematician start writing?" "Do you see a connection between your mathematics and your fiction?" "Will you give up being a professor, now that you're a writer?"

The last is the most insistent of all—people demand to exercise their God-given right to know—in interviews, at book signings, over dinner, over drinks. For the next several weeks I will repeat again and again that I don't think so, and my response will become as mindless as a morning ablution.

NEW DELHI, JANUARY 6, 2001

Vishnu is officially introduced to the world. There is an evening reading at the Habitat Centre to launch the book. My uncles and aunts and extended family are all there—in fact they seem to constitute a third of the audience. In their honor, I decide to end the reading with a sex scene. To my disappointment, they only squirm a little. "Will you give up being a professor, now that you're a writer?" several of my cousins ask.

That evening, I am interviewed on Star TV, on the nationwide nightly news hour. The last time I appeared on a TV screen was when, as a graduate teaching assistant, my calculus discussion section was videotaped for evaluation purposes. It had been a truly harrowing experience to be forced afterward to watch myself fumble on the screen. I am relieved to see that this time my coat and tie make me quite presentable. Even dashing, I think.

NEW DELHI, JANUARY 7, 2001

Kusum auntie calls me up in the morning to tell me that she saw me on TV last night, and why did I let them use so much makeup on my face? She is unconvinced when I protest there was no makeup. "Next time, tell them to use less lipstick," she insists. Sheena phones me later and assures me that it wasn't the makeup, but my entire face, "especially the lip and chin part," which seemed strangely elongated. ▶

3

Journal *(continued)*

On the plane to Bombay, I am surrounded by people reading the Sunday newspapers, a number of which contain my photograph accompanying an interview or review. I am apprehensive that somebody will recognize me. No one does, and my apprehension turns to consternation, then depression. Out of desperation, I tell the lady next to me that there is an awful photo of me in the *Times of India* she is reading. She turns to the article, seems unimpressed, and doesn't talk to me for the rest of the flight.

BOMBAY, JANUARY 8, 2001

They have put up a giant painted billboard outside Crossword bookstore to announce my reading. My mother attends, as does Sheena's sister Sunilla, who covers her mouth and laughs nervously and pretends (for my benefit, bless her heart) to be embarrassed by the racy parts. Mr. Bhatia, my tenth-standard-class teacher, is there, and announces to the gathering that he had always been struck by my "shy and quiet nature" as a student. He is making this up—some years ago, when I met him at a classmate's wedding, he told me that neither my face nor my name rang a bell.

At the reading at the U.S. Culture Center, my old principal, Father Demello, attends. I almost don't read the bedroom scene, but then decide, *What the hell?*

BALTIMORE, JANUARY 24, 2001

The official release date of my book in the U.S. My first radio interview is on *The Marc Steiner Show.* It is live, and a listener calls in. He accuses me of coming from a country whose justice system is based on the "idolatry" of Hinduism. I tell him that India is a secular country, and its justice system is actually inherited from the British. He is not satisfied, and begins to talk agitatedly about monotheism and Judeo-Christian values. The station gently cuts him off.

Later, Steiner announces they have a final caller. I brace myself, but it turns out to be a familiar voice—Freeman Hrabowski, the president of my university. We chat about writing about India even though I don't live there, and how the distance has helped.

Steiner says he has one last question, and asks me if I'm going to stop teaching.

Surely there's only one way I can answer that question if my president is listening, I reply.

TIMONIUM, MARYLAND, JANUARY 24, 2001

My inaugural U.S. reading is in a suburb north of Baltimore. Fortunately, a respectable crowd awaits me—there is a generous representation from the mathematics and statistics department. The reading goes well—so what if the questions afterward are predictable? I realize this just makes it easier to have funny answers prepared. Over the next three weeks, I will perform my shtick nineteen times in all. It's a little like delivering the same calculus lecture every semester—except it's nightly.

Afterward, someone asks my graduate student Alix if I'm funny in class as well. "No," she says quite emphatically, and the other students shake their heads as well. They're right—for some reason, I'm horribly serious while teaching. This somehow feels different, liberating—as if I'm assuming an identity or playing a role. The department chairman sends me an e-mail wishing me all success, but adding that he flinches a bit in saying that, for fear of losing me. I assure him that after three weeks of touring, I'll be ready to do mathematics again.

PHILADELPHIA, JANUARY 25, 2001

This is the home of SIAM, the Society for Industrial and Applied Mathematics. A contingent of four comes to hear me read and take me to lunch afterward. One of them is Ivar Stakgold, who has interviewed me for the latest issue of *SIAM News*. In 1984, Ivar (a well-respected mathematician and also a well-known bridge player) came to UMBC to give a seminar. Afterward, a senior member of my faculty pulled me aside and said that, even though it wasn't his field, he knew that Ivar's lecture could not have been very good, since people who wasted their time on other activities could not possibly do good mathematical research. That's when I knew that if I wanted tenure, I would have to keep my writing secret.

Over the years, I became more keenly aware of this one-track mentality. I remember a junior colleague complaining about another professor's excellent teaching evaluations with, "Does he ever do any research?" Or a fellow grantee at a contractors' meeting of the Air Force Office of Scientific Research commenting about a mutual acquaintance ▶

who had just received a teaching-related grant, "This tells me his research must be going down the tube."

For years, my writing has been a secret rebellion against this attitude. Now, however, I am a tenured full professor. My author photo is splashed across the front page of *SIAM News*. I am irreversibly out of the closet.

Incidentally, I find I am not the only one. After reading the SIAM interview, two professors in my department confess they have a secret passion as well—acting, it turns out, for both of them. One extracts a promise that I will get him a role if my book is ever turned into a movie.

BOSTON, JANUARY 26, 2001

Several friends attend my event. All through my reading, I keep wondering whom I will have a drink with later. Unfortunately, while I am signing books, everyone assumes I will be too busy to do anything with them afterward and leaves! As I stare alone at the TV in my hotel room at 9:30 on a Friday night, I wonder if this is what I have to look forward to for the next several evenings.

SEATTLE, FEBRUARY 6, 2001

My reading is packed, as some others have been before. I am still amazed that people will actually pay money to buy and read something I have written. Very different from publishing a mathematical paper, I think, where it's the author who is expected to contribute toward publishing costs, and where anything with more than twenty readers would probably be a "bestseller."

LOS ANGELES, FEBRUARY 9, 2001

During the reading, I mention that my mother loved the first chapter, but complained that the second was not as funny. An older woman at the back of the audience announces that she hated the first chapter, and rebukes me for creating characters that she found unsympathetic. She starts getting quite animated, upset even, and I am at a loss to understand what exactly in the book has provoked her.

People sometimes ask if I would like to teach creative writing. This woman illustrates why my answer is no. It's so much simpler to teach mathematics, where dissenting opinions are irrelevant and only one answer (usually the professor's—i.e., *mine*) is correct.

DETROIT, FEBRUARY 13, 2001

It's 10:30 p.m., and I have a 6:00 a.m. flight tomorrow. I get to the hotel, make my way to room 315, and stop. The door looks unfamiliar—wasn't 315 the room number in Portland? It must be 815, I think—and go to the eighth floor. Except that's what the room number was in Minneapolis. My key is of no help, because it has only a magnetic strip, not a number. I go to the ninth floor, but that was San Francisco, so I come back to the elevator. As I stand there, wondering whether to go up or down, I resolve to write down the number when I check into my hotel in Houston tomorrow.

Before giving up and asking at the front desk, I try one last time. The number 321 flashes into my mind, so I tiptoe to it, and insert the card into the slot—gently, so as not to alarm anyone inside if this is the wrong room. The light turns green. I'm in!

As I try to fall asleep that night, I am reminded of *The New Yorker* cartoon of the finger sitting upright in bed and saying "Where the hell am I?" Below is the caption, "The moving finger writes; and, having writ, moves on to a three-week, twenty-city book tour."

SILVER SPRING, MARYLAND, FEBRUARY 16, 2001

I've done it. Survived the American book tour, reputedly the most notorious of all. It's wonderful to be at home. I sit at my breakfast table and read the *Washington Post*. I eat eggs the way I like them, scrambled with tarragon. I sip tea from my favorite cup, the one given to me by my Taiwanese graduate student twelve years ago.

The phone rings. It is Katie Collins, the publicist for my publisher in England. She's glad I'm back, glad I'm enjoying my tea and scrambled eggs. Would I be ready by Friday to leave for my three-week six-country European book tour? ∽

First published in slightly different form in The Chronicle of Higher Education.

A Conversation
with Manil Suri

The following excerpted interview, conducted for National Public Radio's Fresh Air *by Terry Gross, aired February 5, 2001, and is used by permission of National Public Radio.*

TERRY GROSS: *Would you describe the character of Vishnu, who's living on the landing of the staircase in this apartment building.*

MANIL SURI: Yeah, Vishnu was a real person, I should say in the beginning. He was someone who was a fixture of my childhood. He would always be on the stairs. He lived on this landing between the ground and the first floor. And he would always say "Salaam" to me. He would often be drunk. He would run errands for people in the building and they couldn't pay him too much because he would just spend it on drinks.

GROSS: *Now is this kind of typical in apartment buildings in Bombay where you grew up, that someone would be living in the landing of the staircase?*

SURI: Yes, it was. Space is at such a premium in Bombay that every little scrap of space is important. Someone like Vishnu would be better off than someone truly on the street, where the monsoons would rain down upon them.

GROSS: *So and was it also typical that they would do odd jobs in return for living on that staircase?*

SURI: It was more like they did the jobs for the inhabitants and were paid for that. And what happened was that there was this symbiosis between them because the people lived on the

66 Vishnu was a real person . . . a fixture of my childhood. He would always be on the stairs. He lived on this landing between the ground and the first floor. And he would always say 'Salaam' to me. He would often be drunk. 99

stairs, and as a result people, robbers, could not come up and rob the apartments. And, of course, they performed errands for the inhabitants as well, and in return they got shelter and sometimes food and money.

GROSS: *Now your book is, in part, about the death of this character. How did the real Vishnu die?*

SURI: Well, I went back home in '94, and Vishnu was very sick. And he was on the steps and I remember someone left a cup of tea for him, and that was untouched. And I was actually not well that time—I had chicken pox—and my mother started giving me reports about his condition. And it only took about two days or something and she was telling me that the police just came and took his body away.

GROSS: *Now the main character in your novel is named Vishnu, and that's the same name as the god Vishnu. What is he the god of?*

SURI: He's the god of preservation. Vishnu is the caretaker of the universe. And it was very interesting, when I started this, I started it as a short story, and I wrote the first chapter and didn't really even think that there's a similarity between Vishnu the caretaker of the building and Vishnu the preserver of the universe. And someone pointed out to me, "Wait a second, you can't write a story, have your main character named Vishnu and not say anything about the god Vishnu." I didn't know that much about Hindu mythology—I hadn't read *The Bhagavad-Gita*— so I started looking at these things and trying to see if there were any dramatic possibilities in them which could somehow be woven into the story.

GROSS: *Now you were brought up Hindu, even though you thought of yourself as an agnostic. Were your parents religious?*

SURI: My father is a very religious Hindu. He actually makes sure that he goes to a church and a mosque and everything to cover all bases. My mother is actually a Sikh. I was brought up Hindu, and then I forget if I was fourteen or fifteen or sixteen or older, but I decided I had to rebel somehow, so religion was one way that I did it, and I just said, "I'm going to become an atheist." And then perhaps the mathematician in me said, "Well, that's not quite fair. Maybe that's too harsh. So let's be an agnostic." That tempers things a little. And that's how I came to writing this novel. At that stage I was an agnostic, and reading these texts was initially a purely intellectual exercise. ▶

A Conversation with Manil Suri *(continued)*

GROSS: *And it became something else?*

SURI: It did, I think. I just feel that my life has changed in many ways. Just the kinds of goals that one tries to aspire toward and the ideals that one has, they have changed.

GROSS: *How?*

SURI: Well, I'll give you one example. Before reading *The Bhagavad-Gita*, I was very obsessed with getting published. I'd tried for many years, and the only thing I had to show for that was one very short thing called "The Tyranny of Vegetables," and that was in Bulgarian. It wasn't even in English. And I couldn't show it to anyone. I didn't even know the name of the journal it was in, because I couldn't read it. It was in Cyrillic.

So after that, after reading this, I just sort of said, "Well, wait a second. I've been sending things out and I've got fifty or sixty rejection letters. Let me just work on this, which is very enjoyable—work on this novel and try to finish it and not worry about what happens afterward."

GROSS: *Now the cliché would be that the math part of your personality is the very rational part and the writer part of your personality is the more intuitive, dreamy part. Would that just be a cliché, or is there any truth to that?*

SURI: I think in math, too, you have to let your mind sort of wander. When I am trying to prove a theorem, for instance, I really have to let go and just let my mind float around and try to maybe even rifle through all the theorems or all the results that I have experienced—I've seen. And it's almost by fluke that sometimes you happen to come upon the right thing. And that process is similar in writing, where you just let your mind wander again and try to come up with characters or situations or ways to resolve different settings.

GROSS: *Now you're doing that kind of high-level math that most people who aren't mathematicians don't really understand. Can you tell us something that will give us an insight into the kind of math that you do?*

SURI: Oh, I'd be happy to fill the rest of the hour with that, if you'd like. I keep threatening people in the publishing business that I'm going to give them a lecture complete with slides and everything, and no one's taken me up on my offer yet. But the kind of math that I do is very applied. I work with engineers. Engineers, especially in mechanical engineering or structural analysis, often come up with very complicated sets of equations which they need to solve to make sure that the components they're designing are strong enough to withstand stresses.

And what my field does is it looks at the methods of approximating these equations that these engineers come up with, abstracts them and analyzes them to see if they do work, if they do work in all possible settings, and gives them some reassurance or validation that their methods are accurate, or if they're not accurate what kinds of errors they can get. It's called numerical analysis.

GROSS: *Now is it a relief, in a way, to work in literature where like the worst thing that can go wrong is that it's dull, but there isn't going to be like a building that collapses?*

SURI: Well, mathematicians like to claim that everything revolves around them, that if some disaster occurs, it's due to the mathematician. But it's usually the engineer who has to shoulder that responsibility. So there is quite a bit of freedom in the abstractions that mathematicians play with. So that wasn't so much of the relief. The relief was that you have much fewer constraints in fiction. You can really take your characters anywhere, pretty much. I mean, you can define them to be anything. In mathematics, since I do applied mathematics, I do have to look at the physical problem and obey the laws of physics and I'm constrained in that way.

There is a branch mathematics called pure mathematics where, again, people start with some assumptions and then just build a theory based on that.

GROSS: *Okay. Well, that's enough about the math, isn't it?*

SURI: Oh, I don't think so.

[...]

GROSS: *Would you describe the neighborhood that you grew up in Bombay.*

SURI: Well, I grew up in one room of a large apartment, and we were the only Hindu family. There were three Muslim families living in different rooms of this apartment. We shared a kitchen with one family. There were some common toilets at the end of the flat. My parents still live there, so a few weeks ago, when I went back, that's where I stayed. Downstairs there's a whole bunch of shops, which have changed somewhat over the years. ▶

A Conversation with Manil Suri *(continued)*

While I was growing up, there was a man who sold paan, a betel nut confection. There was a cigarettewalla, a man who sells cigarettes. The cigarettewalla now has expanded his tiny stall into a giant store, and he's even torn down the wall behind the landing where Vishnu lived and somehow managed to find a way to get into his storeroom that way.

And then there used to be a shop that rented out bicycles that now sells cellular phones.

GROSS: *So you and your parents shared one room?*

SURI: Yes, we did. It was a large room, but it was shared. And people sometimes ask me if I could have written this book in India, and it would have been very difficult, because that's where I might still be staying and there would still be the fights with the neighbors and so on.

GROSS: *What kind of privacy did you or your parents have, sharing one room together?*

SURI: Not much. And every time I go back, it's quite startling. Because in Maryland I live in this house and, you know, there are two bathrooms and I have my own room and everything. And then I'm somehow deposited in this—really it's like a fishbowl, because my parents haven't seen me for a while and they're just always talking to me, and so on, which is great, but certainly privacy is not what I go back for.

GROSS: *What kind of conflicts did your family have with the other families that they shared the apartment with?*

SURI: Oh, just about every kind. You name it. It's just so hard to have a common kitchen. The further complication was that that family was actually the landlord of the entire apartment, so we couldn't really—you know, we always had this worry that, "Well, will we be evicted?" or something like that. So the ones that I remember, there used to be one tank that would feed water to all the families, and that tank usually ran out by noontime or something, and so there were always accusations of the form, "Well, you took an extra bath," "No, you did," and things like that.

GROSS: *You moved to America in 1979 to go to college. You were twenty at the time. What were your first impressions of America? What did you find most wonderful and most disturbing about it?*

12

SURI: Well, the first thing I wanted to do was eat a Big Mac.

GROSS: *Why? What had you heard about it?*

SURI: I'd just seen so much about it, and I, you know, went down to the McDonald's and ordered my first Big Mac and it was great seeing everything on it, and it was awful. It tasted horrible. I couldn't believe it. So in some ways I thought that I knew pretty much everything about America, because I'd seen so many Hollywood films, I'd read so many books; I'd read *Mad* magazine. I'd read Archie comics. And so it was all very familiar, actually. And I just felt myself fitting in. I didn't like Big Macs I found out, but so what.

GROSS: *So what were the movies that really formed your impressions of America before you got here?*

SURI: Oh, there were too many to relate. I mean, I'd had a steady diet of them for I don't know how many years. What was interesting was when I came here, there were all these movies that had been banned in India, so for the first year or so I was just catching up, like *Last Tango in Paris* and even the uncensored *Godfather*. And there were just so many movies.

GROSS: *Was there much sex or violence in Indian cinema?*

SURI: No, not at all. In fact, the classical thing is that, up until recently, in Indian movies, when two people wanted to kiss, when the hero kissed the heroine, they'd duck behind a tree so that you wouldn't see them kissing. And then they came out sort of wiping their lips to show that they'd just kissed.

GROSS: *Now how did that approach to not showing any kind of physical encounter affect your approach to writing your novel?*

SURI: Oh, well, I had to do just the opposite. I had to make sure that I had lots of sex and so on.

GROSS: *Manil Suri, I thank you so much for talking with us.*

SURI: Thank you for having me. ❧

Excerpted interview content denoted by [···].

Author's Picks

BOOKS ON BOMBAY (FICTION)

NO GOD IN SIGHT by Altaf Tyrewala

An undiscovered gem in the United States, this novel has been a big success in India. Like *The Death of Vishnu*, it also combines several story threads (all set in Bombay), but instead of intertwining them in a parallel structure, Tyrewala knots them into a full circle. Filled with engaging characters, the narrative races along with energy and humor.

LOVE AND LONGING IN BOMBAY by Vikram Chandra

The author was putting the finishing touches on this collection when I took a writing workshop from him in 1996. A mesmerizing, kaleidoscopic journey through the city, with the same storyteller relating five different tales that show Bombay in different moods, both dark and bright. Sartaj Singh, who first appeared in this collection, reappears as one of the two central characters in Chandra's epic *Sacred Games*.

THE MOOR'S LAST SIGH by Salman Rushdie

The quintessential Bombay book by Rushdie is, of course, *Midnight's Children*, as I found out while writing *The Age of Shiva*. (Both the tetrapods at Marine Drive and the monkeys on Elephanta Island, which I wanted to write about, had been already unforgettably visited by Rushdie.) *The Moor's Last Sigh,* his other Bombay book, is very accessible and tremendously appealing. For a while, it was

> 66 The author [of *Love and Longing in Bombay*] was putting the finishing touches on this collection when I took a writing workshop from him in 1996. 99

unavailable in Bombay itself—Rushdie's caricature of a well-known local leader earned it a temporary ban in India when it was released.

BOOKS ON BOMBAY (NONFICTION)

BOMBAY, MERI JAAN: WRITINGS ON MUMBAI
edited by Jerry Pinto and Naresh Fernandes

Hard to find, and not to be confused with another book with almost the same name, but well worth the trouble. This anthology is filled with wonderful, quirky essays—a look at the little-known Jewish community in the city, a harrowing account of life in the distant "wild west" suburbs. Naipaul makes a cameo appearance with a hilarious contribution about his attempts to overcome the customs bureaucracy.

MAXIMUM CITY: BOMBAY LOST AND FOUND by Suketu Mehta

A tribute to the millions of inhabitants of the city, chronicling their lives with acuity and empathy, mining wit and humanity from every strata of society. The author uncovers a Bombay that even long-term residents may have never seen. It is easy to appreciate, on the basis of the language alone, why this book was nominated for a Pulitzer Prize.

INDIA: A MILLION MUTINIES NOW by V. S. Naipaul

Although written in 1990, *India* contains sections about Bombay that still crackle with the same religious and sectarian tensions that continue to flare up periodically in the city. As usual, Naipaul's wit is sharp and scathing, his keen eye misses nothing.

BOOKS ON HINDUISM

THE BHAGAVAD-GITA translated by Barbara Stoller Miller

It always amazes me that a text that lies at the center of understanding Hinduism can be so short and succinct. This is the famous discourse that Krishna, disguised as a charioteer, gives to Arjun. The central revelation that forms the heart of *The Death of Vishnu* is the famous eleventh chapter, quoted by Oppenheimer when he witnessed the first atomic explosion. Although several translations are available, it is difficult to match the exquisite lyricism of this version by Miller.

Have You Read?
More by Manil Suri

THE AGE OF SHIVA (January 2008)

Meera is seventeen years old when she catches
her first glimpse of Dev, performing a song so
infused with passion that it arouses in her the
first flush of erotic longing. She wonders if she
can steal him away from Roopa, her older,
more beautiful sister, who has brought her
along to see him.

When Meera's reverie comes true, it does
not lead to the fairy-tale marriage she
imagined. She escapes her overbearing father
only to find herself thrust into the male-
dominated landscape of India after
independence. Dev's family is orthodox
and domineering, his physical demands
oppressive. His brother Arya lusts after her
with the same intensity that fuels his right-
wing politics. Although Meera develops an
unexpected affinity with her sister-in-law
Sandhya, the tenderness they share is as
heartbreaking as it is fleeting.

It is only with the birth of her son that
Meera begins to imagine a life of fulfillment.
She engulfs him with a love so deep, so
overpowering, that she must fear its
consequences.

A sweeping epic embodying Shiva as a
symbol of religious upheaval, *The Age of Shiva*
is the powerful story of an ancient society in
transition and an extraordinary portrait of
maternal love.